WICKED
SERVE

By Grace Reilly

WICKED SERVE

A NOVEL

Grace Reilly

AVON

An Imprint of HarperCollins*Publishers*

WICKED SERVE. Copyright © 2024 by Grace Reilly. All rights reserved. Printed in the United States of America. No part of this book may be used or reproduced in any manner whatsoever without written permission except in the case of brief quotations embodied in critical articles and reviews. For information, address HarperCollins Publishers, 195 Broadway, New York, NY 10007.

HarperCollins books may be purchased for educational, business, or sales promotional use. For information, please email the Special Markets Department at SPsales@harpercollins.com.

Interior text design by Diahann Sturge-Campbell

Library of Congress Cataloging-in-Publication Data has been applied for.

ISBN 978-0-06-338714-0

24 25 26 27 28 LBC 5 4 3 2 1

To Stephanie: thank you for all the love, support, and laughter. You inspire me to dig deeper and dream bigger.

Author's Note

This book contains mentions of domestic abuse, alcoholism, disordered eating, panic disorder, and cheating, as well as explicit sexual content. For more details, please go to my website (grace-reilly.com).

WICKED
SERVE

Nikolai

June

The High Line at sunset is pretty.

Isabelle Callahan at sunset is stunning.

I lean against the park railing, watching as she runs her fingers through a planter of light purple coneflowers. There are other people around, tourists and New Yorkers alike, but I don't pay them any mind. Not when I can admire her dark hair, flung carelessly over one shoulder, and how her airy pink sundress falls over sun-kissed legs.

I adjust my aviators, glad she can't see my eyes.

The ache I feel whenever I look at her hasn't faded, even after weeks of meeting up like this. A night at Little Sister Lounge. An afternoon at the Met. Kisses in the back of cabs and split bottles of wine and walks in Central Park. It's as easy as breathing, and it always leads to the same places: her bed or mine.

It's intoxicating. Dangerous.

Perfect.

Isabelle straightens, pushing her heart-shaped sunglasses up her freckled nose. "You really haven't seen *Legally Blonde*? Ever?"

I shrug. "Isn't it old?"

"You did not just call my favorite movie *old*."

"I'm pretty sure it came out before either of us were even alive."

"And it holds up perfectly." She nudges my shoulder with hers. "We're watching it tonight."

"I thought we were watching *New Girl*."

"This is too important." She scrunches her nose. "I'll even be quiet and let you experience it."

I grin. "No you won't."

She bursts into laughter. My heart skips like a scratched record. I cup her jaw, thumb rubbing over her cheek, and kiss her. She smiles against my mouth as she returns it.

"Elle Woods basically created my style, you know."

"Pink on pink on pink?"

"You like it."

"I do." I play with the strap of her dress. "You look like the sunset."

She shakes her head. "Flirt. You already know I'm coming over." She bends to pick one of the flowers. "Aw, this one has a broken stem."

"Pretty, though." I tuck it behind her ear, touch lingering. She shivers as she steadies my hand, her white-polished thumb pressing against my pulse. Even behind the sunglasses, the endless blue of her eyes leaves me breathless.

I know I shouldn't, but I take out my phone. She's too gorgeous for her own good; this moment needs to be preserved. I've never felt strongly about summer, but lately, I haven't wanted it to end. When fall comes, we'll just be memories to each other. My chest tightens at the thought.

"Smile."

"I thought we said no pictures," she teases.

"I'll delete it later."

"Nik."

I cock my head to the side. "Izzy."

She gasps. "Take that back!"

"What back?" I say, feigning innocence.

"You know what."

I kiss her again, hefting her onto the railing and stepping between her legs.

"Isabelle." My fingertips tap down her spine, ribs expanding with precarious warmth. "My sunshine girl."

CHAPTER 1

Izzy

August

I pick through the M&M's packet for the rest of the yellows, jiggling my foot against the floor. I'm still flushed from practice, hair sticking to the back of my neck uncomfortably.

I spent the summer in dresses, chasing after vendors for my wedding planning internship, so aching legs and chafing after the first volleyball practice of the season is no big deal, but all the same, it'd be great if Coach Alexis could hurry. The longer I sit outside her office, the greater the temptation to check my phone.

It's not like I'm expecting anything new. Nikolai hasn't texted in two weeks. Two weeks is like two *years* when it comes to flings.

I work my way through the rest of the yellow M&M's, then the orange. Why are there even brown ones? The fact that pink isn't a standard color is practically criminal.

I give my phone a tiny peek. No notifications; I don't even need to open my texts. The unfinished thread will still be there, taunting me, and that's just going to make me want to get started on the green M&M's, too.

I know I should delete it. My summer fling is over, and it involved way more dirty bits than feelings. But the last texts that Nik sent me aren't something I can just forget, even if I woke up alone the morning after our last hookup.

I peer down the hallway. No Alexis yet. As soon as our team

meeting ended, I ran upstairs to her office. She can't ignore me if I'm right in front of her door, after all.

I open the thread.

N

You're a beam of light in a person, Isabelle

So fucking beautiful

My heart squeezes tightly.

He can't have meant it. If he meant it, maybe things would be different. It's just a line, no matter how good, and the fact I'm still obsessing over it is several shades of pathetic. It doesn't change the fact that what we had was casual. An exploration in attraction with no promise of anything deeper. A fun time, exactly what I'm good for, and one my family—especially my brother Cooper—*absolutely* can't find out about. He and Nik are two of the top college defensemen in the country, captaining rival programs. They already got into one fight their sophomore year, and that was just because of hockey. The last thing I need is to encourage another, more personal one.

At least Nik is back in Massachusetts at UMass Amherst for his senior year, and I'm in New York at McKee University for my sophomore year. I've never been so grateful for state lines. Soon, I'll forget his crooked smile, and how he handled my body with as much skill as his hockey stick, and especially the way he said my name—always my full name, Isabelle—like a velvet caress.

His mother was my boss this summer, and the first day of my internship, he sauntered into her office without knocking while she was out at lunch. He teased me until I realized who he was . . . and he called me Isabelle from the first introduction. Isabelle, not Izzy, like everyone else.

I can still see him in perfect detail: the blue button-down, sleeves rolled to the elbow. Messy hair, sharp eyes. He stole my M&M's and didn't even eat any—bastard—and scrawled his number on one of my pink sticky notes with a wink that made me go molten.

The rest of the day, I couldn't stop thinking about the way my name sounded coming out of his mouth. I broke down and texted him, and somehow, the first kiss we shared felt like the hundredth. Once we started, I couldn't help but let it happen all summer long.

I stare at those two brief texts until my vision blurs.

"Izzy?"

I whip my head up, shoving my phone into my bag. "Hi, Coach."

Coach Alexis arches an eyebrow. She's dressed casually, just in leggings and a McKee sweatshirt, but the full face of makeup and perfectly placed bleach-blond hair give her a sense of unsettling sophistication. Nik's mother, Katherine, is equally glamorous, but she never made me squirm like Alexis can with a mere look.

"Make sure you take off your necklace before next practice," she says, gesturing pointedly to my diamond *I* charm.

Crap. I thought I got it along with my tennis bracelet and earrings, but since I wear it so often, I sometimes forget it.

"Right, sorry. Um, can I talk to you for a second?"

"Now? We just had the team meeting."

She went over the usual things—the schedule, the importance of sticking with the team during away matches, our practice and conditioning commitments—in her crisp, speech-first-questions-later voice. Honestly, it was more like speech-and-no-questions. She prefers for her plan to be the only plan, which is why my stomach feels like one big knot right now.

My first instinct is to say I can come back later, but I don't know if I'll be able to work up the courage twice, so I nod. "Please. Just a moment."

"Fine," she says, leading the way into her office. "I only have a few minutes."

Like all the athletic facilities at McKee, purple and white dominate the color scheme. Alexis made it glam, of course. The love seat is an inviting shade of lavender, and a chic white chandelier hangs above us. I perch on the end of a leather chair, snow-white with the McKee school logo stamped across the back, and give her my best smile.

"Let me play setter."

She crosses one long leg over the other. "You do a fine job at opposite hitter."

"It's a new position for me."

"It was new last season. This season I expect you to have gotten the hang of it."

"Please, Coach." I swipe my sweaty palms against my shorts. "It's not the position I fell in love with when I started volleyball. I know I can do more for the team as a setter."

She sighs. It's the sigh you might give a toddler who covered herself with peanut butter. I twist my fingers together, excess energy getting the better of me. I bite my tongue so I don't start spewing nonsense.

Last season, she took one look at me and decided I was a second-rate player. I made the mistake of showing up to our first team bonding exercise hungover, and I didn't play my best in practice, and when she integrated the freshmen with the rest of the team, she moved me from setter to opposite hitter. I'm not the best volleyball player in the world, but I love the sport, and I don't want to be sidelined when these four years at McKee are the only time in my life I'll be competing at such a high level. Losing out on the position stung, and losing out on playing time hurt worse. My parents were surprised by the change and, although they didn't voice it, disappointed, too. If there's one thing us Callahans are, it's athletes. My three older brothers—not to mention my retired pro quarterback father—can attest to that.

I accepted Alexis's decision last year rather than fight it, but I know I'm better than that. I hope so, at least.

"You really want to do this, Callahan? You want to go there?"

"I don't—"

"I'm sure you were the best setter on your high school team. But you're not the star here. You're nowhere near the top of the roster." She leans in, drumming her knuckles across the glass top of her desk. "I understand that hearing that is hard. But someone needs to be the one to break it to you that you don't automatically get everything you want just because you can afford to attend a school. I knew plenty of girls like you when I played, and every single one of them had to learn this lesson eventually."

I blink once. Twice. Then one more time, hard enough my eyes sting, so she doesn't see me cry. I knew I wasn't her favorite person, but I didn't think she thought I needed to be taught a *lesson*.

"What, did a football player break your heart or something?" I blurt. "Is that why you don't like me?"

Her eyes flash. "Izzy."

"Sorry, sorry—"

"This has nothing to do with your family. Not specifically. Were there other girls I wish I could have recruited? Other players who were maybe a better fit for the team but whose parents weren't some of McKee's biggest donors? Sure. You're an adult, I don't mind being honest with you. Like I said, the sooner you realize this, the better off you'll be."

"So I wasn't your first choice."

"I'm not saying you're without talent. But perhaps you should be in a program more suited to your . . . level."

I ignore that. I don't disagree with everything she's saying, but there's no need to insult me. "Let me prove to you that I can do it."

"I saw what I needed to see last season."

"This season will be different." I lean forward on my elbows. I don't want to sound too desperate, but I don't know when I'll get this chance again. "Please, I promise. Let me show you that I can do it."

"I'm committed to the starters I have."

"Brooklyn is a senior. She won't be here next season, and by then I'll be a junior. You don't have to put me there right away. Just give me some sets. I'll show you I can handle it for next season."

"I don't—"

"Please, Coach. I love this sport. I'm serious about it. I want to help us win, and I know I can do that best as a setter."

She twists her wedding ring around her finger as she looks at me. I don't dare say another word. After the longest minute of my life, in which I suppress the urge to say at least ten more things, something shifts in her expression.

Maybe it's sympathy. Even if it is, I don't care. I'll take anything at this point. Just half a chance, and I'll run with it.

"Fine. I can tell you're serious about this."

"I am."

"You want my attention, you have it. But you need to focus, Callahan. Work on your grades as much as your technique. Put in extra time in the weight room and in practice. Show me that you have what it takes, and that I can trust you."

I nod. My parents told me as much before I arrived on campus a few days ago. "No distractions."

Especially not when they're wickedly handsome, talented hockey players named Nikolai Abney-Volkov.

CHAPTER 2

Izzy

When I get to the off-campus house I share with Cooper and our brother Sebastian, I chuck my sneakers into the closet and plop on the couch. I undo my ponytail with a groan. Cooper's in the armchair, reading, and judging by the rock music and delicious smells coming from the kitchen, Sebastian's working on dinner.

I glance at the television. "James's last preseason game?"

Our oldest brother, James, plays quarterback for the Philadelphia Eagles. Of the four of us, he's the only one who followed directly in Dad's footsteps. He's an honest-to-God celebrity, the sort of NFL quarterback that inspires thirst-trap Instagram posts and screaming fans and people wanting his autograph, his picture, his time and attention. Dad was the same way, and once Cooper graduates and starts playing hockey professionally, he won't be far behind. Sebastian could have had it the same way as *his* father—Mom and Dad adopted him after his parents died in a car accident, years ago—but he decided to quit baseball at the end of last season to focus on cooking. Something tells me that even as a chef, he's going to garner a lot of attention.

Despite knowing all of this, I still think of them as just my brothers. My ridiculous, freakishly athletic, amazing older brothers. James always buys me a new stuffed animal on my birthday. Cooper has jumped into fights to defend my honor. Sebastian slept on the floor of my room for a *week* when I watched *Poltergeist* way too young and couldn't stop having clown-themed nightmares.

"Yeah," Cooper says, setting his book aside. "He played for a bit in the beginning, he looks good. Did you get to talk to your coach?"

"She's giving me a shot to prove I can handle playing setter."

He smiles warmly. "That's great, Iz."

I beam at his approval.

Sebastian pokes his head out of the kitchen, dishrag in hand. "Dinner in five."

"Ooh, yay." I slide off the couch. "Want me to set the table? We can use my new pink place mats."

He gives me a quizzical look, but before he can reply, the front door opens.

"Someone remind me how illegal murder is," Sebastian's girlfriend, Mia, says as she walks in with Penny, Cooper's girlfriend. "Give me the downsides before I do something I regret."

Penny sighs long-sufferingly as she slips out of her jean jacket. Cooper glances her way, looking as lovestruck as ever as he checks her out. She's definitely about to end up in his lap. I roll my eyes fondly before joining Sebastian and Mia in the kitchen.

Sure enough, I hear her shriek. "Cooper!"

"Super illegal," Sebastian says, his green eyes dancing with amusement. "Pretty sure you can't eat your boyfriend's home-cooked meals if you're in the can."

It sucks to be the fifth wheel when all of us have dinner together, but I love not being the only girl in the house. My brothers just shrugged when I showed them the adorable place mats I picked up at Target earlier this week, and apparently Sebastian already forgot they exist, but I know Penny and Mia will appreciate them.

Well, at least Penny will. I don't think I've ever seen Mia wear anything pink. Not even a *scrunchie*. Sometimes I can't believe that they're best friends, totally independent of their boyfriends. I also can't believe that both Cooper and Sebastian are in relationships, but last fall, Cooper fell for Penny—who happens to be his coach's daughter—and then earlier this year, Sebastian and Mia finally stopped dancing around each other and got serious. James also fell in love at McKee; when he transferred here for his senior year, he met Bex, and now they're engaged with a baby on the way.

Then there's me, fresh off a secret summer fling with Cooper's biggest hockey rival.

Mia gives me a one-armed hug before letting herself get swept up in Sebastian. She wipes a spot of sauce on his cheek with her thumb, wrinkling her nose when he ducks to kiss her.

"Is it Alice?" he murmurs.

"No." She plucks at something on his shirt with her black nails. "Some idiot who probably jerks off to pictures of Elon Musk."

"Ew," I say. "I hate that you put that image into my mind."

She just grins. "How's it going, Iz?"

I shrug as I pull out silverware and grab napkins. Earlier today, I cleaned off the kitchen table and added a vase of flowers. I arrange the place settings, admiring my handiwork for a moment. "This is pretty, right? Do we want wine?"

I glance over and see that they're making out, too. Just fantastic.

"Hello? Earth to the space idiots."

The kitchen timer goes off, and Sebastian reluctantly untangles himself from Mia to pull something out of the oven. Mia looks at me, biting her lip guiltily. "Sorry. It looks great."

"Mm."

"Really, it does. The place mats are a nice touch. Did you get the flowers from Trader Joe's?"

I can't stay annoyed for long. Mia's my friend, and it's always nice to see Sebastian looking so happy. "Obviously. Their bouquets are the best."

"Dinner's ready," Sebastian says, loud enough that Cooper and

Penny can hear. He plates the food—pan-roasted chicken, potatoes, and vegetables all dripping in a sauce that I know firsthand is delicious—and pulls a bottle of white wine out of the refrigerator. "For you, Izzy."

"Aw, Sebby." I take a plate to my usual seat. "You're the best."

Practice left me starving, so I focus on my food while the conversation goes on around me. The skating lessons that Penny and Cooper teach together at the town ice rink are starting up again. Sebastian, who is graduating after this semester, has an interview with a culinary school near the astrophysics study abroad program Mia's doing in Switzerland next year. I lean back in my chair, wineglass in hand. Honestly, we should take a picture of this moment. Mom would be happy to see us sitting down together to eat. That was her hope when she convinced Dad to rent a house in Moorbridge, the town entwined with McKee's campus, for us to use during our college years.

"It's too bad that James and Bex postponed the wedding," Sebastian says.

"When are they doing it now? The spring?" Mia asks.

"Yeah," I say. "Probably April or May. But that means the baby can party with us!"

They were originally going to have their wedding over the summer, but they decided to take their time and make it nice when they've settled into being parents. Bex is due in December, just in time for Christmas. If the baby comes a week early, we might even share a birthday. I smile at the thought. Bex and James are going to make the best parents, and I can't wait to be an aunt.

"Maybe she can be the flower girl," Cooper says. He stretches his arm over the back of Penny's chair, twirling her coppery hair around his finger. She smiles and leans over for a quick kiss.

"I'm already trying to convince Bex," I say, ignoring the tiny spike of loneliness that rises at the sight of them. Sebastian and

Mia are practically nuzzling each other, too. "I worked on a wedding over the summer that had the cutest little baby ring bearer."

"We'll come back for it, of course," says Sebastian.

Penny sips her wine, turning her attention to me. "Speaking of love, how did that summer connection work out, Izzy? Are we finally going to meet him?"

"If she'd ever say who he is," Mia teases.

The question sends my heart into a sprint. I ignore everyone's eyes, Cooper's especially, as I finish my wine. Summer is over. Nik is in Massachusetts and I'm in New York, and when his team comes to play McKee, I'll find an excuse not to go to the game.

It hurts anyway, and I hate that it hurts.

My parents have the gold standard of marriages. My three older brothers are hopelessly in love with their partners. Even though I'm happy for them, it stings to know I'm so far away from that. I'm not brilliant like Mia, or creative like Penny, or determined like Bex. I'm not my mother, seemingly capable of handling every aspect of her busy, colorful life, a husband and four kids included.

It's no wonder that to guys like Nikolai—and especially Chance, my one and only ex-boyfriend, who cheated on me without a thought to my feelings—I'm not the serious option. It's not just that I'm not wife material. I'm barely *girlfriend* material. And fine, I knew the rules when I fell into bed with Nik, but that doesn't mean it doesn't hurt, recognizing that even in different circumstances, I'd never be enough to steal his heart.

"It just fizzled out," I say with a shrug. "You know how it goes."

"Aw, too bad," says Penny. "What about other prospects? Any crushes we should know about?"

"No." My stomach squirms at the lie, but this is easier. I never should have mentioned Nik to them, even vaguely. "Nothing going on. I need to focus on volleyball. Keep my grades up. All that good stuff."

When I manage to escape to my room after dinner, I give my phone another helpless peek. Nothing but that unfinished text thread.

You're a beam of light in a person, Isabelle

So fucking beautiful

Were they lies, or just half-truths? Flimsy, throwaway compliments, good to use on any girl?

Something tells me I don't want to know the answer. If he meant to give me a real goodbye, he would have.

I scrape my teeth over my bottom lip and delete the thread. Summer has slipped into the rearview mirror, and I need to look ahead. If I'm not focused this semester, I have no chance of convincing Alexis to play me at setter, and that's more important than a fling that never had a future. I might not be on the level of my brothers, but it's unacceptable for a Callahan to fade into the background of her own sport.

I doubt I'll ever see Nik again, but if I do, we'll just be strangers. No matter what that does to my stupid, silly heart.

CHAPTER 3
Nikolai

Any property damage, other than the window?"

I've faced a lot of lectures over the years, but no coach—Dad excluded—comes close to the intensity of my grandfather when he's pissed off. And right now? He's focusing all of that energy on me.

I clasp my hands behind my back. As soon as I staggered into Mom's apartment earlier, carrying half the shit I own, she made me change into a suit and sent me to Grandfather's. Like showing up in a collared shirt will do a fucking thing to make up for the fact that I just got expelled from college.

Yet here I am. This morning, I was the team captain of UMass Amherst Men's Hockey. Now I'm not even a college student.

"No, sir. We only broke one window."

Grandfather snorts, drumming his fingers against the arm of his chair. I force myself not to fidget. He has yet to shoot a puck at my face guard and call it training, but in a way, his disapproval is worse than Dad's. It radiates throughout the room like poison. To him, I'm sure, this situation is confirmation of what he already suspects: that I'm the same kind of bastard as my father.

"But this Grady Szabo—"

Donna, his assistant, leans in and murmurs, loud enough I can hear, "One of Nikolai's former teammates. A freshman, new this year."

She smirks as she calls Grady my *former* teammate. Fuck you too, Donna.

"Thank you. Mr. Szabo is still in the hospital, correct?"

I didn't visit Grady in the hospital before I left Massachusetts. A lifetime of playing hockey means I'm no stranger to injuries, but the thought of Grady in that hospital bed—all because I didn't handle my team the way I should have—makes my stomach roll with guilt. Even though I didn't *tell* Grady to get fucked up on blow and try to head-butt some idiot from the football team through a second-floor window, I could have done more. Grady is just a freshman, and now instead of taking reps in practice, he's dealing with a broken leg. Thanks to the shrub he fell into, he avoided a head injury, at least.

"Right," I manage to say. "The rehab will take a long time, but they think by next—"

"Did you know about the drugs?"

"No."

"Don't lie to me, Nicholas."

I grit my teeth. I know he hates the way my name has the unmistakable mark of my father, but still, it's my name. *Nikolai*, not Nicholas. "I'm not lying. I had no idea someone brought drugs."

"The university didn't seem clear on that."

I hesitate. "I needed to be loyal to my teammates."

"So, you knew and lied to them." He sighs, pinching his nose between his fingers. "No wonder my offer of a very generous donation was met with silence."

"I learned more about it after. I didn't know about it in the moment." It's taking all my effort not to snap. "I just want to figure out a way to finish my degree and play hockey."

"Good. Because that's what I want as well." He stands, stepping around his spotless wooden desk, and gives me a calculating look. His eyes are like pieces of flint, his silver hair combed carefully over his temples. He might be old, but he's powerful. You don't get to the point where you own half the buildings in

New York City, plus hundreds around the world, by playing it safe.

The Fifth Avenue penthouse that he calls home is as light and modern as an avant-garde art piece, but his office stands apart, a relic from a time long past. A gas fireplace trimmed with marble stands guard behind his desk. Dark wood paneling gives the entire room a heavy, dramatic air. The last time I snuck in here—to steal a sip of the good brandy with my cousin, Cricket, during an insufferable party—I couldn't understand how easily she flopped onto the leather couch.

Then again, she's fit into this world her entire life. When Mom divorced Dad and we moved from Moscow to New York, I was already thirteen.

Grandfather turns his gaze away as he considers one of the only photographs in the room: my mother, Katherine, embracing her older sister, back when they were eight and ten. Despite the frilly dresses they're wearing, they look solemn. I've always wondered if the photographer threatened to drown their puppy or something.

"I wanted you and your cousin to pose for something similar, but Andrei wouldn't allow it," he says, spitting out my father's name as he adjusts the cuffs of his crisp white shirt. "You should have been here all along. My only grandson, and I barely knew you until you were a teenager."

"It's unfortunate."

"It's unacceptable," he snaps.

Despite his intensity, he rarely raises his voice, so I'm taken aback as much as Donna. She looks away politely.

I swallow the panic that threatens to rise at his tone. The past is past, and right now, I have to figure out what the hell I'm going to do about my senior year of college. "Wherever I transfer, it has to have a hockey program equal to UMass's. Part of the timing of my rookie contract is because of the strength of the—"

"We don't have to worry about that." He gestures to the couch. The crystal decanters on the bar cart next to it wink in the lamplight as he takes out two glasses. "Take a seat."

"Grandfather."

He pours a few fingers of brandy into each glass. "Sit, Nikolai."

At the sound of my real name, I listen. I should have known that his help would come with a price. Grandfather doesn't see much distinction between business decisions and family matters.

"If I do this for you, I need you to make me a promise."

I stare at my glass. No matter how hard I worked in practice, or how well I played in games, I never earned my father's love, but I can still earn Grandfather's. Whatever his bargain is, it can't be that bad.

"Anything."

"Work for me after graduation."

I nearly choke on the brandy. "What?"

"I will help you transfer to another school—one with a good hockey team—and in return, when you graduate, you'll come work for the family business."

"But . . . I'm going to play hockey."

"A couple years spent in an unforgiving league that will tear your body apart? Or worse, joining your father in the KHL? No. I won't allow it."

"You seriously think I'd agree to a contract with my father's team? In *Russia*?"

"He was your first coach."

"He's dead to me." I spit out the words, even though they make my heart ache. I point to the scar on my face. "He gave me *this*."

"I'm well aware."

"Then you don't know me at all."

"I do know you, Nikolai. I want the best possible future for you, and preparing you to take over Abney Industries is the way to make that happen. Did you think I wasn't serious about that? The company can't go to just anyone when I'm gone. It's you or no one."

When I applied to college, Grandfather wanted me to go to Harvard, his alma mater. Harvard's hockey team is excellent, but UMass Amherst had a better coaching staff, so I said yes to their recruiters. He wasn't thrilled about the National Hockey League draft, either, but he still congratulated me when the Sharks took me in the first round. SKA St. Petersburg, the team my father coaches in the Kontinental Hockey League, the Russian equivalent of the NHL, drafted me as well, but I never considered it a serious option. I've made other concessions—studying political science, making it clear that I want my college degree before playing professionally—but never once did Grandfather say that he wanted me to join the family business *instead* of playing hockey.

I stand as the magnitude of what he's asking hits me. "You can't do this."

"This is generous, son." He stands, too. We're the same height, so unless I want to look like a coward, I have to stare straight into his eyes. "You'll graduate from a good university and have another season playing your sport. You'll tell the NHL and KHL that you're retiring, take the job, and start your MBA at Columbia. Now, I would have preferred Harvard for your senior year, but I figured you'd want to stay in the same division. There's a spot for you at McKee University, and the coach is prepared to start you."

At the mention of McKee, the back of my neck prickles.

Before this mess, I had a good summer. Development camp with the Sharks, time spent with Cricket, and messing around with Isabelle Callahan, who just so happens to be the little sister of Cooper Callahan, the captain of McKee's hockey team—UMass Amherst's biggest rival school. I didn't plan that last one, and if he ever finds out about it, I'm sure to get a punch to the jaw like the season before last, but fuck if it wasn't worth it.

If I go to McKee, I'll be on her turf. This time with *Callahan* for a team captain. I'm sure he'd be thrilled to play with me after what I chirped at him about his girlfriend—even if I didn't know at the time that they were dating—when we faced each other last fall.

In my defense, it was the first time I ever saw Isabelle. A minute before the puck drop, and I couldn't stop staring; I blurted out something about her like a fool. Covering it up by taunting Cooper about the redhead he couldn't stop staring at seemed like a smart decision at the time.

Usually when I play, the audience is a blur, but Isabelle stayed crystal clear. Laughing. Talking with her family. Jumping out of her seat to cheer on her brother, her smile so breathtaking that I wanted nothing more than for it to be directed at me. Her hair hung loose around her heart-shaped face, dark and wavy. Absurdly, she reminded me of a mermaid, maybe because of her eyes, blue like the ocean in a storm. If her last name wasn't Callahan, I'd have found her after the game and charmed my way into her bed.

I was prepared to stay the hell away from her when I found out she was my mother's summer intern. I wasn't even going to *entertain* it.

But then I met her for real, and I couldn't resist. Not because her brother would have hated it, but because I knew then, just like I knew the moment I first saw her, that she was special, and special doesn't come around every day.

I've been missing her like hell since we broke off our fling, but I never expected to actually see her again. If I agree to this, we won't just be in the same city for a few months. We'll be on the same campus, in the same small town. I can't risk falling back into bed with her, especially right under her brother's nose.

"McKee? Are you serious?"

"It's an excellent school."

"You can't force me into anything."

"No," Grandfather says lightly. "You're an adult, you can make your own choices. But I'd implore you to make the right one."

"You realize that I'm good at what I do, right? It's my whole life."

"That's what worries me." He clasps my shoulder firmly. "I'm not denying your talent. You clearly inherited many things from your father. But I worry that you inherited too many of the wrong things."

I blink, hard. My mind spins. I could tell him to fuck off, but I wouldn't put it past him to block me from every top hockey school in the country, if only to screw me over for not agreeing to what he wants. I could try to play for a junior league until the Sharks are ready to discuss a rookie contract, but there's a reason why I went the college route. I wanted an education, and I wanted a shot at the Frozen Four. McKee won it last season. Plenty of their core players are still on the team, Isabelle's brother included. There's nothing stopping them from winning it again, especially with me on the ice.

Reaching out to Dad isn't a real option. I never had intentions of playing in the KHL, even if he wasn't still part of that league.

That leaves a spot at McKee.

One more year.

One more *season*.

And Isabelle will be there.

"You say you want to be nothing like him? Prove it. Choose a different path."

Grandfather's words hang in the air for several long seconds, taunting as they pull me in.

I tell everyone I hate my father, but that's not true. I still love him, because he made me the way I am, and while some of it is good—hockey has always been the one good thing in my life—I know I'm lying to myself about not inheriting any of the rest of it. I'm terrified of the day I'll wake up and see him staring back at me in the mirror. It's a piece of shrapnel in my heart, aching with every beat.

And it's why nothing serious could ever happen with Isabelle. What if I tried and fucked it all up? What if I hurt her the way my father hurt my mother for fucking *years*?

I can't have her, but at least I can have hockey for one more season.

"Fine. Call McKee."

CHAPTER 4
Nikolai

I'm barely out of Grandfather's office before Cricket pulls me into a hug.

"I just heard," she says against my shoulder. "I'm sorry, Nik."

I let myself melt into her embrace. She's tall and curvy, with a glasses collection that rivals a Warby Parker store. Today's pair is a truly hideous shade of purple, and since I last saw her, she cut her hair. The dark blond waves used to go to her shoulders, but now she's rocking a pixie cut.

"This is new."

She smooths the sides of her hair. "Do you like it? I figure why not announce myself more aggressively as a lesbian, really scare all the guys on the trading floor."

I snort. Cricket has a flair for dramatics, like someone else I know. Or knew, rather. The last thing I need to think about is how well Isabelle would get along with my cousin. "You look like Kristen Stewart."

Her eyes light up. "Do you really mean that?"

"If you ditch the glasses."

"I like the glasses. They're quirky."

"They're . . . ugh. They're my new team color."

"Oh, so Grandfather did get you in somewhere else. Spill."

I head for the nearest room with some privacy, the sitting room with the grand piano and Jeff Koons sculpture. Cricket's loafers click on the marble floor as she hurries to keep up. Emotion wells in my chest, threatening something deeply embarrassing—

tears—so I gnaw the inside of my cheek and think of the hockey rulebook until it passes.

There's no use mourning the loss of hockey in my life until it actually happens. Once I'm in charge of the corporation, maybe I'll work through my sorrow by buying a hockey team. For now, I have to stay focused on the present, which includes keeping myself in the right headspace to get to work. I'm leaving for McKee first thing in the morning, with just enough time to settle in before classes begin.

"Nik?" Cricket's voice has a soft note to it. I must be tense enough that she can see it. "Seriously, what happened?"

I collapse onto the nearest couch and drop my head into my hands. "I deserved to get expelled."

"That's not true."

"A freshman is in the hospital because I fucked up." I lift my head as she sits next to me. "The team was my responsibility."

"But they weren't your drugs. I don't get why you didn't just say—"

"Because John is at UMass on scholarship," I interrupt. "His family doesn't have ten houses, Cricket. He doesn't have a fortune to fall back on. If UMass had expelled him, his future would have been over. I could take it. He couldn't."

I've never had a best friend, but John Hayes comes close. We roomed together freshman year, and he's the only one on the team who knows the truth about my father. He can be an idiot, and bringing coke to a team party was monumentally stupid. I care about him, though, and I wasn't about to snitch on him. Loyalty to the team is everything.

Even if because of it, the team isn't mine anymore.

"But it was his choice, not yours. You should have told them the truth."

"He's my friend and teammate. And my responsibility as

captain." I manage a smile. "And look, it all worked out. Grand-father is very generously letting me finish my degree at McKee, so long as I come work for him right after."

"Are you serious?"

"Yes."

"He can't do that."

"He can." I'm not even all that bitter. The world revolves around Joseph Abney, and there's no point in fighting it. If he gets his way—and he will get his way—that will be me eventu-ally. The one with more power and wealth than he knows what to do with.

I can think of worse lives to lead. Not everyone gets what they want; that's a fact. Some people don't get anything, whether it be loving families, fulfilling careers, or romantic relationships. I should have known that I was one of the unlucky ones.

"He knows you're going to play hockey professionally, right? Like, for millions of dollars?"

"Why make millions playing a sport that will wreck your body when you can make billions in a boardroom?"

Cricket stands, practically vibrating with indignation. "Did he say that?"

"No," I say, tugging her down. "It's fine."

"This is the definition of not fine."

"I thought you didn't understand why I love hockey so much anyway."

She's never played a sport seriously, outside of tennis, and that was just to pad her college applications. She thinks it's strange that it's practically the air I breathe. An unsavory reminder of my father, not an expression of something I want on my own merits.

Who knows, maybe all of them are right. I wouldn't have this love without him giving it to me.

I wonder what he'd say if he knew I'm going to walk away.

He'll learn about it eventually; he keeps tabs on me. I promise myself over and over that I'll stop taking his calls, but then he finds a way to draw me back in. I hate how good it feels to speak Russian with him, never mind the panic attack I have to fend off after I hang up.

"I don't. But I know it's important to you, which is good enough for me. Honestly, Grandfather can be such a prick sometimes."

"The company should be yours, you know."

"It was never going to be mine." Her tone is neutral enough, but I catch the flare of frustration in her eyes. Grandfather has never taken her as seriously as she deserves, which is ridiculous considering how brilliant she is. Right now, she's working for a venture capital firm, wiping the trading floor with the other associates, but I know she'd prefer a spot on the Abney Industries board. "It was always going to be yours. He didn't have a son, but at least he has a grandson, and because you're a man and I'm not, you will always be the better choice."

"Nikolai?"

I tear my gaze away from Cricket's at the sound of Mom's voice.

My mother has always been an elegant woman. In Russia, that meant expensive furs and perfectly coiffed hair, but without the influence of my father, she's embraced her natural tendency for the bohemian, just as high end as possible. Today she's in heels and a sundress that Isabelle would call periwinkle, her blond hair curled gently around her shoulders.

She takes off a pair of red sunglasses and carefully tucks them into her purse. "Did you have a chance to speak with your grandfather?"

"I'm leaving for McKee in the morning."

"Oh, good." She kisses me on the cheek. The non-scarred one. In the wrong mood, she flinches when she looks at me, trapped in a memory, I'm sure. I look so much like my father, she doesn't even watch me play hockey anymore. During my first game in America after we left Dad, she took one look at me, froze, and fled; she sent a car to take me home when it ended.

"McKee?" she adds. "You'll have to tell Izzy I said hello. It was so nice to have an assistant who really understood things."

I had no doubt that Isabelle was excellent at her job, but I smile at the confirmation. Mom has no idea we were involved with each other, but in other circumstances, I like to think she'd have approved.

"I'm sure she'll be thrilled."

"I don't understand why they had to expel you. Like we haven't given that school enough money."

"It doesn't matter."

"Of course it does, honey. I know you chose to go there for a reason."

"Grandfather is making him work for the company when he graduates," Cricket says.

Mom blinks. I can't quite tell, but I think that surprised her. "I'm sure he has his reasons."

"Nik has *hockey.*"

"And look how well that worked out for his father," she snaps. She flushes. "I mean—Nikolai, sweetie—"

"It's fine." I step around her. "I have to pack."

"Let's get lunch before you leave. Or dinner. Any restaurant you want."

I swallow around the debris in my throat. I've never blamed my mother for staying with my father as long as she did—he's a magnetic force, charming and downright seductive when he wants to be—but still, I hate to think of the years she spent covering her bruises with makeup and making excuses for him. Our relationship is fragile, a dance where neither of us knows the steps. Distance aside, I'm glad she's here and happier than she was before. She has her wedding planning business now, and all the friends she knew before she ran away with Dad brought her back into the fold. *Grandfather* welcomed her back, despite their fractured relationship, and part of me can't help but be grateful about that, too.

"Sure," I say after a too-long pause. "That sounds nice."

Cricket pounces the moment Mom leaves the room. "You're going to Isabelle's school? *That* Isabelle? Did I hear that right?"

"It doesn't mean anything."

"How is she?"

"No idea. You know that."

"Okay, sure, like you haven't stalked her on Insta."

"It doesn't matter that she's going to be there." I scrape over a scuffed spot on the floor with my shoe. Of course I've searched for her Instagram, but I'm not about to admit that. Half the photos on her grid are of her with her family; our childhoods couldn't have been more different if we tried. "I'm going to be on her brother's team, and he already doesn't like me, remember?"

Cricket's eyes widen. "Oh, shit. Right."

"And anyway, she can do better than me," I say, scrubbing a hand through my hair.

Better that she settles down with a guy who deserves her, someone her brothers will never have to worry about when it comes to treating their little sister right. Someone who won't dread the day his relationship turns him into his father.

"That's not—"

"It's true." I make myself smirk. It's a mask, and normally Cricket would be exempt from seeing it, but the last thing I need is her encouragement. I couldn't even bring myself to give Isabelle a proper goodbye the last day of her internship; I left her asleep in

CHAPTER 5

Izzy

The semester technically hasn't started yet," Victoria says as she drags me by the hand to Haverhill House. "Listen to Alexis after tomorrow."

I dig in my heels, stopping both of us in our tracks. I got dressed when she showed up at the house, armed with makeup and assurances that we'll only stay at this party for a little while, but Coach's words are still echoing in my mind. She didn't explicitly tell me not to party, but surely "no distractions" also means "don't get shit-faced at senior housing."

On the other hand, Victoria does have a point. I'm sociable by nature, and maybe I'll be able to focus on my classes better once I've scratched the party itch. Just a little, mind you. A couple of beers, a few dances, maybe some flirting. I could definitely use the latter, because I'm not going to forget about Nikolai until I find the right distraction.

"Two drinks," I say, trying for a stern tone. Victoria's lips twitch as she fights a smile. "Two drinks and like fifteen minutes of dancing. That's it."

"Yay!" She pulls me into a sticky hug. The late August air is irrepressibly humid; it's going to be a swamp at Haverhill. Hopefully the beer is semi-cold. "This is going to be so much fun."

Aside from being my best friend, Victoria is an excellent volleyball player. She plays libero, and even as a freshman last year, she led the defense with conviction. We met in middle school during volleyball camp, and we've only gotten closer over the years.

Balancing the intense sports schedules of four kids wasn't easy for my parents, and whenever a tournament of mine wasn't at the top of the list, her family would keep an eye on me. We'd eat pizza in bed at the hotel while *Friends* played on the television, and the next day, try our best to dominate every set we played. I still get warm fuzzies whenever I think about how excited we were when we both got into McKee.

She marches down the sidewalk, forcing me to jog to keep up. "These heels aren't meant for fast movement, you know."

"The faster you go, the sooner we can get you laid."

"I said *flirting*, Torie."

"The best way to get over a breakup is with a rebound."

"And you would know? You and Aaron are practically an old married couple."

Victoria is dating Aaron Rembeau, the goaltender on Cooper's team. It's serious enough that she spent the majority of the summer at his family's lake house in Michigan, tanning on his boat and bonding with his cousins. A tiny, selfish part of me hates that it worked out so well with her hockey player, but I shove that deep. Maybe I'll get to plan the eventual Rembeau-Yoon wedding.

She smiles, twirling her hair around her finger. Thinking about Aaron's six-pack, I'm sure. "Yeah. I love that goof."

"Anyway, Nik and I were never dating. There's nothing to get over."

"You spent the summer screwing all around Manhattan. And the Hamptons." She stops at the crest of the hill, putting her hands on her hips. Haverhill House—which is actually a collection of regular houses that the university bought and converted into off-campus housing for seniors—glitters just beyond, light spilling from the windows. "And wasn't a yacht involved? I watched those private stories like a hawk."

"It wasn't his—whatever. It doesn't matter. He's not even here." I take a couple of halting steps. Damn these stupid heels. "Wait *up*."

The guy at the door gives us an appreciative look-over before waving us inside. The price of admission to a party like this—looking like a snack—never fails to gross me out, but I know I didn't dress like this *for* the men at the party. Sure, they can look, but I squeezed myself into this tight yellow dress, strapped my feet into these death-heels, and put on a full face of makeup because I love looking hot.

"Drinks?" Victoria yells over the scream-shouts of Olivia Rodrigo.

Someone got a strobe light in here, making the throng of bodies dancing and chatting and hooking up look almost alien. The whole scene is already giving me a headache, but I dressed up and came all this way, so I just smile and nod.

I chug one beer, then another, and cut myself off there. Victoria does the same, then pulls me to the dance floor. We jump to the music, singing along to the lyrics and letting our high ponytails whip around. Sweat drips down my temple; it's as humid in here as it was outside, but I know it just adds to the shine on my face. Glittery highlighter, clear lip gloss. Winged eyeliner that Victoria applied with a steady hand.

After a couple songs, I start to notice the stares. My heels make my legs look extra-long, and my bright dress is practically a beacon in the flash of the strobe light. Victoria spins me around, laughing as I nearly lose my balance. I do the same in retaliation, and we fall over each other. I'm only buzzed, but I can't stop smiling. The energy of the music and the crowd around us is acting like magic, weaving a spell that keeps my hips moving.

Someone grips my wrist, turning me around.

It's absurd, but I feel a pinch of disappointment when I see it's just another guy with a too-charming smile. Strong jaw, trim waist, looking like he wishes he could taste me.

Nik is hours away, in Amherst. I have to get my head on straight. I'll never move on if I can't prove to myself that I'm capable of it.

I muster a smile of my own, so the guy pulls me close, grinding against me. I sway my hips to the music, breathing in the sour smell of his sweat. His hand skims up my side, settling on my rib cage. Possessive, even though I don't know him. I turn in his embrace, hoping to at least ask his name. He takes that as permission to brush his fingers just above my ass.

The smile slips off my face. Why do guys always want to jump to sex? I'm sure if I gave him the right look, he'd find an unoccupied room in this house and pull a condom from his wallet. He's not unattractive. He has a nice smile. If we met in class instead, and he asked me to dinner, I'd probably say yes. I don't want to fall into last year's pattern, settling for hookups that never led anywhere.

And yeah, fine, I spent the summer scratching that itch with Nik with no expectation of more. But despite the casualness, Nik cared about me. He might not have cared enough to stick around until I woke up, that last morning, but I didn't mean absolutely *nothing* to him. The first time we met up, I asked him if he only wanted to sleep with me because it would be something to lord over Cooper. But he shook his head and said he noticed me for the first time last year, at the game UMass played at McKee. He said I was special, and I believed him.

A beam of light in a person.

So fucking beautiful.

The way he said my name never failed to make my pulse race.

"Isabelle," someone says into my ear.

It was just like that. Just like—

My heart skips a beat.

I glance over my shoulder—and meet Nikolai's gaze.

I'd know that face anywhere. Tousled brown hair and a face full of tantalizing angles. Deep, practically sinful eyes. A scar that slices from the bottom of his eyelid all the way to his jaw, giving his face undeniable seriousness. He commands—no, *demands*—attention.

And here he is, looking at the guy dancing with me like he wishes he could rip his head off.

I don't hear the music anymore. I don't feel the sweat on my skin. I don't notice anything or anyone but him, smirking at me like he never left.

"Sunshine," he purrs. "Did you miss me?"

CHAPTER 6
Nikolai

To my credit, I don't punch the guy pawing at Isabelle. I don't react when he tries to punch *me*, either, curses falling from his mouth like confetti. I do turn when he calls her a bitch, and my glare is enough to make him melt into the crowd. Drunken asshole.

I grip her hand in mine as I lead her away from the dance floor, through the house, and finally to the backyard. When I feel the hazy night air, I take a full breath for the first time since I realized I wasn't imagining her.

She jerks her hand away. "Nik?"

I shove my hands into the pockets of my jeans, studying her. I didn't come to the party to find her—I just wanted to blow off some steam before I meet my new coach tomorrow—but she was impossible to ignore, dancing in the middle of the crowd. At first, I told myself I'd finish my beer and leave before she noticed me, but then she started dancing with that asshole, and something about the way she stiffened in his arms set off my alarm bells. I know I don't have any more of a right to her than him, but fuck if I don't feel that way. She was mine for three months and she's still mine, never mind the weeks of silence. How the hell could I have thought this would fade the moment she wasn't in my mother's office every day? That I'd be able to stay away?

"It's really you," she breathes. "How—"

"Do you know that guy?"

"What?"

"He's not your boyfriend, is he?"

She flushes deeply enough, I can see it in the moonlight. "No. He's just some guy."

"He was getting pretty familiar." I work my jaw. "You seemed uncomfortable."

"I had it handled."

"Did you?"

She just narrows her eyes. "What are you even doing here? Why aren't you at school?"

It doesn't surprise me that we crossed paths so soon. We've been magnetic since our very first kiss, shared in the back of the car on the way to my place after I took her to dinner at Per Se. Her strawberry lip gloss, the mischievous tilt of her smile, the way she moaned when I pressed her against the wall of the elevator with my hand up her skirt—I couldn't forget it if I tried.

Right now, she's in a tight yellow dress with tiny straps, her tan legs accentuated by heels. Her hair is in a smooth, high ponytail, but a couple loose pieces frame her face artfully. Glitter sparkles on her cheeks and across her collarbone.

If I leaned in for a kiss, would she push me away, or pull me closer?

"Remember the wedding in the Hamptons? Sagaponack?" I take a step in her direction, backing her against the nearest tree. She swipes her tongue over her lips. The glitter on her cheeks sparkles like stardust. "We split that bottle of Dom rosé."

A tiny, surprised smile melts away some of the wariness in her expression. I'm still a live wire, but that smile relaxes me. After weeks of missing her, I'm hungry for every detail. I've been telling myself that the distance will help, but it hasn't, and now there's no distance at all. I drink in the ocean of her eyes, resisting the impulse to press my body against her warmth.

It should feel wrong. It's not summer anymore, and anyone

from the party could see us. But I don't want to move away, and she must not either, because she doesn't even twitch.

In the heels she's wearing, she's almost as tall as I am. It would be so easy to kiss her. I'd lick the gloss away, and she'd give me a delighted smile before nuzzling closer, the way she did all summer.

"I remember," she says. Her eyes search mine. "We went skinny-dipping."

"It was freezing."

Her smile widens. "You mean invigorating."

"I wouldn't have gone in, except I was afraid you were going to drown." I return her grin. "Would have been an inconvenience to the wedding guests."

"You're so full of shit," she says with a snort.

I can't help myself; I cup her chin, tilting her face up. She's so pretty, I can't stand it. All summer long, I kept coming back to her. I'd promise myself that I'd break things off, but then I'd think about the prospect of never holding her again, never kissing her, never tasting her, and my reservations went straight out the window.

"You danced for me, before that. On the sand, with your hair loose. Do you remember that, too?"

Her breath catches. "Of course. You thought it was silly."

I shake my head. "No way."

"You totally did."

"You're remembering it wrong."

"Oh, am I?" She crosses her arms over her chest, which pushes together her small, perfect tits to the point of distraction. "You're the one who just showed up on my campus out of the blue, and now you're calling me a liar? Wow."

"Our campus."

"What?"

"I thought for sure your brother would be going around telling everyone he knows." I nearly tug on her ponytail, but stop myself at the last moment. "Interesting."

"Telling everyone what?"

"UMass kicked me out." I keep my eyes trained on hers as the back of my neck heats up. It's one thing for my family to find out—you can't lose approval you never had in the first place—but admitting this to her is embarrassing. I don't regret what I did, even as the reality of it sinks in, but that doesn't mean I feel good talking about it. "I just transferred here."

"Oh, Nik," she says, voice soft. "What happened? Are you okay?"

Even though I spent the summer with her, I'm surprised by her immediate empathy. She's sweeter than anyone deserves, me especially.

"I'm fine."

She takes my hand in hers and squeezes. "But you loved it there. You told me."

"Yeah. I did." I swallow, glancing at our interlocked fingers.

She presses her lips together, but instead of asking about the details, she shakes her head. "I can't believe you did this."

"What?"

"Why here?" She pokes me in the ribs, hard, as she pulls away. "You can't just show up here, talking about the Hamptons. Acting like—"

"I didn't have a choice."

"Oh, I'm sure," she says, a flinty note in her voice. "A family like yours, and you couldn't wrangle a spot at one of a dozen other fantastic hockey schools. You had to come here and make it that much harder for me to move on."

"You don't know the situation. My grandfather—"

"You can't leave and then show up and ask if I miss you," she snaps. She swipes at her cheeks, messing up her glitter. "That's not fair."

"Izzy?" someone calls. "Where'd you go?"

"Here!" Her voice is perfectly cheerful, as if she didn't just spear me through the chest.

The moment my feet hit the sidewalk outside her building, I regretted it. But I couldn't bring myself to say goodbye, and part of me thought it would be better for both of us if we didn't have a chance for emotions. Yet it hurt her. *I* hurt her. I can see it in her eyes.

A girl with pin-straight black hair walks over, a frown on her glitter-covered face. Her dress is a similar style to Isabelle's, tight and bright, but green instead of yellow.

"Um, what's going on?" She looks at me, then Isabelle. "Is something wrong?"

"No," Isabelle says. She links arms with her friend. "Let's just go, we have early practice tomorrow."

"Isn't that him?" her friend says in a stage whisper. "You know?"

Isabelle just starts walking. "Come on, Torie. Let's go."

Before they get too far, I call her name. She turns, biting her lip. I should have kissed her when I had the chance.

"We should talk."

"I don't know." Something flickers in her gaze, too quickly for me to catch. "You're the one who left without a word."

CHAPTER 7

Nikolai

Meeting a new coach is always stressful. Meeting a new coach *and* the guy whose sister you slept with all summer? After you chirped at him about his girlfriend, no less? That's nightmare fuel.

I tap my fingers against the arms of my chair as I wait in Coach Ryder's office. I can't stop fidgeting. It's a nice space—albeit very purple, like everywhere else in this hockey facility—and under other circumstances, I'd want to take a closer look at the trophies and awards behind the desk. Larry Ryder is a Harvard man, which is about the only thing Grandfather approves of in this whole clusterfuck of a situation.

I refuse to let my last season end with anything less than me holding up the national trophy, so here I am. Waiting. Hyperaware of the fact I'm back in Isabelle's vicinity. After she left last night's party with her friend, I got smashed enough that I could almost forget what she told me. Eventually, I dragged myself to my dorm, and to my first class this morning.

I wonder if she's at practice right now. I'll bet she looks fantastic when she's in the middle of a volleyball match. Tight jersey, short shorts, those cute knee pads . . . If I saw her, I'd have to resist the urge to drag her over by the ponytail and lick the sweat away from her temple.

That kind of thinking isn't doing me any favors, especially since it looks like she never wants to talk to me again, so I tip my head back.

Jesus. There's even purple on the ceiling.

The rest of the campus seems nice, although I haven't explored much beyond getting to class and . . . whatever this place is called. The Markley Center, I think. An assistant coach took me through the players' lounge, the dry locker room, the main locker room, the practice ice, the arena—a sea of purple stands and a huge crown painted on center ice, in case I forgot where I was—the staff offices, the medical center, and the gym. There's another gym that any athlete on campus can use, as well as a wellness center and a spa. Athletics has always been a strength of McKee University, and the facilities prove it.

I wish it were enough to make up for living in a dorm room again, and figuring out an unfamiliar campus, and getting used to a whole new coaching system. I'm off-balance and on edge, but at least I can swim in the athlete-only pool whenever I want. Lucky me.

Coach Ryder walks in, Cooper at his heels. Ryder's pale blue eyes are like chips of ice, but they seem friendly enough. Even though I'm sure he hasn't played in years, he looks fit, ready to lace up if necessary.

He shakes my hand firmly. "It's a pleasure, Nikolai."

I smile. I've had plenty of coaches since my father, and the first impression matters every time. "Same here, Coach."

"This is Cooper—well, you two are acquainted with each other." Ryder's smile turns wry. "As you know, he's team captain."

Cooper looks different without his hockey gear on. I wonder if I look different to him as well. His dark hair is longer than mine, curling over the nape of his neck. We're the same height, give or take half an inch, and I'd bet our weigh-ins are around the same, too. I keep a neutral expression on my face, even though I can't stop thinking about the apology I owe him. Me and my fucking mouth.

After a beat, he sticks out his hand for me to shake. "Can't say it's a pleasure, but here we are."

His blue eyes are the exact same shade as Isabelle's. The second I notice that, my breath sticks in my throat. I return the handshake quickly.

"Here we are," I echo.

"Have a seat, gentlemen. Let's discuss how this is going to work." Ryder gives each of us a long look, then sits back with a nod, as if we passed some sort of test. "Lucky me. Two of the top college defensemen in the country, and I can pair you on the same line."

Cooper spares me a glance before saying, "Sir, what about Evan?"

"Evan can work more closely with Jean. I know you've had your differences in the past, but you're on the same team now. We all have the same goal, and that means working together."

Cooper looks as if he swallowed a lemon, but he just nods. I suppress my smirk. An unexpected bonus in this whole mess: seeing Callahan sweat.

"I'm expecting leadership from both of you," Ryder continues. "You're both seniors, and the younger guys will look to you for guidance. We're lucky to have so many upperclassmen on the roster right now, in terms of our chances at getting to the finals again. If you work together to get the team culture to a good place, combined with clean play, we're going to crush the competition."

"Hear that, Volkov?" Cooper says.

"I ought to be asking you that."

"Still sore about that punch?"

"Cooper, son," Ryder says mildly.

Right, Cooper is dating Ryder's daughter. Must be nice to have your girlfriend's father call you "son." I have no doubt that Coach runs his team the way he wants to run it, but I need to make sure

I don't piss off Cooper any more than I already have. The last thing I want is for him to convince Coach to cut my ice time in favor of someone else.

It's for the best that I didn't kiss Isabelle yesterday.

"I want you to clear the air," he adds. "Do it now, before you're on the ice together. This isn't going to work without trust, and trust doesn't come without honesty."

At that last bit, he levels me with a look that feels more like an X-ray. For a split second, I think about Isabelle, but there's no way he'd know about that, or—thank fucking God—what I said about his daughter before I knew who she was. He must mean the circumstances around my expulsion from UMass. And possibly the dozens of other insults I've hit Cooper with during the games we've played against each other.

Guilt gnaws at me as I think about what I said last year. Telling a guy that his girl looks like she'd give good head is never a classy move. And normally on the ice, classy isn't what matters the most, but I should have reined it in.

Ryder drums his knuckles on the desk, then stands. "I'll be outside. Don't fuck up my shit, boys."

When the door shuts behind him, I turn to Cooper. "I'm sorry for what I said about Penny last year. I didn't realize you were dating, but regardless, it was stupid and dickish and crossed the line."

I don't dare add what I said about Isabelle. Hopefully he was so focused on what I chirped about his girl, he'll have forgotten the asinine thing I led with: *Where have you been hiding that sister of yours, Callahan? You'll have to introduce me.*

"It *was* an asshole move."

"I know. I really am sorry."

"I . . . thank you." He looks me over, eyes narrowed. "You got expelled?"

"Technically speaking."

"What the fuck does that mean?"

"I got kicked out." Talking about it over and over is getting exhausting. "But it wasn't my fault."

He laughs shortly. "I'm sure."

I jerk my fingers through my hair. John deserved to stay at UMass. There's no point in getting angry about it now, even if I miss the way my life was before. "One of my guys brought blow to a team party. I didn't know about it until after a freshman got fucked up and hurt himself. That's it."

He's quiet for a long moment. "You covered for your team-mate."

I incline my head.

"That's surprisingly decent of you."

"It's the right thing for a captain to do."

"The guys have heard some rumors. To them—"

"I put the team at risk and got my family to clean up my mess?"

"They listen to me." He stands, pacing to the window. "I can tell them the truth, and they'll drop it."

Huh. I figured he'd make me sink or swim, even after my apology, but I guess I shouldn't have underestimated his drive to win. If there's one thing I understand, it's that. "I'm surprised you'd offer."

"You can be an asshole on the ice," he says, looking out the window, then back at me, seriousness in his expression. "I understand why, and you used it to destabilize me more times than I like to think about. But we're on the same team now. I don't want the situation that got you here to fuck things up for us."

"I'll tell them myself." I join him by the window. "It'll sound better coming from me."

"Fine," he says, scrubbing a hand over his beard. "But it's my team, Volkov. Don't forget that."

My heart drops straight to my stomach. I worked just as hard as he did to become captain, but none of that matters now. He's a lucky bastard. His relationship with Ryder. His future in hockey. His family, his girlfriend. He won, and he doesn't even know it.

"Don't call me that."

"It's on the back of your sweater."

"Not anymore." I already told the assistant coach this, and he just nodded and said he'd mention it to the equipment manager. "I'm just going by Abney now. Mother's side of the family."

"But your father—"

"We're not close." If I'm going to fully commit to being an Abney, I might as well start now.

"Okay," he says slowly. "Fine. But I want you to do something for me, too."

The last time I agreed to this, it didn't lead anywhere good, but I nod. "What?"

He drops the smile. "Stay away from my sister."

I stare at him for a beat too long. "I don't know what you're talking about."

"Bullshit. I know that she worked for your mother this summer. She told me that you never even met, and maybe that's true. But I remember what you said about her last fall. You didn't just jaw about Pen. You spoke about Izzy, too."

Goddamn it, of course he remembers. He must have locked onto the fact that I wasn't shit-talking for no reason. Even then, I was paying too much attention to Isabelle. Thinking about possibilities I had no right to imagine. I smile casually, even though my pulse is racing.

"I was just making conversation, Callahan."

"You sure about that?"

I manage a short laugh. "No offense, but she isn't the kind of girl I go for. Cute, but . . ."

The lie sounds wrong in my mouth, but it seems to work, because Cooper's shoulders relax.

I was wrong. Isabelle's eyes aren't the exact same as her brother's.
Hers have warmth that never goes away. But Cooper? He can be
a shark when he wants to be.

And I know it because I'm the same way.

Partnering us together might make McKee the strongest team
in Hockey East—but it could just as easily implode.

"Good," he says, a hint of amusement in his tone. "Because she
can do way better than you."

CHAPTER 8

Izzy

I shuffle forward in line at the Purple Kettle, playing with the stack of rings on my index finger. I've been up since five; I started the day with a swim before hitting the gym. Caffeine is definitely in order before my two boring classes: statistics and philosophy. I met up with Victoria, who is taking stats with me, and Ellie, our friend and teammate, on the walk over. If this line hurries up, we'll have enough time to enjoy our iced coffees outside before class begins.

That's a big if. Mia isn't working today, but if were, the line would be going a lot faster. She doesn't like when people *dither*.

"This is taking forever," Ellie says with a sigh. "I need to be in class soon."

Victoria just shrugs. "Aren't you going to one of those huge classes that doesn't take attendance?"

"They still take attendance."

"No way."

"They do. With the clicker question thingy."

"That sounds fake."

"Why do you think they ask you a question when you walk in? They want to know who's there to answer it."

Victoria pokes me. "Is that true?"

"It sounds legit to me." The group at the head of the line finally finishes ordering, so we're able to take a big step in the direction of the register. "And why do you care, anyway? You never miss class."

"I like the fantasy of it," Victoria says. "It's like coming from just a cock. It never happens, but it's fun to think about."

Ellie makes a face. "Straight people terrify me."

"The elusive vaginal-orgasm-by-cock," Victoria continues, nodding sagely. "Although you can ask Iz about it."

"Oh my God, shut up," I say, glancing around. The guy behind us has AirPods in, but really, anyone could be listening. I regret telling her that Nik actually made me come, sometimes without even touching my clit. With everyone else I've slept with, Chance included, I had to fake it. "You're the worst."

"Maybe Shona and I should try it," Ellie says. "With a toy, obviously."

"Wait, what?" I say, whipping my head around so fast my hair nearly hits Victoria in the face.

"It's new," Ellie says. She's blushing, pink bangs falling into her eyes. "So don't—"

"This is the best news ever! I *knew* you guys were flirting."

Victoria squeals. "So you have Shona, Izzy has her—"

"Don't you dare. I haven't even seen him since the party."

"Right," she says, dragging out the word. "I'm sure."

I'm not lying; in the week since the party, I've stayed away from Nik. It's been harder than I'd expect, at a school this large, but it's like when I really want a pair of sold-out shoes and suddenly it seems like everyone is wearing them but me. A couple days ago, as I walked past the athlete gym, I saw him bench-pressing enough weight that I almost started drooling. Just yesterday, I nearly ran into him in the quad, but hid behind a shrub before he noticed me.

I still can't believe he showed up out of the blue, asking me if I missed him.

Of course I missed him; I missed him before I even lost him. But that's not the point. We were never dating, which means I don't have the right to be upset by how things ended. The only thing more pathetic than getting upset at your former fling in a stupid party outfit complete with *glitter* would be pining over him, and as long as I avoid him, I can try to move on. Maybe I'll get lucky and he'll be gone for the NHL by Halloween. He told me over the summer that he wants his degree first, but a girl can dream.

"Really," I say. "I'm chill. I'm moving on. My crush on Harry Styles is returning."

I wonder what Nik thinks of McKee girls. Who knows, maybe he's hooked up with a new girl each night this week, enjoying the fact that male athletes on this campus never have to go looking for company. Maybe the next time I see him, he'll be holding hands with some gorgeous girl who—

"Izzy," Ellie says, nudging my arm.

"Are you going to order?" the dude behind the counter asks.

I blink, my green-tinged daydreams scattering. "Oh, sorry. Yeah. Can I get an iced coffee with a pump of vanilla syrup?" I pull out my card, hoping to foot the whole bill before Victoria or Ellie offers, but someone else beats me to the chip scanner.

"No latte today, Isabelle?" Nik asks, tilting his head to the side as he tucks his credit card back into a leather wallet.

My heart jackrabbits as I glare at him. He's got a smug look on his face, as if he's thrilled to have surprised me. First the party, and now this. Where did he even come from? I glanced around when we arrived to make sure I wasn't about to run into him, and I thought I was safe.

"This is the best day ever," Victoria whispers. "Free coffee *and* a show."

He looks good today, dressed in a gray T-shirt and dark wash jeans that I'm sure cost a couple hundred dollars each. I know what his wardrobe is like. Damp hair curls over his forehead. A leather messenger bag hangs from one shoulder, and somehow, the pen tucked behind his ear looks attractive, not douchey. He gives me a lopsided smile; it's always a smirk, thanks to his scar.

I straighten. At least I put on more than just mascara this morning.

"I was about to pay for that."

He hands me my drink. "I figured one more coffee run couldn't hurt. Old times' sake."

My cheeks erupt in what I'm sure is a very noticeable blush. He bought my morning coffee at least a dozen times over the summer. I drank whole milk iced lattes with the most colorful flavors on the menu: orange, lavender, raspberry. He always got a black iced coffee, bitter enough to make me scrunch my nose when I kissed him. The best mornings were the ones when he could hang out with me for a while, instead of rushing off for a session with his trainer.

I stab a straw into the coffee lid. There's no point in bringing up those memories. "Come on," I tell Victoria and Ellie.

"What, no thank-you?"

I want nothing more than to thank him, except my thank-you would involve a kiss, so instead, I try for a smile. A polite but dismissive one, like you'd give the weird old guy staring at you on the subway platform. "Thanks. I need to get to class."

"How is volleyball going? Did you talk to your coach yet?"

"It's fine. And I did." I step around him, ignoring the fluttering in my belly. "I'm going to be late."

He flashes my friends a smile before guiding me forward, fingers brushing the small of my back. "I'll walk you."

I march to the door, knowing he's right on my heels. Outside, before I can escape, he stops me in my tracks with a hand on my arm.

"Please, Isabelle. Let's find a time to talk." He glances around as he tugs me behind the nearest tree. The September sun filters through the still-green leaves. "I know you have a match later, but what about tomorrow? Dinner?"

I bite my lip, brushing the hair away from my face. I should have put it up before I left the gym; it's annoyingly windy outside. Somehow, it doesn't surprise me that he knows my volleyball schedule.

"There's nothing to say."

"We both know that's not true."

I practically fling my hair over my shoulder. A piece falls back over my eyes. "Look—"

"Here," he says, pulling a scrunchie out of his bag. A pink scrunchie, to be exact. A scrunchie I lost one day after an impromptu and ill-advised trip to Jones Beach with the guy holding it out.

I stare at it like it's poisonous. "You found it? And kept it?"

He gives it a shake. "It's yours."

Our fingers brush as I take it, sending a tiny, delicious lick of warmth through me. I smooth my hair into a ponytail, willing away my flush. It's just a scrunchie, after all.

"Found it in my cupholder," he adds, half smiling. "Remember when you—"

"Why are you toying with me?" I bet I could finish his sentence; he's thinking about when I put my hair up to blow him while we were both sunburnt and sandy and craving cold beers. I banish the thought. "You never—we never—"

His gaze doesn't leave mine. "You know me better than that."

"We can't do this." I take a step back. "Summer's over."

"And things look a hell of a lot different now."

"So?" I blink, emotion crowding my throat. "You can't tease me just because I'm the convenient option."

"Is that what you really think I'm doing?" He traces the side of my face, fingers hooking on my chin.

This close to him, I feel the power in his body—and remember exactly how he used that to make me scream. Every intimate encounter before him ended in disappointment, but he made me feel so wanted, so good. A tangle in the bedsheets meant orgasms so intense I cried and him praising me for it in his lowest, roughest voice.

Good girl, Isabelle. So perfect for me, like sunshine after a storm.

I want to melt into him, but instead, I steel my spine. "I'm sure dozens of girls are dying for a shot with McKee's newest hockey star."

He tugs on my ponytail, gaze darkening. "And I haven't noticed a single one, sunshine."

My heart skips a beat or five. The ponytail move is bad enough, but calling me *sunshine* again?

I should leave. Go to class. He's just saying whatever he thinks will get me to agree to one last hookup, and I'm falling for it. And yet I can't help but sway closer, inch by breathless inch . . . until my lips brush his.

My entire body sparks at the light contact. I relish his sharp intake of breath, gripping his shirt even tighter as I swipe my tongue over the seam of his lips. His familiar, clean scent makes me shiver. He slides an arm around my waist, holding me close, my coffee nearly spilling over our shoes.

For one perfect, sparkling moment, it's July again, and I'm drunk on him.

Then my eyes open, and reality crashes through. I jerk away, hitting my hip on his bag and stumbling.

"Sorry, sorry. That was just—a thank-you. A thank-you for the coffee."

It's just a kiss. Kisses don't count for anything.

I make a break for my building, and this time he doesn't try to follow me.

CHAPTER 9
Nikolai

Five missed calls from Dad.

The news took longer to reach him than I thought it would.

I ignore my phone, trying to focus on the reading for my class on modern Russian politics. I pick up my highlighter, but the words—English and Russian alike—swim in front of my eyes. I wonder if Donna enrolling me in this class is Grandfather's idea of a joke.

My phone buzzes yet again. The girl sitting across from me raises her head, smacking her bubble gum.

"This is a quiet room," she says, pointing to a sign on the wall.

I scowl at her as I silence the phone. She just blinks at me, clearly equally annoyed, before going back to work.

I spoke Russian to Isabelle three times: once because she asked if I was fluent, so I replied Да, and waxed poetic about how pretty she looked in the dress she was wearing, and two times while she was asleep. "Sunshine" describes her perfectly in English, but the Russian term of endearment, солнышко, solnishko, translates more directly to "little sun," and that's what I think of when I look at her.

I haven't seen her since she pressed her lips to mine and ran like she hadn't just awakened every nerve in my body. If I'd been thinking clearly, I'd have dragged her back and told her exactly what I think about our summer fling.

Instead, she slipped through my fingers again.

My phone lights up with yet another call.

"Maybe you should take that," the girl says.

"Maybe you should mind your own business," I mutter as I stand, grabbing the phone.

I leave the quiet room and duck into an alcove in the hallway. I run my hand through my hair, rubbing the back of my neck, as the call connects. A cold tendril of panic hooks into my heart. I know I should block his number, but whenever I try, I can't quite make myself.

Five minutes. I'll give him five minutes.

"Dad?" I say in English.

"Only six calls this time. That's an improvement."

I've heard people call Russian a harsh language, but that's not true if you understand it, and it always sounds extra-smooth coming out of my father's mouth. I can imagine him perfectly, even though I haven't seen him in person since my eighteenth birthday, when the no-contact custody agreement ceased. Tall and broad-chested, with a long, handsome face. A crooked nose, but that's to be expected after a lifetime of playing hockey. Brown eyes like mine, and the same defined jawline. He has a face that looks good on camera. Even when his teeth were all chippy, his smile would draw stares.

I stand straighter, despite the fact he's thousands of miles away and can't actually see me. He used to hit my legs with his twig to correct my posture while skating, and it stuck.

I shouldn't answer when he calls. However talented and charming he is—and believe me, plenty of people think he's a great person, an excellent ambassador for Russian hockey—I shouldn't keep letting him into my life. He's a manipulative asshole when sober and worse when drunk. He controlled as much of my life as he could, and hurt my mother, and then eventually hurt me, that New Year's Eve so long ago.

Sometimes I wake up drenched in cold sweat, unable to

breathe. And sometimes . . . sometimes I wake up missing him. He put me in the hospital, and I haven't eradicated the part of me that still loves him.

"What do you want?" I ask, switching to Russian. "I'm in the middle of something."

"Visit me."

I nearly drop the phone. "What?"

"You haven't seen the club. I think you'll change your mind once you tour it and meet everyone."

"Change my mind about what?"

"I was always your best coach, Nikolai. You don't need more college."

"You have to be kidding." I laugh shortly. "I'm not going to play for you."

"Are you so sure that team in California will want you now? From what I heard, you made quite a mess."

That team in California. Like he doesn't know all the teams in the NHL; he spent a disastrous few years playing for the Penguins before injuries forced him—and his wife, and three-year-old son—to Moscow. He revived his career, but never made it back to the NHL.

"It's none of your business."

"You're my son. Of course it's my business."

"I thought you wanted me to play for the NHL." I'm glad I'm speaking Russian now, because I'm getting angry, and I doubt anyone passing by understands what I'm saying. When I was little, my father dreamed of making a comeback in the league through me. It shifted, once he retired from playing and started to coach professionally in the KHL, but I figured that wish wouldn't have just gone away. Not completely. "Isn't that where the money is? You always said things would have been different if you stayed in the league."

Would they really have been different? Would he have loved my mother more? Would he have loved *me* more?

He sighs. My body tenses at that sound, anticipating a raised voice. But when he speaks, his tone is calm, almost flat.

"We're prepared to make you a very generous offer."

For a moment, I consider telling him about my deal with Grandfather, but as much as I'd love to shock him, he'd just find a way to turn it around for his benefit. In truth, the Sharks organization wasn't thrilled to hear about my expulsion, but I'm a talented enough prospect that they let it slide—provided I have a good season with McKee and continue to show progress. I should have told them to forget it, but I couldn't make myself open the door to that conversation. Not yet, anyway. Some delusional part of me must think there's a chance I can convince Grandfather to change his mind.

"No amount of money will ever make me say yes to playing for you." I say the words in English, practically spitting them out. "I'd rather play for nothing than wear your jersey."

"Everyone has a price, Kolya."

At the sound of the old diminutive for my name, my heart nearly stops. It's a speck of affection, barely anything, and yet it resonates with me like a half-remembered dream.

"Don't. Don't—call me that."

"It's your name, no? The name I gave you." His voice is a soft blanket. "Nikolasha, I remember how tiny you were when I first held you."

I bite the inside of my cheek so hard I taste copper. My fingers go numb. I curl and uncurl them, trying to get the feeling back.

He's manipulating me. He's sour that he lost me to Grandfather when Mom divorced him, and he wants me back. As long as I remember that, I'm safe. He can't hurt me again, whether it's with fists or velvet-wrapped words.

A girl with long, dark hair rounds the corner. Yellow tank top. White denim skirt. Volleyball bag.

Isabelle.

"If everyone has a price, you'll have to try harder to find mine."

I don't wait to hear his reply. I end the call and run down the hallway. Isabelle's eyes widen when she notices me, stopping in her tracks even though she nearly collides with a guy carrying a stack of books.

"Nik? What's going on?"

She started calling me Nik all on her own, just like I called her Isabelle from our first conversation. Nik isn't Kolya, but I love it even more because it belongs to her. Kolya is a dagger, but Nik is a kiss.

I try to find the right words to set her at ease without getting into the phone call, but nothing comes out of my mouth. I just shake my head.

"Let's—here." She yanks me into the nearest closet, shutting the door before tossing her bag aside. "What's going on? Who were you talking to?"

My throat feels as if it's being welded shut. I shake my head again. "It's nothing. Just . . . nothing. I'm fine."

She cups my jaw. "You can talk to me."

Her blue eyes are wide with concern. I turn my face into her palm, chest twinging sharply at the ghost of affection. "I can't."

"Nik."

"I can't," I repeat, voice cracking.

She pushes closer. I tremble at her warmth, overcome with the desire to hold her. I fumble for the doorknob, but before I can turn it, she reaches up on her tiptoes and brushes her lips to mine.

My mind short-circuits as I breathe in her perfume. Bright, delicate citrus, like always. I whirl us around, pinning her against the door. She fists her hand in my shirt, urging me into another kiss.

"You're okay," she whispers.

I guide her onto her tiptoes. When I run my hands over her hips and thighs, she gets the idea and hooks her legs around my waist. I groan at the shift in position, dropping my head to her shoulder. The looming panic attack ebbs away, bit by bit.

"One more time," I murmur against her neck. It's selfish to ask this of her, but I can't help myself. "Distract me. Please, Isabelle."

She nods, tangling her hand in my hair and giving it a tug. I kiss her again, openmouthed and openly desperate. I feel her smile against my lips like she missed this as much as me; as if the other day at the coffee shop wasn't nearly enough.

This is so much better than arguing with Dad or trying to forget Grandfather's plans for me. It's the one thing in this whole situation that's bearable. She made the world fall away all summer, and she's doing it again right now with each kiss and each scratch of her nails down my back. I pull down her shirt, giving me access to her tits. Her nails dig in as she gasps. My dick throbs.

I hope she leaves marks with her pink manicure.

"Nik," she says, her voice wobbly as I press fevered kisses to the tops of her breasts.

I gently bite one of her nipples as I drag my hand down her side, bunching up her skirt. When I brush my fingertips over her panties, she moans into my mouth. My jeans are starting to get uncomfortable, but I ignore that in favor of teasing her. I know how easily she comes when I touch her just right.

"Isabelle." The name most people call her is cute, but her full name is beautiful. I love the way it sounds in my mouth.

"More," she gasps. "Please."

In other, less hurried moments, I've coaxed her into begging, but I don't have the patience for it right now. We're in a closet in the middle of the goddamn library. I'll control myself better in the future. Just . . . not yet. Not until I hear my name on her lips as she comes one more time.

I nudge her thin panties aside and slide a finger into her. She whimpers when I add another, curling both in search of that place that makes her fall apart. I kiss her all the while, getting both our mouths messy with spit. Her intake of breath lets me know I found her G-spot, and as I rub it, she arches her back as best she can against the door.

"Nik." Her ankles dig into my lower back hard enough to make me grunt. *"Nikolai."*

"Shh, sweetheart. Not so loud."

I wish I could taste her. I have half a mind to slip to my knees and lick her out against the door, but that'll make her come louder, and anyway, if I taste her again, it'll be that much harder to forget. I angle my thumb so it brushes against her clit with each stroke of my fingers. Her eyes are open, wide and blue in the dim of the closet, her lashes perfectly curved. Her breath comes in short pants. She's close.

I press our foreheads together, clenching my stomach as lust swoops through me. I'm skirting the edge just from this, and by her pleased smile, she knows it. I push a third finger into her. She's trembling, clenching around my fingers so tightly I can barely move them. With the next touch of my thumb against her clit, she says my name sharply. I muffle her loud cry as she comes.

I'm right on the edge, balls drawn up tight, but manage to rein it in. I pull out of her slowly, resisting the temptation to lick my fingers clean.

"Perfect girl." I let her down gently, tugging her skirt and panties back into place. "So fucking perfect when you come."

If possible, the praise makes her blush even deeper. We stare at each other for half a beat too long before she reaches for my waistband. I shake my head, pulling her away with the hand that isn't covered in her slick. I want that hand for when I jerk myself into my fist.

"Let me help."

"You should get back to whatever you were doing." I clear my throat; my voice sounds hoarse. "I'm sorry for interrupting."

"You must be aching."

"I'll take care of it."

It's one thing to pleasure her, but another for her to do it to me. If I have any chance at keeping my desires at bay, that door needs to stay locked. Not just shut. Locked, key tossed away. She made me come better than anyone I've ever been with, and the last thing I need is to experience that again. Besides, this was reckless of me. Selfish and reckless. I need to keep my distance.

She hesitates, eyes searching mine. "You're sure nothing's wrong?"

"Really. I'm fine."

She kisses my cheek, right over my scar. I shiver, resisting the urge to pull her into my arms once more.

"If you say so," she whispers into my ear. "I don't like seeing you sad."

CHAPTER 10
Nikolai

I pull the jersey out of my locker, staring at the gleaming 16 stitched on both sides.

The home sweaters for McKee aren't terrible. Deep purple with white accents, a crown splashed across the front. If I have to wear it, at least I get to keep my number. I make a face at it anyway. Like everything else in this locker room, it's entirely too purple.

Mickey, the starting center, gives me a glance as he fiddles with the tape on his stick. "You okay there, man?"

Our lockers are next to each other, with Cooper's on my other side. Since I was last here a few days ago, someone added my name and number to a metal placard over my slot. It's strange to see Abney there, instead of Volkov, but I can't deny the sense of satisfaction it gives me.

"Fine, thanks." I shove the home sweater back into the locker and pull out a practice one instead. Today is the first whole-team workout, and I'd be lying if I said I wasn't nervous. "How's it going with you?"

He rips the end of the tape carefully and curves it over the handle. "Fine. That last reading was a bitch, wasn't it? I'm dreading the quiz."

Right, we're in the same economics class. I didn't think it was so bad, but I just make a noncommittal noise. "Full pads, right?"

"Yeah. Today won't be too intense, though. Ryder likes to ease into it."

As the rest of the guys filter in, I work on sorting through my gear. Cooper nods at me shortly when he enters, continuing his conversation with one of the other guys on defense, Evan Bell. He claps Evan on the shoulder before settling next to me. He's clearly comfortable with everyone on this team, and meanwhile, my choices are to pretend I can hold a conversation with him, complain about economics class with Mickey, or sit in silence and listen to everyone else's laughter. I miss John and the rest of my old teammates. We've talked since I left UMass, but it's been uncomfortable. I don't know what to say to make things go back to the way they were.

Cooper nudges my side. "Hey, Abney. You want to talk to them today?"

Say what you want about Cooper Callahan, but he's been good about remembering what I said about my last name. Calling me by my father's name anyway would be an easy way to get a shot in, and he hasn't gone there.

It's almost enough to make me feel bad about accosting his sister in the library the other day.

Almost, but not quite.

At least I kept myself in check, in the end. She looked so goddamn pretty in that white denim skirt. The moment she left, I leaned against the door and jerked myself with my slick hand until I came into my fist, thinking of the way her voice broke around my name.

Now that there are more guys in here, I can't help but notice the stares. A gangly kid who must be a freshman nudges his friend, and both of them give me a quick look before putting their heads together and whispering. I know I have a reputation that extends throughout Hockey East and beyond—most guys with a pro player for a father get at least some attention, even when said player didn't have an illustrious NHL career—but it's always weird to see it in action.

"Hey, Volkov," someone else asks from across the room. "Is it true that you knocked both of Emerson Hull's front teeth out with one hit?"

"What about Coopy?" Evan asks. "He wouldn't admit if you chipped him up."

"That's inconclusive," Cooper says, a hint of amusement in his tone.

I *definitely* made him swallow a tooth sophomore year, but he did it to me first. I went a little too far with my insult—something about getting back to the football field, I could hear his daddy calling—and he clocked me in the jaw. I punched him right back, and the resulting fight led to twin suspensions.

"What about that hit on the Vermont goalie, what's his name," another guy says. "Right into the net. I saw the tape."

"Worth the penalty," I say, since half the guys in the room are staring at me—and especially the scar, I'm sure. I scrub my hand through my hair. People assume that I got it thanks to a hockey injury, a skate to the face or something, and I never correct them.

Starting on a new team sucks under normal circumstances, but this is particularly awkward. I played against most of these guys for at least one season, if not more, and looking around, I can recall plenty of tense moments. Every team has instigators; it's not like my style of play is unique, but it's one thing to fuck around with your opponents to knock them off their game and another to skate on their side of the ice.

"It's so cool that your dad played pro," the skinny freshman says in an eager voice. "Too bad the Penguins didn't stick with him."

"Did he coach you?" his friend asks.

Caught off guard, I nod. "Um, yeah. When I was younger."

"That's sick. You're so lucky."

I almost snort, but keep myself in check. Lucky. That's one way to put it. I stand, tugging off my T-shirt.

"Whoa, man," Mickey says. "Did you fuck a werewolf?"

Cooper whistles. "You must've been doing something right."

Oh, *fuck* me. Isabelle left marks on my back, and I forgot about them until this moment.

"Yeah, well, I'm settling in." I force a smirk. "Have to find a way to occupy myself until the season starts."

"Amen to that," Mickey says. "We should go out sometime. Callahan's gotten boring since he fell for Ryder's daughter."

Cooper just shakes his head. "I feel sorry for you."

"Yeah, totally," I say, even though the thought of intimacy with anyone other than Isabelle sounds about as appealing as drinking paint thinner.

"I've definitely heard more about you off the ice than on, man," another guy says, to everyone's laughter. "You're a legend."

You get caught hooking up with a chick in the locker room before a playoff game *one* time, and suddenly everyone in the conference thinks you've got game. I mean, I know I do, I've never had trouble finding hookups, but the chatter about it is ridiculous. It's just sex, and as long as everyone involved has a good time, it's no one's business but theirs.

One of the other defensemen, Jean, leans over. "Dude. Did you really sleep with an entire women's figure skating team?"

"I heard at the same time," someone else adds.

"Hey," Cooper says mildly. "Keep it respectful."

"I think my dick would have fallen off if that was true." The guys hoot at that, and one of the freshmen flushes beet-red. "Anyway, I don't kiss and tell, gentlemen."

"I hope you're getting ready in there," Ryder drawls from the hallway.

I get into my gear, and I'm grabbing my stick when someone's voice cuts through the rest of the chatter.

"Why are you here?"

I look over my shoulder. Aaron Rembeau, the goaltender, stands with his pads half-on, glancing around at the rest of the guys. The side conversations fade out. "No offense, but it's a little late for a transfer. Coop, do you know?"

I know what he's really asking. He doesn't have to say it aloud. He wants to know if he can trust me. If they—the team that already existed long before I showed up—can put their faith in me as a teammate. My stomach tightens. I glance at Cooper, who just raises an eyebrow. Letting me have the floor, like he promised.

"I know you know me as the captain of the Minutemen," I say, looking around at the guys. My new teammates. "And I thought that's what I'd be doing this season, too. But I fucked up, and I was lucky enough to get a second chance here. I'm excited to be a Royal."

"Fucked up how?" Evan asks.

I relay the story quickly, and hopefully for the last time. It gets uncomfortable for a moment; drugs are the one thing you never want to fuck with during the season, but gradually, everyone relaxes. Mickey even claps me on the back when I finish talking. I miss my former teammates like hell, and I think everyone can hear that in my voice.

What matters is getting to the Frozen Four. Holding up the Stanley Cup isn't in my future, but at least there's a chance of ending my college career on a high note. Looking around the room, I can see why Coach is confident. Aside from the strength of the upperclassmen, there's a hunger in the air, anticipating the start of the season, and that's a language I will always understand.

I stride to the door. "Let's go. We're not going to win it all if we don't get started."

"Yeah," Cooper says, a hard note in his voice. "What Nikolai said."

Fuck. I didn't mean to play captain in front of everyone; it just slipped out. A few of the guys titter, looking between us. I wait for a rebuff, but after a stifling pause, Cooper grabs his stick, too.

"Come on," he says, shoulder knocking into mine as he passes. At the command, the team jolts into action.

During warm-ups, I stick to myself, so I don't risk saying anything even more inane. I can't stop putting my foot in my mouth when it comes to this guy. I was serious when I agreed with him that the team is his; I'm not trying to steal the position out from underneath him. He has the support of everyone in the locker room, and that didn't happen accidentally.

Which is why I'm not at all surprised when, during our scrimmage, Cooper slams into me so hard, my stick goes flying.

I spin out, the world flashing purple and white as I collide with the boards. I stare at the ceiling for a moment, stars swimming in my eyes. My body protests, but not terribly. It was a good check. If it had happened during a game, he wouldn't have ended up in the box.

I spit out my mouth guard, trying to catch my breath.

He stands over me, holding out his hand.

I'm sure everyone is waiting to see my reaction. If I'm going to take his hand and get up, or if I'm going to challenge him. I'm not an idiot; I know the guys won't embrace me without proof I'm one of them. Hell, Cooper is waiting too, his bare hand still outstretched, glove tucked underneath his arm.

"Take it. That's the last time I'll ever hit you."

I think of Isabelle and nearly laugh.

But I grip his hand, and he helps me to my feet. Our eyes meet. A beat passes in absolute silence.

I don't sense trust yet, but I do sense respect. That's going to have to be enough for now.

"Grab your stick," he says, skating backward with a gracefulness that's hard to match, even for me. "Your turn."

CHAPTER 11

Izzy

W ait wait wait," Victoria says from her perch on my bed, brandishing her chocolate milkshake. We beat Merrimack in a hard-fought match earlier, and stopped for ice cream in downtown Moorbridge on the way to my house to do homework. "Back up."

"Yeah," Ellie says. She's on the floor, textbook abandoned at her side, surrounded by several of my stuffed animals, including my favorite, a worn pink rabbit very cleverly named Pinkie. Once Victoria asked about the "Russian Situation," any pretense of a post-game study session fell away. "This happened in the *library*?"

"Sounds hot to me," Shona says with a shrug, her thin, dark braids falling over her shoulder as she scratches Tangy behind the ears. Of all my friends, she loves Shona the most; she's barely given me half a glance in the past hour. I would be offended if I weren't secure in the knowledge that at least she loves me more than Sebastian. "Then again, he's very hot. Like, I'm gay as hell, but I can still appreciate him."

"The scar is a game changer," Victoria agrees.

I duck my head to hide my blush. The first time I worked up the courage to touch Nik's scar, he startled and grabbed my wrist, but after a moment he nodded, giving permission. We were in my bed, awake past midnight, the sounds of the city providing a soundtrack to an otherwise quiet moment. He trembled when I brushed my lips to his cheek, and I felt victorious, even as my heart ached for him. A scar like that can't have a funny story, after all.

"So, he dragged you into a library closet, *Beauty and the Beast* style—"

"Does that happen in the movie?" Ellie interrupts.

"—and had his way with you, but then he kicked you out—"

"Well, I did the dragging," I say, my blush deepening.

"—can I not finish?" Victoria says with faux exasperation. "He kicked you out before he let you touch the goods. Did I get that right?"

I make a face as I sip my cotton candy milkshake. "Technically speaking."

Whatever was going on with Nik the other day, I enjoyed the outcome. I just wish he had let me touch him back, or at least told me what was wrong. I should be glad that nothing else came of it—he didn't text me after, even though I half expected it—but the thought of that being the end of our connection makes me sad, not relieved.

"Technically speaking, you kissed him again first," Ellie says. She leans her head against Shona's shoulder. Shona turns and kisses her. I smile at the sight; they're so cute together.

"Ugh. Thanks for the reminder."

She shrugs. "What do you want to happen?"

"She wants to bone him again, obviously," Victoria says.

Shona snorts. "You should move on, Iz. Let the summer be the summer."

"Why didn't he just . . . let me return the favor?" I shake my head slightly. "Maybe he realized he isn't into me anymore."

"I don't think that's it," Victoria says dryly.

There's a knock on my bedroom door. "Izzy?"

I choke at the sound of Cooper's voice. At least we weren't screaming Nik's name or something equally embarrassing.

I pull open the door. "What's up?"

Cooper leans against the doorway, shooting my friends a grin. "Hello, ladies. Nice match."

Victoria perks up. "Is Aaron with you?"

"In the living room."

"Babe!" Victoria shouts as she runs down the stairs. "I thought you said you had practice!"

"Yeah, didn't you have practice?" Cooper and Aaron came to the match earlier, to cheer us on, but they had to leave early to get to the rink.

"Coach took pity on us and kept it short. Can I talk to you for a moment?"

I narrow my eyes at Ellie and Shona as I scoop up Tangerine. "If you make out, don't mess up my stuffed animals. Especially Pinkie."

When we're in the hallway, I hug the cat closer. "Everything okay?"

"You played really well today." He gives me a half hug as he pats Tangy's head. "You'll be back to playing setter in no time."

"I hope so."

"I know so." He lets out a breath. "Look, I know he wasn't around over the summer, but now that he's here . . . you haven't seen Nikolai, right?"

The cotton candy taste in my mouth turns acrid. Hopefully he didn't see us together and this is just him being overprotective. It was reckless to kiss Nik right by the Purple Kettle. Even more so to go into that closet with him.

"Um, no? Why would I?"

He shrugs. "No reason."

"Why, did he say something?" I hope I sound casual, even though my belly is doing somersaults. On one hand, I hope that Nik never brings me up to Cooper, ever, in any capacity, but on the other . . .

"Not exactly," he says. "Look, I'm not saying there's anything wrong with keeping things casual, but Nikolai makes it an art form. I've seen him with girls after games, and I've heard the stories. If he makes a pass at you, turn him down. You'll just end up getting hurt."

The other day, Nik said he hadn't noticed any of the girls at McKee. Was that true, or just a lie? In the library, he seemed desperate for me, but that doesn't mean he hasn't been that way for anyone else.

I glance away. I hate to lie, but it's not like anything is going to come from this. "Cooper, come on. I doubt he even knows who I am."

He shoves his hands into his pockets, rocking on his heels. "It's just—I remember how messed up you were about Chase."

I redden. "Chance."

"Stupid name," he mutters.

"That was ages ago."

"And I still wish I had the chance to defend you." His voice strengthens. "He was a scumbag. Cheating on you was bad enough, but breaking up with you on your birthday? I should have kicked his ass."

I stiffen at the mention of that ruined seventeenth birthday. My excitement slipped into confusion the longer I waited for Chance to pick me up, and then it became devastation when I realized what he was doing instead. *Who* he was doing instead. The mere thought twists my heart, yet I bristle at Cooper's words. The wound Chance left was only exacerbated by last year's hookups, and my summer with Nik didn't help the way I wanted, either. Doesn't mean I want to admit that to my brother.

"I can take care of myself, you know."

"I didn't say you couldn't. But I'm your brother, Iz. I want you to be happy."

My indignation fades at the earnest look on his face. He's always been overprotective, but it comes from a good place. He doesn't have anything to worry about, anyway. I know that things could never go anywhere with Nik. Soon, he'll get bored, and whenever we cross paths on campus, he'll pretend he doesn't know me. Same as the guys I hooked up with last year. Same as Chance, when he wasn't parading his next conquests in front of me.

"I'm happy. Really."

Mostly.

CHAPTER 12

Izzy

Whenever I head to the gym early—something I'm determined to make a habit this season—I call my dad.

He wakes up ridiculously early to work out too, even now. He retired from football ages ago, but the drive to stay fit hasn't gone away. We have a stacked gym at home; adding the indoor basketball court really took things to the next level. When I'm home, I'm usually able to wrangle him, and anyone else who is around, into playing some casual volleyball.

I finish changing into my bathing suit, a one-piece that's pink enough to put Barbie to shame, and tie my hair into a tight bun before dialing his number. You're not supposed to bring phones into the pool area, but it's so early that I'm the only one around.

"Good morning, darling," Dad says, answering, like always, on the first ring. "At the gym?"

"The pool today. I'm getting back into laps, for stamina." I sit by the edge, letting the water run over my calves. This is the pool that any athlete at McKee can use, which is nice because it's separate from the main pool. It's smaller than true Olympic size, but always comfortable and inviting. "How are things with you?"

"Your mother and I are going to play pickleball this morning."

"I thought you said it was an insult to tennis?"

"She's very taken with it. I suppose it can't be the worst thing in the world."

"I'm sure it's fun. It's a net sport, I can get behind that."

He chuckles. "And how has volleyball been?"

I take a breath, thinking about how to frame this. We have a winning record, and successfully navigated a difficult double-header against Albany. I even earned a compliment from Alexis after a snappy move to keep a crucial rally going during the Merrimack match, so all in all, it could be worse, but I've played opposite hitter each match. No setter yet, even for a few plays.

"It's fine," I say eventually, kicking my feet. "We're 3-1 right now, with two matches coming up against UConn."

"That sounds promising."

"We're better than them." I think of Brooklyn's presence on the court and nod to myself. "Definitely better. We should win both."

"Has your coach given you playing time at setter?"

"Not yet."

"But you spoke with her about your frustrations.'"

Yes, and she thinks you bought me a place on the volleyball team. I worry my lip as that thought runs through my mind. There's no use mentioning it to him. It's not like anything she said wasn't true; my parents have contributed heavily to the university. They're a big part of the reason why the library is adding to its fiction collection and the football facilities are getting upgrades in a few years. Neither of them came from money, but then Dad got into the NFL and started winning, and things snowballed from there. His second career in broadcasting has been one of the most lucrative ever for a retired athlete, and they funnel a lot of their resources into the Callahan Family Foundation, an organization my mother runs that works with various sports-related charities.

I do wonder what he'd say, though. My parents were never the type to complain to coaches—Dad knows better than anyone how important it is to form your own relationships with them, and we'd never get there on our own if they tried to clean up our messes—but I wouldn't put it past him to try to talk to Alexis if he knew the truth about how our conversation went.

That would be *so* mortifying.

"Yeah. But it's not like I'm going to play setter right away. She's paying attention to how I'm doing with what I'm given now."

"And I'm sure it's going very well," he says, in a voice that brooks no argument. "Just like your efforts in your classes this year."

I've always ragged on my brothers for calling Dad "sir" when having serious conversations with him, but when he uses that tone, I can understand the urge. This is the same guy who led his team to three Super Bowls, after all. When he wants something to happen, he expects it to be done. I didn't do terribly in my classes last year, but I still got a stern talking-to about buckling down.

"I did well on my first philosophy paper."

"Good. I want to hear those kinds of updates all semester, darling."

"Yes, sir," I say, mostly teasing.

He sighs; I can imagine him pinching his nose between his thumb and forefinger. "Isabelle."

I smile at the exasperated note in his voice. My mom is one of my best friends, but I've always had a special relationship with my dad, too.

I'm his only daughter, and his youngest kid to boot. His last Super Bowl win is one of my earliest memories; he held me on his shoulders while he celebrated on the field, confetti flying everywhere. I was obsessed with princesses at the time and absolutely *loved* when he dressed up as one too, so instead of donning a Super Bowl Champion cap, he put on a plastic tiara. He didn't care that he was on camera, or that his teammates and coaching staff surrounded us. He held the Lombardi trophy in one arm and me in the other, crooked tiara on his head and glitter on his cheeks, and that photograph ended up on the back of every newspaper in

New York. I have a copy of *The Daily News* framed in my bed-room at home.

"You took a big step forward this summer," he adds. "I'm proud of you. Your mother and I have friends who attended the Heyman wedding, and they were very impressed by the work you put into it."

"Oh, that's cool." I know he's just trying to compliment me, but after the conversation with Coach, it feels uncomfortable. "Mom's the one who got it for me, though. She met Katherine at that charity thing and heard she was looking for an intern, remember?"

"And you're the one who took advantage of that opportunity. There's nothing wrong with that. Who knows, maybe you'll end up being a wedding planner after you graduate."

Even though I loved every moment of my summer internship, I have zero idea what I want to do with my future. I wish I had a set path like my brothers. James has never wondered about his future, and Cooper hasn't either. Sebastian changed course when he moved on from baseball, but he knew exactly where to go next. But volleyball isn't going to be a career for me. I'm only major-ing in communications because it's a neutral course of study that could lead in a bunch of different directions. Including wedding planning, I suppose, but I wonder if it would truly be enough for Mom and Dad.

I know that they want me to be the best version of myself, but sometimes it's hard to shake the feeling that their expectations are not that high. I can't help but wonder if some part of them thinks I'm not worth taking seriously, and all this talk of pushing my-self is just that: talk. I've always been coddled, always protected. Spoiled.

"Maybe," I say eventually. "I need to get started on my swim."

"Good. We'll talk soon about coming to some matches, okay?"

After I hang up, I drop straight into the water, deep enough to touch the bottom before coming back to the surface. Cool water streams down my face. I settle myself against the wall, flexing my toes.

I doubt I'll get any time at setter when they do watch me play. I'll just have to do the best I can at opposite hitter and hope I have a good match.

I lunge into my first lap, doing the breaststroke from one end to the next. I work up a rhythm quickly, flipping against the pool wall to launch into each lap. After a few minutes of going as hard as I can, my limbs start to burn, but I keep pushing. My mind remains stubbornly crowded with thought after thought, and there's one I can't shake.

Nikolai. Cooper's rival, now his teammate. So much for state lines separating us.

It doesn't matter anyway, because I'm not letting what we did in the library happen again. Even if it helped distract him from whatever was going on, Shona's right; I need to let the summer be the summer. Eventually, I'll feel fond when I think of him. Probably.

There's too much chlorine in this pool. It's making my eyes sting.

Only a silly girl would let herself get distracted by a boy.

I accidentally swallow a huge gulp of water and start coughing. I stop mid-lap, rubbing my chest. I'm definitely crying a little, and not from the chlorine, but fuck it. It feels like I'm treading water in my actual life, trying to balance everything on my head while I keep it high enough to breathe.

The door behind me clicks open and shut, echoing loudly in the high-ceilinged room.

I whirl around, stiffening when I see who just interrupted. "You've got to be kidding me."

CHAPTER 13

Nikolai

I swipe my access card to open the athlete gym. It's still dark out, the sun struggling to make its way over the tops of the trees.

The door shuts with a click as I stride down the dark hallway. This early, no one else should be around, and that's what I'm banking on. I ease my way into the men's locker room, settling on one of the benches to open my bag.

By our apartment in Moscow, there was an indoor pool. On the rare days I didn't have hockey, Mom would dig out my bathing suit, grab a book, and bring me there to play for a few hours. No Dad, no hockey, just Mom watching with a smile while I showed off how fast I could swim from one end to the other. I started playing hockey with the older kids from the time I was five, and even then, I was one of the best on the ice. A break to do something just for fun was a treat.

Swimming isn't an official part of my training routine, but it's as relaxing to me now as it was when I was little. During hockey games, my mind races with constant decision-making. Swimming involves no thoughts at all.

And right now, I can't stop thinking about Isabelle. The library, the party, the whole goddamn summer races through my mind on repeat.

When I left her sleeping, I stood by the bed for the longest time. She looked beautiful, her dark hair spilling down her bare back, her pink mouth curved like a bow. She had orange nails—Creamsicle, she called them—and little diamond studs in her ears. Her favorite stuffed animal, a worn-out pink bunny, stood guard on the nightstand.

I nearly climbed back into bed beside her.

Instead, I brushed a kiss to her forehead and eased out the door.

I told myself she deserved a clean break, and I knew if I stayed, I'd selfishly try to convince her to keep things going. I must be even more of a bastard than I realized, because now, I can't bear the thought of letting her go. The moment I see her, my desires take over. I spark like a match.

True attraction is magic. I've slept with plenty of women whose beauty I could recognize without it actually doing a thing for me. I'd get turned on just fine, but it wouldn't be bone-deep and irresistible. It wouldn't leave me needing more. I never daydreamed about them, or wondered how they were on a random Tuesday morning, or bought their coffee just because.

And I know part of that has to do with my own guardrails. I've been reckless plenty of times in my life, but never when it comes to romantic feelings. If I took things too far, and it spiraled out of control the way my parents' relationship did, I'd have no one to blame but myself.

Isabelle is in a category all her own. When I'm around her, I can't focus on anything else. We could be in the middle of a hurricane, and I'd just stand there like a goddamn fool, cataloging the raindrops on her face.

All the more reason to stay away. No more parties, no more coffee, no more closet hookups. She deserves so much better than an asshole like me, no matter my feelings.

I throw my bag into one of the lockers, even though I'm sure no one else is going to come in, and open the door to the pool.

I freeze as I stare at the girl in the middle lane. There's no mistaking that pink one-piece. Not when I peeled it off her myself one June night.

The universe must seriously hate me.

The door slips from my hands before I can decide whether to leave, shutting loudly enough that Isabelle turns her head.

So much for escaping.

"You've got to be kidding me," she says.

Her hair is in a sleek bun. Water droplets cling to everything; her earlobes, her eyelashes, her lips. I take a step forward, unable to help myself. "I promise I'm not stalking you."

"This campus has never felt so small."

"I know." I take a few steps forward. "You're everywhere I look."

"You aren't supposed to be here anyway," she says, a stubborn note in her voice.

"But I'm glad I am."

When the words leave my lips, I realize they're true. I am glad to be here. The situation aside, it led me back to Isabelle. Even if nothing permanent can come of this, being around her in any capacity is better than not being around her at all. I like knowing she's on the same campus as me, never far away.

She blinks, her expression shuttering. "You keep saying things you don't mean."

"I'm not a liar, Isabelle." I take a couple more steps, until I'm on the edge of the pool. This is a terrible idea, but I owe her an apology or ten, and I want nothing more than to do it while she's in my arms.

So I jump in.

"Nik!" she shrieks as I surface, hair plastered to my forehead, water up my nose.

I grin at her. "Warmer than the Atlantic, for sure. I'd skinny-dip in this."

She wrinkles her nose, even as she smooths my hair back. "You're such a *boy*."

I wrap my arm around her, tugging her into the shallow end. She lets me, although she has a frown on her face. I push her against the wall of the pool as I brush my lips to hers. The moment she kisses back, something unwinds in me, relaxing my limbs. I taste chlorine on her lips. She's deliciously warm, letting me crowd her with a leg between hers as she wraps her arms around my neck. We had dozens of moments like this over the summer, giving in to that itch wherever we were. If we weren't somewhere private, we'd make it private enough. I never laughed more than during adventures with her, and that has to count for something.

I can't date her, and I can't fall for her, but I can't give her up, either. Not yet. Even if I'm running the risk of any tenuous trust with her brother falling to pieces.

"I'm sorry," I whisper against her lips.

She pulls away, her eyes searching mine. "You didn't say goodbye," she says haltingly. "You left me like it meant nothing."

"I know."

"Did it? Am I the idiot here? Caring about you when you didn't give a shit about me?"

"No. It was never like that."

"Then what?" She kicks at me underneath the water. Her voice gets stronger. "What the fuck, Nik?"

I hesitate. Once I explain myself, I can't go back. The truth always changes things. She might decide to put up a real barrier, no matter my feelings, and I'll have to respect it.

But if she doesn't—if we fall back into what we had before—

I fist my hand in her hair and pull her into another kiss. Deep, lingering, until I can't breathe anymore.

"I didn't say goodbye because I didn't want to." I stroke my thumb across her cheek. "I didn't want to shut the door on us."

CHAPTER 14

Izzy

I'm shivering, but I've never felt so warm.

Nik's words hang in the air, winding through the memories crowding my mind. Days on the beach. Nights in the city. Slow mornings wrapped in daisy-patterned bedsheets and afternoons in deep blue. Frozen lemonade and outdoor markets and matching white linen. A fire in my belly, laughter in his eyes. Love bites and chocolate kisses and echoey museum exhibits. Tequila in my mouth and salt on his lips. Midnight dim sum and noontime beers and *New Girl* on mute in the middle of a thunderstorm.

This warmth is different from the sparks that erupted the first time he kissed me, and much more dangerous.

He didn't want to say goodbye.

I drag my hands down his strong back. "I woke up alone."

"I know." He sounds serious, thoughtful. "I thought . . . it would be better, I guess. Cleaner, for both of us. I knew if I tried—"

"There was nothing clean about it." I shake my head, replaying the moment I realized he wasn't in my borrowed summer apartment. I waited too long to see if he would come back, and felt like such an idiot once morning turned to afternoon, and eventually evening. Just like Chance on my seventeenth birthday. "It hurt, Nik. It made me feel like . . . like everything you told me over the summer was fake. Like whatever we shared—"

"It wasn't fake."

I press my lips together tightly. My heart does cartwheel after cartwheel.

"It wasn't fake, Isabelle," he says quietly. "It was real, all of it. Real enough that I knew if I tried to say goodbye, I'd just beg for more instead."

My breath stutters. "Then you should have said something."

"I know," he says quietly.

Even if it was real, there's a reason why we didn't make plans past August. He has his life and I have mine, and they don't fit together. He might think he wants me, but if this keeps going, eventually he'll realize just how much better he can do.

Yet he's here, looking at me with hunger in his eyes. He's especially handsome like this, his broad chest on display, dark hair slicked back, water droplets dotting his still-tanned skin. I almost trace my fingers down his rib cage—but then I remember the library. Did he push me out to try and control himself? Is he as much of a live wire around me as I am around him?

"I'm supposed to be focusing this semester," I say, nails digging into his skin. "No distractions."

"Calling me a distraction, sunshine?"

I manage what I hope is a casual enough shrug. "If the shoe fits."

"Your brother warned me away from you, you know. I may have said something about you to him last fall."

I sigh. "Oh, Nik."

"It was the first time I saw you." He presses a soft kiss to my cheek. "I was unfairly distracted. I couldn't say *nothing* about the prettiest girl in the stands."

I can't stop my smile. Just a tiny one, though. No wonder Cooper talked to me about him the other day. "Stop it, you're going to make me blush."

"Good." He leans in, his warm breath making me shiver anew. "You know, I think I like you soaking wet best."

My pussy actually throbs at that. I gasp in surprise. He just grins.

"What?" he says with fake innocence. "The beach, the pool . . ."

I hit his shoulder lightly. "I can't even with you."

The amusement fades as seriousness takes over his face again. "It can be our secret. What we do together is no one's business but ours, anyway."

I shouldn't say yes. He might be able to handle it, but I know I won't. My romanticism has bitten me one too many times, and I can already see how this will end. Eventually, I'll feel too much. Eventually, he'll move on, and my heart will be the one in pieces.

But he's holding me close right now. He's looking at me with warmth in his eyes.

The last time my heart felt this fragile, and I trusted a boy anyway, the road led to nothing but pain. It flutters all the same, begging me to give in.

I run my fingertip down his scar. "Just until we work it out of our systems."

"Everyone needs a little stress relief now and then. Especially athletes."

I nod seriously. "It should be on training plans."

He laughs—his best laugh, deep in his chest and absolutely infectious—and scoops me into his arms, carrying me out of the pool.

"I want you inside me," I say, breathless with laughter. I dig my nails into his skin for emphasis as I cross my legs over his lower back. "Since you didn't let me help you come last time."

"One of my stupider moments," he says as he throws open the door to the men's locker room.

I press a wet kiss to his ear. "At least you know it."

"This fucking pink bathing suit," he growls.

"Pretty, right?"

He practically slams me against the nearest bank of lockers as he kisses me, hands grabbing wherever they can reach.

"Pretty?" He laughs shortly as he massages my ass. "You look good enough to eat."

I tug him even closer, core clenching at his words. "What's stopping you?"

He drags the straps of the bathing suit down far enough to free my tits. He groans, licking his lips before pressing his face to them. I've always been self-conscious about them—they aren't much to look at, and even less noticeable when I'm wearing a sports bra—but I learned over the summer that he likes them like that. His hand fumbles into the locker for his bag, pulling out a condom. I shiver as the cold metal of the locker seeps into my skin.

He lifts me again, so easily my belly swoops. "Don't want you to freeze on me."

He strides to the nearest shower stall and runs the water, drenching both of us all over again. The heat makes me moan. I'm already on edge, anticipating the stretch of him inside me. He sucks my necklace into his mouth as he pulls my suit off the rest of the way. His hands dig into my hips as he maneuvers me against the wall.

"Spread those legs for me," he murmurs.

He drops to his knees.

I steady myself with a hand in his hair. He grins up at me, lopsided as always, and runs his hands down my thighs. He guides my foot to his shoulder, putting me on display for him, his other hand grounding me so I don't slip. I drag my teeth over my bottom lip as I look at him.

"Beautiful," he says.

He's beautiful like this too, and I open my mouth to tell him so, but then he presses his face against my pussy, and my mind short-circuits. I hold on to his hair tightly enough it must hurt, but he just moans against my slick skin. Desire pools in my core like lava. He finds my clit easily, teasing it with his tongue, making me jerk against the shower wall.

Hopefully if someone comes in, my moans are muffled enough that we're not interrupted. I can't help but get loud when it comes to him.

He licks lower, rubbing my clit with a finger instead. I arch my back as best I can, given the wall. He pinches the aching nub, making me whimper.

"Next time we do this," I say with a pant, "we need to be horizontal."

He pulls away, mouth shining. "I like the sound of that."

I dig my foot into his shoulder. "Don't stop."

He rubs his fingers through my soaked folds before sliding one into my core—and pressing the other against my asshole. I yelp, feeling my blush all the way to my ears. He never fucked me there, but he did finger me plenty.

His smile widens. "Such a princess."

"More," I say, voice breathy. "Nik, come on—"

He works the finger in all the way, moving it in tandem with the one in my cunt, and licks my clit again. I feel like I'm on fire, burning up from my ears all the way to the tips of my toes, as he keeps teasing, giving me just enough to hover on the edge. Right when I think I'm about to come, he backs off, dragging it out until I'm begging.

Finally, he nibbles my clit, and I explode at the pleasure. I cry out, slapping my hand over my mouth belatedly. His laughter vibrates against my sensitive skin as he gives me another lick before withdrawing his fingers. He helps me plant my feet on the floor of the shower.

"Should have opened this before," he says, cursing as he tries to tear the condom packet.

I pull his cock out of his bathing suit, running my hand down the long, thick length. Seeing the evidence of his arousal—that eating me out got him rock-hard—makes me moan again. It's one thing to hope that you're being sexy enough to affect someone else, and another to see it in action. I swipe my thumb over the reddened tip. He groans, jerking his hips.

"Wait, wait. I need to get inside you."

"I can't believe you didn't want me to do this," I say, twisting my hand just the way he likes as I give him a pump.

He sucks in a breath. "Wasn't about not wanting, sweetheart."

I shake my head as I help him roll on the condom, but I'm smiling. He cradles my face in his hands, kissing me deeply enough, I can taste myself. He turns me around, planting his hands on my hips to guide them against his. His cock presses against my ass, thick and achingly hard, as he hooks his chin over my shoulder. He brings an arm around my middle, hand flat against my belly, and nudges my legs apart.

"So goddamn sexy," he says, voice low and rough, as he sinks into my cunt, inch by tantalizing inch.

He's careful, but not gentle, pounding into me exactly the way I've been missing. He must be as desperate as me, because he moans into my ear with each thrust. Even though I just came, my body ramps up again, clenching around him. He smacks my ass, making me gasp sharply.

"Harder," I whine, even though my legs are shaking with the effort to keep standing. "You can do it harder."

"Good fucking girl," he says, punctuating that with a particularly deep thrust. "You need it like this, don't you? Rough like me."

He spanks me again, hard enough I feel the sting. I whimper against the tile. He teases my clit, sparking an even deeper level of pleasure. His thrusts get short, erratic, as he drags us both to the edge. When he spanks me a third time, the tips of his fingers catch on my cunt, and the burst of delicious pain shoves me right over the peak. I cry out, voice echoing in the shower stall. He grunts, blunt nails digging into my skin, as he tenses and spills into the condom.

My body trembles with aftershocks as he kisses my shoulder. He massages my bottom, murmuring praise. My toes curl against the tile floor; I missed his commanding touch so much. He unlocks something in me that no one else has been able to reach.

"Isabelle," he says finally, his voice breaking on the word. "You feeling good?"

I smile to myself. My name always sounds wonderful coming from him, but it's never better than when he's wrung out with pleasure.

I squeeze his hand. "So good."

We can do this a few more times. Maybe a few *dozen* more times. We became friends this summer, friends who slept together, and there's no reason we can't keep it going. Like he said, it's no one's business but ours. It's hardly a secret if there isn't much of a secret to keep.

He pulls out, reaching to shut off the shower. We're quiet for a moment, but no one comes barging in, so I reach up and run my fingers through his hair, giving him one more kiss for good measure. We make out for a long minute, just enjoying the quiet.

"God," he says eventually. His chest, glistening with water, heaves; he hasn't caught his breath yet. "That was so fucking perfect."

"Stress relief," I say, trying and failing to keep my smile in check.

He holds out his hand to help me out of the shower. "Coffee before class? We can go to the Starbucks off campus."

CHAPTER 15
Nikolai

September 15th

Cricket
How are you settling in?

I've never been so sick of the color purple

Promising start

It's fine

I guess

Grandfather had fun picking out my classes and I can't switch any of them

And I presume Isabelle's brother hasn't attempted a duel for her honor yet

Are you rewatching Bridgerton?

Think about how much more fun life would be if we still had duels

The inner workings of your
mind must be fascinating

You're hilarious.

Really, how is she?

I have no idea

Annnnd you're a terrible liar

I'm FaceTiming you in 5

Just fantastic

Oh, shush. We can practice my Russian

You're still taking that?

Think about how much it'll piss off
Grandfather when he realizes we
can gossip about him secretly

September 18th

Sunshine

Where's Bainwright Hall?

It's next to the arts center, why?

Is your brother usually this ridiculous?

This sounds promising

I've been wandering around campus for two fucking hours

With all the freshmen

Reminder: I am not a freshman

I do like an older man

Trying to find this hidden . . . flag? Old sweater? Trophy? I don't even fucking know

Aw, team bonding time, how adorable

Nothing about this situation is adorable

It's a flag, and if he hid it in Bainwright, it's probably on the fourth floor landing

September 20th

Sunshine

Practice is finally over

Your brother needs to figure out how to pass the fucking puck

I will absolutely not be relaying that to him

☺

Come over later? We can order in

Ooh, yes please

September 24th

Sunshine

I saw a bit of your practice today

Omg

Nik!

I was nearly late but I made it, thank god

Stop distracting me in the mornings

You looked good, though

All sweaty

You have such a fetish

No comment

Suuuuuure

Coach would have killed me if you interrupted

> I know, don't worry. No interruptions

> I haven't watched much volleyball

> But I could tell you were locked in

Why do I have the feeling this is
going to go in a dirty direction

> No puns, just an hour to kill
> before conditioning

> Open invitation

Sounds like you're about to have
plenty of physical activity

> Nowhere near as fun, though

> Second floor classroom, like last time

. . . I'll text you when I'm at the building

"GOOD," I SAY, stopping the puck with my stick. "That's a much better pass."

Micah, standing on the blue line, smiles at me. "I think switching up the grip helped."

"Try it again."

While he sets up, I glance at the bench. Cooper's in the middle of a conversation with one of the assistant coaches, but he gives me a cordial nod. We ran into each other a couple days ago and started chatting about the freshmen on the team, and I agreed to give Micah, the promising but gangly kid who wishes the Penguins stuck with my dad, some extra help during practices. Part of me bristled at Cooper's obvious attempt at trying to contain my leadership tendencies while throwing me a bone, but all the same, I don't mind helping out. Especially with Micah, who is more wide-eyed enthusiastic about playing at the college level than anyone I've ever met. I might not be able to do much for that poor freshman Grady, but at least I can help Micah improve.

Ten more minutes, though. Ten minutes, and then I get to catch up with Isabelle. I already saw her this morning, during yet another pool workout that led to a shared, steamy shower, but I'm itching for even more stress relief. If the match wrapping up now went well, we can celebrate, and if not, I'll console her. Preferably while horizontal, for either.

"Nice." I stop the next pass. "Feel the power in the rotation?"

My phone buzzes in my pocket. Once, twice, a third time. I'd bet my favorite skates that it's Isabelle; she always has a lot to say.

I suppress my smile. I can't deny how fun it is to sneak around with her. We were discreet over the summer, of course, but it's one thing to have all of New York City to play with, and another to be on a college campus with half her family. Whenever I see her and there's nowhere private to say hello, I wink at her. Her cute blush is worth the risk. Hopefully we don't work this out of our systems for a good long while.

When practice finally ends, I give Micah a couple takeaways and book it before anyone can trap me in a conversation. I hurry to my dorm, nearly jogging along the lighted walkway, and smile when I catch sight of Isabelle lounging against the front door. She's still in her uniform, the royal purple jersey with 10 stamped across the front standing out against her fair skin.

I back her against the building as I kiss her, my hand reaching for her ponytail and tugging.

"Hi," she says breathlessly.

"Did you win?"

"You didn't check your phone?"

I shrug. "I wanted it straight from you."

She winds her arms around my neck, giving me another peck. "We absolutely crushed them."

"Atta girl. I wish I could have seen it."

I hear the footsteps of someone approaching, so I tug her around the corner, and in the process, manage to knock over a recycling bin. It clangs loudly as it hits the ground. Isabelle freezes, giving me a wide-eyed look. The guy who just walked out of the building pauses, but continues on his way.

As soon as we're alone, she bursts into laughter. "You're such a nuisance," she teases as we crouch to clean up the mess. At least it was recycling, not trash. "This is Bryant Park all over again."

I snort at the memory. The New York Public Library had an art exhibit in the park in July, and there may have been a teeny, tiny issue involving a display that, to be clear, looked a lot like a regular tree. "Purely accidental."

"You knocked over half the exhibit!"

"And they should have bolted it down, if they didn't want anyone leaning on it."

Her grin sparkles in the early evening light. "It wasn't so much leaning as like, a mauling—"

I cut her off with another kiss. "Is tonight the night we finally finish *New Girl*?"

"Oh my God, please. Then we can start *Gossip Girl*!"

"I never agreed to that."

She tugs me to the door, practically bouncing with excitement. "Oh, shush. It'll give you all the warm New Yorker fuzzies."

CHAPTER 16

Izzy

I stare at the sign hanging on the door to the pool with dismay. "You have to be kidding me."

After what went down in the pool shower, we couldn't resist going back, and over the past few weeks, Nik and I have combined actual swimming workouts with another kind of cardio. No one suspects anything, and I'll never object to starting the day with an orgasm in the showers and an off-campus breakfast run. We're just enjoying each other's company for mutual stress relief, after all.

Today, though? The pool's closed for maintenance.

Nik squints at the sign. He still looks sleepy, which would be adorable if not for the fact I can't shove him into the pool to wake him up. I've been careful not to spend the night at his dorm, so I rarely get to see him like this.

"Huh. That's a bummer."

I unwind my hair from its bun and shake it out. "A bummer? You mean a catastrophe."

He stifles a yawn. "We have another option."

"Going back to bed?" I say hopefully.

"No." He smirks. "Going for a run."

I groan, flopping my head back. "No. No way."

"What? It's cardio."

"It's horrible cardio, unlike swimming, which is wonderful."

"They're not really that different."

"The fact you don't think they're different makes you the weird one."

"There's a trail the next town over that I've been meaning to check out." He winds his arm around me. "I'll run at your pace, sunshine. It'll be fun."

I narrow my eyes. The words *fun* and *run* should not go together, even if they rhyme. There's a reason why I never went running with Nik in Central Park, despite repeated invitations and attempts at bribery. Of course I *can* run; I've gone on runs with my family for years, but it's so *boring*. And yet . . . if the choice this morning is between spending time with him on some stupid trail or not having it at all, I know my answer. I didn't wake up early and sneak out of the house for nothing.

"Fine. But you're buying me pancakes after."

His fingers dig into my hip. "Sure."

"Chocolate chip pancakes. Like, the huge ones that take up the whole plate."

"Got it."

"And a pumpkin spice latte." I smile at him sweetly. "Even if you think it's an affront to coffee."

"Any other demands?" he says, mouth twitching.

I pretend to think, tilting my head to the side. "Well, if you wouldn't mind throwing in a few orgasms . . ."

I trail off as he makes a low noise, looking every bit the wolf to my rabbit. "Run, Isabelle."

Spoiler alert: it's not fun. We've been running for fifteen minutes, and I'm already sweaty, aching, and vaguely itchy. But Nik is clearly having a great time, and I know he's slowing his pace for me, so I just smile and focus on sticking to the path. I'll bet that when he goes on runs by himself, he tracks his blood oxygen levels and eats that gross gel stuff for the electrolytes.

October's in full swing now, so the forest around us looks like a box of jewels, each glowing shade more beautiful than the last. At least I'm warm enough that the chilly morning air feels pleasant. It's not the pool, but it's something.

I give him an appreciative look. He's ridiculously easy on the eyes when he's like this. I never thought the leggings-plus-athletic-shorts look was an especially hot one, but clearly, I wasn't checking out the right guys. Combined with the way his hair flops invitingly over his forehead and his fitted black T-shirt, I need to be careful I don't run right into a ditch.

"Chuck and Blair are getting together, right?"

I arch an eyebrow as I dodge a tree root. "You'll have to watch and see."

"So that's a yes."

"I didn't say anything!"

"When I asked about Dan and Serena, you gave me a straight answer."

"So?"

"So, I know Blair's your favorite, which means you want to keep what happens to her a secret, to watch my reactions." He laughs at the expression on my face. "I'm right, aren't I?"

"To be fair, basically everyone dates on that show at some point. It's the most incestuous friend group ever." I dance around a puddle, grimacing when the toe of my shoe gets wet. "And yes, I will judge if you don't have the right reactions to Queen B."

"I can't get over how I'm supposed to believe they're in high school."

"I went to a Long Island version of Constance, but the biggest scandal we dealt with was the art teacher trying to pass off a student's work as her own." I poke him in the side. "What about you?"

"You should talk to Cricket, not me. She went to Dalton."

"Isn't Dalton coed? You didn't go there, too?"

"I mostly had tutors, to keep up with hockey training." He

snorts, shaking his head. "She threw some really wild parties, though. Flew half her class year to Ibiza for her eighteenth birthday."

"Holy crap, your cousin is a badass." I wanted to meet Cricket over the summer, but our schedules never aligned. It was for the best, anyway; only a girlfriend would meet family like that. From the way Nik talks about her, she's the closest thing he has to a sister.

He nudges me playfully. "What about you? You've probably had some fun birthdays."

"Um, yeah. My family has this tradition—each birthday is like, Izzy Day, or Cooper Day. We do something fun and exclusive together."

"That's sweet. What was your best one?"

My heart seizes. "Um . . ."

He frowns at the look on my face. "Sore subject?"

"No, I've had some good ones. Just not recently." I should move on, talk about something else, but for whatever reason, I keep going. "It's just, my ex-boyfriend stood me up on my seventeenth birthday. And I didn't really celebrate last year, either."

I look at the ground, so I don't see the pity in Nik's eyes. That birthday was supposed to be the first Izzy Day I spent with a partner, not just my family. They still made it as special as they could, but it wasn't what I wanted. Especially not when I was reeling from Chance's betrayal.

"Oh," he says. "Shit, Isabelle. I'm sor—"

"It's not a big deal," I interrupt. I pause, leaning against a tree to catch my breath. "It happened ages ago."

I put enough firmness into my voice that he doesn't press, although he gives me a lingering look. I just lift my chin. He pushes me against the tree as he kisses me. The bark scrapes my shoulder blades. He breaks away, but doesn't stop touching me, hands running down to press into my hips and inch up the fabric of my shirt.

His brown eyes have flecks of gold in them. Somehow, I never noticed until just now. I push back his hair, studying him.

He kisses me again. It's the kind of kiss that holds the promise of *more*. His mouth in more sensitive places. His fingers tracing more than just my midriff. He pushes his leg between mine, and I gasp, biting his lip. My hands twist in the back of his shirt.

"We're finishing the run," he murmurs. "Even if I want nothing more than to see you on your knees."

I'm dizzy, suddenly. It must be the lack of caffeine. My brain is dying for pumpkin spice. "You *did* promise me orgasms if I ran with you."

He nips my bottom lip. "But not when, sunshine. Keep up."

He takes off, running down the trail at full speed. I stare at him in outrage for a moment—he's always a tease, but that's just *evil*—before sprinting after him. The trail curves, half-overgrown with bushes, but I run right through them, ignoring my stinging legs. His laughter echoes in the forest, spurring me even faster. I finally catch up to him, and whether he's slowing his pace or not, I don't care; I tackle him into a pile of leaves.

"Oof," he says, muffled underneath me. "See? You can run."

"Bastard," I pant. "Of course I can run, I have three older brothers to keep up with."

He yanks me down by the ponytail. I laugh and kiss him again and again.

CHAPTER 17
Nikolai

Isabelle plops on my bed, cold pizza slice in hand. "I'm so glad you live on an all-gender floor. The bathroom is marginally less gross than it could be." She pauses to bite her pizza before adding, "Although I'm still surprised you're living in a dorm at all."

"I didn't want to put anyone out last minute," I say as I reach for another slice of pizza. We both prefer it topped with vegetables, a summertime discovery that delighted her to no end. "It's not like I need more space. And anyway, it's better now that I replaced the furniture."

Back in the city, I'd stop by the office after Mom left for lunch with a couple slices, plus a Fanta for her and a seltzer for me. When she waltzed in an hour ago, pizza box in hand, I tossed it on my desk and busied myself with a different sort of feast. Not that she put up a protest, of course. She knew what she was getting into when she showed up still dressed for practice.

"This bed is definitely better," she says teasingly, stretching out her long legs. I let my gaze linger—she has a cute freckle on her knee that I can't stop staring at—until she blushes, swatting at me.

Prettiest stress relief I've ever seen.

I gesture to her with my pizza. "Interesting shirt choice."

She glances at her chest. Usually, she goes for a soft maroon T-shirt of mine that I suspect will go missing one day, but tonight, she opted for my favorite band shirt. We saw Rift over the summer, when I snuck her into a club with a surprisingly hard-ass bouncer, and even though she pretended to hate the music, by the end of the night, she was scream-shouting the lyrics with me as we danced.

"This is the terrible metal band you took me to see, right?"

I press my hand to my heart. "You wound me."

"Okay, fine. They had a couple good songs." She sips her Fanta. "But generally speaking, your music taste needs help."

She reaches for my phone, but I grab it before she can. "No. No more Carrie Underwood on my workout playlists."

"It was *one* song—"

"One song that blasted to the entire team in the middle of warm-ups."

She huffs. "Which is not my fault. You're the one who volunteered your phone." She lunges for it. I hold it over her head, making her scowl adorably. "Come on. I promise this is going to be cooler."

"Who?"

She climbs into my lap, still reaching for the phone. I almost tickle her—it would be so easy—but she's so sensitive to that, she'd probably kick me and send the pizza flying across the room. I learned that the hard way last week. "Ariana Grande?"

"Ugh."

"Dua Lipa."

"No."

"Sabrina Carpenter?"

I heave a sigh at her hopeful face. It's hard to say no when she's swimming in a Rift T-shirt, a bit of pizza sauce on her cheek. I swipe it away with my thumb. "Fine. One song."

She already has my phone in her hand, cackling to herself as she fucks up my Spotify algorithm again. It's not like I actually mind; it's just too fun to wind her up first. Even though we're back at school, along with everything that entails, it's been as easy between us as it was in New York City. I don't know if I'd have been able to move on if I stayed in Massachusetts. It's not the sex, although the sex is fantastic. I just like being around her, as long as I don't think about the eventual end. Somehow, whenever I spend time with her—even if it's stolen moments like this on a Tuesday evening—I feel lighter. Calmer.

I kiss her, pizza breath and all. "How was practice?"

"Pretty good, actually. Do you remember Brooklyn Ortega?"

"The senior setter you keep fangirling over?"

"She's amazing." She finally relinquishes my phone. "She heard I'm looking to get back into the position and offered to do extra practices with me."

My heart does a delighted backflip. "That's great."

"Yeah." She wiggles happily as she returns to her pizza. "I hope Alexis will notice."

From what I've heard about Isabelle's coach, it's best if I never meet her. I'd have a hard time holding my tongue. Over the years, I've played alongside plenty of guys who think they're owed something just because they're on the team, but I know Isabelle isn't like that. She's putting in the work, and extra practices with Brooklyn will help even more.

"I'm sure she will." I put my hand on her knee, squeezing. "The stuff I've been doing with Micah is really helping him."

She smiles as she tucks her hair behind her ear. "I'll be too embarrassed to face my parents otherwise. It's bad enough to have my brothers asking about it whenever I get home from a match."

I make a sympathetic noise. "You never told me how you got into it, you know."

"Volleyball?"

"Yeah."

"Well, I had to do *something* athletic," she says. "You get it."

"True. I don't know what my father would have done if I didn't like hockey." I don't want to think about it, either. I shove the thought aside. Everything that I went through to become the best when I was young—if I hadn't loved it, it would have been pure torture.

"By the time I was, like, four, James was already playing football. Dad tried to get Cooper into it, too, but he decided he wanted to play hockey. So I tried dance, specifically—"

"Ballet?" I interrupt.

She digs her elbow into my side. "How did you know?"

"Something tells me that baby Isabelle was very enamored with pink tutus."

"Yes," she says with a sigh. "The tutus. The greatest advertisement ballet could ever come up with. But it was so rigid. I just wanted to move to music, I didn't want to learn specific steps."

"You're still an excellent dancer."

"You're not half-bad yourself."

"Did you go into volleyball, then?"

"No. I tried soccer first, and then softball. Both were fine—just not enough to make me want to really work at it, you know? And then, when I was in middle school, my dad took me to a charity volleyball game. And it clicked for me." As she talks, her voice brightens. "I loved how fast-paced it was, and all the coordination and teamwork. I went to volleyball camp—that's how I met Victoria—and joined a club team that fall."

"That's nice," I say, my heart squeezing fondly. "I'm glad that you discovered it."

"I want to feel that again. I was really involved with my team in high school, I was a leader, and now it's just . . . it's like I'm on the outs." She frowns at me. "Are you feeling this way, with the new team?"

"I think it's normal." I've always felt . . . apart, somehow, from my teammates, and so far, McKee hasn't proved to be an exception, even if I've gotten dinner with the guys a few times and worked on my economics homework in the team lounge with Mickey. Isabelle, though? I can't imagine her not finding a place on her team. "Maybe the thing with Brooklyn will help."

"Maybe." She knocks her shoulder against mine. "I can't get over the thought of you playing with Cooper."

"He's really good," I admit.

"Of course he's good. He's a Callahan."

I yank her shirt hem; she sticks her tongue out. She shrieks as I drag her close by the legs. "Nik—"

I kiss her, my hands skimming underneath the shirt. I wish she could spend the night. For some reason, I sleep better when she's around, and that's been true since the first time we shared a bed. "Then you're good, too."

CHAPTER 18

Izzy

The volleyball sails over my head, way out-of-bounds. On the other side of the net, Victoria shrugs. "Whoops?"

"That was terrible," I call as I chase after it.

"You weren't paying attention."

I spare Coach Alexis a glance as I scoop up the ball. Her gaze sweeps over the gym, clearly missing nothing. I adjust my headband, hustling back to Victoria. We're doing an easy serving drill in pairs before practice truly begins, but that's no excuse for sloppiness.

"Your face is all red," Victoria says, easily catching the ball after I lob it over the net.

I stick my tongue out, even though my legs *are* aching. Nik and I have been switching off the swims with runs, and I have to admit that the runs are growing on me, even if they leave me feeling like jelly.

"Haven't you been getting plenty of cardio?" she says. She holds on to the pole holding up the net, opening her mouth in an exaggerated orgasmic O as she tilts her head back. "Oh, give it to me harder, you big, sexy Russian—"

"Yoon," Alexis calls. "A little more effort, please."

I'm fighting to keep a straight face when she adds, "You too, Callahan. You're running like you've got cinder blocks on your feet."

"Sorry, Coach," we chorus. Victoria serves the ball to me. I catch it, set up for a serve, and smack it over the net to her. She has a weird look on her face, as if she just stepped on a slug.

"What?"

"Nothing."

"It's obviously something." I put my hands on my hips. "Is it Aaron?"

"No, we're fine. Although it's getting tricky to remember when you're supposed to be with me."

"Has he said anything?" I feel bad whenever I tell my brothers I'm hanging out with Victoria when I'm actually meeting up with Nik, but until now, she hasn't minded. It's easier than making up details about something else. Fortunately for me, neither of them seems all that suspicious about why I keep leaving the house so early and getting home so late. I've never been so grateful that both of them are in relationships.

"No." She shakes her head for emphasis before serving again. "It's just . . . this seems kind of involved."

"What? We're just friends."

"You're sleeping with him."

"We do normal friend things, too. We're watching *Gossip Girl* together. He's forcing me to listen to this Russian metal music, which, don't tell him, isn't actually that bad."

"See, that's weird."

I dribble the volleyball a little harder than necessary. "I thought this is what you wanted for me."

"It is. But it's sounding kind of domestic."

"And I can't have that?"

"No. Ugh. This is coming out all wrong." She ducks under the net to my side of the court. I look around nervously, but Alexis is on the other end of the gym, lecturing a couple freshmen for sneaking away after the last road game. "I just don't want you to get hurt, Iz. This could get messy."

"We're friends and we're having fun." I cross my arms over my chest. I know I'm not the kind of girl who'd get a shot at more with someone like Nik, but I don't need my best friend to tell me that. "And that's all I want."

NIK WORKS HIS hands underneath my pleated plaid skirt, nibbling down my neck. "Tights? Really?"

"It is—ah—freezing out." I put my arms around him, gasping as he lays me out on a table. My cheeks flush, as much from the position as the look on his face when the skirt rides up. I can't believe he's looking at *me* like I'm the prize, instead of the other way around.

This classroom, a little nook of a room on the second floor of the building where I have philosophy class and he has a Russian politics seminar, has become an unintentional meetup spot for us. Friends have routines, right? Ours just happen to involve making out and then some in the twice-weekly overlap between our classes.

Totally normal stress relief. Victoria has no idea what she's talking about.

"Allow me to warm you up, then." He kisses me for real, one hand winding in my hair, the other dancing down my side.

"I'm presenting in class," I warn. "I can't be late."

"Practice it now," he says, skimming his lips along my jaw. "What's the topic?"

"Um—Kant." I dig my hands into his navy-blue cable-knit sweater. I couldn't resist tugging him into the room as soon as I saw it. The collar is unraveling in a way that feels rich boy intentional, and I'm not sure why that's so hot to me, but I'm not about to question it when he's on the verge of ripping my tights. He better not mess them up too badly; it took ages to pick out the right outfit for this presentation. I'm even channeling Blair Waldorf with a headband.

He does rip them. I give him an exasperated look, but he just strokes me through my panties, hooking his thumb underneath the elastic. "What about him?"

"His views on moral philosophy and how they differ from— Nik, fuck." I arch my back as he rubs my clit through the thin fabric. Why are his fingers so damn talented? "If I fail this assignment, I'm blaming you."

He smiles, easy and self-assured . . . and then presses his face against my inner thigh. "I'm dying for a taste," he murmurs. "I want you lingering on my tongue when I walk into that fucking seminar."

Someone jiggles the door handle. We freeze, looking over. He curses as he pulls away from me.

I sit up, hastily tugging down my skirt to hide the rip. "You locked it, right?"

"Yes." He helps me off the table, smoothing my collar over my sweater. I comb his hair back; it's falling into his eyes. "I've never seen anyone even walk into this classroom. There are tarps over half the shit in here."

"I should go to class anyway." I grab my bag, checking to make sure my notes are inside. Usually, I'm good at oral presentations, but this philosophy class has been kicking my butt. I'll be lucky if I manage a B. I open the door carefully, breathing out a sigh of relief when it's obvious that no one is lingering outside. I step into the hallway, Nik on my heels.

"Hey, Izzy!" Cooper calls.

My heart drops straight through my body. I plant my hand against Nik's chest and shove him into the classroom. I yank the door shut, plastering a smile on my face, just before my brother reaches me.

"Hey," I say brightly. If Nik left marks on my neck, I'll kill him. "What are you doing here?"

"Taking Penny to lunch." He adjusts his Yankees cap, peering at me. "What were you doing in there? You okay?"

"Just, uh, practicing for my philosophy presentation." There's a knock on the door. I thump my heel against it, keeping my smile intact. "You know how stuffy these old buildings get. I've been boiling since they turned on the heat. Which feels earlier than usual? It's earlier than last year, right?"

"Right," he says slowly. "Well, I'm sure you'll crush it." Instead of moving on, he leans against the door, snapping his fingers. "Oh, hey. Seb switched his shift at the restaurant, so it's just us for dinner later. I was thinking ramen and that show you like? The one where they work on yachts?"

"Below Deck?"

"Yeah, that one. I love that show."

"Sure. That sounds nice."

"Cool." He gives me a one-armed squeeze. "Good luck. Tell me about it later."

As soon as he rounds the corner, I push the door open. My heart is slowly clawing its way back into my body, but now I'm all jumpy. Hopefully my presentation won't be first. And hopefully Cooper bought my lie about practicing.

"Seems like you handled that well," Nik says from his perch on the end of the teacher's desk. He swings his legs, grinning like the Cheshire cat.

"That was Cooper, you know." I cross my arms over my chest, scowling. "Why is this campus so *small* sometimes?"

He shrugs. "What'd you tell him?"

"You seem way too calm about this."

"No harm done, right?" He slides off the desk, sauntering to me, and tugs on my arms until I uncross them. I melt into his embrace—just for a moment—as he kisses me.

"You're such a nuisance," I grumble, twisting out of his grip.

He pinches me. "Brat."

"Make me pay for it later," I shoot back. "I'm going to be late."

"Tonight?" he says. He keeps his voice light, a contrast to the dark promise in his eyes.

I give him a honey-sweet smile. "Unfortunately, I just made dinner plans with my brother." I heft my bag over my shoulder, striding to the door. As I open it, he says my name. I look over my shoulder. "Yeah?"

Something shifts in those golden-brown eyes. He's quiet a beat too long.

"One, good luck on the presentation," he finally says. "I know you can do it. And two . . . will you have lunch with me and my mother?"

CHAPTER 19

Izzy

zzy!" Katherine says, jumping up from her chair to hug me. "I was so thrilled when Nikolai told me you'd be coming."

I hug her back, happy to see that she's dressed as glamorously as ever. The patterned shawl she's wearing would look frumpy on almost anyone, but on her, it transforms into something elegant. I admire how she owns her wardrobe, rather than let the clothes wear her.

As I sit, she gives her son a much more reserved kiss on the cheek. Given the brief times I saw them interact over the summer, it's clear that they're not as close as I am with my parents. He didn't go into any detail, but I could tell he was relieved when I agreed to come. While I'd have done it even if I hadn't interned for Katherine, it's nice to see her again.

"I figured you'd want to catch up with your favorite intern," Nik says, draping his suit jacket over the back of his chair before taking a seat next to me. When he picked me up earlier, I nearly drooled at the sight of him. It's impossible to look bad in a two-thousand-dollar suit, after all. "It's been nice to have a friend on campus."

A friend. It's the most accurate way to describe what I am, even if the word makes my stomach twinge.

I just smile, arranging my napkin in my lap. "Yes. We've run into each other quite a few times now."

She smiles at us both, clasping her hands together. She's wearing expensive rings on every finger except the left ring. We were discreet around her; I don't think she ever suspected that we were hooking up. "And how are you, Izzy?"

"Good." I open my menu. Katherine originally suggested Vesuvio's, a restaurant in town, but when I told Nik that's where Sebastian works, he got her to agree to a fancy little place in nearby Hudson instead. "I've been busy with school and volleyball."

"My new intern isn't half as good as you," she says as she opens the wine list. "The other day, she ordered powder blue tablecloths instead of baby blue. It completely threw off the momentum of the reception planning."

I wince. I made a mistake like that exactly once, and corrected it before she even noticed. "Yikes. I'm sorry."

"Not everyone appreciates the details like you do." She turns her attention to Nik, twisting around one of her rings. "Your grandfather wants to know how things are going."

"They're good," Nik says, glancing at me. "School is fine. Hockey is fine."

"Good." She takes a sip of water, pressing her lips together. "Call him soon, please."

He nods. "I will."

They both fall silent. I needlessly adjust my napkin as I look between them. A little stiffness, I expected, but this is just awkward.

"Are you in town for the hockey opener tomorrow, Katherine?" I ask after we order our food. "I wish I could make it, but I have an away match."

A selfish part of me is grateful that I won't have to pretend to only cheer for Cooper. I'd definitely feel unwarranted jealousy if I noticed girls wearing Nik's jersey, too.

"Oh, I don't think so," she says, fiddling with her rings again.

I blink. "Really?"

Nik's foot nudges against mine. I give him a look, but he ignores it. Katherine asks him a few more questions about his classes, and he replies to each one, offering just enough information to be a complete answer, but not enough to encourage conversation. I gulp my wine, grateful that the server didn't card me.

"I'm going to the powder room for a moment," she says eventually, reaching for her purse. "Be good, you two."

I turn to Nik as soon as we're alone. "She doesn't go to your hockey games? Ever?"

He shrugs. "It's not her scene. Hasn't been since she divorced Dad."

"Not her—she's your mother."

"An astute observation."

"Why did you bring me here?" I bite my lip. "Just so she'd focus on me, not you?"

"I brought you here because I wanted a friend with me." He leans in, his hand brushing over my thigh. "And because yes, she likes you and misses you. Which is more than I can say about our relationship."

"Oh, Nik." I can't imagine being so formal with my own mother. "Why? What happened?"

He looks at me with the flickering, hesitant expression he wore when he asked me to lunch in the first place. "Ask her about how work is going. I thought you might enjoy talking to her about some of your old clients."

WHEN WE FINALLY wrap up the meal, Nik gives Katherine a perfunctory kiss on the cheek before going to get the car. I spent the lunch chatting with her about work; he seemed content to listen, chiming in occasionally with a comment or question. It was nice to talk wedding planning specifics again, even if the discomfort never faded. It might be boring to most people, but I actually do like pondering the differences between powder blue and baby blue and the respective vibes they bring to a reception.

"I'm so happy to see that Nikolai is finally dating someone," she says as she slips into her coat. "And that it's you, especially."

I freeze with my scarf halfway around my neck. "Oh. We're not . . . we're just friends."

"Well, even that," she says, although she raises an eyebrow. "I've never seen him with many friends."

"He has his teammates." I fight the urge to add something about how she'd know that if she went to his games. It's not my place to overstep like that, even if I do have my own relationship with her. Whatever happened to cause this rift between Nik and his mother, I'd be willing to bet it has nothing to do with hockey. I'm glad that he wanted me to help him today, even if it was just because I'm someone who knows her.

She has a frown on her face, as if her mind is elsewhere.

"I just worry about him," she says eventually. She pats down her blond hair, so different from his. He must look more like his father. Her eyes are blue instead of brown, and she has a rounder face. "He's always been a loner. Never brought girlfriends around, either. But he does look at you in a way I haven't seen from him."

My breath catches. Of course she'd want to see that, if she thinks he's lonely. She's just reading into things.

Not for the first time, I wonder what led to her divorce from Nik's father. It seems like his dad isn't part of his life at all.

"It's been nice to be his friend." I step onto the sidewalk with her, bracing myself against the chill in the air.

"You'll keep in touch, won't you?" She hugs me again as Nik pulls up in his car. "We can talk about next year. If I didn't scare you away from the industry, that is."

"Really?"

"Of course," she says with a smile, looking more like the woman I remember from the summer—ready to go to bat for her clients at a moment's notice—than whatever happened over this lunch. "You have a big heart, Izzy. That's rarer than you'd think it would be."

CHAPTER 20
Nikolai

I shut the textbook with a groan, leaning back in my chair. The air in this part of the library is stuffy, and I've had a hard time holding back my yawns. I'd like to be unconscious, but now that the hockey season is in full swing, if this paper about the sociopolitical climate in Western Europe ahead of World War I is getting written at all, it has to be now. It doesn't matter what my grades are, but I won't give Grandfather another thing to hold against me. After lunch with Mom last week, I called him, and he droned on for an hour about the moves he's making to give me the best possible start at the company. It was a relief to cut him off once I had practice.

It was an even bigger relief to have Isabelle there for the lunch. Mom had fun talking to her, and I didn't have to suffer through too many stilted questions. My father's ghost lingers whenever we're in a room together, but Isabelle chased away those shadows, at least a little.

"Nik?"

I jolt, the legs of the chair hitting the floor with a crack. My heart leaps as I look at Isabelle standing in the doorway. She had a match this evening, but she's dressed normally, her damp hair falling over the collar of her orange sweater. She swipes at her nose; it looks like she's been crying.

"Hey," I say worriedly. I kiss her cheek as she settles next to me at the table. "You okay? How was the match?"

She makes a face at my computer screen. "This looks complicated."

"It's fine. What's the matter?"

"And you wrote half of it in Russian."

"I'll translate it later." I nudge my leg against hers. "Match didn't go well?"

She arranges herself in a pretzel on her chair. My legs hurt just looking at it. Even though the quiet way she's holding herself has me concerned, I can't help but smile as she leans her head against my shoulder. She smells like her signature citrus perfume.

"What do you do when you make a mistake during a game?" She fiddles with her necklace. "Do you just . . . keep imagining it? Like, on a loop in your brain?"

"Is that what happened?"

She lifts her head, lip caught between her teeth.

"Of course I do." I take her hand, stilling her fingers. "It's worse than getting destroyed when we watch tape."

She lets out a breath. "I ruined a rally. It cost us the lead in the set."

I know enough about volleyball now to understand what she's talking about. "Did you lose the set?"

"Yeah. And it was the . . ." She shuts her eyes. "The tiebreaker for the match."

"Shit. I'm sorry."

"I'll bet whatever mistakes you've made, they're not that bad."

"Oh, I've done that, too. Last season, I completely misread a play. Puck went right through my legs and into the back of the net. It helped send your brother to the playoffs."

She winces. "Okay, that's pretty bad."

"And I thought about it way longer than I should have. I don't think I slept for a week." She doesn't quite smile, but she doesn't look like she's about to cry, so I'll consider that a victory. "I just kept imagining it, over and over."

"That's basically what's happening." She keeps chewing on

her lip. "If I can't even handle what my coach is giving me now, how the hell am I supposed to convince her to give me more responsibility? We should have won."

I drape my arm over the back of her chair. "Do you want advice, or do you just want me to listen?"

"Advice." She kisses me softly. "And thank you for asking."

"You're not the whole team. That play might've been on you, but your teammates could have stepped up throughout the match to make sure it didn't come to a tiebreaker in the first place."

"Fair enough," she grumbles.

"Plus, mistakes happen. They'll happen again, to me and to you, and the only thing to do is get back out there and do better with your next opportunity."

"You know how closely she's watching me."

"And I know that you're rising to the challenge." I tug gently on the ends of her hair. "Will vending machine candy make you feel better?"

When I come back with a packet of M&M's, I see that she spread out her own books, apparently content to settle in for a late-night homework session alongside me. She smiles as she takes the candy. "I have stats homework to do. Although I'm really not good at this class. James would be, he's great at math. Cooper and Sebastian always get straight As, too. And I'm just . . . ugh. I've never been good at it."

I suppress the face I want to make. She compares herself to her brothers way too often, but I don't want to upset her again by bringing it up. I know her family is competitive, but I hate the way it makes her feel inferior.

"Want help?" I say instead. "I've taken a lot of statistics for my major."

"You have to write your paper."

"It's not due until next week." I drag her textbook between us. "What topic are you up to?"

My phone buzzes on the table. I glance at it, stomach tightening at the number. Dad, calling yet again. If he had his way, I'd be in Russia for a tour with SKA St. Petersburg over Thanksgiving break. I silence the phone and slide it into my pocket.

"Do you need to get that?" she says.

"It's nothing. Spam." I clear my throat, peering at the textbook. I wish I could say for certain that I won't be returning the call, but I know I will. Just when I'm alone. "Oh, variable data. Riveting."

She fiddles with her pen—pink, of course; my heart squeezes with fondness—giving me a look that lingers longer than I'd like. "Are you sure? You already helped me tonight."

"So? I can keep going." I lean in, delighting in the way she shivers as my breath washes over her ear. "All night, sunshine."

She jabs my side. "Don't you dare try to make math sexy."

"That sounds like a challenge to me."

She glares, but I catch the way her lips twitch. "Fine. Teach me about variable data."

I'm about to answer when I remember the fall festival in Moorbridge that she mentioned to me in passing the other day. Going into town together would be risky—there's a reason why we go to the pool so early, and why we're careful about who sees her come to my dorm—but she'd love it. I know we're just friends, and I ought to be reminding myself of all the reasons why I could never be with her, but for an evening, it'd be nice to pretend we're more.

"If you promise to sneak out with me tomorrow." I can tell she's intrigued by the way her eyes light up. "Maybe you can finally give me that tour of town you've been promising before the festival."

CHAPTER 21

Nikolai

I still can't believe you haven't really been downtown," Isabelle says, balancing on the edge of the sidewalk like she's walking a tightrope. Overhead, the last vestiges of sunset fade out in favor of the stars. "Do you do *anything* but school and hockey?"

"Well, there's you."

She wobbles in place, her mouth dropping open. "Oh, that's dirty."

"You walked right into it, sweetheart." My lips twitch as I steady her with a hand on her back. She's wearing a pair of ripped jeans and a pumpkin-patterned top with an oversized yellow cardigan. Her hair's loose, held away from her face with clips. When I met her on the sidewalk just around the corner from her house, she looked around with exaggerated carefulness before leaping into my arms for a kiss. "Are you sure you're not cold?"

"I've endured way worse for the price of being on theme."

"Do you want my jacket?"

She eyes it longingly. "Nope."

"You sure?"

"Absolutely." She lifts her chin, candy corn earrings bobbing. "Cold? What cold?"

I peel off the jacket and drape it over her shoulders. She scowls, but burrows into it all the same. I hide my smile as she surreptitiously sniffs it.

"It's on theme. Black leather is very Halloween-ish."

"I like the way you think." She jumps off the curb, taking my hand. "Moorbridge is so pretty, come on."

She leads the way into the heart of town, past rows of houses already decorated for Halloween. Most of the storefronts are closed by this time of night, but streetlamps and strands of orange lights looped around the trees illuminate everything. The restaurants are still busy; as we pass, music and conversation bleed into the air. She points out the arcade, the bookstore, and the movie theater. The bakery apparently sells used records, but only on weekends, and the noodle shop on the corner has great lunch specials.

"Which you'd know if you came here as a freshman," she says as we round another corner, heading for the park. "So really, I'm acting like your tour guide right now. I should've done this ages ago."

"Movie specials on Tuesdays," I recite obediently. "And the arcade sells beer, but the slushies are better."

She beams. "You're listening."

"Obviously." I push her against the nearest surface—the brick exterior of what looks like a bar—and give her a rough kiss. The gloss on her lips tastes like pumpkin spice. "What's this?"

She twists around. "Oh, Lark's. College bar. I'm sure the guys will drag you here eventually."

The name rings a bell; Mickey mentioned it the other day. The season has gotten off to a rough start, so we haven't had much reason to celebrate, but I like knowing where we'll go when we turn things around. Visualizing victory is half the battle.

"What about you?" I run my fingertips over the exposed part of her midriff. "If I came here after a win—"

"Love the confidence," she says, her voice hitching, "but—"

I take a step back as a couple guys leave the bar, and she cuts herself off. They look like students, chatting among themselves as they decide which direction to go in.

"Ugh." She yanks on my shirt until I follow her behind a car. She crouches, observing the group with a scowl on her face.

"Why are we hiding?" I whisper into her ear.

She jumps, shaking her head. "I hooked up with the guy in the red shirt a couple times last year."

I snag my thumb in her belt loop and pull her closer. "Him? Really? What's his name?"

"What, are you jealous?"

I give the guy a closer look. Backwards baseball cap, red T-shirt just tight enough to show off his muscles, and a cocky sneer on his face. I tighten my grip on Isabelle. "He looks like a douche."

"Don't get too excited," she says, rolling her eyes. "He wasn't that great."

"In bed?"

She's blushing furiously, which is adorable, but I don't let her off the hook. "He wasn't as good as me, was he?"

"Nik."

"I'll bet he didn't fuck you as good as I do." I suck on her earlobe, earring and all. "And that you didn't come as hard when he touched you."

She shudders. Her hand covers mine. "I didn't."

"Didn't what?"

"Didn't come." She jerks out of my grasp, steadying herself. She flops the arms of my jacket over her hands, her gaze settling somewhere near our feet. "He didn't make me come."

I straighten. "Oh."

"I faked it." She shoves her hands underneath her armpits, rocking back and forth. "Which I know is so embarrassing, okay? I don't think he noticed, but I didn't want to run into him again if I could avoid it."

"That's not embarrassing."

She snorts, passing me on her way back to the sidewalk. "Sure."

"Really," I say, hurrying to catch up. "Sounds like a him problem. You come when you're with me."

She crosses the street, heading for the park—and the festival—on the other side. I barely glance at the road before jogging across as well. I reach for her wrist, holding her in place gently. She looks over her shoulder with a surprisingly vulnerable expression.

"Did I say something wrong?" I rub my thumb over her wrist. "You come when you're with me, right?"

"Yes." We're under a streetlamp, and the light is bright enough that I can see the blush on her cheeks. "Yes, God, of course. But before, I never . . . not with him, or anyone else."

"Never?"

"Let's play a game," she says, a determined edge to her voice. "A question for a question."

"Isabelle."

"I ask you a question, and if you answer, you get to ask me one back."

She's looking up at me with so much fire in her eyes that I have no choice but to back down. "What kinds of questions?"

"What's your favorite animal?"

"That's not . . ." I trail off. "That's not a real question."

"Sure it is." She takes my hand, leading me down the sidewalk. The park entrance is to the left; this close, I hear the live music. Something country, rising over the noise of the festival-goers. "Everyone has a favorite animal, and it's weird that I don't know yours yet."

"What's yours?"

"I'll tell you when you tell me yours."

I pay the entrance fee for both of us, waving away the offer of change. "Um . . . dogs? I've always wanted a dog."

"Didn't have one when you were a kid?"

I think of Dad and suppress the urge to make a face. "I thought it was my turn to ask a question."

"True. Have to respect the game. Ooh, they have apple cider."

We get paper cups of hot cider and meander through the crowd, stopping at a couple of booths. Kids with face paint and cotton candy run around us, and up ahead, a group of people dance to the band. Most of the people here must be from Moorbridge, not the university, because I see lots of young parents and old couples. She takes my hand again, a comfortable anchor, as we peer at a jewelry stand.

"What about you?" I finally ask. "Favorite animal?"

"I love koalas. I won't consider my life complete until I hold one."

"That's not what I was expecting."

"They're so cute, Nik! Their noses!"

"Don't most of them have chlamydia?"

"What? No way."

"I've definitely read that somewhere."

She takes a sip of her cider, frowning. "That's so sad. They're too cute to get STDs." A woman holding a squirming toddler throws us a look as she passes. Her eyes widen. "Whoops."

"That one's on me," I say with a snort.

She sighs dramatically. "Okay, what about your favorite ice cream flavor?"

"Don't have one," I say, guiding her around a puddle so she won't ruin her sneakers.

She stops in her tracks so suddenly, we almost stumble into the next booth. "What? That's impossible."

I shrug. "Obviously it's not."

"Because every flavor is so delicious and you can't pick?" She shakes her head. "No, even I have a favorite flavor."

"Which is . . . ?"

"Usually it's—nope, not until you answer."

I play with her hair. "Guess I'll never find out, then."

"This is tragic." She finishes off her cider and tosses the cup into the nearest trash bin. "Are you allergic to dairy? Wait, is that why you never put milk in your coffee? You've always been mysterious about that."

"Some people just like their coffee black, you know."

"Some people? You mean psychopaths." She wrinkles her nose, considering me. "How have you lived on Earth for twenty-one *whole* years without deciding—"

"My dad never let me have sweets," I admit. I hardly ever say anything about him aloud, so the words feel weird in my mouth. "I just never ate ice cream or anything like that growing up."

She looks genuinely upset for me. "Who doesn't give a kid ice cream?"

I think of Mom sneaking me sour candy after swimming and chocolate after tough losses. When she didn't agree with something Dad decided, she'd rebel in her own quiet way. She didn't always get away with it. "Sometimes my mom would buy me candy."

"That's not the same thing."

"Isn't it?"

She brushes her lips against mine, the taste of pumpkin mixing with apple. "Okay, new plan." She gives me a mischievous smile, practically dancing in place. "And I'm very committed, so don't say no."

CHAPTER 22

Nikolai

An hour later, I'm stretched out on a bench in a quieter area of the park next to Isabelle, spoon in my mouth as I ponder if mint chip is better than pistachio. She's sitting cross-legged, a cup of cotton candy ice cream in hand, watching me like I'm playing an overtime period in the Stanley Cup Final.

It's adorable. I've been putting on a show for her for the past ten minutes, dutifully tasting each flavor and giving her a verdict. One of the things I like best about her is how much she cares about everything—whether that's the welfare of koalas or *Love Island* drama or if I have a favorite ice cream flavor—and I don't want to disappoint her.

"I don't know, I still like coffee best," I say, shaking my head.

When she walked into the ice cream store and declared that we needed as many tasting cups as possible, the two girls manning the counter, alone in the shop and taking advantage of the quiet to listen to a murder podcast, giggled the entire time they filled a tray with mini scoops of ice cream. Isabelle made conversation with them so seamlessly that in a matter of minutes, we learned that they go to Moorbridge High, they're applying to colleges out of state, and they both love birthday cake ice cream the best. She's so good at making herself at home with other people, a skill that I've never been able to master.

"Are you dating?" one of the girls had asked bluntly as I paid and shoved all the cash in my wallet into the tip jar.

"No," Isabelle said, balancing the tray carefully in her arms. "We're just friends."

"Good friends," I added before I could help myself.

Worth it, since she beamed at me on the way out the door.

Now, she groans, tipping her head back. "Coffee? Could you *be* more boring?"

"What? The espresso bits were yummy."

She gives me a sideways look, mouth full of ice cream. "Okay," she says once she's swallowed. "I don't think I've ever heard you use the word yummy, so I'm still considering this a success."

"Pistachio is a close second," I say, mostly to make her groan.

"Are you secretly a grandmother? Coffee, pistachio. What about rocky road? Or cotton candy? Even mint chip would be a better pick."

"Isabelle," I say with faux seriousness, "cotton candy was the worst."

She gasps. "You take that back."

"It was even worse than birthday cake."

"I regret everything."

I burst out laughing. "It's so easy to wind you up."

"You're the one being ridiculous," she says, poking me in the ribs.

"I think you like it," I say, catching her hand before she can withdraw it.

"Nik?"

"Yeah?"

"Why didn't your dad let you have stuff like ice cream?"

I stiffen; I can't help it. "He just . . . I had a training plan."

She sets her ice cream cup in the tray and moves the whole thing to the end of the bench so she can scoot closer. I put my arm around her, even though suddenly, moving feels so incredibly difficult.

"But you were just a kid," she says, resting her head on my shoulder.

Part of me wants to deflect, to make her laugh or kiss her, but she's looking at me so earnestly that I can't bring myself to do it.

"He wanted me to play hockey professionally from the moment I was born. I learned to skate before I learned to run."

"So? My dad played football professionally, but he treated us like kids. Even James. He didn't try to turn us into little athlete robots. What about your mom?"

"It wasn't like that."

It was, but I can't bring myself to say so. Not to her. Not when it would skirt too close to the actual truth. I don't want her pity and I don't need her indignation. Or worse, for it to ruin what we have.

"But if he controlled what you *ate*—"

"It's fine, Isabelle," I interrupt. "It's not as bad as it sounds."

She lifts her chin stubbornly. "But—"

"Drop it."

My voice is a touch too loud, and sitting this close to her, I can see how it makes her eyes shutter. She unwinds herself from me. Fuck. I can almost hear my father's voice, his raspy laughter. I work so hard to act nothing like him, but the moment someone touches that nerve—even her—I want to snarl.

"I'm sorry," she says, an uncertain note in her tone. "I just thought . . . we've been sharing a lot . . ."

It's not her fault. She doesn't know.

And she never will.

"We should go back." The tips of my fingers are going numb; I dig them into my palms. "I'll walk you home."

"I can walk myself."

"I'm walking you back." Frustration colors my words. I feel ugly, I feel broken, I feel like I'm breathing through a punctured lung. Panic tries to dig its claws in. I have to stave it off long enough to drop her at her house. "I'm not leaving you alone in town at night."

"Fine," she snaps. "Not to the door."

"Obviously not."

Her eyes are glassy, the ocean on a day without a breeze. I reach for her, but she turns her shoulder, effectively cutting me off. My stomach rolls. If I'm not careful, I'm going to throw up every bit of the ice cream.

"Obviously," she repeats.

I try to take her hand, but this time, she doesn't interlace our fingers.

CHAPTER 23

Nikolai

I rip off my helmet as I leave the ice, striding down the corridor to the locker room. My fingers flex with the urge to hurtle the helmet into my locker, but instead, I take a breath. My father was infamous for destroying equipment after losses, and other than the occasional broken stick, I try not to give in to the impulse. It's something I can control, even when I want to curse and see something crack for my own satisfaction.

I missed Cooper's pass.

I was a foot away from where I was supposed to be and fucking missed it, and we lost the game.

0-3 on the season so far. It's officially a trend, and trends like that don't get you anywhere near the Frozen Four.

I'm winded, my body aching with every breath. I took a shot to the ribs earlier, and even though my gear protected me, I can feel it.

And I'd do it again, and again, and again. I'll put myself in front of the puck as much as possible to make a stop, and I'll go for hard checks that result in true collisions, because if there's one thing I've always known how to do, it's put my body on the line for the game. I put my mouth on the line, too, trying to keep the chirps fresh, and that's led to more than a few altercations.

No wonder Grandfather finds the whole concept of hockey distasteful.

The rest of the guys shuffle in. It's silent, as if everyone is holding their breath, running over their role in the game like I am.

"That was on me," Aaron says. He's dripping in sweat, eyes wide. "Fucking misread it."

I spit out my mouth guard and flop onto the bench to begin the arduous process of peeling off layer after layer of gear. "No. That was my fault. There shouldn't have been a shot in the first place."

"But—"

"You were great all night," I say shortly. "I'm the one who missed the pass in the first place."

Cooper takes off his helmet, shaking out his hair. We all stink; I'm sure he's as sore as I am. He glances at me, his chest still heaving.

"It was one play," he says, but I hear the frustration in his voice loud and clear. When we're on the ice together, we should be working as a true pair, not misreading each other on simple fundamentals.

I wince as I pull off my chest guard. It's not terrible—I've cracked ribs before, and this is definitely not that—but still, I'm going to request an ice bath. I've heard all the jokes about Russians and the cold, but nothing settles me after a game, or even a tough training session, like the shock of freezing water.

"No showers yet," Ryder says as he comes into the room, flanked by the rest of the coaching staff. "Let's talk for a moment."

"That sucked," says Micah.

Maybe I should be spending less time building him up and more time paying attention to drills with Cooper. I hate the way my mind races after a bad loss, but I can't help myself. It's a fair question. There's another game in a few days, and I'd rather catch the puck in my teeth than lose again.

"It did," Ryder agrees, carefully tucking his clipboard underneath his arm. "But it's early in the season. Don't beat yourself up too much—the mental game is as important as the physical one."

The guys grumble, but everyone knows it's true. He goes over some of the high points of the game, but mercifully doesn't call out me as the reason we lost. Dad would have, though. He was always happy to point out my mistakes in painstaking detail. If I fucked up badly enough, he'd throw my helmet or break my stick himself.

I wish I could text Isabelle to vent, but we haven't spoken in a few days. Not since I snapped at her for asking about Dad. I've tried to find a way to apologize, but every time, I just think about the look in her eyes, those shifting emotions swirling around like fog in a crystal ball, and delete the text.

I drag my hand down my face. At least I didn't panic in front of her.

As one of the assistant coaches takes over, sketching out the schedule for the next few days, Ryder gestures for me and Cooper to follow him out the door. Even though I'm still in half my gear, I join them in the training room across the hallway. Ryder seemed plenty calm in the locker room, but without the guys watching, his demeanor changes, gaze hardening as he draws himself up to his full, considerable height. He stares at us for a long moment, arms crossed over his button-down.

"I thought we let bygones be bygones."

"Sir?" Cooper says.

"We have," I say, swiping my fingers through my sweaty hair.

"What did I tell you before we started the season? I need you on the same page, providing leadership."

Cooper and I glance at each other.

"We're doing that," he says.

"Then why," Ryder says with exaggerated patience, "does it seem like you're seeing each other for the first time whenever I send you out there together?"

"We just—"

"Sir," I interrupt. "The loss was my fault, I know that, but—"

He puts up his hand, cutting us both off. "Get a beer together."

I duck my head. Next to me, Cooper shifts his weight from side to side.

"Get a beer together," he repeats, pinching his nose between his thumb and forefinger. "Do *something* together. You can't just show up for practice, go your separate ways after, and expect to trust each other enough not to fuck up when the game's on the line."

Cooper wipes his forehead with his sleeve. "The team's been spending plenty of time together."

"Don't misunderstand me on purpose, Callahan."

Cooper blinks. I don't blame him; Ryder usually calls him by his first name instead of last.

"Not the team. The rest of the guys are picking it up." He looks between us with seriousness in those pale eyes. "The two of you. You're supposed to be leading the team, and I have the sense you haven't been alone together since you met in my office."

I swipe my tongue over my lips. "It's Cooper's team. He's the one they listen to."

"That doesn't mean you have nothing to offer."

"He's been putting in a lot of work with Hazelton," Cooper says. He turns to me. "The young guys look up to you."

I nearly do a double take. I know he asked me, but truthfully, I didn't think he'd noticed how much I've been mentoring Micah. The kid needs it; he's been slowly improving with extra instruction. "And everyone respects you."

"Which I appreciate," Ryder says, softening slightly as he claps our shoulders. "But I want more from both of you. Spend some time together, get to know each other. The more effort you put in, the faster you'll click."

I swallow my reflexive protests. I've tried to stay out of Cooper's way because I don't want him to get suspicious about whatever's going on with Isabelle or mess up his relationship with the team, but Coach is right. This loss fucking sucked, and doing it over and over would suck even more. A losing season isn't acceptable, not when the stakes are this high. This time next year, Cooper will be making a name for himself professionally, and I'll be in my high-rise office, imprisoned in tailored suits.

"Okay," I say. "Understood, sir."

"We'll have a playdate," Cooper says, a touch dryly. "He can help me with the team formal."

Ryder gives him an exasperated look. "You haven't even started planning it, have you?"

I nudge him, suppressing a wince at the ache of my ribs. "Your place or mine?"

CHAPTER 24

Izzy

I bounce on the balls of my feet as I dribble the volleyball, waiting for Coach Alexis's whistle.

We're doing a scrimmage, half the team against the other, and I've been playing setter the entire time. One more point, and my team will win. She didn't say it explicitly, but if I can prove to her I know all the current plays and their signals, she'll give me a spin at setter during our next match, after the break in the schedule.

It also happens to be a match that Mom and Dad are attending, which explains the nerves zinging through me right now. They came to one of my other matches, a few weeks ago, and Dad made a face when he realized I was playing opposite hitter. It was brief, but I saw it.

Alexis nods at me. I jump into action to serve, since it's my turn in the rotation. The ball stings my palm just right as I hit it, sending it over the net in a perfect arc. I run into position, setting up Shona's pass for Ellie, who spikes it down onto the opposite side of the court with an authoritative smack. Too easy. Alexis's whistle blows, punctuating the point.

"Yes!" Ellie says, clapping me on the back.

I spin in a circle, my heart sprinting with a heady mixture of excitement and satisfaction. It wasn't a real game, fine, but it was *something*, and I know I totally rocked it.

"Excellent way to end practice," Alexis says as she walks onto the court. Her pullover is white today, with gold jewelry accenting her look. "This was pretty successful for both sides, regardless of the score. And nice job calling those plays, Izzy."

I beam as Victoria gives me a sweaty hug. "Thank you."

If I get to show that off during an actual match, I'll be thrilled. I smile as I shake my hair out of its ponytail, wrapping my headband around my wrist.

Alexis looks around the group. "We've got tape, so let's break it down now, and I'll let you go after that. Grab some water and change first. Good work, ladies."

While everyone heads into the locker room to take a breather, I hang back, hoping to catch her eye.

"Yes, Izzy?" she says.

I swipe my headband-turned-wristband over my frizzy hair. "Was it . . . enough?"

She glances at her clipboard, making a note, before replying. "We'll try it out for at least a couple sets at the next match and go from there."

"Wait, really?" I nearly hug her, but manage to contain myself.

"Really," she says, quirking an eyebrow as if she can't believe I just asked that. "You've been putting in a lot of work and improving. Wasn't sure you had it in you, Callahan."

A backhanded compliment if I ever heard one, but I don't care. Not right now, at least. Mom and Dad will see me play setter again. Suddenly, I feel lighter.

An hour and a half later, I walk up the porch steps to my front door, keys in hand. I run my fingers through my shower-damp hair. Sebastian has work tonight, but at least Cooper's home, judging by his truck in the driveway. He's going to be pumped when he hears about practice.

I open the door and do a double take.

I haven't spoken to Nik since the ice cream disaster a couple days ago, and now he's in my house.

Sitting on the couch.

Laughing with Cooper as they play something on the Xbox.

I freeze like a rabbit in an open field. They've clearly been at this for a while; a half-eaten bowl of popcorn sits on the coffee table alongside seltzers. Tangerine, curled on the armchair, blinks her orange eyes at me as if to say, *weird, right?*

"—just get dinner or something, for the team formal," Cooper is saying. He glances over casually. "Hey, Iz. How was practice?"

"Good," I say automatically. "What . . ."

Nik looks over too, his fingers continuing to move on the game controller. "Your sister, Coop?"

"Dude." Cooper nudges his side in a bro-ish manner that makes me blink like Tangerine.

"What? I've never met her. Isabelle, right?"

He's just acting right now, because for some reason he's in my house, hanging out with my *brother*, and I know that, but still, my pulse races. I shouldn't draw attention to us by staring, but I can't make myself move.

"Yeah," I finally say, even though I want to scream. "I usually go by Izzy, though."

"Izzy," he repeats. "I'm Nikolai."

My nickname sounds wrong in his mouth.

He's wearing a neutral expression, but I see the emotion in his eyes. It's something, but it's definitely not enough after days of missing him. I pushed too hard, asked too many questions about too sore a topic, but that doesn't mean I want whatever we are to fall apart. I'll take *good friends* over *my brother's stranger of a team-mate* any day.

Even if he's in my living room, getting to know my brother like he didn't know me first. Like I'm not the one who *deserves* to know him better. I almost throw my lanyard, but ball it in my fist instead.

His messenger bag is behind the couch, slumped next to Cooper's backpack. His own lanyard hangs out of a side pocket. I wait until they're both looking at the television again before leaning down and carefully swiping it.

"Cool," I say with as much casualness as I can muster. "Well, have fun. I'm going out."

"What?" Cooper says. "You just got home."

"I'm going out," I repeat, heading for the stairs. I take them two at a time, yanking my door open and shutting it loudly enough, I know they can hear.

When Nik walked me home the other night, he kissed me on the street corner. That's as far as we went, because I didn't want to risk anyone walking outside at the exact moment he left me on the front porch. I was especially glad to have the privacy when he backed me against a tree and framed my face with his hands, staring at me with wide, unreadable eyes before he leaned in and finally, finally kissed me.

Did he feel as desperate as I did? Did something spark in his heart when we touched? I could have imagined it; his eyes were nearly silver in the moonlight. But I didn't imagine the way his body felt pressed against mine, or the sugary taste of his lips, or the way he whispered my name—my full name, as always—before leaving me to walk the last half block on my own, still wearing his jacket.

I wish he could have walked me to the door.

No. I wish he *wanted* to walk me to the door.

I stride to my closet and pull it open.

My most delicate lingerie. A dress that hugs my curves in all the right places. Fresh makeup, a comb through my hair, and diamond teardrops to match my necklace and tennis bracelet.

I make sure he gets a good look at me as I walk downstairs.

"You have a date or something?" Cooper asks. "You've been going out a lot lately."

"Something like that," I say as I pull my jacket out of the hall closet. "Don't wait up."

He frowns. "Call me or Sebastian if you need someone."

The look Nik is giving me could burn this house down.

I wave on my way out the door, and watch him fight a snarl.

This is a gamble—but I feel good about my odds.

CHAPTER 25
Nikolai

Isabelle Callahan is going to be the death of me.

Looking at her in my bed, I realize I'm pretty fucking okay with that.

She's on her stomach, calves crossed in the air, her hair tossed carelessly over one shoulder. When I click the door shut—she left it unlocked so I'd find her exactly like this, I'm sure—she flicks her gaze to mine before turning her attention back to her book.

I can't believe she stole my keys from right under my nose.

I lean against the doorway. "You swiped my keys."

She turns a page in her book.

I run my hand over my jaw. I peel off my jacket and toss it onto the desk chair. I wish I could see inside her head, figure out what she's thinking. All I know is that I feel off-kilter. I didn't intend to hang out with Cooper at her house, but he asked, and I couldn't say no, after our conversation with Coach. Yet the look on her face when she saw me with her brother . . .

I didn't really think she was going out with someone else, but for half a second I considered it, and I hated it so much, I wanted to march out the door after her and stop her from getting in her car.

"Aren't you going to ask me how my date's going?" she asks.

"If this is about your brother, he's the one who invited me over."

She keeps reading.

"Isabelle. Look at me."

A tight white dress. Seashell-pink lipstick. Her long, strong legs, swinging back and forth like she's having a goddamn picnic, not camping out on my bed. Everything about her is so sexy, it makes me dizzy. My dick ached the entire Uber here—I declined Cooper's invitation to drive me home, and I was too impatient to walk—and she has to know it. She didn't put on that dress and those fuck-me pumps without wanting to make it so.

It's calculated. Measured.

Thank fucking God she's not on a date with someone else.

She's not really reading. She's waiting. She took out the game board and set up the pieces, and she wants me to roll first. I lean against my closet door, crossing my arms over my chest.

"Looks like your date ditched you."

"He's a little late." She finally looks at me, marking her place in the book with her finger. "Between you and me, I think he's hanging out with my brother instead."

"If it's for the good of the team," I say lightly.

She sits up, arranging her body with delicate preciseness. She looks like a princess, hair cascading down her back, legs pressed together and angled to the side. Her eyes, however, are stormy.

"I thought the last date I had with him went well," she says, picking an invisible bit of lint off her skirt. "I'd give it a seven out of ten."

My jaw twitches. "Only a seven?"

"We hit a wall. And I'm sorry about that. But then he doesn't text—you know how I hate when guys don't text."

"I can imagine."

She sighs, sounding put-upon. "As if that's not bad enough, I find out that he's hanging out with my brother. Acting like he doesn't know me at all."

I'm itching to break character, but I just shake my head. "You have to know it's not like that."

"Isn't it?" She presses her lips together. "I spent all this time getting ready, and he's late."

I take a step closer. Just one, as careful as she's being. This is a dance. Her game.

"Maybe I can help."

She snaps her gaze upward. "He'll be upset if he sees me with someone else."

Another step, and another. I cup her chin in my hand, brushing my thumb over her lips. Her eyes flutter shut, body relaxing into my touch.

"Take it out on me," I whisper.

Slowly, slowly, she slips to her knees. My breath hitches.

She drags her fingernail down the hard bulge in my jeans. I curl my fingers in her hair, just lightly, wanting her to guide the moment. She undoes my pants, taking out my already-hard cock.

She reaches between her legs. Heat pools in my stomach and lower, making my body tighten with anticipation. Her hand shines with her own slick as she grips me, mouthing at the tip with the tiniest, most perfect sigh.

"Atta girl," I say hoarsely.

She manages to smile, even as she takes more of me into her mouth. She works me over with her hand, just the way she knows I like. Her tongue presses against the sensitive underside, making me jerk, fingers tightening in her hair. She moans, and the sound emboldens me; I wrap her hair in my fist and pull. I'd recognize that intake of breath anywhere.

She looks up, eyes sparkling, and gets me back by running her nail down the vein in my cock.

I hiss, resisting the desire to push further into the warmth of her mouth. She teases me with each lick, each shallow suck, until she takes me into her throat. Her lips look pretty as fuck stretched around my dick, lipstick smudged. I sink deeper without entirely intending to, but she takes it. My perfect girl takes what I give her, trusting me not to choke her.

"Breathe through your nose," I remind her. I watch her relax and reward her with a gentler tug on her hair. "That's it. You're being such a good girl for me."

Only for me. I don't want her on her knees for anyone else; this is a sight for me and me alone. Other guys didn't know how to treat her right. A girl like her needs it dirty, no matter how sweet she seems.

I thrust deeper, rough enough to make a claim. She shuts her eyes again. Tears leak from the corners, her diamond earrings swaying with our movements.

"You get me so fucking hot." My voice drops to a callous whisper. "What if I came down your throat? Would you drink every drop?"

She manages a moan, the vibrations going straight to my dick. I let out a strangled curse, thrusts faltering. My balls draw up tight, the pleasure building to a fever pitch in my gut. However much I love when she swallows my seed, I love coming inside her more. I ease her off my cock, hand curling over her cheek. I will myself to calm down long enough to get inside her.

"Easy, sunshine," I murmur as I help her to her feet.

I turn her around, pressing a kiss to her bare shoulder as I inch down the zipper of her little white dress. She's breathing shallowly, each touch sparking more soft, addictive noises.

The dress falls from her shoulders. I press close, wrapping my arm over her middle, letting her feel the weight of it. She turns her head, seeking out my kiss. I reward her with one, my tongue slipping into her mouth. I reach down with my other hand, pushing aside the flimsy fabric of her panties, and work two fingers in deep.

"Nik," she says immediately, her voice high and breathy. "Babe, oh my God—"

I scrape my teeth over her pulse, then kiss it. She shudders in my arms, pushing against me until I thrust my fingers, plunging in and out with less finesse than raw, bone-deep need. I want her coming on my fingers and again on my cock, and I want to hear it. Yet technically, we're still playing her game. Dancing around each other.

"Let him hear what he's missing," I order.

She gets louder and louder, whining each time I pinch her clit, until she's teetering on the edge. I add a third finger and curl all of them inside her, and she comes with my name on her lips.

Fucking hell, I love that sound. My dick is throbbing so badly, I hiss as it presses against the small of her back. I urge her onto the bed, grabbing a condom from the nightstand before joining her.

"Come here," she says, reaching up to kiss me, her nails combing through my hair.

I rip the wrapper with my teeth and roll the condom on, then prop myself up to get a good look at her. I'm always breathless around her, but this is a special kind of torture. She's still half-wearing the dress, her delicate, light pink bralette visible alongside the ruined matching panties. I messed up her hair, and there's a smear of lipstick across her cheek. She strokes my arm, her chest rising and falling rapidly.

An errant tear slips down her face. I wipe it away with the hand that's still soaked in her slick.

"Good?" I check, just to be safe. "I didn't push you too much, did I?"

She shakes her head, then drags me between her legs. "Please."

That one little word has me on the fucking edge again. I tear her panties off and press against her as her legs wrap around my still-clothed body. Her heels hook at my back, encouraging me to push into her.

"Fucking hell," I groan when I'm inside her all the way. Pleasure sparks down my spine at the feel of her tight core. I thrust shallowly, and she squeezes tight around my cock as if in answer. I move for real, then, shoving her several inches up the bed accidentally. She reaches for the slats in the headboard, steadying us both.

"Come on," she says, a satisfied smirk on her face. "You can give it to me harder."

No doubt she knows by now exactly how easily she's able to unravel me. I thrust again and again, bending my head low to kiss her. My hair falls into my eyes as I build up a rhythm, but I shake it away so I can see the unbridled pleasure on her face. My hips snap forward and back, drawing enough noise from her that there's no way other people in the hall don't know what we're up to.

Fuck it. Let them hear her. When I'm deep inside her again, I freeze with difficulty, rubbing her clit. Her hips nearly come off the bed, even pinned by my body. Her eyes are wild, desperate. I move again, touching her clit all the while. When she's trembling so hard I can feel it, I press a chaste kiss to her cheek, so different from the rough thrusts.

"Let go, sweetheart."

"Nik—"

"For me, Isabelle."

I slam home one more time. She cries out loudly as the orgasm hits her, and that combined with her tight fucking pussy sends me over the edge as well. I come with a moan, the tension leaving my body at once as I sag against her. After a long moment, I try to pull away, but she holds me still.

"Don't wanna squish you," I mumble.

"I like it." She skims her nails over my nape, making me shiver. "You didn't even get undressed."

"I'm sure we look ridiculous."

"Everyone on your floor must hate us."

I snort, kissing her temple. Eventually, I ease out of her and settle us on our sides. Spooned against me, I'm able to truly hold her, my heart beating a possessive tattoo all the while. I always worry about pushing her too far in bed, and she always gives it back as good as she takes it.

"Nik," she murmurs into the twilight. "I really am sorry."

I skim my nose over her bare shoulder. "And I'm sorry I overreacted."

"But I pushed." She twists to look at me. "I just . . . I want you to know I'm here. When you are ready to share."

I trace over her hip. After I dropped her off around the corner from her house, I sat on the curb until my nausea passed and I could feel my hands again, but it wasn't easy.

I should be pulling away. Better not to play the game at all than try and lose. I can't have more with her, no matter my possessiveness, and the other night made that crystal clear.

And yet, selfishly, I kiss her cheek. "Spend the night."

"Cooper will wonder where I am."

I reach for her purse, pulling out her phone, and type out a text one-handed. I hit send. "Now he won't."

She huffs a quiet bit of laughter. "You better not make me late for conditioning."

CHAPTER 26

Izzy

I finish up in the bathroom and slip back into Nik's room, giving him a tentative smile. I couldn't stand the sight of him with Cooper when everything was so precarious with us, and I'm glad about what just happened, but I still feel fragile. On edge. I could have sworn that something about the way he looked at me as he told me to come for him was . . . different. Possessive, and not just in the way guys naturally get when they have a woman in their bed. This felt ravenous, as if he'd have torn apart whoever asked me on a date instead.

There's more to his past than he's letting on. Whatever led to his parents' divorce, whatever makes him stiffen at the mere mention of his father—there's a deep wound there, and I'd bet anything that it has to do with his scar. If he's truly been as lonely as Katherine claimed, I doubt he's told many people about it. Perhaps no one at all. The thought makes me want to wrap him up in a hug.

I curl beside him in bed. He tucks a bookmark into the mystery novel he's reading, setting it aside as he puts an arm around me. We were just as intimate as ever, and yet this feels more dangerous than being on my knees for him. Despite all the time we've spent together, I haven't stayed over at his dorm. I always drive back, calling him as soon as I get to the house. Maybe this is reckless, but I *did* make Cooper believe I was going on a date. We might as well milk it for all it's worth.

"The Rift shirt again?" he says, plucking at the sleeve.

"You need to do laundry."

"Call the dry cleaner, you mean."

I shake my head fondly. "I was wondering how your shirts have perfect creases."

"Mm." He kisses my hair. "Like I'd insult my suits with the school washing machines."

I twist, so I can kiss him properly, and revel in the way his hand slips down to press against my lower back. I let myself get lost in his clean scent, our shared minty breath, the way he shivers when I cup his jaw. When we eventually break for air, his eyes are gleaming. He turns off his bedside lamp, plunging the room into darkness. My eyes slowly adjust to the moonlight drifting in through the window.

He kisses me again, hard enough our teeth scrape together.

"Can I ask you something?"

I nod, twisting in his embrace so I can trace down his bare chest.

"Did you mean what you said the other day? No other guys have made you come?"

I'm glad he turned off the light, so he can't see my blush. When I saw Jeremy, who I slept with three times last year, outside of Lark's, I panicked, and blurted out that secret. I'd hoped Nik forgot about it, given all that happened after, but apparently, I'm not that lucky.

"Yeah," I say, focusing on his sternum. "No one else. Just you."

I expect gloating, but instead, I get a scowl. "No one took care of you properly."

"I'm grateful," I admit. I almost stop there, but something pushes me to continue. Maybe if I open up more, eventually, he'll do the same. More than that, I *want* to share this secret with him. "In high school, my boyfriend Chance, he . . . he made me feel like it was my fault that I couldn't do it, that it was why he had to cheat on me with a bunch of other girls in our class."

"Is he the guy who broke up with you on your birthday? He did that *and* he cheated on you?"

I nod. "I know it's stupid."

I don't miss Chance, not even a little, but I gave so many firsts to him, and they weren't even good firsts. If I could go back, I'd erase the entire relationship, start to finish. I offered him so much of myself, and he trampled it all. I was never enough for him, not in general and definitely not in bed, and he turned my trust into a joke.

Nik swears softly, his scar thrown into sharp relief by a stripe of moonlight. "I'm sorry."

"We were together for ages. And then the night we were going to celebrate my seventeenth birthday, he stood me up. I found out that he had been cheating on me pretty much our whole relationship." My heart lurches at the memory. "He has another girlfriend now, by the way. I guess it wasn't that he couldn't be faithful, he just didn't want to try for me."

"He's a fucking asshole," he says shortly. He pulls me even closer, tucking my head underneath his chin. "There's no excuse for that."

I drag my teeth across my lip. Tears prick my eyes, more out of embarrassment than sadness. I stopped crying over Chance long ago, but I haven't gotten past the mortification of realizing my entire relationship was a lie.

"I guess. And when I got to college, I . . . I still couldn't do it, no matter who I was with. Orgasm, I mean. I thought something was wrong with me. But I met you, and it's been different."

His fingers dig into my hip. Grounding me in this moment, in his bed. "You deserve to feel that good. To be taken care of."

"Maybe." My voice wobbles.

At least we're in the dark. Like this, I can pretend there's still plenty of distance between us.

He wipes away an errant tear. "Definitely, Isabelle." His voice sounds so quiet, so serious, but then it takes on a more playful edge. "Where is this guy now?"

I squint at him. "Nik."

"Just asking."

"He goes to college in Indiana."

Whenever I'm home on Long Island, I wonder if I'm going to cross paths with him. Fortunately, that hasn't happened, but never say never. Part of me dreads holiday breaks for that reason. I have zero idea what I'd say to him if we were face-to-face. Probably nothing.

Nik makes a contemplative noise. "None of those guys realized how rough you need it, huh?"

"*I* didn't even know. How'd you figure that out?"

"I just did what I wanted to do to you," he murmurs against my ear. "What I imagined from the first moment I saw you."

"Dirty," I whisper back. "I can still feel you, I hope you know that."

"Good," he says, the weight in that one word making my belly clench. "I'd have failed if you couldn't, sweetheart."

CHAPTER 27

Izzy

It's endlessly unfair that when men want to dress classily, they get to throw on tuxedos, whereas women have to deal with skirts and open-toed shoes. I'm freezing, bouncing in place despite the fact we finally made it from the sidewalk to the inside of the laser tag place. This silky black dress looks fantastic on me, and yes, I helped Cooper and Nik come up with this idea for the team formal, but I wasn't thinking about the weather when I decided to go all *Miss Congeniality*. I spare Nik another glance. It's *also* unfair that tuxedos do so much for guys. I haven't stopped sneaking looks at him since he swung by the house earlier to set things up for the afterparty, and I'd be embarrassed if it weren't for the fact he's done the same to me. He's still looking at me now as he leans against the wall, ankles crossed, hands in his pockets. *Grinning.*

He could put James Bond to shame, especially with that scar. He has no business looking this hot or showing me so much attention, especially surrounded by the entire hockey team. It's been a week since our conversation about Chance, and if anything, he's taken it as permission to get bold. We nearly got caught in the pool locker room the other day, thanks to his insistence that one orgasm wasn't nearly enough.

"Gentlemen," Cooper says, clapping his hands together. "And your invited guests. Welcome to the team formal."

"It's . . . laser tag?" a skinny freshman I don't recognize asks.

Cooper snaps his fingers, pointing at him. "Yes. But not just laser tag. Nikolai and I—"

"And your sister," Nik interrupts.

I stand taller, hoping the blush doesn't show on my face. I won't lie, it's weird to see them becoming friends. Or at least friendly enough to plan this event together. When they approached me in the library earlier this week to ask for help deciding on a theme, I nearly spit out my coffee. They wanted to just do dinner—boring—but I convinced them that they could bring the formal vibe to an activity the guys would actually like. Cue the laser tag. I also persuaded them to keep the dress code, because the only thing more fun than running around half-tipsy in the dark is to do it in themed costumes.

"—and Izzy, yes, party planner extraordinaire, have created a game that will test you," Cooper continues. "Challenge you. Make you regret only renting your tuxedo, Hazelton"—everyone laughs at that, including the skinny freshman who must be Hazelton—"and most importantly, bond you as a unit."

"By playing laser tag?" Evan drawls. He brought his boyfriend along tonight, a guy named Xander. According to Cooper, it's new, but Evan's happier than he's ever seen him. They do look adorable together, casually holding hands . . . like how Penny's lingering by Cooper, and how Sebastian's resting his chin atop Mia's head. Oh, and not to mention Victoria and Aaron, looking absolutely lovesick. Maybe it wasn't such a good idea to tell them to open it up to partners and friends, too. I'm bombarded by romance everywhere I look.

"Not just any laser tag," Nik says, a dramatic note in his voice. "We're playing capture the flag."

I grin as the guys all start talking over each other. It might be strange to see Nik and Cooper getting friendly, but it's nice, too. They put a lot of work into this plan, so their teammates better appreciate it.

"Are there actual flags?" Aaron asks.

"We get to shoot each other, right?" another guy calls.

"Haven't you ever played laser tag?" Cooper says. "It's going to be a bloodbath."

"A bloodbath of fun," Nik adds, letting his Russian accent, usually very slight, hit more strongly than usual.

I raise an eyebrow, and he throws me a wink.

Electricity zings down my body. I don't dare look at Cooper; hopefully he didn't notice. This might've been my idea, but I'm playing with fire tonight. I know it, and I know Nik knows it . . . and yet I can't help but blush at that wink.

"We'll split into two teams," Cooper continues. "I'll captain one, and Abney will captain the other. We're all playing as secret agents trying to secure vital intelligence—the other team's flag— before the enemy."

"What's the prize?" someone calls out.

Cooper turns to Nik, who says, "One free pass on practice . . . and front-row seats to any NHL playoff game you want, on me."

Just like we thought, the prize is a total hit. I give Nik another small smile as we split into teams. Maybe he's finding a place on this team after all.

Fifteen minutes later, I hitch my skirt around my waist as I dart from one fake rock to the next, blue plastic gun in hand. It's dark in here, aside from the glow-in-the-dark props and the laser gun flashes. Even though a truly terrible throwback soundtrack blares from hidden speakers, I'm hearing way more of the overly dramatic shouting, teasing, and laughter. I pass Penny chasing after Cooper—she ended up on Nik's team, whereas I'm on Cooper's—and spot Sebastian tugging Mia behind another fake rock, presumably to make out with her. (They came for the booze and the excuse to dress up, anyway.) Victoria raises her hand in a wave as she passes me; she's hot on Aaron's heels. I wonder if she's going to smack him or kiss him when she catches him—either is possible, given how he grinned when they ended up on opposing teams.

A guy on Nikolai's team fires a shot at me, but I twist before it can hit the target on my vest. Mickey shot me right at the beginning of the game, but otherwise, I've done a good job of retaining my lives. Cooper sent me, Evan, and Hazelton on the offense, hoping that we can sneak around the edges of the room to grab the flag waving tantalizingly on top of the red team's tower. Even though the prize doesn't matter nearly as much to me, I'll never turn down a challenge. I'm a Callahan. I've been trained since birth to dominate games.

I skid behind a large rock, peering over the top as I aim my gun. I see a flash of red and shoot, ducking before they spot me. Nik's team flag waves in the distance. I want to see the look on his face when he realizes I'm the one who stole it. The next place for cover is a little far ahead, but if I time it right—

A familiar hand curls around my wrist.

"Isabelle," Nik says, still using that pronounced accent. I should laugh at how ridiculous it sounds, but for some reason, it makes my nape prickle. "When did you betray me for the enemy?"

I smile sweetly. "Who says it was my betrayal?"

"I'm wanted in twenty-seven countries," he says, sounding for all the world like he just walked out of an action movie. Someone should bottle that rasp and sell it. "And yet I'm risking it all to see you."

"You're so ridiculous."

He presses his gun into my side. "If the pretty girl won't cooperate . . ."

"I'm terrified," I deadpan, although I shiver, lips twitching into a smile, when his hand curves over my hip. "How did you even find me?"

He says something to me in Russian. My eyes widen. He's only spoken the language to me once or twice, and that's because I asked him to. I know it's his voice, obviously, I'd recognize it anywhere, but the way it catches on the syllables is smoother, sexier. He adds something else, grinning at the look on my face. The noise of the game melts away.

Yep. Russian is officially way sexier than English.

"While that's unfairly hot," I say with a tremble, "what—"

"It's impossible for me not to notice you," he says. There's depth in his voice, as if saying this is costing him something. "You walk into a room and I know it's you, instantly, solnishko. You couldn't hide from me if you tried."

"That word." My pulse hammers wildly. He said it once, presumably when he thought I was asleep. "I remember it."

His hand digs into my thigh, just under the slit in the dress. I hook my fingers in his tuxedo jacket, pulling him even closer.

"It's what I think of when I see you." His nose skims up the side of my neck; he kisses my ear. "Little sun."

My breath falters as he gathers my hair over one shoulder. He sucks on the spot over my pulse until there's no doubt it'll leave a hickey. A claim. I feel warm, and not from the pre-gaming we did at the house. I'll have to be careful to cover it with my hair, but right now, I don't care.

I freeze as the realization hits me. *I don't care.*

I wish I could walk out of here wearing his hickey, his tuxedo jacket; I wish I could pepper his face with lipstick kisses. I wish more than anything that I could kiss him in front of everyone, my brothers included. But claiming comes with a label, and he's never used that word to describe me. Solnishko is beautiful, but it's not the same as *girlfriend*.

I ease away, trying to find the right words—any words—to combat the sudden tumble of my heart.

"Nik," I whisper, breath hitching.

He pulls me close once more. "Yes, solnishko?"

My hands feel slick; I nearly lose my grip on the stupid plastic gun. I wet my lips, searching those gold-flecked eyes. I have no idea what to say. All I know is that I don't want to lose this, in whatever form I can have it. We wouldn't be kissing if the lights came on, no matter what he whispers in my ear.

So instead, I raise my laser gun to his vest and shoot him in the ribs—right as Evan pulls down the red team flag.

CHAPTER 28

Izzy

I jog off to the bench on the side of the court, grabbing my water bottle and taking a big gulp. We're between sets, so I shouldn't tear my focus away from the match, but I can't help but look for my family in the stands. My volleyball matches don't draw the same kind of crowd that you see at McKee hockey or football, so it's easy to spot them right at the end of one of the higher rows. Mom's wearing a cashmere turtleneck, and Dad a collared shirt. Sebastian has on an atrocious geometric sweater that I'm sure Mia hates.

After my match is over, we're going straight to the hockey game. They're playing UMass Amherst—a traditional pre-Thanksgiving rivalry game—which means more to Nikolai than the rest of the team combined. He wouldn't admit it to me during this morning's run, but I'm sure he's nervous.

One more set to get through first. After, we'll either have a winning record again, or slip back in the standings.

"Let's huddle up, ladies," Coach Alexis says.

I give my parents another quick look before joining the huddle. Dad's sitting with his elbows balanced on his knees, fingers steepled in front of him as he takes in the scene. I'll bet he noticed my miscommunication with Shona last set just as quickly as Alexis did. She only played me at setter for the first set, then switched to Brooklyn.

I took it without complaint, like everything else this season, but relief washes over me as she says, "Ready to set again, Izzy?"

I nod. "Yes. Definitely."

"Good." She quickly outlines the plan, monitoring the clock that's counting down until we need to take the court again. "Remember, a short set means we don't have room for mistakes. We practiced the moves for this situation, so just stay focused and we'll be able to head into the final stretch of the season with a win."

We come in close and count *one-two-three-McKee*, then break with a cheer. Brooklyn pats me on the back before I take the court. I smile as I adjust my elbow wrap. It shouldn't feel different with Mom and Dad here, but it does.

Alexis is right, we practice these kinds of situations all the time. I know the moves, I know the signals. We're receiving the serve first, so I get into position just behind my front row attackers, Ellie and Shona. Victoria's behind me with the two other back row players, her long-sleeved black libero jersey a contrast to our home purple.

St. Francis serves. The volleyball comes over the net like a cannon, but our defensive specialist dives to hit it back into the air. It goes high enough that I'm able to set it up for Ellie, but they block her attempt at a spike, and the ball falls on our side of the net.

We all come into the huddle. "Watch out for nine," I say, gesturing to the St. Francis attacker who blocked Ellie's move. "She's the strongest. If we're going to get past her, it'll be by placing it where she can't reach."

Adrenaline zings through me as we set up for their next serve. Everything but the court melts away.

This time, a rally gets going, each side diving to keep it alive at the last moment. Finally, Shona buries it in the back corner, and we tie it up. I give her a high five as we reset. Out of the corner of my eye, I see Mom and Sebastian cheering.

But we lose the next point. And the next. St. Francis keeps serving, and we keep flubbing the move that will break the pattern. They're so deft at placing the serve, we're on our heels each rally.

I gesture to Alexis, who calls for a time-out. I take a quick drink of water on the sidelines, listening intently as she goes over the set so far and the adjustments she wants us to make. I shuffle through the formations mentally, nodding when she tells me which ones to try out and which substitutions she's making. We line up to provide more man coverage for the next serve, and finally get a break when St. Francis's weaker attacker misreads the ball.

"Back in it, back in it," I call as we huddle again. "Let's go."

We wrestle back another point, and another. There's always some give-and-take in a match, and I can sense the power shifting with every hit of the ball. St. Francis might be better than us on paper, but we've been forcing them off-balance all afternoon, and with the right shove, we could topple them over. I switch up our formations, refusing to give them a chance to get comfortable. Next rally, Victoria makes an incredible save to keep the ball in the air, and I'm able to capitalize with a perfect set to Shona. We win the point, putting us tantalizingly close to the majority we need to seal the victory.

"Almost there," I say in the next huddle. It's time for us to rotate, and I'll be serving. "I'm going to try a short serve."

"They won't expect it from you," Victoria says, bouncing on her heels.

"Good plan," Shona says. "Let's end this."

I set up to serve in the 5 spot, but keep it short, just floating it over the net. St. Francis handles it, but barely; we kill the rally with a quick set of moves. I pump my fist. My observations—and instincts—paid off exactly as I'd hoped.

We're a point away.

I give Dad one more glance. He's looking at me the way he looks at James during the two-minute warning in football, on edge and barely blinking. My resolve solidifies, sending a shiver down my back. I don't just want to win. I want to win with an ace.

I flex my knees as I dribble the ball a few times, envisioning exactly where I want it to go. I take a deep breath in through my nose, setting up as I exhale. As I throw the ball high into the air, I jump with perfect form—and send a rocket of an ace right into their back corner.

Match. Point.

"Yes!" I shout, jumping wildly. "Hell yes!"

Victoria collides with me midair, throwing her arms around me. "Izzy!"

I hug her back, relief and elation coursing through me. This is what I've been missing since I started playing volleyball at McKee. I feel like I'm back in high school again, heart soaring in the aftermath of a tough tournament win. The rest of our teammates join us, cheering and patting me on the back. Brooklyn congratulates me, and even Alexis has a smile on her face.

After we untangle ourselves and shake hands with the St. Francis team, I stay on the court. I don't want to leave this moment yet, especially with my family in the stands.

Sebastian pulls me into a hug before either of our parents can, smiling broadly. "That's how you win a match!"

I hug him back. In a moment like this, it's easy to remember the hours spent practicing volleyball in the home gym with him and James and Cooper. Sometimes our schedules kept us apart, but that only made it more special when we could bond like that. My technique wouldn't be as good as it is without those hidden, foundational pieces.

"What are you even wearing?" I say with a laugh as he lifts me into the air.

"I lost a bet with Mia."

I narrow my eyes. "Do I want to know?"

"Honey," Mom says, arms open wide. She squeezes me tightly, her hair tickling my face. "You were incredible."

I flush. "I don't know about that."

"You were," Dad says. Under the gym lights, his hair looks extra silvery, his eyes a more serious blue. I let him wrap me up in the best hug I could ever want, burying my face against his shoulder. "You've always had a wicked serve." He kisses the top of my head and adds, "Proud of you, darling."

"I'm sure you want to celebrate with your teammates, but the hockey game starts soon," Mom says. "Still want to come with us?"

"Obviously she does," Sebastian says, a touch dryly. "She spent two hours picking out her outfit."

I roll my eyes. Even if I hadn't promised Nik that I'd be there, I'd want to go. He won't have any family at this game, despite its importance, and he deserves to have *someone* in his corner.

I can't wear his number, but at least I can cheer for him.

CHAPTER 29

Nikolai

My first goal of the season goes in so quickly that for half a second, I think I missed it. Bated breath for the tiniest of moments, and then the arena explodes with noise from the crowd and, even better, the horn. I barely have time to turn before I crash into the boards with Cooper and Mickey and the rest of the guys, all of them hollering.

"Fucking A!" Cooper shouts, pounding on my chest. "That was sweet, dude!"

I wrap my arm around him. "Your assist!"

It's rare that you come onto the ice for a fresh shift as a defenseman and find your partner passing you the puck in perfect position to get a shot off, but I turned UMass's lapse in concentration into a point. We're up 4-1 now, with only a few minutes to go in the last period.

A couple feet away, John stands with two of my former teammates, looking at our impromptu huddle. He nods at me before skating to the UMass bench. We spoke briefly before the game for the first time in weeks, and it was stilted, strange, even though we made dinner plans.

Something inside me pinches tightly, but only for a moment. It can't banish the adrenaline rushing through my veins. I usually score a good number of goals each season, on the higher end for a defenseman, and not having one yet was bugging me. Cooper got one when we played Vermont last week, after all; I couldn't let myself get too far off-pace.

Before the game resumes, I look behind the net. Just once. I've been avoiding it all night, for my sanity, but I've been aware of Isabelle all the same. She's standing next to Penny, her body pressed against the glass like she wishes she could melt right through it. Her smile is so wide, it takes my breath away. It's lucky I scored the goal this period instead of last, when our net was on the other end of the ice.

I wish more than anything that I could skate over, acknowledge her somehow, but I restrain myself. It's not just a matter of Cooper not noticing. She's with her parents and Sebastian, too.

Aaron's able to block the last-ditch efforts by UMass to get another goal or two in before the buzzer, and I leave the ice sweaty and grinning. I spot John before he can head into the visiting locker room.

"Hey, man." I give him a thump on the back. "Wanted to catch you before I went in."

"Nikolai," he says, taking a step back. "Good game."

"Thanks. You too."

He just gives me a tight smile.

"For dinner, I have this great burger place picked out. Their specialty is this bacon—"

"I actually think we're heading back to campus," he interrupts.

"Oh. Tonight, you mean?"

"Yeah. Sorry about that."

I blink, tapping my stick against the floor. "That's . . . that's fine. We can talk some other time."

"Sure." He claps me on the shoulder briefly before catching up with the rest of his team. Even though they lost, they look animated, chatting with each other—and not one of them gives me half a glance.

I tug off my helmet. Sweat drips from my temple down the side of my face. I shove my hair back, trying to ignore the pit in my stomach. Where's Isabelle? Even a glimpse of her before I head into the locker room would be enough to settle the discomfort.

I spot her purple sweater, her dark hair threaded with matching ribbon. Her laughter is a beacon, rising above the other noise in the tunnel. She spots me, quirking her lips in a tiny smile. I hope like hell that she won her match earlier.

As I watch, Cooper and Penny join her and the rest of the family. Sebastian says something to Cooper, who gives him a playful shove. All of them laugh. It must be nice to have family at your games. Mom's a nonstarter, and Cricket's usually too busy to make the trip. I can't imagine Grandfather setting foot in this building, let alone watching an entire hockey game.

As if sensing my lingering gaze, Cooper gestures to me. "Hey, Nik. Come meet my parents."

I SETTLE INTO my chair, resisting the urge to put my arm around the back of Isabelle's. Her mother invited me to dinner with the family as soon as she heard my plans with my old teammates fell through. I should have made up an excuse not to come, but I have the sense that it's hard to say no to Sandra Callahan when she's made a decision.

Reminds me of Isabelle. Her fingers brush mine underneath the table for the briefest moment before retreating.

I suppress a shiver. I shouldn't have sat next to her, either, but Penny is busy hanging over Cooper, and Sebastian's girlfriend met us at the restaurant, so I had limited options. And besides, I'm happy to be celebrating with her; she won her match earlier while playing setter. It took all of my self-control not to embrace her the moment she shared the news with Cooper.

I absolutely shouldn't trace the seam of her jeans underneath the table. In fact, I should scoot my chair further away.

Richard Callahan looks up from the wine list, his gaze lingering on me. If I wasn't sure before where Isabelle got her eyes from, now there's no doubt. "That was an excellent goal."

"A little late, but appreciated anyway," Cooper says, smirking at me from across the table.

I snort at Cooper. "Thank you, sir."

"It must have been strange, playing your old team," Penny says.

The sting of John's rejection hasn't gone away, but at the same time, things feel easy with my current team. Since the team formal, I've been more relaxed. The locker room celebration, the silly Turkey trophy, the joint interview Cooper and I gave since the game was televised—none of it was a hardship. I didn't wish I was boarding the bus back to Massachusetts.

"Yeah," I say. "But I've settled into the McKee system by now."

"You're all my dad talks about," she says. She kisses Cooper's cheek. "Well, both of you. He's going to be so sad when you're in the NHL."

"The Sharks still hold your rights, yes?" Richard asks.

"Yes, sir. But they haven't come to collect yet."

Isabelle stiffens slightly, even though she's talking to Mia. I haven't told her about my deal with Grandfather, and if I tried, I don't think she'd understand. How could she, with a family that goes out to dinner together to celebrate wins?

"And what does your grandfather think of this?" Richard asks. "I've met him a few times. I've gotten the sense that sports aren't exactly within his . . . scope of interest."

"You're not far off the mark," I admit.

"Your mother certainly seemed proud, when I ran into her the other day," Sandra says.

I blink. I'm sure Sandra talks about Isabelle and her brothers all the time, but I'm a constant reminder of the part of my mother's life that she wishes she could forget. I can't imagine her casually bringing me up in conversation.

"I'm so glad that the summer worked out for Izzy," Sandra continues. "The business your mother built after her divorce—but I'm sure you don't want to talk about that."

"It's fine. I was thirteen."

"I've had four thirteen-year-olds. It's not an easy age."

"Mom," Isabelle says. Her fingers find mine again.

I squeeze hers, grateful for the support, even if she doesn't know the whole picture. My mother might've been able to seamlessly fall back into the world she grew up in—a world Isabelle shares a slice of—but I don't have that option. Even next year, working whatever job Grandfather thinks will suit me, I'll be an outsider. You can bring a cat in from the cold and give it a bed, but that doesn't do anything about the claws.

"It's a shame that your father's NHL career wasn't longer," Richard says. "I know plenty of men who didn't get what they deserved from their sport. It can be brutal."

"He preferred the KHL anyway." I haven't had to fall back on that lie in a while. I'm not sure how much of a lie it is anymore, anyway. The last call we had, he told me to visit him for Новый год, the New Year, since I didn't make plans to see him over Thanksgiving break. I felt like punching something after I hung up, panic clawing at my throat.

"And you have no interest in going back?"

Cooper snorts. "Dad, he's ranked higher than me. His talents would be wasted in the KHL."

"You know we basically have the same rank. And I have no intentions of setting foot in Russia again." A moment passes, and then I realize what I just said. Fuck. "I mean, I was born here. I did live in Russia for a long time, but my home is here now."

I cover Isabelle's hand with my own, nails digging into her jeans. She turns to me, under the guise of listening, but I catch the worry in her expression. There and gone in a blink. My breath hitches. I'm breaching a space I don't belong in, no matter how friendly her parents are or how easy things have become with Cooper. I'm the piece that doesn't fit, and if Isabelle hasn't started to realize that before, she definitely will now.

"Do you think in Russian?" Mia asks, tilting her head to the side. "If you were young when you moved there?"

"Usually. Sometimes English slips in, or German."

"German?" Isabelle says.

"Thanks to an overly enthusiastic tutor at my first American school. My grandfather—" I stop, feeling my face flush. "He assumed I wouldn't be able to speak English fluently, when I arrived. The tutor was pleasantly surprised, and taught me German instead."

I don't know why I just admitted that; I'd nearly forgotten about it until now. There's a beat, and then—

"Cooper failed French," Sebastian says with a grin. "Twice."

Cooper sighs, long-suffering. "Why write the words like that if you don't pronounce half the letters?"

"I think Jean would be able to answer that question better," I say.

"He *does* speak French? Prick. He pretended not to when I needed help with my homework."

The tension in my chest eases. When did it become this easy? Homework in the team lounge, trash-talking during video games, drawing up drills for the guys to work on, and now this, dinner with Cooper's family. Dinner with *Isabelle's* family. Part of me wants to wrench my hand away from hers. But another part—a louder part—wishes I could kiss her here, at the table. She deserves that, and moreover, I want it.

CHAPTER 30

Izzy

I shuffle downstairs without bothering to cover my yawn. Tangerine's sitting on the back of the couch, her head tilted to the side imperiously.

"Did Cooper not make it home?" I ask quietly as I give her a scratch between the ears. "How rude."

"He stayed over at Evan's," Sebastian says.

I look up, blinking at the sight of him dressed for work. Black slacks, white shirt; he must have a serving shift this afternoon. He leans against the mantel, sipping from a mug shaped like Snoopy.

"What time is it?"

"Just past nine." He checks his watch, nodding to himself. "Want some coffee?"

I scoop Tangerine into my arms and give her a cuddle. "Yes, please."

As we sit at the kitchen table, I shake my head, trying to banish the fog swirling around my brain. I didn't drink that much at the restaurant, just a glass of wine, but after, I hung out with Victoria and the rest of the team, and Brooklyn busted out the margarita mix. I take a sip of coffee, nearly gag from the bitter taste, and dump in another spoonful of sugar.

Last night was fun, but however much I love my teammates, I wish I could've spent it with Nik. After dinner—a raucous event that left me breathless, half from laughter and half from Nik's hand on my knee where no one could see—Mom and Dad dropped him and Cooper at Lark's so they could celebrate their win with the rest of the team. I almost asked to tag along, but Victoria was already calling me, and anyway, I didn't trust myself not to do something stupid while drunk. It was hard enough to restrain myself after the hockey game. I only managed it because we were around my family. If we'd been alone, I'd have congratulated Nik on the win with a lot more tongue and a lot less clothing.

I can't stop my smile, but mask it with another, much better sip of coffee. Maybe, if his hangover doesn't hurt worse than mine, we can get brunch somewhere. I wish I could just invite him over, but even with Sebastian at work, there's the risk of Cooper walking in the door.

"Hit it pretty hard last night, huh?"

I look at Sebastian over my mug. "Why do you sound like Dad?"

"I'm not judging." He takes another sip of coffee. "Just observing."

"It's weird," I grumble.

"Is there anything you want to share?"

"No." I narrow my eyes. "Why are you *looking* at me like that?"

"What's going on with you and Nikolai?"

I nearly choke. "What?"

"I saw you together, at laser tag." He sets his mug on the table with a too-loud thump. "I didn't say anything then because I figured it was just a hookup. But then last night, the way you were looking at him . . ."

I glance at Tangerine, curled neatly on the windowsill. Her tail twitches back and forth, as if she's waiting for an answer, too. Just looking outside makes me shiver. It might be sunny, but there's no mistaking the fact it's almost Thanksgiving.

"I wasn't looking at him like anything."

"If that's how you want to play it."

"I'm not trying to play anything." I run my fingers through my tangled hair. I hate lying to my brother's face, but truthfully, I've been lying for months now, so what's one more on top of the pile? "He's just Cooper's teammate."

"And Mia's just some chick from the physics department."

"It's not like that."

"Then what's it like?"

"Fine. God." I bite my thumbnail, huffing out a breath. "We've just . . . we've hooked up a few times. We spent some time together over the summer, and then he transferred here . . . but it's just casual and—ugh, why am I telling you this? It's so not your business."

"I saw the way you looked at him, Iz."

I cross my arms over my chest. I'm wearing one of Nik's shirts—a nondescript maroon T-shirt that I stole from him after I discovered he was hoarding my favorite pair of panties—but Sebastian doesn't need to know that either. "So what?"

"If it's really casual, and I'm wrong, great." He sits across from me, his father's necklace peeking out from his collar. "But you looked like you really care about him. And I know what it's like to hold back with someone you have feelings for."

My heart lurches. "There's nothing to hold back."

"Okay," he says, leaning back in the chair. "Maybe it's different. But in the beginning, with Mia—"

"It's not like that."

"Maybe not," he says lightly. "But I know you, Izzy. You care about so many things, I see it every day, and I *don't* want to see you get wrapped up in a guy who won't commit to more. I want you to have what you deserve. You're a romantic person, and—"

"Maybe I just want to screw him," I snap.

I say it to startle him, but he doesn't even flinch. It doesn't make me feel good, either. I've kept the realization I had during laser tag locked up tightly, but that doesn't mean I don't feel its presence. It's getting harder and harder to hold on to the lie; to deny that I want more with him. Telling him about Chance, hearing him speak Russian to me . . . it drew out something that I can't shove down entirely.

"Then that's great," he says. "Enjoy it. But the Izzy I know isn't a casual person."

"Is this about Cooper?" I stand, the chair scraping against the floor. My head throbs. "Because it's not his business either."

"No. And I'm not going to tell him, in case you're worried about that. But I'm leaving for Geneva after Christmas. I want to make sure my little sister is okay before there's an ocean between us."

Even though I want to hurtle my coffee mug at him, I soften. "You sound like you're going to stay there forever."

"Maybe," he says. He sounds serious enough that I freeze. "I mean, I'm going wherever Mia's going. If she decides that she wants to go to graduate school in Europe after this program, I'm staying there with her. I can cook wherever I am."

"Oh." I chew on my lip. "That's . . . romantic."

"Make sure you're getting what you really want, whatever that is. That's all I'm trying to say." He squeezes my arm as he walks past me to put his mug in the sink.

I force myself to breathe.

The closer I get to Nik, the more certain I am that I could fall in love with him.

Maybe I'm halfway there already. He's smart, he's funny, he's achingly charming. Last night, I wanted nothing more in the world than to wear his hockey sweater. But there's a reason why flings aren't in the same categories as true relationships.

If I could fall for him, that means my heart could break, too.

"I have to go to work," Sebastian says. "But I'll be around later, okay?"

"He's a good person, Seb." I cross my arms again, holding on to my elbows like they're anchors. "I'm . . . I'm glad he's here."

"I'm glad, too." He gives me a half smile. "If you decide it's going somewhere, don't hide it."

CHAPTER 31

Nikolai

I've never seen a volleyball match in person, but the instant it begins, I learn two things:

One, volleyball is awesome.

Two, Isabelle is electric on the court.

I haven't seen her since before Thanksgiving break, although we texted throughout it. I never celebrated Thanksgiving in Russia, for obvious reasons, but the version I know, a catered meal and a table full of Grandfather's business associates, doesn't seem quite right. Hers was packed with football and talk about her niece, who is due soon, and she ate homemade everything, even the pumpkin pie. I, meanwhile, hid in the butler pantry with Cricket after the staff left to finish off the open champagne.

As good as it was to catch up with her, I think I'd have liked Isabelle's version better.

I balance my elbows on my knees as I lean forward on the gym bleachers, tracking her movements. She's playing opposite hitter right now, and she keeps glancing at a girl with dark curly hair before arranging herself ahead of the serve. I'd bet that's Brooklyn, the senior she's been practicing with. She served earlier—I still don't fully get how the rotations work, but to be fair, I was inside her the one time she tried to explain it—and watching her jump to hit the ball sent a jolt straight to my dick.

Here's another thing I'm learning: it's fucking hot, watching her play. Her ponytail, her knee pads, those tight shorts, even her goddamn elbow wrap has me on edge. I teased her when she breathlessly told me that the pads I wear for hockey made her wet, but now, I don't have a leg to stand on.

I wonder if she'd chuck a volleyball at my head if I tried to haul her into a closet after the match.

Her team wrestles another point from the opposition. They're behind this set, and since they lost the first, they need a win to even things up. During a time-out, Isabelle's coach substitutes her with someone else. She perches on the end of the bench, drinking from her water bottle. When she meets my eyes, she winks.

I scrub my hand over my jaw. At least I'm essentially alone on the bleachers. There isn't much of a crowd for the away team, given the fact we're all the way in Boston.

The restaurant I chose for dinner tonight is definitely fancy enough to warrant heels and diamonds; the dress I brought for her already hangs in the closet of my hotel suite. The day after Thanksgiving, I went to Cartier and finally put one of my credit cards to good use. A girl who loves pink like she does deserves rose gold, after all.

She deserves everything. I've known that since the moment I met her, but the night she told me about Chance, it hit me again. I can't erase what he did, but hopefully by surprising her here for her birthday—her Izzy Day—and spoiling her the way she deserves, I can give her some better memories.

The set ends in a victory for her team, and they head into the third with a fresh spark of energy. She's playing setter this time around, directing the action on her side of the net. During one particularly difficult, long-lasting rally, she loses her balance and hits the gym floor.

I nearly get up, but manage to keep myself in check. She stays on the floor for a moment, her chest rising and falling rapidly. Victoria jogs over, her hand held out. When Isabelle takes it, I breathe again, although she's grimacing.

Her coach strides onto the court, asking a question. Isabelle shakes her head as she replies. Her coach gives her a look, and she stares right back, chin lifted stubbornly.

I lean forward. She's described the setter position as a leadership role, especially for the team's offense. Sounds like a center in hockey, if you ask me. Mickey would have to be knocked out stone-cold before Coach could drag him off the ice midgame.

Same for me. My heart squeezes, because there's no way that fall didn't hurt, but at the same time, I understand it. I admire it. She's a tough person, of course she is, but seeing it in action is something else.

The set resumes with her on the court, and even though I catch her wincing a few times, she settles into the groove. I'm starting to catch on to the intricacies: the huddle in between points that helps set up the formations, and the way the ball height varies for different moves. She uses hand signals to make adjustments, just like a quarterback before a snap. After a hard fight, they win the set, which ends the match. When the celebratory huddle breaks up, she hurries across the court to me, eyes sparkling.

I hurry down the steps two at a time, pulling her into a perfect, sweaty kiss. She lets me, but after a moment slips away from my grip, adjusting her headband. "It's six hours between here and New York, you know."

"I wanted to see the birthday girl."

She shakes her head with a tiny, pleased smile. "My birthday isn't for another week."

"And I've been dying to watch you play, you know that." I tug on her ponytail. "Are you okay?"

She crosses her arms, as if daring me to fuss. "That's why we wear knee pads."

"What, you mean it's not for sex appeal?"

She rolls her eyes fondly. "I should go to the locker room before Coach kills me."

"Come out with me tonight. An early Izzy Day celebration."

Her breath catches. "Wait, really?"

"Really."

She throws her arms around me with a squeal. "Oh my God. You're the best." She steps back. "But I'm supposed to stay with the team."

"I'll have you back in time."

She frowns at her uniform. "And I don't have anything to wear."

I dart in for another kiss, speaking in Russian and then translating to English, mostly to feel her shiver. "I'm at The Newbury. You don't need a thing but yourself, sunshine."

I BUTTON MY shirt in front of the window, gazing at the Boston skyline. I've seen enough cities to mark New York as my favorite—my home—but there's a certain energy about Boston that makes me itch to explore it. This close to wintertime, the days are short, so it's already dark, the lights from windows and streetlamps and cars illuminating the scene like so many candles.

I didn't experience true wealth until thirteen, when my mother brought me back to America for good. My face was stiff with stitches, and I kept scratching the cast on my broken arm. I remember fidgeting so much in my new suit that she snapped at me just before Grandfather met us in his foyer. His handshake, and eventual hug, felt foreign, but at least it was gentle.

I couldn't stop staring at his home, with its opulent details and uniformed staff and intense quiet. Since it was early January, it was still decorated for Christmas, and I felt a twang of longing as I stared at the tall, trim, perfectly decorated tree in the living room. I never wanted for anything in Moscow, and our apartment was the nicest in our building, but comparing those luxuries to his would've been like pitting a Prius against a Ferrari.

I'm used to the wealth now, but I rarely take advantage of it. My Mercedes, sure. Clothes, no problem. I don't protest when Grandfather greets me each birthday with a new Rolex watch. But a hotel suite like this, booked on a whim, and the Cartier necklace resting in its case on the coffee table? This is on a different level. It's a reminder of the amount of money I have at my fingertips.

I've never been so glad to spend it.

I move on to my tie, then my cuff links. I opted for a navy-blue suit, to match the dress hanging in the closet, and looking at my reflection in the window, I know I made a good choice. I can't do anything about the scar, but the rest of me is plenty put together. You'd hardly know that my favorite thing in the world is playing a violent contact sport.

There's a knock on the door; I told reception to send Isabelle up when she arrived. She reaches for a kiss as soon as I open it, but stops short as she looks me over.

"Oh, wow," she says, smoothing my suit collar.

"Something tells me this should be resulting in more kisses, not less."

She shakes her head, lips pressed together in a smile. "This is just . . . wow. All of this for Izzy Day?"

She spins in a slow circle, taking in the details of the suite. I asked for the best available, and the space definitely delivers. There's a gorgeous wood-burning fireplace in the living room, views of the Boston Public Garden from the bedroom, and an enormous freestanding tub in the pristine white bathroom. I'm already having visions of eating her out in that bathtub, should I be so lucky.

"I know you missed out on a few," I say, my heart jumping. I'm risking bringing up bad memories for her, but hopefully, we can make good ones tonight instead. "I wanted to make up for it."

I swipe the jewelry case from the table and open it, holding it out to her.

"Oh my God. Nik, that's way too many diamonds."

I cock my head to the side. "I'm talking to Isabelle Callahan, right?"

"And it's rose gold," she practically whispers. She meets my gaze. "I *really* don't have anything to wear."

"Check the closet."

She hurries to the bedroom. I lean against the doorway, not bothering to fight my smile, as she pulls open the closet. She gasps at the ball gown, a deep ocean blue that I know will match her eyes perfectly, but it's the white fur stole that she pulls out.

"This is beautiful. Is it vintage?"

"It's my mother's." I join her in front of the closet. I stopped by Mom's apartment before I drove to Boston, and she didn't mind me taking it out of storage. "It was a present from my father, back when they first got married."

Before things changed, I think but don't add.

"She didn't . . . take much, from Russia, but she did bring this. I remember her wearing it a lot when I was a kid."

"And you want me to wear it." Her eyes are shining. She blinks rapidly before pecking me on the lips. "You drove all the way to Boston with this? For me?"

"I wanted you all to myself." I take the stole from her gently and set it on the bed, then pull her close. She's in leggings and a thick sweater with a Patagonia jacket. She must have blow-dried her hair before she came over, because it falls in gentle waves over her shoulders. She looks stunning just like this, no dress or diamonds required, but I'm still relishing the thought of her dripping in finery. The stole has a complicated past, and when I look at it, I can't fully shake it, but it'll be beautiful on her. "I thought we could make a better birthday memory. Together."

And maybe when we return to New York, I can take her to dinner without hiding it.

"Oh, Nik," she says softly.

"Happy birthday, solnishko." I give her a luxurious, lingering kiss. "Let me dress you."

CHAPTER 32

Izzy

My breath crystallizes in front of me as I laugh at the dirty joke Nik just told. He has a mouth on him when he wants to use it, and tonight, he's been full of laughter and wit, unabashedly kissing me all over Boston. He presses the button for the crosswalk by our hotel, but there isn't much traffic this time of night, so I tug on his hand until he runs across the street with me. My feet are freezing in my heels, but my shoulders are snug underneath his mother's stole. My laughter turns breathy as we hit the sidewalk on the other side.

"Reckless," he murmurs in my ear, but I can sense his amusement. He walks me to the building, pressing me against it. His eyes glitter in the light from the streetlamp as he gives me his trademark smirk.

Maybe it's the bottle of wine we split over the tasting menu at Menton, but I've never felt heat like this.

I trace his scar. A million wishes crowd my mind, yet I manage to hold them inside.

"Maybe I like being reckless with you."

He presses his cold lips to mine.

I know that Nik's family is wealthy—I spent the summer working out of his mother's outrageous apartment on the Upper East Side—but somehow, I never quite registered the level until tonight. College has a way of leveling the playing field; I've snuck into his dorm all semester. He could've bought anyone out of their housing, and yet he chose to keep a low profile.

Maybe it's the hockey player in him. He's no stranger to sacrificing comfort for an end goal. Or maybe it has something to do with his parents' divorce. I saw the depth of emotion in his eyes, that night with my parents. Hints at secrets I don't know if I'll ever learn about from his lips.

The rose gold diamond necklace I'm wearing is utterly gorgeous. I don't even want to think of the price. I doubt he just had it, like the stole, which means he bought it for me. All to give me a better birthday.

Is a necklace just a necklace to a guy who has more money than he knows what to do with?

I wind my arms around his neck, biting his lip. His grip on me tightens as he lets out a startled moan. Tantalizing warmth pools in my belly. The freezing air bites through everything but the fur, but I can't stop kissing him.

Faintly, I hear music. Instrumental, delicate, like so many of the songs I listened to during my internship.

"Do you hear that?"

"Must be a wedding."

"In the hotel?" I glance at the entrance. "Our hotel?"

He arches an eyebrow. "Feel like dancing?"

At my grin, he leads me to the hotel entrance, his expression growing haughty. "An hour and a half late. Utterly ridiculous." He inclines his head to the doorman. "You'd think she actually liked her cousin, the amount of time she spent getting ready."

I force myself to scowl, not laugh. "*You're* the one who got the time wrong. And you changed your suit three times."

"And *you* gave the driver the wrong address," he says, raising his voice so reception hears it. "We drove around half the city for an hour like fools."

"If you were so certain I was wrong, why didn't you correct me sooner?" I give him a sweet smile when his mouth shuts. "Precisely."

"The reception is down the hall, sir," the woman behind the front desk says.

"Thank you," he replies, sounding so perfectly exasperated, I nearly lose it and ruin the whole thing. He looks extra hot when he scowls, even if it's pretend. "Finally, someone who listens to me."

He throws me a wink.

"It must be so difficult to be you, darling," I say dryly.

At the entrance to the ballroom, a young woman wearing a headset, with a clipboard tucked underneath her arm—something so familiar I miss it, deeply, for a moment—smiles at us. "Welcome. What's the name?"

She's busy staring at Nik, so I peek at the clipboard.

"Alan and Yvette Bancroft." Yvette sounds like the kind of woman who would wear furs. "Well, won't it be soon, honey? When you finally get the balls to propose, I mean."

The woman's lip twitches.

"Stacy will kill us if we miss another moment," I add, sliding my arm through Nik's and tugging him into the room before the woman can protest.

As I take in the ballroom, decorated from ceiling to floor in shades of white and icy blue, I sigh audibly. Summer might be wedding season, but a winter wedding? When it's done well, there's nothing better.

"Were you so easily swayed by handsome wedding crashers during your internship?" Nik teases.

"Absolutely not," I say, plucking two glasses of champagne from a passing server. "I was a professional."

"And your professional opinion of this?"

I turn in a circle, hungrily taking in every high-end detail. Delicate, shimmery decorations combine with the breathtaking chandelier above to give the illusion of stars sparkling on a clear winter night. They must be in between dinner service and dessert, because most of the guests are on the dance floor, moving in elegant circles to the string quartet. They somehow managed to make the balloon arch behind the musicians look classy—no easy feat, Katherine rarely signed off on balloons—and the white orchid centerpieces? I want the florist's contact information. I'd love to have been the one to pull off a reception this impressive.

"It's stunning." I shake my head as I sip the champagne. "Look at the flower arrangements! The cake!"

"I've missed how excited weddings make you."

I couldn't fight my smile if I tried. "Did you know this was happening?"

"I figured you'd be up for a little fun." He grins; there's no doubt he liked playing pretend as much as me. "I'm glad I chose this dress for you."

I look down at the sequin-studded, midnight-blue ball gown. It's the perfect fit, a detail that didn't escape me when he buttoned me into it earlier. "It does suit the theme."

"It suits your eyes." He holds out his hand. "Dance with me, Isabelle."

"Yvette, you mean."

"No. I mean my Isabelle."

My Isabelle.

Sebastian's words echo in my mind, despite my best efforts to keep them at bay. I'm terrified to ruin the delicate balance we've struck. I know I need to tell Nik about how I feel; I owe him that honesty—but not yet. Not here.

Not on a perfect night like this.

He sweeps me onto the dance floor as a new song starts. It's slow and romantic, perfect for dancing. In the middle of the crowd, the bride and groom sway as one, looking at each other lovingly. I smile, even though I have no idea who they are. A wedding isn't a love story all on its own, but it is a symbol of whatever road the couple has been on and where they want to go in the future, and I've always found that beautiful.

"They look happy," I murmur.

Nik pulls me close, one hand on my hip, the other holding my palm. I put my free hand on his broad shoulder, letting myself get as close as I can without tripping over his feet. He spins me, then pulls me back in, guiding our shared movements. Jumping on the dance floor at a college party isn't the same as a waltz like this, and despite loving to dance, I don't do it enough. The give-and-take of our bodies leaves me breathless. Soon, I'm yearning for more contact, more warmth, more of the promises he's giving me with his gaze.

This is the best Izzy Day I've ever had.

Somehow, I manage to contain myself as we dance through the next three songs. If anyone realizes we don't belong, they keep it to themselves. At the end of the third, the last bars of music fade into the air without immediately leading into the next. I press a fevered kiss to his lips.

"You dressed me." I scratch my nails down the back of his neck, underneath the collar. He dragged on lacy scraps of lingerie and the dress; he clasped the necklace around my throat and knelt to guide my feet into the shoes. "Are you going to undress me, too?"

The desire in his eyes makes my breath catch.

Plenty of guys have admired me, complimented me—but no one, *no one*, has looked like he's desperate to breathe the same air as me.

"Slowly." His voice is so low, so rough. "As slowly as I can make myself, because the moment you're in nothing but that necklace—"

I drag him out of the room by the tie.

CHAPTER 33

Izzy

By the time the elevator door dings, Nik has me in a bridal carry.

The silken dress slides over my legs like water. It's ridiculous, because all he did was press me against the elevator wall and kiss me on the short ride up, but I'm on edge already. He unlocks the door to the suite without putting me down, then kicks the door shut. He strides right through the tastefully appointed living room to the bedroom, setting me on the bed—and slipping to his knees.

"No nightcap?" I tease.

He runs his hand down my calf. I let out a small sigh as he takes off my heel; my feet have been aching since the walk back to the hotel. He slips off the other heel, sets both aside, and starts to rub my feet.

"I'm finding myself hungry again." His serious, sensual eyes settle on me. "I'll need something more than a drink."

A moan escapes my lips as he presses his thumbs against the arch of my foot. I kick my leg reflexively. "You promised to undress me."

"I did, didn't I?" He moves to the other foot. I knew his fingers were talented in other regards, but this is new. "Gorgeous girl."

My belly tightens with want as slick gathers between my legs, but despite my pleas, he just keeps massaging my feet. By the time he rises, turning me around so he can set the stole aside and undo the row of buttons marching down my spine, I'm forced to bite my tongue to keep moans from spilling out with each touch. He tosses his jacket and tie aside haphazardly, but at my look, carefully drapes the dress over the chair in the corner.

He doesn't bother undressing me further.

Instead, he takes his time rolling up his sleeves. We didn't turn on the lights, and the shadows sharpen the angles of his face.

"Arrange yourself however you like," he practically purrs.

My nipples go taut, rubbing against the textured fabric of my bra. The sky-blue straps crisscross over my rib cage, leading down to matching panties. By the way his gaze darkens, I know he can see the wet spot on the front, the undeniable evidence of my arousal.

As if I could be anything else when he's like this. Dominant, yet graceful. Noting the part of me that craves it, and offering to pull me in. I haven't seen this side of him in full force since the summer.

I take a step back, then another, until my legs hit the bed.

I let myself fall.

"You still want me on my knees?" he says with amusement.

I nod breathlessly, sitting up on my elbows. Even better than his deep tone of voice is the way he looks as he sinks to his knees again. No hesitation, just raw lust etched into every inch of his beautiful face. He settles between my legs, pressing them open with his wide shoulders, and lets his breath ghost over the front of my panties.

I whimper, my hand drifting to my breasts. I pull my bra far enough down that I can twist my nipples between my fingertips.

At his curse, I smile at the ceiling—but it doesn't last long when he nuzzles over the damp silk. His hands dig into my hips as he licks the fabric; he scrapes his teeth over it with enough pressure I gasp. Fingers slide over the top of the panties, then lower, pulling the ruined fabric aside so he can give me a proper lick. I think he says something, but I can't hear it over the buzzing in my ears, the urge to lift my hips even though he has me so thoroughly pinned.

And when his teeth catch on my clit, a finger pushing into me, my hips do come off the bed.

"So fucking delicious," he says, kissing my thigh wetly. "You taste like you were made just for me."

I can't reach his hair from this angle, but I wish I could; I want to pull and pull until he's breathless, too. I wish I could speak, but I seem to have lost that capacity. When I try, I just whine. He dives back in, fingering me as he licks and nibbles and sucks. My core tightens, seeking more friction. I'm warm from the tips of my ears to the soles of my feet. He adds another finger, stretching roughly. I whimper, twisting in his grasp until he holds me down and seals his mouth around my clit, turning my desire molten.

His name finally bursts from my lips as I climax, swept away in an unyielding surf of pleasure. I struggle to angle my elbows so I can get a glimpse of him, even as he continues to use that talented mouth and curl his teasing fingers.

He noses through the trimmed hair around my clit as his gaze meets mine.

Mouth slick. Eyes dancing.

I can't see his grin, but I can feel it.

I muster up enough attitude to feel worthy of the necklace that's still around my throat.

"Are you going to just stare, or get back to work?"

The words hit the mark; his body goes rigid. Pressing a quick kiss to my hip, he rips off my lingerie, then the rest of his clothes. He settles against the headboard, as comfortable as a panther in a tree.

I wet my lips, staring at his smooth, muscled chest, his strong legs, and especially his hardened length, framed by neat, dark hair. He's the picture of carefully contained power, and even though he wrung me out with his mouth, I want more.

He strokes himself lazily, and I nearly whimper aloud, clenching around nothing.

By the way he raises his eyebrow, he knows it.

"Crawl to me, Isabelle."

The order—because it is an order—hangs in the air for the slightest of moments. He doesn't push, and I know if I shook my head, he'd pull me into his arms and ask where things went wrong, if my knee still hurts from earlier, but that's not what I want. I've always found safety in the ways he pushes me, and this is no exception.

So I crawl.

He keeps stroking himself, and I crawl, inch by inch, up the bed. Deliberately slow. A show for him, clad in nothing but the diamond necklace, my hair long and loose around my shoulders. My breasts sway with each movement. I just came, but I honestly think I could climax again from the position, the exposure, the look on his face as he drinks in the sight of me.

When I'm close enough, he doesn't tease; he drags me straight into his lap.

"My good girl." He squeezes my ass with both hands, massaging lightly. "You're going to sit on my cock and take every fucking inch."

I scratch my nails down his perfect torso. He's ridiculously built, each part of his body honed for the sport he loves so much. I take his cock in hand, giving it a firm pump. He's rock-hard, skin flushed and wet with precome.

I tilt my head to the side. "You promise?"

Part of him wants to roll me over; I see it in the way his eyes catch, but he grabs the condom he pulled from his wallet as he undressed and hands it to me. I roll it down, a little inelegantly, and with enough pressure to make him hiss. He checks between my legs, just to make sure I'm still plenty slick, and I don't miss the hitch in his breath when he realizes just how soaked I am. He kisses me, hand tangled in my hair, as he lifts me up.

I slide down his cock inch by agonizing inch. He's the biggest I've ever taken, and I love it regardless of the position, but this is a special kind of torture. The slow drag of him against my core, the way his fingers dig into my skin as he fights not to buck into me. When I bottom out, I'm practically panting, and he looks exactly as wrecked as I feel. He rubs my clit, easing any discomfort.

"Slowly," he murmurs. He helps me move on his cock, kissing my throat when I let my head fall back.

Each movement loosens moans from my throat. I try my best to move myself up and down, but before long, I'm trembling with effort as well as arousal.

"This is"—I gasp as he gives my clit another firm rub—"a core exercise."

His startled laughter makes me soar. "You're doing so well, sweetheart." He guides one of my hands to the headboard and the other to his chest, for leverage. "Give me a little bit more."

"I want to come with you inside me."

"I know." He takes pity on me, planting his hands on my hips as he snaps his own upwards. I cry out sharply. "I fucking want that too, want to hear those sweet noises from you while I fill you up."

Another thrust, and another. I bear down, meeting each of his movements with one of my own. I press my nails into his chest so hard it must hurt, but he doesn't even flinch. His intense eyes never leave mine, the hunger stark in his expression even as he's getting his fill. It's as though he could devour me entirely and still want more.

I squeeze around him as we move together, pleased when it makes him moan. The pleasure grows and grows, bringing me to the peak. On one of the downward thrusts, he catches me against his chest. He holds us still, and with aching slowness, takes one of my nipples into his mouth and sucks.

I come with a scream, the tension seeping out of me in a rush. I wind my fingers through his hair, lifting his head. He crushes his mouth to mine. I bite his lip because I can, and I smile when I feel him spend inside me, holding on to me so tightly I know I'll feel it tomorrow. He whispers my name, over and over, as we float down from the high.

I don't protest when he untangles us, but I reach for him when he comes back to bed after getting rid of the condom.

We're close enough that I can see the gold in his eyes. He tucks my hair behind my ear, a tender smile on his face.

I wonder if I'm the only one who has ever seen that smile. The only one to touch that scar.

I open my mouth, to say—I don't know what. Despite what we just did, the night feels paper-thin. Anyone, even Nik, can say the right things and touch me in the right ways, and still not want to stick around.

"I started the bath," he says. He traces a pattern onto my hip. "It's big enough for us both."

A bath sounds nice. Much safer than the conversation I don't even know how to begin.

"That *is* a spectacular bathtub," I mumble against his shoulder.

He scoops me up, holding me with a fraction of his strength. "Need you clean before I can get you dirty again, sweet solnishko."

WHEN I WAKE, the bedroom, with all the evidence of last night strewn around, is bathed in morning light.

Nik's spooning me, breathing softly, a hand splayed over my

middle. Our feet are tangled together. I rub my face against the pillowcase as I smile, covering his hand with mine.

Every kiss, every touch, every word we shared, comes rushing back. The whole perfect birthday night, from start to finish, in color film.

If you decide it's going somewhere, don't hide it.

I rub my thumb over the back of his hand. He has a bruise on his finger. He'll need to tape it before his next game.

I'll tell him over breakfast. I'll tell him that I want to put a label on this, and stop sneaking around, and if last night wasn't a fluke, if it wasn't a hollow moment without a heartbeat—

Reality slams in a second later.

The team. The bus back to campus.

I dive across the bed for my phone.

"Isabelle?" I hear Nik ask, his voice rough with sleep.

I fumble to unlock my phone. A dozen missed texts and calls greet me. Victoria, our other teammates, Coach Alexis.

I should have been on that bus three hours ago.

CHAPTER 34

Izzy

"Do you understand?" Coach Alexis says again. "I expected better of you."

I dig my teeth into my trembling lip. When we finally got back to campus, I practically threw myself out of Nik's car in my haste to run to her office. I've apologized ten different ways since I sat down, but nothing has made her budge.

You stick with the team during away trips. Always. Plenty of my teammates have snuck out like I did to go to parties or clubs, but they all know that when the bus to campus pulls up the next morning, you have to be on it. *I* know that, and I fucked it up anyway. No amount of explaining or groveling can erase that fact.

I suppose I ought to be grateful that she's not suspending me or kicking me off the team, but in a way, this punishment is worse. My second chance, ground to dust. I'm still on the roster, but I'll never be the starting setter.

It takes me a moment to be able to manage more than a nod. "Yes."

"I can't expect someone I don't trust to lead the team. That's just how it is."

I suppress another string of pleas.

"And it's a shame, because you've been playing well. If not for this, we'd be having a very different conversation."

The only good thing about this conversation is that I haven't lied. Not once. Yes, I went out with Nik instead of staying with the team. No, I didn't ask permission. Yes, I missed the bus. I haven't lied about it, not a single word.

I'm so tired of lying to my family. Tired of pretending that Nik doesn't mean a thing to me when he's becoming everything.

Last night shouldn't have happened, but I can't bring myself to regret it.

"I understand." I clear my throat, willing strength into my voice. "And again, I'm sorry."

"You can go."

I nearly knock over a side table in my haste to get to the door. By some miracle, I haven't cried in front of her, but I know that tears will start flowing the moment I'm free from the confines of this stupid, magazine-glossy office.

"Callahan?"

I freeze with my hand on the door handle.

She gives me a look that could crack ice. "I hope that boy was worth it."

When I shut the door, I press my fist to my mouth, swallowing a sob. I expect to see Nik waiting, but I'm alone. In case Alexis is planning to leave her office, I jog down the hallway, peering around corners for him.

Eventually, I hear his voice. He's speaking Russian, so I don't understand a word, but still, I relax at the sound. I enter the gym lobby, making a beeline for him; he's pacing by the door, face taut.

"No," he says in English, an edge to his tone, "I didn't—"

At the sight of me, he stops midsentence and hangs up the phone. I lurch into his arms. He hugs me tightly.

"How did that go?" he asks quietly, into my hair.

"About as well as you'd expect."

"I could talk to her."

"Absolutely not."

"What did she—"

"I messed up." Alexis's parting shot to me echoes in my mind: *I hope that boy was worth it.* "It was my fault."

"I'm the one who went to see you."

I shake my head. "None of what I did this season matters." Tears streak down my flushed cheeks. "How well I played, all the extra work I put in—she's not giving the starting setter position to someone she can't trust."

"That's bullshit."

I untangle myself from him, shoving at the doors to the building so hard, they bounce against the brick. Cold air blasts me in the face, setting off shivers. I didn't bother to throw my coat on for the dash from Nik's car to the building, and now I'm regretting it.

"I'm sorry. It's my fault, I'm the one who kept you out all night. Are you sure I can't—"

"God." My breath blows out like smoke in the freezing air. "I can't do this."

"Do what?"

If the night we just shared meant to him what it meant to me, then this lie isn't hiding a crush. It's hiding a spark that could easily grow into a wildfire. Yet around everyone, we act like we don't know each other at all. Moment after moment this fall—even during the dinner with my parents—we acted like near strangers. I shoved it down and pretended it didn't matter. That *we* didn't matter. Volleyball just fell to pieces, and if I have to keep pretending that Nik is nothing to me, I'm going to break.

I whirl on him. "Lie. I can't lie anymore."

He opens his mouth. Shuts it. I wipe my face roughly.

"Isabelle," he says finally. His eyes are wide; he swipes his tongue over his lips. He fists his hands, then relaxes them, over and over.

I know he knows what I mean, and yet he doesn't say anything else.

I jerk my hand through the tangled ends of my hair. Words crowd my throat, but it's an effort to string them together. "Part of me was relieved, in her office." I laugh hollowly. "Relieved that at least I didn't have to lie about you."

"What did she say?"

"It doesn't matter." I haven't truly let myself think about what this means yet. What kind of future I'll have on the team. What a disappointment I'll be to my parents the instant they hear what happened, and why. It's all background to the sight of Nik so still, his expression so pained. The five feet between us may as well be a canyon.

"Of course it does. She has to know it was a mistake."

"I don't care." Another fucking lie, but at least it makes him take a step forward.

"Isabelle," he says again. His expression is so stark that it would scare me if I had enough room in me to feel anything but heartache.

"I can't lie to my family like this." My voice cracks. "I can't sneak around anymore, especially if it's going to get in the way of everything else, for someone who isn't . . ."

"What are you talking about?" His voice sounds odd and flat.

I convinced myself that casual with him felt different because I actively made the choice, but in the end, the path twisted in the same direction. I felt something for him from the start, and I thought he did too, especially after last night, but maybe he's better at keeping people out. There's so much he hasn't shared, especially when it comes to his family. Maybe I'm the idiot again, shoving my feelings at anyone who gives me a second look. Letting myself believe this was going somewhere, that the trust went in both directions, when I'm not enough for him.

"You might be capable of holding yourself apart from everything and shutting out your family, but I can't do that."

A twitch, as if I just slapped him. "My family has nothing to do with this."

"And mine has everything to do with it," I shoot back.

He doesn't react with so much as a blink. He may as well be a statue. Cold. Unbothered. Letting me drown in front of him.

"I can't do it anymore," I whisper. "Not unless it's for real, Nik. Is it for real?"

Something flickers in his eyes at the break in my voice, but he doesn't answer.

Last night, he called me *his Isabelle*. Now he doesn't say a word. Tears press at my eyes to the point of pain. If I take in a full breath, I won't be able to hold back my sob. No answer, but it's answer enough.

I somehow manage to open the door and escape back into the warmth of the gym.

I think I hear my name, but he doesn't follow. Wishful thinking, like every other moment from May to now. Last night didn't matter. None of it did.

At least I manage to find a quiet corner before the tears fall.

THE SHOT OF tequila tastes extra smooth going down. My belly's on fire, my limbs loose. I slam the glass on the table alongside the rest of the guys—football guys, maybe lacrosse, it doesn't matter—and throw my hands up as they cheer for me.

I smile. The whole room's gone hazy, thanks to that fifth . . . no, sixth . . . shot. Something about the tequila makes me think of summer, but I can't remember the specifics now. I don't want to remember the specifics ever again. Floating, fuzzy—it's so much better than wallowing. So much better than reliving that ice-cold expression. How Nik didn't say a word when I laid myself bare.

I stagger backwards, nearly tripping, and someone steadies me, his hand lingering on my waist before I sidestep. Terrible Christmas music. Tons of sloshed students looking to blow off end-of-semester steam. I lived at parties like these all last year, twirling in my heels and glitter, drawing stares from every direction. Why the hell did I stop?

I drown the answer in another shot.

When I showed up at Victoria's dorm, already dressed to party, face blotchy, she took one look at me and hauled me to the bathroom to do my makeup. No I-told-you-sos, just waterproof mascara and higher heels.

Before everything, we were going to go to tonight's hockey game, but this is way better. This has booze, and sugar cookies, and no hockey players whatsoever. It's free of things like volleyball, and lectures, and staring into the eyes of someone you think you knew, only to find a stranger looking back. Screw that. Screw everything but this. Frenetic energy and breathlessness and someone pulling me to the dance floor.

"Take it easy on the shots," Victoria says in my ear, hauling me away from the football-or-lacrosse guys. "Let's dance instead."

I hug her, rocking us both to the weird dance remix of "Jingle Bell Rock" playing from cheap speakers.

"You smell like beer," I say, smacking her cheek with a kiss.

"And you smell like a bottle of Patrón."

Someone passes by with a tray of shots, and I grab two. Victoria grimaces, but handles hers while I handle mine. It's such a cheap brand, it makes my nose smart, but I like that, too. It adds yet another log to the fire burning in me. Multicolored lights twinkle at the edges of my vision as I twirl around, commanding attention, as always.

I can burn brighter. That's my specialty. I burn and I burn until I'm nothing, until I'm alone again.

I'm not sure how I end up on top of the table, but once I'm there, I'm dancing. I rip a garland away from the wall and drape it around myself like a feather boa as I sway my hips. Someone changes the song to an especially sultry rendition of "Santa Baby," and I launch into a proper dance, singing along to the lyrics. I trail my hand down my throat, the front of my green sequined dress, and toss my hair over my shoulder as the crowd whoops.

If you decide it's going somewhere, don't hide it.

I hope that boy was worth it.

I can't do it anymore.

I spin. The table buckles.

I hit the floor, and the strands of Christmas lights wink out like stars.

CHAPTER 35

Nikolai

I'm not sure how I make it to the rink. One minute I'm standing in the cold, trapped in a panic attack as I look at Isabelle's tears, and the next I'm in the locker room for the last game before the break in the season, managing an approximation of a smile.

There were some steps in between. Resisting the impulse to smash in the window of my car. Leaving bruises on my forearms because I dug my nails in too deep. Scowling at my phone as I remembered snatches of the argument I had with Dad before Isabelle came out of her coach's office. Breathing in the smell of her forgotten coat. Trying, and failing, to calm my rising nausea. I dragged myself out of that anxiety-ridden haze inch by painful inch, but by then, it was too late.

"You coming?" Mickey asks.

At the sound of his voice, I startle. I've been staring at my locker, gloves in hand, for God knows how long. I just can't get the image of her standing there with tears in her eyes out of my mind, or stop hearing the way her voice hitched as she told me she couldn't do this anymore. Panic robbed me of speech, of movement, and it all came crashing down.

I somehow manage to get onto the ice, and it's only then that I realize Cooper isn't there. I'm partnered with Evan for the opening shift. I give him a look, and he just shakes his head. "Later," he mouths.

I glance at Coach, but he's busy talking to one of the assistants, so instead, I ready myself for the face-off. Hockey never stops.

Not for panic, not for heartbreak. Hockey is my father's voice, as impossible to ignore as a punch.

Nausea threatens again, but I shove it down. I haven't eaten since last night, so there's nothing for my stomach to chuck up. Dad would scoff if he saw my stick shaking against the ice like this.

The whistle blows. I burst into action. I've been training all my life, so my body takes over, working on autopilot. My mind goes blank when I'm on the ice, and the second my skates hit the bench in between shifts, Isabelle's face is all I see.

I let her run from me while she was reeling, even after she told me what Chance did to her. Even after I already hurt her that way once before. She asked if what we have is real, and I was too trapped in my mind to give her a fucking answer.

My hands are numb again. Trembling.

I can't believe I let her go.

"Nik," Evan says, clapping my shoulder with his gloved hand. I startle, looking around. I'm the only guy still sitting on the bench. "The period's over. You okay?"

On the way to the locker room, Ryder stops me. "Cooper's not going to make the game, so I need you to step up even more." He sighs, brows drawn. "He's dealing with a family emergency. Something with one of his siblings—son?"

I race down the hallway. Fucking skates. Can't move in them off the ice. I skid into the locker room, shouldering past the guys, and pull my phone out of my bag.

It can't be Isabelle.

Can't be.

If something happened to her after I left—if after my own fucking panic sent me spiraling and I let her go, she ended up *hurt*—

No texts, but I have a new voice mail. I swallow as I raise the phone to my ear. I don't recognize the number.

"Nikolai, it's Sebastian. I got your number from Izzy's phone, sorry."

I sit on the bench with a thud.

"I know we don't know each other that well, and I don't know where you and Izzy stand right now, but she was at a party and she—she got hurt. She's at the hospital. Bethel-Ross."

My heart leaves my body. The trembles turn into full-on shaking. There's more, but I don't bother listening to it. I yank off my skates, shove my feet into street shoes, and grab my bag. All around me, my teammates are chatting and laughing, but I can't hear them over my pounding heartbeat.

Fuck distance, fuck reservations, fuck secrets.

I have to see her. Now.

"What's going on, man?" Aaron asks.

I sling my bag over my shoulder. "Tell Coach I'm sorry."

"You're leaving?" Mickey says.

I don't bother answering. I can make apologies later, after I'm sure Isabelle is okay. On the way out the door, Evan meets my gaze. He does a double take as he puts two and two together.

"I'll tell Ryder," he says.

CHAPTER 36

Nikolai

Isabelle Callahan," I repeat breathlessly, swiping back my sweaty hair. "Where is she?"

The woman behind the counter looks me over, no doubt taking in the hockey uniform I'm still wearing, pads and all. I didn't want to stop for even a moment to change; I raced to the hospital as fast as I could without getting pulled over.

"They just transferred her upstairs," she finally says.

"What room?"

"It's family only."

"I'm her— Please, I need to see her. Now."

The woman glances at her colleague, who shrugs. She sighs again as she turns to me.

"She's on the third floor. But—"

I sprint to the elevators. She shouts something, but I ignore her, slipping into the first one that opens before anyone can stop me. I don't give a fuck if they haul me out of the building in handcuffs, so long as I can see her first.

On the third floor, things are quiet, lights dimmed for the evening. I don't see a sign of her or her family in the first part of the floor, so when a doctor opens a set of locked doors, I slip by into the next section. A nurse pokes his head up from a desk to the right. I ignore whatever he asks.

Further down, I see two guys—Cooper and Sebastian—guarding one of the rooms. Blood roars in my ears as I skid over to them. Cooper looks up when he hears me approaching, his eyes going wide. My stomach twists at the sight of the unmistakable pain on his face.

"Abney? What are you doing here?"

"You're here," Sebastian says. I catch the relief in his tone.

"I have to see her." I take a step forward. "Let me inside."

They give each other a look.

"Please," I say, my voice breaking. "Please, Cooper, don't keep me from her."

I see the moment his bewilderment clicks into understanding. Betrayal. Sebastian dips his chin in a nod, and Cooper stands, dragging a hand down his beard.

"Please," I say again. "I'll explain it all later. Just give me five minutes with her."

"There's nothing to explain," he says. His laughter sounds harsh in the otherwise silent hallway. "I understand it all. I thought we were teammates, Nik. Friends."

"Coop," Sebastian says, his voice low.

Before Cooper can say anything else, Penny walks over, holding a tray of coffees. She takes a few tentative steps forward, her gaze darting between me and her boyfriend. "Honey? What's going on?"

Cooper doesn't look at her. He keeps his eyes, as piercing as they were that first meeting between us, trained on me. He looks fiercely protective. Ready to tear off my limbs. I can't even begrudge it, because it's what Isabelle deserves.

"Cooper?" Isabelle calls from behind the door. "Sebastian?"

My knees nearly buckle at the sound of her voice. At least she's awake, and aware of the fact her brothers are outside the room. Whatever happened to her, it can't be that bad.

Cooper's expression doesn't change, but he steps away from the door. "Five minutes. She has a concussion."

I slip inside the darkened room before he can change his mind.

I notice her hair first, spread out on the pillow like a dark halo. She's in a pale blue hospital gown, an IV attached to one wrist, a soft cast on the other. She looks tiny in the bed, tucked into the stark white sheets.

I realize abruptly that I haven't been to the hospital since I was a teenager. Not since it was me in the bed, wincing as the doctor told my mother that it was lucky the glass didn't hit my eye. I can still picture her face in perfect detail. The smeared red lipstick, the way her hand shook as she held it over her mouth, and above all, the blue-black bruise on her cheek. I shove the memory away.

"Isabelle," I whisper.

She turns her head slowly enough, I know it hurts. I yank off my sweater, my gear, dumping it all uncaringly on the floor until I'm just in my under-layers. I ease into the chair next to the bed, reaching out to take her hand in both of mine. She has stitches on her forehead, and the beginnings of a bruise extending from her temple to her cheek. I duck my head, willing myself to breathe, as the tension in my body eases.

She's safe. She's looking right at me.

"Nik," she says, her voice equally soft. "What are you doing here?"

"What happened, sweetheart?"

"My brothers know you're here." She squeezes her eyes shut. "Oh God."

"It's okay." I force myself to stay relaxed, to stave off the panic. "Don't worry about that right now."

Tears spill down her cheeks. "I'm so sorry."

"You don't have to apologize for anything."

"You don't have to be here, you had—"

"I know," I interrupt. "I don't care about that. Nothing mattered except getting here to see you."

"But earlier . . ."

I brush my lips against her cheek, featherlight. "I was an ass-hole, earlier. You were right. It's real, Isabelle."

Her breath catches audibly. I kiss her on the lips, relief zinging through me when she kisses back.

"Are you okay?" she asks, rubbing down my bare arm.

Of course she's asking me that, even though she's the one in the hospital bed. I squeeze her hand, overcome with fondness.

"I had a panic attack." She stays silent, taking that in. I swallow as I continue. "It happens sometimes, and I just . . . I shut down. But it's not an excuse, and I shouldn't have left you alone. I'm so sorry."

"Panic attacks?" She shifts closer to me, wincing.

"I'll tell you everything. I promise." As I say the words, I know they're true. I'm scared out of my mind at the prospect of sharing my past, but I'll do it anyway, for her. Only for her. "But right now, you need to rest."

More voices outside. She bites her lip as she looks at the door.

"It's probably my parents," she says, the words careful and measured. "If you want to go."

Fresh worry slams through me as I take in—really take in—the depth of her injury. She's going to have a scar on her temple; there's at least ten stitches there. Hopefully this is only a minor concussion, and she's being observed as a precaution.

"No. I'm staying."

Half a day spent thinking I fucked things up was more than enough for me. I might lose her one day, because a brightness like hers can't linger with my darkness forever, but today isn't that day. Not yet.

I stand as the door opens. Isabelle's mother stifles a small cry at the sight of her daughter and hurries for the bed. Her father, flanked by her brothers and Penny, stops when he sees me.

"Nikolai," he says. "What a surprise."

I don't hesitate before reaching out my hand to shake his again. "I didn't introduce myself properly the last time we met, sir."

He raises an eyebrow. "Oh?"

I spare Cooper half a glance before answering, "I'm Isabelle's boyfriend."

CHAPTER 37

Izzy

Nik's words hang in the air for the longest ten seconds of my life. The day has been a blur, from this morning to the party to the hospital, but I see this moment in perfect clarity.

Nikolai. My boyfriend.

Joy rushes through me like wildfire.

When I woke up this morning, I knew I couldn't handle sneaking around anymore. I didn't *want* to do it. And I thought I lost him over it, only now . . . now he's in front of my family, declaring himself mine.

Which makes me his.

"Yes," I say. "We're together."

Dad blinks, but that's the only sign of surprise he gives. There's still worry on his face, worry for me, thanks to my own stupidity, yet he glances at Mom and says, "We're happy to hear it."

"Of course." Mom's eyes shine as she strokes my hair. She looks Nik over. "You came from the game?"

"As soon as he heard," Sebastian says.

Seb must have been the one who told Nik what happened. I lift my chin in a silent thank-you, and he nods. He's not quite smiling, but I can tell that he's pleased.

Then I notice Cooper, looking at me and Nik like . . . like he can't believe what he's seeing.

"Cooper," I say, my mouth going dry.

"What did you do to her?" he asks Nik.

"Nothing," I say quickly. My head throbs, and I wince. Nik

settles his hand on my shoulder, a comforting weight. "He didn't do anything."

"Victoria said she was upset," he says, still looking at Nik instead of me. The hurt on his face sends my heart into a fresh sprint. "Not just because of what happened with her coach. About an argument. She said she argued with a friend, but it wasn't a friend, was it? It was you."

"Cooper," I say again. "Stop it."

He doesn't know a thing about what really happened, and I won't betray Nik's confidence about the panic attack. I watch Nik closely, waiting for that frozen-over expression, but aside from a wince at Cooper's words, he seems okay. I squeeze the hand on my shoulder, reminding myself that he promised to tell me the whole story. Whatever it is, I'll find a way to help him.

"No," he says. "You're right. This is my fault."

"No, Nik, it isn't." I struggle to sit up properly, but a flash of pain makes me grit my teeth. Nik holds me in place. The doctor said I was lucky to get away with a minor concussion, but I still feel like someone hit me with a sledgehammer.

"What did you say?" Cooper presses. "What did you do to make her go to a fucking daytime rager?"

"Let's go outside," Sebastian says, grabbing Cooper's arm. "Come on."

"Do you have any idea what it felt like to get that call from Victoria?" he continues, shaking Sebastian off. "What it felt like to tell my parents that my little sister had a goddamn head injury?"

"Baby," Penny pleads. "Sebastian's right. We should go outside."

Nik steps around the bed, eyes alight.

"Yes," he snaps. "Because I got it from Sebastian."

"She hasn't been to parties like that in ages—"

"My heart fucking stopped when I heard—"

I press a hand to my mouth. I threw up earlier, and despite the anti-nausea medication the nurse gave me, I might do it again. I was half-unconscious during the drive to the hospital, but I re-member the panic on Cooper's and Sebastian's faces. Whatever Nik thinks, this was on me. My stupidity. My mistake. My nose smarts, tears filling my eyes.

"Enough," Mom interrupts, pulling herself to her full height. She crosses her arms over her chest tightly. "*Enough.* My daughter is hurt, and she needs rest, not shouting, and especially not from people who care about her. Cooper, Sebastian—go home."

Cooper clenches his jaw. "But—"

"Now," Dad says sharply. "You need to calm down, son."

He nearly protests further, but allows Sebastian to guide him out of the room.

"And you," Mom adds to Nik. "Go home and clean yourself up. And eat something, you look dead on your feet."

"I can stay."

"Go," she says, in a voice that leaves no room for argument. "We'll take care of her. If you calm yourself down, I'll let you back in this room. That goes for her brothers, too."

They stare at each other for a long moment, but eventually, Nik nods. He sweeps his gear into his bag and slings it over his shoulder.

"Talk to him," I say, grabbing his hand. "Please."

He nods. "I will. And I'll be back later." He leaves me with another kiss.

As the door clicks shut behind him, Mom sweeps back her hair, a tight frown on her face. "I need to figure out what's going on. Let me find the nurse."

When we're alone, Dad bends over and kisses me lightly on the forehead, right above the stitches, before settling into the chair next to the bed. He groans, tipping his head back. For a minute, we don't speak. I fiddle with the tape on my sprained wrist.

"I'm sorry, Daddy," I say quietly.

"It's okay, darling. I'm just glad you're safe." He gives the monitor a glance as it beeps softly. There's no anger in his expression, only weariness and concern. Same as when I broke my arm at nine, concussed myself for the first time at thirteen, nearly got arrested at seventeen. This is the latest disappointment, and I have to face it. "Why don't you tell me what really happened?"

CHAPTER 38

Nikolai

By the time I reach the hallway, Cooper is gone. I take the stairs to the lobby, slipping past the nurse from earlier before she notices me, and step into the cold, clear evening. The sweat on my body dried long ago, but I'm still filled with adrenaline, relief and guilt warring inside me.

I had no idea I was going to introduce myself like that, but it felt right. It was the only answer I could give, the only one that mattered. Things haven't been casual for a long time, and honestly . . . maybe they never were. I have no idea when or how the other shoe will drop, but for now, I want nothing more than to belong to her, and for her to belong to me. My Isabelle. Even if it shatters my shot at belonging on my last hockey team.

"—were going to tell me," Cooper is saying.

I step around the building quietly. Cooper stands with Sebastian and Penny underneath the light of a streetlamp. He has his back to me, frustration evident in the stiff set of his shoulders.

"It wasn't my news to tell," Sebastian replies, his voice clipped.

"And then you *called* him?"

"He deserved to know."

Cooper makes a noise of disgust. "When it's his fault this happened?"

"You *don't* know what happened. Neither of us do." Sebastian takes a step closer to his brother, arms open, placating. "What if it had been Penny? You'd have bitten my head off if I tried to keep that from you. He deserved the choice about whether to show up."

"And he did," Penny says as she rubs Cooper's back. "He looked like a wreck. He cares about her."

For a moment, I consider finding another way to my car. I doubt anything I could say right now would make things better. But Isabelle asked me to talk to him. I can't go home without trying.

"I do care," I say, stepping out of the shadows. "What happened—it *was* my fault, but I care about her."

Cooper studies me. "How long?"

"What?"

"You know what I mean. How long?"

I hesitate. "Since the summer." I'm not sure how the fuck to approach this, what Isabelle actually wants me to share. "It was just casual at first, we didn't label anything, but now . . . it's not."

"Why?" He crosses his arms over his chest, practically spitting out the word. "Did you do it to have something else to taunt me with?"

I laugh shortly. "No. Jesus, no. I did it because I *liked* her."

"And you've been keeping it secret the whole time? Both of you?"

"It wasn't your business," I say, unable to keep the growl out of my voice.

"She's my sister and you're my—my teammate. I'd say that means you could have said fucking *something*. In Ryder's office, you even lied and said she wasn't your type."

Exhaustion settles into my bones, dousing the anger. I nearly sway on my feet. "And who do you think wanted to keep it a secret?"

"What do you mean?" Sebastian asks.

I stare at Cooper. Of course I had my own reasons for wanting to keep my connection with Isabelle quiet, but fuck it, he needs to know this. "You know that she compares herself to you—all of you—constantly, right? She thinks you're all amazing and perfect and that she'll never be the same way. She couldn't stand the idea of you judging her. And now I see why."

"Shut the hell up," he says, voice low.

My head throbs, even though I'm not the one with a concussion. I put up my hands. "Come on, Callahan. Hit me."

I'd welcome the pain, after hurting her. I might not have concussed her myself, but if I hadn't had a meltdown, if I'd just fucking *stayed* with her, she wouldn't have gone to that party. She wouldn't be in that hospital bed, hooked up to a monitor to make sure her brain is okay.

I swipe my tongue over my lip, smirking. "I know you want to."

Cooper takes a step closer. I keep my hands up. This is all I'm good for, when it comes down to it. Dishing out pain and taking it. I keep that cocky fucking smile on my face, as if my heart isn't aching.

"Wait," Sebastian says. "Stop, guys."

Penny stifles a gasp as I bridge the rest of the gap, looking into those blue eyes, so like Isabelle's. She'll be upset that I goaded her brother into this, but I can't make myself stop.

"Go on," I breathe. "Hit me for fucking your sis—"

"No," Cooper snarls. He raises his hand—but swipes it through his hair, not at my face. "I'm not going to hurt someone my sister cares about, you asshole. Get the fuck out of my face."

He steps around me, striding away. Sebastian races after him. Penny lingers, biting her lip. My eyes smart as I stare up into the streetlight.

"I'm sorry," she says finally. "He'll come around."

"I don't care," I lie.

"I'm glad Izzy has you." She squeezes my arm as she walks past. "Get some rest, Nikolai."

CHAPTER 39

Izzy

James collapses next to me on the couch. "Jesus, that feels good."

"Want some punch?" I tuck my legs underneath me as I adjust my plaid velvet dress.

We're the only ones in the living room right now, admiring the tree while Christmas music plays softly. Sebastian, Mom, and Penny's dad's girlfriend are in the kitchen, working on our traditional breakfast-for-Christmas-Eve-dinner with Mia, Penny, and Cooper to keep them company. Bex is napping—I don't blame her one bit for taking advantage while there are plenty of babysitters in the house—and last I checked, Dad was watching football with Penny's dad, Larry, Coach Ryder. It's an almost perfect Christmas Eve, especially since I'm aunt to Charlotte Callahan, the cutest baby in the world. I'm glad I'm not the only December birthday in the family anymore.

With Nik in the city for Christmas, however, it's less sparkly than it could be.

When we finally got around to discussing the holiday, we decided it would be best to spend it with our respective families. His grandfather expected his presence at his Christmas celebrations, and James and Bex were already coming with itty-bitty baby Charlie, not to mention the fact that Cooper and Nik haven't spoken since the beginning of the month. I should be enjoying the break from school, and from thinking about my future in volleyball, but I'd rather be with Nik than alone here.

"Milk punch?" James asks.

I lift my glass. "Sebby's special recipe."

Instead of getting up for his own, he swipes mine and takes a sip.

"Hey," I protest.

"I know my daughter is perfect"—he stops as I snort, raising his eyebrow—"but would it kill her to nap? Even a little?"

"I was a very fussy baby. Ask Mom about it."

"That's true," Dad says as he walks into the room with Larry, a tray of sugar cookies in hand. James and Bex's dog, Kiwi, trots at his heels. Whenever they bring him over, he can't get enough of Dad. "You screamed all hours of the night."

"See?" I say, snatching back my punch.

"I'm not sure that's the flex you think it is," James says dryly. "Are those the cookies you made?"

I smile, sitting up straighter. "All by myself."

"Let's hope we don't get food poisoning, then," he says, eyeing them suspiciously.

I kick his leg. I'm not wearing shoes, so it's not that effective, but *still*. I'm capable of handling a simple sugar cookie recipe. Kiwi begs for a cookie with his adorable brown eyes, but I just pat his head.

"Penelope did that as well," Larry says, giving us an amused look. "Kid had a set of lungs on her."

"Something about daughters, perhaps," Dad says, clapping his hand on James's shoulder. "You're doing a great job so far, son."

James groans, tipping his head back, but he's smiling. Despite the stress of having a new baby this late in the season, he's been ridiculously happy. Charlie came a few weeks ago, after a fortunate midweek labor that allowed him to be at Bex's side the whole time without compromising football. No one would have minded if they chose to have Christmas by themselves in Philadelphia, but they didn't want Charlie to miss even one holiday with her grandparents and newly minted uncles and aunt.

"How is Nikolai doing?" Larry asks me.

I snag a cookie, thinking about how to answer. He's worried about the rift between him and Cooper, and I don't blame him. The hockey season has been on pause for the holidays, but that's only going to last so long. Soon, they'll be back on the ice together, and if they're at each other's throat, that won't keep their winning record going.

I have no idea what happened after they left the hospital. Later, I explained everything to Cooper, and apologized for keeping it secret for so long, but still, he didn't budge on telling me about the argument they had. Nik's been just as tight-lipped about it.

Both of them are being idiots. It's not like I can talk, but *still*.

"Fine," I say eventually. "He's in Manhattan with his family."

"They do need to hash this out," Dad says. He drums his fingers on the arm of the couch. "They both care about you, darling."

I make a face as I bite into the cookie. Not because of the cookie, although it definitely doesn't come close to Sebastian's. Cooper and Nik were on the way to becoming good friends before everything happened, and I hate the thought of them losing that forever. Especially if it's because of me and my own stupidity.

"You're sure he doesn't want to come to Long Island?" James says. "Even for a little while?"

"He's busy."

"Busy, or avoiding Cooper?"

I stuff another cookie into my mouth. "I told Cooper I wanted them to make up for Christmas."

"And what did he say?"

"He told me to talk to my boyfriend."

"Why don't you call him? Maybe he'll want to come after all."

I doubt it, but I guess it's worth a shot. Christmas Eve is my favorite night of the year because of my family's traditions, yet if Nik had invited me to the city, I'd have said yes.

I slip into Dad's office to make the call. There aren't many hall-marks of the holiday in here; just a garland around his desk, courtesy of me, and a little ceramic tree next to the computer, courtesy of Mom. I perch on the edge of the couch, looking at the awards, the framed newspapers, the case with his three Super Bowl rings.

I'm fully aware of the differences between hockey and football—when Cooper was younger, he wanted nothing more than to rub them in Dad's face—but still, I know in my bones that one day Nik and my brother will hold up the Stanley Cup. I doubt it'll happen on the same team, but it'll happen for them both somehow.

And I want them to be supportive of each other when it happens.

It felt so necessary to lie, not just to myself but to everyone around me. Now that the burden doesn't exist anymore, I see how heavily it was weighing on me. There's still so much to talk about, not least Nik's panic attacks, but at least this massive secret isn't lingering. I can call him without pretending he's someone else.

I smile as soon as I hear his voice. "Hey. Merry Christmas."

"Merry Christmas." I wonder if he needed to step away from the party to answer my call, or if he was already alone. I don't hear background noise, so I'm guessing the latter. "I've never gotten used to celebrating it so early."

"Oh, right. Russian Orthodox Christmas is different."

"Yeah. And the new year is a bigger deal anyway."

"All the same, are you having fun?"

He laughs shortly. "Define 'fun.'"

"That bad, huh?" I pick at a loose thread on my skirt, hesitating. It's just a question, after all. It's fine if he can't get away tonight. "If you want . . . you could come over. Dad and Larry were asking about you."

"I don't know."

"Please? It'll be fun. You might not get here in time for dinner, but we always play Monopoly after."

"I don't want to ruin anything."

"You wouldn't. Besides . . . you have to make up with Cooper eventually."

"Isabelle," he says, sighing.

"You do," I say, stubbornly lifting my chin even though he can't see me. "You're not just teammates. You're friends. I explained everything to him."

"Everything?"

"Not that. Of course not. But you didn't force me to go to that party and get drunk, Nik. I made that choice all on my own."

"Because I let you go."

"I'm the one who ran. You didn't have to follow me."

"But I should have."

"You *could* have." I wish I made this a video call; I want to see his face. We've been dancing around this topic ever since the hospital, and while we were busy with the end of the semester, it was easy to ignore it. "But I don't blame you for not doing it, okay? I could have stayed. I could have realized you were hurting and helped you instead of running away."

I wish I had stayed. I wish I had never said that comment about his family. I wish so many things went differently that day, even though I don't regret the eventual outcome. I wouldn't give up my new relationship with Nik for anything, but he's hurting, and I didn't do a thing to ease that hurt. I just made it worse.

"I'm glad, where it led," I add. "I'm glad to have you and I want you here with me for Christmas."

He's quiet for a long moment. "Okay, sunshine. Give me your parents' address."

CHAPTER 40
Nikolai

Snow drifts from the heavens as I stand in Isabelle's parents' driveway.

The driver offered to carry my bags to the door, but I declined. The entire ride from the city to Port Washington, I stared at the passing Christmas decorations on front lawns, trying to ignore the pit in my stomach. I thought by the time I arrived, I'd have calmed my nerves, but I need another moment.

Even in the dark, it's easy to see that this isn't just a house. It's a home. It's absolutely beautiful, a towering cream-colored colonial with a wraparound porch and twin pines on the front lawn, but I'm drawn to the crooked wreath on the front door and the multicolored lights hanging from the roof. Light spills from the windows on the first floor, illuminating the silvery Christmas tree in the front hall. Isabelle's family is well-off, and even from the outside, I can tell that her parents have used their wealth very differently than Grandfather. The party I just escaped was stuffy, formal, and utterly boring. Whatever's happening inside, I can guarantee it's none of those things.

Cricket caught me on my way out the door and told me to have fun, and I think she meant it as a serious reminder. New Year's is just around the corner, after all, and with it, the anniversary of the night everything shattered.

There's a family inside. Isabelle and her parents, her siblings, their partners. A real family, complete with well-loved holiday traditions. Even though she invited me, I'll be the odd man out. An interloper, especially in the same room as Cooper.

It takes me three tries to press the doorbell.

A blond woman with pretty hazel eyes opens the door. She's wearing an oversized red sweater and leggings. Beaded Santa earrings glint through her hair. As she takes me in, her smile grows so wide, I nearly turn around.

"You must be Nikolai!" she says. "I'm Bex. Come inside. Can you believe it's actually snowing on Christmas Eve?"

She ushers me into the house before I can escape, fussing immediately with my coat. I set down my suitcase and bag of presents, unwinding my cashmere scarf. "It's nice to meet you."

"And I'm so glad to meet you. Izzy's told me a ton about you."

"Yeah?"

"Of course I have," Isabelle says, stepping into the foyer. "Hey, Nik."

I nearly drop my coat. Fuck, I missed her, even if it's only been a week since break began. I'm so caught up staring at her beautiful face that it takes me a second to notice she's holding a baby. She steps closer. Stitches still mark her temple, but they look better than before. Her red-and-green plaid dress hugs her body like a glove, accented by the matching bow in her hair.

She kisses my cheek, smelling of sugar and pine. "This is Charlotte Callahan."

"We've been calling her Charlie," Bex adds fondly. "That nap didn't last long, huh?"

"She wants to stay up to see Santa, obviously," Isabelle says.

The baby is utterly adorable; she has a little mop of dark hair and bright, inquisitive eyes. She's dressed in a onesie patterned with stars. I've never been around a baby in my life, much less one barely a few weeks old, so I have zero idea what to do in this situation. I settle on waving at her.

"She's perfect, right?" Isabelle says. "She already loves her auntie."

"Yeah," I say, even though I'm not looking at the baby anymore. "She's perfect."

"Let me see if she's hungry." Bex carefully takes her daughter from Isabelle, giving my shoulder a squeeze. "We're so glad you're here."

The second we're alone, Isabelle leaps into my arms. I handle her weight easily, staggering backwards just to make her laugh. She threads her fingers through my snow-damp hair, kissing me deeply.

"Thank you," she whispers. "I missed you."

"I missed you, too." I let her down slowly, groaning as my hands curve over her ass. "How is everything?"

"You missed dinner, but Mom left a plate for you, if you're still hungry." She smooths the collar of my dark green sweater. I wore a suit to Grandfather's party, but changed into more casual clothes before leaving the city. She frowns. "Although now that I think of it, it's mostly sweet stuff. You won't like it."

"That's okay. I should talk to Cooper first."

"Yeah?"

I play with her bow. "You're right, we need to talk."

Even if the thought makes my entire body tense. I acted like an asshole outside the hospital, trying to bait Cooper into taking a swing at me. I'm loath to admit it, but I'm glad he had the cooler head. I doubt Isabelle would have kissed me like that just now if I had brawled with her brother in a parking lot. Regardless of my guilt over my role in her injury, it would have been a step too far.

She searches my eyes, nodding at whatever she sees in them. "He's in the den."

THE CHRISTMAS TREE in the front of the house looked professionally decorated, a magazine piece rather than a feature of a real home, but the one in the den is perfectly imperfect. It's smaller and spotty in places, but the strands of colorful lights, homemade ornaments, and what has to be an entire package of tinsel make it all the more appealing. Antique Christmas knickknacks cover the mantel above the crackling fireplace. The rug spread across the wooden floor is faded and worn, and the furniture doesn't quite match. There are family photos everywhere, as well as a wall of books and old-fashioned DVDs. This room is different from the other glimpses I've caught of the house so far. It's private. Warm and inviting and very much family-only.

I pick up the nearest photograph. A little girl with dark hair who must be Isabelle beams at the camera, flanked by three boys. They're on a beach, waterlogged and in the middle of working on a sandcastle.

I give the picture a smile as I set it back on the shelf.

"Outer Banks," Cooper says from his spot in front of the fire. "We went every summer as kids."

"You look very concerned about the structural integrity of your sandcastle."

He looks over. He's wearing a sweater with a snowman on it, a bit of whimsy that doesn't match the serious expression on his face. He stands, shoving his hands into his pockets. "I expected you sooner."

"My grandfather wasn't thrilled that I left."

"I'm sure Isabelle is happy to see you."

"She is my girlfriend," I say, mostly because I can. But Cooper doesn't give me the satisfaction of scowling. "What, no objections?"

"No," he says shortly. "Like I told you before, I know she cares about you."

"But you wish this wasn't happening."

"You gonna keep putting words in my mouth?" He prowls in my direction. "You've always been good at it, I'll give you that."

"If you've missed my chirps, just say so." I lean against the bookcase, crossing my ankles, and smile. "Happy to oblige."

His jaw twitches. "You can be such a prick."

"For sneaking around with your sister?"

"I'm not my sister's keeper and you know it."

"Then what?" I tilt my head to the side. I know I should be slowing things down, but I can't help it. Maybe it's my own self-loathing, or the guilt I can't shake. Maybe it's just the fact that Isabelle deserves better, even if no one is saying it. My voice gets stronger. "For letting her get hurt? For trying to get you to take a swing at me?"

"No," he says, his voice louder now. "Although that was a dick move. I'm fucking *pissed* that you—"

"Both of you, shut the fuck up." A man strides into the room, blue eyes ablaze. He looks a little older than us; he must be the eldest Callahan sibling, James. "You want to yell, fine, but do it outside, because my wife is trying to put our daughter down so she won't scream all night, I'm running on two hours of sleep, *and* I have to play the Cowboys next game."

Cooper and I freeze. James shoves us in the direction of the sliding doors banked across one wall. "Go. Now. Have your pissing match, because you need to get over this, but do it where you won't disturb the rest of the goddamn house."

He slides open the door, letting in a rush of cold air, and pushes us onto a snow-covered porch. Behind him, the family is gathering in the den, even Coach Ryder and his partner. Fantastic. Isabelle hurries to her brother, saying something to him, but he just responds by locking us outside.

Extra fantastic. I slip on ice and struggle to right myself. My socks are already soaked through, and the only solace I have is that Cooper isn't wearing shoes either. If I freeze to death, at least he's coming with me. He gives me a glare that could melt the snow around us.

"Great fucking job."

"He's your brother," I shoot back. "And you were the one yelling."

"Because you keep trying to bait me." He swipes his hand through his hair. "And anyway, you're the one who lied."

My heart sinks. "Cooper—"

"I don't care that you're together, Abney. I really don't."

I search his expression, but I can tell he's being honest. The weight on my chest lightens, despite the emotions running through me. "At the beginning of the season—I thought you hated me."

"Hated you?" he scoffs. "I thought you could be too much of an instigator, and a bit dirty sometimes, but I never hated you. If anything, I was jealous."

"What?"

He shrugs. "You're better than me."

"You're talented too, man." I shake my head, shivering. My feet are going numb. "Why'd you warn me away from Isabelle, then?"

"I was trying to protect her from a guy I figured wouldn't be serious." His mouth twists; he barks out a laugh. "Didn't matter, obviously."

"It's . . ." I hesitate. "It's always been different with her."

"She told me everything. Listen—I'm sorry for what I said at the hospital."

"And I'm sorry I tried to goad you into fighting me."

He reaches over for a handful of snow from a nearby table, packing it into a ball. "Like I said, I won't hurt someone my sister cares about."

He throws the snowball. I don't duck in time; it hits me in the face. Cold bursts across my senses.

I brush away the snow with a grimace. *"Seriously?"*

"Didn't say anything about snowball fights." I think I catch a hint of amusement in his eyes, but it's gone in a blink. He packs another snowball. "You lied to my face for months. I'm your teammate, and I thought we were becoming friends, too. And yet you were lying to me."

"We were both lying." I spy a snow-covered bench and scoot towards it, careful not to fall on my ass. Cooper's next snowball hits my shoulder as I pack one of my own. "And not just to you." I throw the snowball. He twists, but it still hits him in the chest. I work to make another, swiping my half-frozen tongue over my lips. "And we *are* friends."

"I don't know, are we?"

"Yes," I grind out as yet another snowball hits me. My next one smacks him in the face, to my satisfaction. "We're friends. We're about to die out here together because your brother is a psychopath, I'd say that makes us fucking friends."

"Good," he snaps.

"Great," I shoot back.

"Get inside before you both freeze to death!" Isabelle shouts from the doorway.

"I'm sorry," I say, finally. I inch closer to him, gritting my teeth against a particularly chilly gust of wind. "I'm not sorry about being with her, but I'm sorry we didn't tell you. We tried to keep our feelings at bay, but . . ."

"It has a way of sneaking up on you," he finishes.

I just nod.

He meets me in the middle of the porch and pulls me into a hug. I blink in surprise, hesitating before squeezing back.

"Did you mean what you said?" he says, quietly enough no one watching through the now-open door can hear. "She doesn't think she's as good as us?"

"Yeah." I slick back my soaking wet hair. Hopefully once we're allowed inside, Isabelle can sneak me into the shower, because this chill sure as hell won't go away on its own. "And I'm sure it's worse now, after what happened with her coach. She's amazing, but she refuses to see it."

"She hasn't said much about it." He steps back, glancing at the house. "I don't even know if she's going to keep playing volleyball."

"She should." I haven't wanted to push her on the topic, but I know she still loves the sport.

"Thank you for telling me." He shakes his head. "That's just not true."

"Of course not." I rearrange the cuffs of my sodden sweater. "She's way better than you, you bastard."

He laughs—a real, deep laugh that I can't help but join in on—and claps my shoulder. "Come on, let's play Monopoly. I'll even let you be the toy soldier."

"There's a toy soldier piece in Monopoly?" I ask as we enter the blessedly warm house.

Isabelle looks torn between kissing me and clawing my face off. I shake my wet hair at her. She sticks out her tongue as freezing water splashes her.

"You're so—Coop, what are you doing?"

Cooper holds out a plastic bag filled with random objects, none of which look like actual Monopoly pieces. I haven't played in years, but I know that much.

"Come on, man," he says, shaking the baggie. "Best piece for you."

Isabelle's eyes widen. "Don't take it, Nik."

I glance around the room. Coach is clearly relieved that Cooper and I didn't murder each other, and Richard actually looks pleased, as if we passed some sort of test. James is still scowling, but he raises his hand in a two-fingered salute when our gazes meet. Penny looks as if she wishes she could throw another snowball at Cooper's face, and Sebastian and Mia are clearly holding back laughter. Sandra sighs and says something about idiotic boys as she leaves the room with Ryder's girlfriend. I hope she's fetching towels.

"Is it a trap?" I say.

"No," James drawls.

"Not unless you want to be cursed," Sebastian adds.

Cooper cocks an eyebrow. "Are you going to listen to those assholes, or me, your new best friend?"

Isabelle knocks his hand away. "Shush. We're playing in teams again, and we're going to crush you. Now hand over the button."

CHAPTER 41

Izzy

"You sure they don't mind me staying with you?"

I glance over my shoulder at Nik. "They know we're having sex."

"I'm sure you have a guest bedroom. Or I could sleep on the couch."

"And disturb Santa? No way." I open the door to my bedroom, waving him inside. "No one is going to lock you outside again, I promise."

He groans. I grin at him as I flip the light switch. What James did *was* effective, after all, and Cooper suffered right alongside him. Aside from trying to convince Nik to take the cursed toy soldier game piece—which, for the record, no one has tried on any of my brothers' significant others—the evening went smoothly; he even ate three sugar cookies after he heard I'm the one who made them. Sebastian and Mia pulled off a suspicious Monopoly victory, and we ended the night with *The Family Stone* and glasses of Irish cream. I ought to be ready to pass out, but instead, I'm all fired up. And possibly a little tipsy. I'm glad I'm not the only one going to bed without a partner tonight.

"Whoa, sweetheart," he says, stopping in his tracks. "This is a lot of pink."

I flick his cheek. "You knew this about me."

"And that's an army of stuffed animals."

I scoop an armful of stuffies from the bed, dumping them onto my desk. He's right, the walls of my room are pink, as is the rug on the floor, my bedding, and even the fan on the ceiling. The furniture is a uniform white; while the bed is bigger now, I still have the desk and rocking chair my parents bought for me when I was little. The bench underneath the picture window, one of my favorite places in the house, is covered in throw pillows in various shades of pink, with more stuffed toys keeping guard. The exterior Christmas lights provide enough of a glow that I can see the snow-covered trees outside.

Nik peers at a shelf full of volleyball trophies, then trails his finger over the spines of the books nestled into the built-ins above my desk. He lifts an eyebrow as I move even more stuffed animals. "How many do you have?"

"I'm not sure, I've never counted."

"Liar."

I bite my lip, smiling. "Okay. About two hundred, if you count the ones I brought to school."

"That's terrifying. And impressive."

Desire lurches through me at the fond expression on his face. "Come here."

He gives me a cream-and-whiskey kiss. I try to focus as he draws a finger up and down my spine, but it's hard. He smells deliciously clean, and his sweater, a fresh one that he changed into after the snowball fight, is ultrasoft cashmere. I rub my cheek against his shoulder, gasping when his hands work underneath my dress.

"This fucking dress," he rasps. "I've wanted to peel it off you for hours."

Despite the dirty words, he makes no move to back me against the bed. He slowly hikes the dress up my thighs, my bottom. I bite his lip, giggling breathlessly at the way it makes him moan. "Consider it an early Christmas present. Although you'll be very impressed with my real one tomorrow morning."

"Oh, shoot. That reminds me, I left all your presents in the city."

I jab him in his rock-hard abs. "Now who's the liar?"

"Don't worry," he says, grinning as he ducks in for another kiss. "I have plenty of presents for you."

"You already gave me a present." I scratch my nails through his hair. "You made up with Cooper. Although I don't know why he had to throw a snowball at your face."

Something about that makes him go still.

"Look, I . . . I tried to goad him into taking a swing at me, outside the hospital."

"You *what*?"

"I know," he says shortly. "It was stupid."

I unwind myself from him, tugging down my dress. "I told you to *talk* to him!"

"And I'd just seen the evidence of what happened when I let you go," he snaps. "I would've deserved that punch."

I cross my arms over my chest. "I know you hockey players like to talk a big game about throwing punches—"

"You had a concussion," he interrupts, his voice quiet, intense. "There's a scar on your face, and that won't go away. Ever. And it could've been so much worse, Isabelle. I've seen what it's like when it's worse."

My retort dies in my throat. "What do you mean?"

"It doesn't matter," he says, clenching his jaw as he looks away.

I wait for him to add something else, anything else, but he doesn't. Great.

"Like I told you, it was my choice to act like an idiot," I say eventually, grabbing a nightgown from my dresser and striding past him to the en suite bathroom. "You didn't need Cooper to punish you, or whatever the hell you thought you deserved."

As soon as I shut the door, I yank the dress over my head, balling it up and throwing it into the corner. I'm cotton-mouthed, a headache starting up behind my temples. What's it like when it's worse? An accident? An argument? It didn't sound like he was talking about himself, even though his scar makes mine seem like a scrape.

I get ready for bed slowly, half expecting to be alone when I come out, but Nik's still there, dressed for bed as well. I breathe easier as I take in the sight of him, shirtless and barefoot in a pair of black sweatpants, head hanging low. At the sound of the bathroom door shutting, he looks at me, a tight, unreadable expression on his face.

I walk to the bed. "If we're going to date, we need to trust each other."

"I know."

I slip into his lap, my arms around his neck. I sigh with relief when his hands settle on my hips. I tilt his face up, searching his eyes for some glimmer of whatever he's holding back.

"I didn't protect you," he says eventually. "I wasn't *there* to protect you. And you're right, I wanted to be punished for that. Even if it meant pushing Cooper to a place we couldn't come back from."

"I never asked for your protection," I say softly.

He cradles my jaw, rubbing his thumb over my skin. "All the same."

"You promised you'd tell me everything." I kiss him. "Please, Nik."

He shakes his head. "Thank your brother for keeping his head."

"It's just me. I'm not going to judge you, whatever it is."

"Not tonight, Isabelle." He sounds exhausted, as if this conversation is aging him. "I haven't pushed you about volleyball. Don't push me on this."

I shift in his lap. "That's not the same."

"Isn't it?" he says. "Have you faced your father yet? I've seen you compare yourself to your brothers over and over—"

"You don't have siblings," I interrupt. "You don't know what it's like."

"I watched you spend an entire season chasing after what your father wanted."

"What I wanted."

"I know what it looks like when you're doing something for family."

"So tell me about it!" I burst out, my nails digging into his back. "Tell me about it, because I don't know. Who was on the phone when I came out of Alexis's office? Why don't you want to go back to Russia? Why do you look at your mother like she's on the other side of a wall?"

He flinches. I can't help it, I press further. "Did you even tell her about us? Does she know, or are you planning on bringing it up the next time I'm your buffer?"

"She knows," he says shortly. "And in case you were wondering, she's thrilled. She sent you a Christmas present. Cricket, too."

"Oh," I say, the emotion leaving me in a rush. "Nik, I didn't . . ."

"It's late," he says, that bone-deep note of tiredness still in his voice. "And I'd like to go to sleep next to my girlfriend and wake up on Christmas morning with her in my arms. Can we do that, solnishko?"

I don't trust myself with more words, so I nod. There's tenderness in the way he lifts the covers for me, and in the kiss that he brushes against my forehead. When he comes back from the bathroom with minty breath a couple minutes later, he eases next to me slowly, as if I might already be asleep. I roll over, and he wraps an arm around me, urging me closer.

I plant my face to his chest and breathe.

CHAPTER 42

Izzy

"Do your boobs hurt?" Penny asks, tilting her head to the side as she sips from her mug. "I've heard the nipples chafe."

Bex makes a face, readjusting Charlie in her arms. "Unfortunately. I'm happy I can do it, but it's not that fun."

Mia and I share a look. While Mia is very much on the no kids train—a sentiment Sebastian is happy to share—I want kids one day, but I have to admit, not much about newborn parenting is appealing. You get a cuddly baby, yes, but that same baby is going to make chafed nipples seem like the least of your worries. I feel bad for Bex that James had to travel to Dallas for his next game, but at least she has us.

I hold my mug of spiced tea close, letting the steam drift over my face. It's nice, sitting at the kitchen table with Penny on one side and Mia on the other, and Bex across from us, nursing her daughter. If someone told me back in high school that a couple years later, all three of my brothers would have significant others to bring home for the holidays, I'd have laughed. And yet here we are—and I have Nik, which, even a month ago, I wouldn't have believed either.

"Do you have, like, a salve?" Penny continues. "Or does that make her not want to eat?"

Bex holds up a tin. "Christmas gift from Sandra. And no, she doesn't seem to mind it."

"Fortunate," Mia says. She bites into another one of the peppermint cookies Sebastian made this morning, then scowls at it. "Okay, I seriously need to stop eating these. Christmas was a week ago."

"He hasn't gotten the memo yet," I say cheerfully. "And I'm not going to tell him to halt the baking deliciousness."

"Oh God, no, never," Penny says.

Mia rolls her eyes, but she's smiling. Her default state when it comes to my brother.

"Have you started packing yet?" I ask.

"Ugh, don't remind me."

"It should be easy for you," Bex teases. "Three black shirts, two pairs of black jeans, and your laptop."

"You forgot Sebastian's old jersey," Penny says. "Which, in case you didn't know, she sleeps in."

Mia's eyes widen. There's a scuffle underneath the table; I'd bet the Hermès boots my parents got me for Christmas that she just stomped on Penny's foot. "I told you that while I was drunk."

"And it is *so* adorable," Penny says, a satisfied note in her voice.

Mia just flips her the bird.

"Hey," Bex says, covering Charlie's eyes. "Not in front of the baby."

"I am looking forward to getting away from McKee," Mia says, hugging her knees to her chest. To Bex's point, she's wearing a NASA sweatshirt and black leggings. "I've never traveled . . . well, anywhere, really. I'll happily take Switzerland."

"I wish I didn't have to go back," I admit. "Let me run away to Switzerland with you."

The week in between Christmas and New Year's has been blissfully uneventful, even though I still feel a tug of emotion whenever I think about Christmas Eve. Nik has been here, bonding with my family, sleeping beside me every night. He loved the Rift tickets I gifted him, and surprised me with a bracelet to match the necklace he gave me in Boston, plus half a dozen other wildly extravagant presents. All week, we've kept things light, but tonight is New Year's Eve, and once it passes, we'll be that much closer to the start of next semester.

And I'll be that much closer to facing volleyball again.

Nik might have his own expectations to live up to—expectations that I'm sure involve his father, even if he refuses to talk about it—but he doesn't know what my family is like. I didn't just fail. I imploded. Everything spilled out of me at the hospital; I told Dad about my season with Coach Alexis, and my fight with Nik, and my idiotic choice to go to that party. He listened and, instead of getting into it, just hugged me and told me to rest, but I know there's a longer interrogation coming.

"Is it volleyball?" Penny asks tentatively.

I need another cookie for this. I break it in half with a bit too much force, sending crumbs everywhere. "At least the season is over."

"There's spring league."

I scowl at the cookie. Stupid spring league.

"You are going to do spring league, right?"

"It's optional."

"You can't get back into your coach's good graces if you don't do it."

I smash the cookie, letting the pieces fall over my plate. I'm making a mess, but I don't care. Penny's eyes narrow with concern; she fiddles with the end of her fishtail braid. Bex makes a soft noise, patting Charlie's tiny back.

"Maybe I don't," I retort. "Maybe I quit."

The breath leaves my lungs in a whoosh. Every time I've thought about volleyball lately, my thoughts have looped back around to that one painful, surprisingly tempting word. When the doctor in the hospital told me that I'd be able to get back on the court in a few weeks, he smiled like he expected me to be thrilled. I was supposed to feel that way, but I didn't. I didn't feel anything approximating happiness or gratitude or even relief. I just felt empty and tired.

"That's bulls—bullcrap," Mia says.

"Seb quit baseball. Did you call that bullcrap?"

"Sebastian quit baseball for another career," Mia says evenly, refusing to rise to my admittedly weak bait. "One he's better suited to anyway. That's not the same and you know it."

"At least he could have made baseball a career, if he wanted." I dig my nails into my palms. "Volleyball doesn't lead anywhere after graduation. It's not the same as him or James or Cooper or—or Nik. It doesn't mean anything anyway."

"That's not a reason to quit," she says.

I ignore her. "And now that I screwed myself over, my coach will never give me what I want. She might not even play me again. Definitely not at setter. What's the point of putting myself through all of the preparation for a team I don't have a place on?"

"You can keep—"

"My whole life shattered when I tore my ACL," Penny interrupts. "I didn't skate competitively again."

"That's not the same," I say. "That wasn't your fault."

"Wasn't it?" she says. "If I'd been focused during that routine, maybe I wouldn't have fallen."

"I didn't get injured. I broke a rule."

"And your coach is a bitter bitch," Mia says. "Sorry, Bex."

"I'll let it slide," Bex says. "It's true, anyway. She's never liked you, which has everything to do with her, not you."

Penny undoes her braid, shaking out her hair. "Look. The point is, I learned to love it again. I love my job at the rink. I love teaching classes with Cooper. I love lacing up my skates and practicing—even though I'm not preparing for a competition."

I sigh, rubbing my forehead. The skin, freshly devoid of stitches, still feels tender. It's definitely leaving a scar, albeit a much smaller one than the slash on Nik's face. "It's not the same."

"Isn't it?" she says. "You're an athlete. Screw anyone who is making you think otherwise."

It's a nice sentiment, but it doesn't change the fact that everyone around me is amazing at their sports. I've tried my best to keep up, but I've been chasing my family since the moment I was born. I blink, focusing on my half-empty mug. Sometimes the kind, logical thing feels like a slap.

I stand, taking my tea with me. "Okay."

"Izzy," Penny says as I walk out of the kitchen. I gnaw the inside of my cheek. I know she's just trying to help, but I'm not in the mood to hear it. It was stupid to bring it up in the first place.

In the hallway, someone tugs on my sleeve. I'm expecting Penny, but it's Bex. She adjusts Charlie from one arm to the other.

"Can we talk?" she says. "Just the two of us?"

I nod warily. "If it's about volleyball—"

"It's not, although I agree with them, for the record," she says. "It's about my wedding."

I stand straighter. Finally, something way more fun to think about. I've been waiting for this ever since she and James postponed the original one in August. "Did you get in touch with Katherine?"

"I want you to do it," she says. "I'll pay you, of course."

I laugh slightly. "I'm not a wedding planner."

"When I spoke to Katherine, she agreed to help, but she wanted you to lead it."

"She didn't mention . . . Really?"

"Really." Bex touches my shoulder comfortingly. "You're still thinking about doing this for a career, right?"

For the first time since the hospital, I feel a hint of excitement. Volleyball is fraught right now, even if doing spring league would mean more time with Victoria and the rest of our friends. But planning Bex and James's wedding, with some help from Katherine? It would be like last summer again. Maybe even a real stepping-stone to a future career. I haven't stopped thinking about the wedding that Nik and I crashed in Boston.

The warmth fades as something occurs to me. "Are you just asking because of what happened?"

"Of course not. I asked you because you're talented and passionate. The fact you're my future sister-in-law is the cherry on top."

"Aren't you legally married already?"

Her eyes sparkle. "You and I both know it won't count for real until I walk down the aisle."

I rock on my heels, my mind already full of color schemes and fabrics and venue options. "I . . . I need to talk to my parents."

CHAPTER 43

Izzy

Dad sends the volleyball over the net in a neat, if unpracticed, arc. I set, then spike it myself, the same routine we've been doing for the past hour. Instead of hitting it back, however, he catches it, giving me a pleased smile.

"You've definitely improved."

I run my fingers through my ponytail. "I practiced a lot last season."

The unspoken part of my sentence hangs in the air uncomfortably. I stare at the floor of our home gym, blinking hard. I've loved every second of the past hour, but whenever I think about spring league or next season, I'm filled with dread. At least the thought of planning James and Bex's wedding gives me the good kind of nerves. *If* I say yes.

"Isabelle," he says, coming around the net. "You're upset, darling."

I startle at the use of my full name, wiping away a trickle of sweat from my brow. I sit on the built-in bench along the wall, sipping from my water bottle.

"Aren't you?"

He tosses the volleyball aside and joins me on the bench, stretching out his legs. The left one has a scar down the knee; an old football injury that required surgery.

"Yes," he says, after a moment. "Of course I'm upset. But not about what happened."

"I promised you I'd play setter again, and now that's not happening." I have to whisper it. I thought I could take this conversation, but two seconds in, I'm already faltering.

"And I don't care about that."

Tears prick my eyes. "How could you not?"

He sighs, rubbing his scarred knee. "Well, I'm relieved you didn't hurt yourself too badly, for one thing. And I don't agree with the way your coach has handled things, even if it's her team to run how she sees fit."

"You wanted me back at setter." Nik's words echo in my mind before I can banish them. Even though I tried for myself, I can't deny that I tried for my father's approval, too. My whole family's approval. I wanted to be worthy of the Callahan name, the way my brothers are.

"I knew what that position meant to you, so yes, I wanted you to try to win it back."

"And I failed you."

He blinks, quiet for a moment. "Is that what you really think?"

I worry my lip between my teeth as I stand, needing distance. Even though the gym has high ceilings and plenty of space, it feels tiny, a box without an escape. I turn my head, refusing to look at my father.

"Isabelle," he says again.

"You know what I'm talking about." A tear runs down my cheek. I wipe it away roughly. "Don't act like you don't."

He stands too, reaching out as if to give me a hug. I turn, shaking my head.

"I've never been enough." My brittle voice cracks on the words. "Not for you, not for our family."

He sighs heavily, the lines on his face more pronounced, somehow. "Darling—"

"You've accomplished everything you ever set out to do," I interrupt, my voice gaining strength. "James followed in your footsteps, and Cooper is massively talented, and Sebastian has this whole new passion to explore, and I'm just . . . here. Failing." I sniffle. "Don't deny it."

His shoulders sag; something flickers in his eyes. "Isabelle, I've never once . . . All I care about is your happiness."

"You care about us being the best."

"*Your* best. Not the best."

I shake my head tightly.

"Yes," he insists. "Come here, honey. Please."

I can't bring myself to step closer, but I don't protest when he wraps me in a hug. I shut my eyes, trying to breathe.

"Not enough?" I make a soft noise. I feel him shake his head. "It breaks my heart to hear you say that. Our family wouldn't be complete without you. And that has nothing to do with volleyball."

"But I failed," I whisper.

"You made a mistake, one that you can learn from and move on. That's all it is." He strokes my hair. "Do you remember what you told me when you started playing?"

"Not really."

"You were so excited." He eases away, meeting my eyes. "You said that you had so much fun, and that you just made friends with a girl named Victoria, and that you wanted a pink volleyball, if they made them."

"I remember the pink volleyball."

He laughs softly. "I think I got you half a dozen, just in case."

"Because you could tell I had a shot to be good at a sport, finally."

"Because I could tell you really loved it," he says, voice gentle but firm. "And I remember being so thrilled—not because you found a sport to play, but because you found something you loved to do, and made friends doing it. I would've felt the same if it was theater or art or, I don't know, pickleball."

I smile despite myself. Just a little, wobbly with emotion. I tried out a lot of other hobbies—the summer of piano was torture to everyone's ears, I'm sure—but volleyball stuck like nothing else.

"What if . . . I don't want to do spring league?"

He considers that. "Because of your coach?"

I shake my head, tucking my hair behind my ears. "Bex asked me to plan her wedding, and I think I'd rather focus on that. At least for now. She'll pay me and everything, and apparently Katherine already said she'd help."

"Darling, that's wonderful," he says, the concern vanishing from his face.

"Really?"

"That sounds like an excellent plan to me." He gives my shoulder a comforting squeeze. "You're allowed to take a breather. And you're allowed to stop if that's what ends up working best for you. Play again if you still love it, but don't do it for me."

I search his face, even though I can sense the truthfulness in his words.

"You promise?"

"Of course." He kisses my temple. "You're my daughter, and I love you."

"Everyone should say those words more often," Mom says, the door to the gym shutting behind her with a rush of cold air. "Did I miss practice?"

I look at Dad. He just raises an eyebrow. Before, I'd have said it was a challenge, but now I recognize it as encouragement. I pick up the volleyball and toss it to Mom. "Guess who has a wedding planning gig?"

Half an hour later, I'm breathless with laughter, watching Mom jostle Dad for the volleyball. I'm not sure when our straightforward practice devolved into a volleyball-basketball hybrid, but I'm not complaining.

"Your point! Your point!" Dad says, throwing the volleyball like it's a football. It sails through the air, landing in front of me with a smack. He lets Mom push him against the gym wall, kissing him.

I wrinkle my nose, but I'm smiling. "I'm going back to the house."

"Start your playlist for New Year's karaoke!" Mom calls. "Rich, don't you *dare*—"

Outside the gym, I hurry down the path to the house, still beaming. I didn't bring a jacket with me, and it's cold enough that my breath looks like smoke. I feel so much lighter. I should have had that conversation with Dad weeks ago. I'm not entirely certain where I stand with volleyball right now, but at least I have some time to think. To reflect.

I round a corner and see Nik leaning against a tree, his back to me as he talks to someone on the phone.

"You're back from training early!" I smile even wider, stepping around a patch of ice. Nik and Cooper went to a nearby rink for a skate, and I wasn't expecting them back until dinner. "Guess what?"

He looks over. His face is a stiff mask. The phone falls from his fingers, hitting the ground. He flinches at the sound, eyes wide, hand curling and uncurling in a fist. His body is as tense as when we argued after my conversation with Alexis.

I stop in my tracks. My heart starts to pound. Last time, I thought that expression meant he didn't care, but I know better now. I take a couple careful steps forward. "Babe? What's the matter?"

"It's New Year's Eve."

"I know," I say, still inching closer. "Novy God in Russian, right? I looked into it a bit, I thought maybe we could—"

He shakes his head once, violently, effectively cutting me off.

His chest rises and falls rapidly. His scar stands out like a brand. I pick up his phone, tucking it into my pocket, and cup his cheek with my cold hand.

"Talk to me, Nik, please."

He says something in Russian, then curses in English, then knocks my hand away.

"My father . . ." He trails off, clenching his jaw. "My father, he . . ."

"What?" I say, searching those wide, panicked eyes. I want to hug him, but I'm afraid he'll push me away again. "He what?"

His eyes shutter. "He tried to kill my mother on New Year's Eve."

CHAPTER 44

Nikolai

Isabelle stares as panic twists my insides. I'm skating at full speed into a brick fucking wall. Half of my body is numb, the other on fire. I retch, turning to press my face against the rough bark of the nearest tree.

I've never said those words aloud before. Not like that. Whenever I've spoken about that night—the night my father put me in the hospital and we finally, finally left—I've kept that to myself.

The world hasn't shattered, now that I've said it. But I do feel different. A little more broken than before, as if the last piece of me just cracked. I gag again. My lungs are burning, but I can't get in enough air.

"Hey," she says softly. Her hands cover my trembling shoulders. She pulls me away from the tree, wiping my mouth with her sleeve. "It's okay. I'm here."

I squeeze my eyes shut. "Leave me alone."

"Come inside, it's freezing out here."

I try to twist out of her grip, but she's tenacious. There's a burning in her eyes, a fierceness I don't deserve. She half drags me to the house, and everything blurs as she takes me upstairs. My feet feel like stone. Each breath is a knife, twisting into my lungs. I struggle to push my father's voice out of my head. I can't quite manage it, and I definitely can't banish the memory of my mother's tearstained face, or the raw scream that sent me running from my room—

"Nik," a blue-eyed angel says. Her thumb rubs my scar tenderly. "Take a deep breath."

I try to focus on her. My panic attacks have never made me pass out, but I feel pretty fucking close right now. I sense a hand squeezing my arm, another running through my hair. I twist, retching yet again.

"Okay," she says—distant, as if I'm underwater. "Breathe through your nose, hang on."

She leads me to the bathroom, her hand cool and dry on the back of my neck as I flip the toilet lid and vomit. She says something else, but I can't hear her. I can't hear a thing but the conversation with my father, echoing over and over, and my own ragged breathing.

It's never been this bad. Never this absolute. He said my name—not Nikolai, not Nik, but Kolya—and I unraveled completely. Usually, I manage to keep my past in a lockbox, but it's all I can think of now. A million painful moments, sprung open by that one word.

And the conversation itself, taking a hammer to the week I've had with Isabelle's family. He's planning a trip here. To New York. Not tomorrow, but soon. It's been three years since I saw him in person, and now . . .

"Go," I say roughly. "Please."

She blinks, and I realize that I said it in Russian. I swallow, trying to find the right words in English. When I manage it—or something close enough—she just shakes her head.

"You know how to breathe," she murmurs. "Focus on it, honey. Do it with me."

Tears prick my eyes. I press the heels of my hands against them. I don't cry. I'm especially not going to cry now, in front of Isabelle. I take one shaky breath, and then another.

I used to hear my mother cry at night. She'd deny it, in the morning, but I heard it, just like I heard the arguments.

Something must show on my face—a shard of pain too large to bury fast enough—because Isabelle hugs me. I stay still, losing myself in the lemony scent of her hair. I should work up some sense of embarrassment at the sweat on my body and the sour smell of my breath, but I can't.

"Hug me back," she urges. "It'll help."

She feels fragile. Breakable. I knocked her hand away, outside, and it would be all too easy to shove her away now. I don't want to hurt her, but I could. I could give her the marks my mother would hide with makeup, after a particularly bad night with my father.

If you won't come home, I'll just have to travel to see you, Kolya.

I force myself to focus on her warmth. I don't hug back, but inch by inch, I relax. My breath comes easier. The lingering nausea fades, although my body begins to ache with exhaustion. I could fall asleep here, on the bathroom floor.

Isabelle finally steps back. I see the disappointment on her face, but she just grabs a washcloth from the cabinet and wets it.

"Use some mouthwash," she says, wiping my face. "I'll get you a glass of water."

"Thank you," I say when she's at the doorway.

She stops, giving me a hesitant smile. "You're okay."

I just nod, pulling my sweat-soaked shirt over my head.

"And I'm here for you." She digs her teeth into her bottom lip. I notice how cute that is, and it makes my heart skip a beat, even with the lingering effects of the attack. "If you don't want to talk about it now—"

"Tonight." I clear my throat. "Let's talk tonight."

CHAPTER 45

Nikolai

Isabelle spreads the blanket on the cold sand, smoothing the corners. She gives me a faint smile as she pulls another blanket out of her tote bag. "Are you going to sit down?"

I sit, carefully, shoving my bare hands into my pockets. She drapes the blanket over my shoulders. When she suggested ditching her family's New Year's plans, I thought we'd hang out in her room, but she had the sliver of beach attached to her parents' property in mind. The Long Island Sound is flat and dark, moonlight dancing across the surface.

Since that night at thirteen, I've spent every New Year's Eve alone. I thought I'd spend this one alone, too, but instead of going back to the city after Christmas Day, I've stayed with Isabelle and her family. I should have expected Dad's phone call today, of all days, and yet I fooled myself into thinking he'd drop it after our last argument. Visiting me. What a fucking joke.

She nestles into my side, sharing the blanket. The tip of her nose is red.

I slide my arm around her. "Are you too cold?"

"It's a pretty night," she says. "And we're alone here."

I'm pretty sure that means she's freezing, but she just raises an eyebrow, as if daring me to call the whole night off. I swallow around the block in my throat. When I promised her the truth, I didn't think about how I would give it—and what it would feel like to be faced with it. I never envisioned sharing these pieces of myself with someone. Cricket and I have never spoken about it in depth. When I confided in John, I told him the barest details. But Isabelle deserves more, even if I don't deserve *her*.

"But you're cold," I say, flicking her nose.

She doesn't smile. "Who were you on the phone with? Your dad?"

I look at the water. "Yes."

"He still lives in Russia, right?"

"Yeah. He coaches a hockey team in St. Petersburg. He's been doing it since he retired from playing."

"Is that where you grew up? Before you moved here?"

"No." A wave laps in our direction gently. I look at it instead of Isabelle; I know the pain is showing on my face. "I grew up in Moscow."

"But your dad played for the NHL."

"For a few seasons." Her hand finds mine, lacing our fingers together. I finally look over, steeling myself with a breath. The last time we were on a beach together, she convinced me to chase her into the waves. "It's a long story."

"I figured." She squeezes my hand. "Talk to me, okay? Trust me, baby, please."

I stretch out on the blanket, taking her with me. It's a clear night, with a nearly full moon overhead. She curls against my side, a welcome warmth. Her fuzzy pink knit cap tickles my cheek.

I haven't found many reasons to trust in my life, but I do trust her.

"My parents met in Europe," I say, watching a cloud drift over the moon. "My mom took a gap year after high school. My dad was in the KHL farm system, playing some exhibition game in Sweden. Somehow, they ran into each other, and apparently it was . . . instantaneous, whatever connection they shared. Dad was interested in playing for the NHL, and Mom encouraged that. Even though my grandfather hated it, she brought him back to America with her, and he worked his way onto the Penguins."

"Why did he hate it?"

"Pretty sure he thought my dad was a douche. Maybe he thought my dad wanted his money. I don't know." I laugh shortly. If Grandfather is anything, he's a good judge of character. "My mom didn't care. I haven't spoken about it with her that much, but my dad was—is—this really charismatic guy. He's funny, he's confident, he's easy to get along with when he's in a good mood. She fell in love, and eloped with him when she got pregnant with me. But the NHL didn't go well. He had a few rough injuries, and things never really took off. So when I was three, he went back to Russia."

"And your mom went, too?"

"Yeah. We both did. Obviously, I don't remember what it was like when they lived in Pittsburgh. But all my early memories are in Russia. I started hockey pretty soon after we moved, and my dad coached me personally."

"That must have been intense for your mom. A huge difference in culture."

"I'm sure she would have hated it even if my dad didn't start hitting her."

I say it without thinking, without filtering. A beat, and then Isabelle gasps. My heart stutters. Even though I meant to tell her, it's one thing to think it, and another for it to leave my lips.

"I thought it would be something like that." She's quiet for a moment. "What you said earlier, I figured . . . Oh, Nik."

I shut my eyes. My chest feels tight. Not as bad as earlier, but not comfortable, either. "Yeah."

"Poor Katherine," she whispers.

"I don't know when it happened for the first time." I drag my teeth over my lower lip. "We've never really spoken about it. But it was always there. Always a possibility. They'd be fine for months, and then something would happen, Dad would get drunk and lose his temper, and Mom would just . . . act like things were normal, after. She'd cover up the marks with makeup and bring me to school. They argued about me a lot. I figured that out early on. She didn't like how hard he pushed me in hockey."

"Like with your diet?"

I can hear the distaste in her voice. Small, needle-sharp memories flash through my mind. Skating laps when I messed up in practice. Hours and hours of ice time, working until I nearly puked. Picking over every mistake I made in a game. He couldn't be the best, but I could be, and I wanted to be. For him, for myself, and for the future in the NHL that he always expected me to have.

"Stuff like that. But I didn't care. I loved hockey, and I loved his approval." My voice breaks. "Years went by, and I didn't say anything. I didn't protect her."

"You were a child."

"All the same."

"You were a *child*," she repeats. She presses her lips together, shaking her head. "You weren't responsible for any of it."

I blink, looking away. "I could have said something, Isabelle."

My teachers, my other coaches, even the couple that lived in the apartment next door. I could have said *something*, but I didn't. I acted like everything was fine, even though I heard the shouting, the crying, the slammed doors and breaking glass. I convinced myself that the charismatic version of my father—someone who bought my mother extravagant gifts and surprised her with date nights and told me how proud he was of how I played—was the real version. Maybe that's what Mom did, too.

"Nik, did he ever . . . hurt you like that?" The question hangs in the air like our breath.

I sit up, the blanket slipping away. I've hardly felt the cold, but now I shiver. "Not like that. He could be mean, and he pushed me too hard in training too often, but he took out his drunken anger on her."

"But something did happen." She hesitates. "On New Year's Eve?"

I ease away from her, swallowing as I focus again on the surf. I know I have to keep going—I can't tell half the story, not with her—but each sentence feels heavy. The exhaustion from the panic attack earlier hasn't gone away. I sift through the memory to find the words to describe it.

"They were getting ready for a party," I say eventually. "The team was having an event for the holiday. I don't know why they started arguing, and Mom's never said, but I think it had something to do with me. Dad had been talking about maybe sending me to a hockey training program—a boarding school in Chelyabinsk. But whatever it was, it was bad. Both of them had been drinking, and I remember Mom shouting back at him, which she didn't always do."

"You were thirteen?"

I nod. Thirteen. Old enough to push back on Dad, just a little. I remember our own arguments from back then. My devotion to hockey never wavered, but I wanted more privacy. More time with my friends. I'd started to understand that not everyone lived the way we lived, and that while not everyone's father was a hockey star, they weren't all bad-tempered alcoholics, either.

"Usually, I tried to stay out of their way." I ball my hands into fists, my nails digging into my palms. Coward. "But I had a bad feeling. I . . . I made it to their room in time to see him throw her to the floor."

A tear runs down Isabelle's cheek.

"She worked hard to learn Russian, you know. And it's not an easy language to get the hang of if you're not a native speaker." I shake my head slightly, remembering how she'd read the newspaper out loud for practice. "She wasn't that great at it, but she lived there for years and didn't want to be left out when Dad and I spoke to each other. All the same, I never really heard her try. Until then. She was pleading with him, utterly terrified, and there was something about the way he stood over her, like she was nothing, that made me just . . . I was afraid he'd kill her."

My voice cracks on the last sentence. If he'd done it, it would have been just me and him, alone. Utterly alone.

"Nik," Isabelle whispers.

I shake my head again, rougher this time. "I started getting into it with him, finally, but I wasn't that big at thirteen. He slammed me against the wall, broke my arm. And threw his drink at my face."

"Is that how you—"

"Yeah."

She sniffles, wiping her eyes. "Fuck."

I huff out a ghost of laughter. "Yeah. Fuck."

"But you left after, right?"

"Neighbors heard us and called the police. I guess that night, at the hospital, Mom finally got in touch with her father. They were estranged for most of her marriage, but in the end, he helped us leave. I haven't been back since."

Isabelle leans in, slowly and carefully. I'm expecting a kiss on the lips, but she presses a chaste one to my scar instead. I blink. This time, when she puts her arms around me, I hug back.

"I'm sorry, Nikolai," she whispers. "I'm so sorry."

"It's not like you had anything to do with it."

"You know I don't mean it like that." She squeezes me tightly. "None of it was your fault."

"It's complicated."

"It's really not," she says, a firm note in her voice. "You deserved better."

I'm too tired to argue the point right now. It's a nice thought, anyway.

"It's okay."

"No. It's not."

We breathe in tandem for a few shiver-filled minutes. She slips into my lap and gives me a proper kiss. Comfort. Reassurance. A signal to come back to the present, with her. I should take her to the house, get her warmed up, but I don't know if I could face seeing any of her family right now. I kiss her hard enough our teeth clash, feeling something wild take flight in my chest.

I haven't shared my future with her—not yet, even though I know I need to sooner rather than later—but now she knows my past.

"No," I agree, my breath against her ear making her shiver anew. "It's not."

CHAPTER 46

Izzy

"Do you really want to go?" I finish my mascara, wiping the corners of my eyes delicately. Nikolai sits at the foot of my bed, lacing his boots. "If you want to stay home, I can, too."

He shakes his head as he stands, adjusting the sleeves of his black pullover. "No, it's okay. It'll be nice."

"I'm sure everyone else is hungover." I snort, tossing my makeup back in its bag. "We'll be talking to the wall."

The New Year's Eve karaoke was still going strong by the time Nik and I got back from the beach. We snuck upstairs with glasses of champagne and spent the rest of the night ensconced in my room. I fiddle with my new bracelet as I look at him, trying not to full-on stare. I'm grateful that he chose to share his past with me last night, but it was heavier than I could have imagined.

He didn't deserve a childhood like that. Not at all. The mere thought of it is enough to set me on edge, but I know he needs normalcy right now, not more anger. And if normalcy looks like brunch with my siblings, then all the better.

"I'm dying for some coffee," he says, kissing my cheek. His hand lingers on my waist as he takes in my outfit. "You look beautiful."

I tuck my hair behind my ears. I'm just wearing jeans and a chunky sweater, but it's nice to hear the compliment anyway. "You'll love this diner. It was my favorite, growing up. I can't even tell you how many times I've been."

"Let me guess, they make a good pancake."

"Thin, crispy edges, and they take up the whole plate. So good."
I snag my purse. Hopefully everyone is actually awake. When I
stopped by the kitchen earlier, I only saw Sebastian, slumped over
the kitchen table with a half-drunk mug of coffee. I asked him
how much they drank last night, and his answer was totally inco-
herent. "Let me guess, you're looking forward to plain scrambled
eggs and rye toast."

"What's wrong with rye toast?"

"Everything," I mutter, peering into the foyer.

Behind me, Nik barks a laugh. Sebastian waves from his spot
next to the front door.

"Where's everyone?" I ask.

He checks his watch. "Bex doesn't want to come, but the others
should be down in a second. Everything okay?"

"Yeah," Nik says smoothly, wrapping an arm around my middle and tugging me to his chest. He kisses my hair. "I wanted
Isabelle all to myself last night. Sorry."

Before Sebastian can reply, Mia stomps down the stairs, in the
middle of putting her hair into a topknot. "I knocked on Cooper's door six times. Either they're asleep or they're fucking, and
I don't care which, but they're not going to get between me and
my mimosa."

Two hours later, I nestle against Nik's side, half-drunk mimosa
in hand. The six of us—Cooper and Penny eventually emerged
from his room, mostly conscious—are squished in Shed House's
corner booth with nothing but crumbs left on our plates. I happy-
danced through every bite of my chocolate chip pancakes, and
Nik even ordered eggs Benedict instead of his usual boring breakfast. I don't miss my hometown when I'm at McKee—Moorbridge
is pretty enough to make up for it—but whenever I come here,
I'm reminded of good memories. We ate here as a family the
morning Dad announced his retirement from football. Victoria

got the server to add a scoop of ice cream to my pancakes after my breakup with Chance. My school volleyball team stormed in monthly for milkshakes and fries.

Nik traces a finger along the seam of my jeans as he steals a sip of my mimosa.

"What happened next?" he asks. "With the game?"

Cooper, energized by coffee and booze, has taken it upon himself to share some of my greatest hits from childhood, and since he hasn't told Nik about how I got my first period in the pool or the time he and Sebastian caught me kissing my Shawn Mendes poster, I've let it slide. I raise an eyebrow, waiting for him to finish. This one is pretty epic.

"So then," he says dramatically, "she spots James with the ball and *leaps* for him. Barefoot, tutu and all. Sacks him right to the ground."

"No way," Nik says, eyes widening. He turns to me. "How old were you again?"

I finish off the mimosa with a grin. "Six."

"Which made him . . ."

"Ten," Sebastian says. "I remember our mothers shrieking."

"Worth it," I say, punctuating that with a sweep of my hair over my shoulder. "James was so mad at me."

"Yeah, because I was open all the way down the field," Sebastian says. "I'd have taken it to the end zone for sure if he managed to throw it."

"Sure," Cooper says, drawing out the word.

"You keep telling yourself that," I add, smiling sweetly at him.

"I'm just imagining you flying through the air with the tutu on," Mia says.

"Bear in mind it wasn't a cute ballet pink," Cooper says. "It was this horrendous hot pink—"

"It was not horrendous," I interrupt. "It was sparkly and awe-some."

"I'm sure you looked adorable," Nik says. "And the flying tackle doesn't surprise me at all. You're a little hellion when you want to be."

"You want this little hellion."

"Mm," he says, ducking to kiss me. "It's such a hardship."

"Ugh, stop," Penny says. "You two are so cute."

Cooper rolls his eyes as the server comes over with the check, but I catch the smile on his face. Thank God. After we pay, I lead the way to the street, bundling into my coat as I weave through the tables.

It's a chilly but clear afternoon. Christmas decorations still dominate the main downtown strip. Even though the holiday has come and gone, the window decorations make me smile. I hurry around the corner ahead of everyone else to peer at an elaborate toy train set chugging away in the window of the hardware store. It weaves around a little North Pole scene, complete with penguins ice-skating on the frozen lake in the center of town. I put my palm to the glass, trying to spot penguin Santa.

I catch sight of a man's reflection in the window. "Nik, look at these itty-bitty little penguins."

"Hey, Izzy."

I know that voice. I whip my head around. My stomach drops at the sight of Chance, of all people, standing on the sidewalk. Same mop of blond hair. Same sharp blue eyes. He's broader than I remember, and somehow taller. The mustache is new as well, but the cocky smile is the same.

He looks . . . good. I hope I don't have chocolate on my face. I press against the glass as my heart rate kicks into gear. He takes a step closer, but doesn't go in for a hug.

I shove my hands into my coat pockets. "Um. Hey. What are you doing here?"

"Waiting for my girlfriend," he says, gesturing to the boutique next to the hardware store. "Didn't want to look at all the girly shit, you know?"

"Oh." I attempt a smile. My palms are slick with sweat, despite the cold air. I wish I didn't drink that third mimosa. "You . . . you have a girlfriend?"

There's no way I'm giving him the satisfaction of knowing that I stalked him on Instagram. I wonder if he's still dating that pretty blonde, or if he moved on to someone else by now.

"Been dating a year and a half now," he says. "Her name's Madison."

My heart sinks. A year and a half. That's the entire time we've been in college.

"We met during move-in day freshman year," he continues. "She's a dancer. And pre-med."

"Wow," I force out. "She sounds very, um . . ."

"It's nice to be with someone serious," he adds, his gaze running up and down my body. He takes another step, backing me against the building. "Someone driven. My old man approves."

My scalp prickles with discomfort. He's assessing me, determining if the way I look now matches up with his memories. His dad never liked me. I remember the looks I got whenever I went to his house. I glance around, but I don't see Nik or my family.

"Right. Sure."

"What about you? I remember the fun we used to have," he says, lingering on the word *fun*. "Working your way through the suckers at McKee? I'd ask what you're studying, but I don't think they have a major in party planning."

He laughs, as if expecting me to play along with his idiotic joke. I ignored his mean streak while we dated, but it was always there, ready to say something cutting. I made way too many excuses for him before the truth came out. I try to keep my chin high, but the comment hits its mark, just like he intended. My cheeks burn with embarrassment.

I finally catch sight of my brothers. Sebastian is pressing his lips together tightly, and Cooper looks like he's about to launch himself at Chance.

But Nik is the one who strolls over. "Party planning, no. Communications, yes." He slips his hands into his pockets, the picture of casualness, even though I catch a flash of intensity in his eyes. "You know, I was hoping I'd meet you one day, Chase."

I bite the inside of my cheek as I ease away from Chance. One step, then another. A hand steadies me. Mia, glaring daggers, flanked by Penny, who's staring at him like he's a particularly disgusting bug. Cooper and Sebastian step on either side of Nik, adopting that same faux-casual stance. I don't know if I've ever seen so much ice in Cooper's eyes.

Chance scowls at Nik. "It's Chance."

"Right. Whatever." Nik leans in, a smirk on his lips. He has an inch or two on Chance, and definitely more than a few pounds of muscle. He picks at his nails, letting Chance squirm for a moment. "So, *Chance*. Give me one good reason why I shouldn't smash your head through that glass window."

Chance startles, but he masks it with a sneer. "Interesting."

"What's interesting?" Sebastian says darkly.

"Is she a frigid bitch in bed with you, too?" he drawls. "Or did she learn some new tricks by now?"

He's addressing Nik, but he looks past him to me. Tears threaten to spill down my face. He's the one who cheated on *me* and made our relationship into a joke on my goddamn birthday, and yet I can't move. Can't think of a retort.

"Hey," Nik says sharply. "You don't talk about her like that."

"Shut the fuck up," Cooper adds with a growl.

Nik presses in, forcing Chance to flatten against the window. "You're a cheating scumbag, and—"

"Go away," I interrupt, finally finding my voice. I wrestle my arm away from Mia and take a few quick steps forward. He can't just stand there and insult me in front of my family and my boyfriend. "Unless you want me to walk into that store and tell your girlfriend about how much of a dick you were to me. I'm sure she'd be interested to hear all about her perfect, *serious* boyfriend's past."

The color drains from Chance's face. "Fucking bit—"

"Look at me." Nik yanks Chance close by the lapels of his jacket, but doesn't raise a fist. "If you ever run into her again, you keep your mouth shut and walk away. If I hear that you've talked to her, if you've so much as looked at her—I'll fucking destroy you."

"The same for us," Cooper says.

"All of us," says Penny.

Mia grins. "I won't hesitate to go for your balls. Just so you know."

"That's your cue to take your sorry ass somewhere else," adds Sebastian.

Nik keeps Chance pinned for a long, tense moment. "You understand?"

"Yes," he finally grits out. Nik lets him go with a little shove. He hurries into the boutique without so much as a backward glance.

"Are you okay?" Nik asks, immediately coming to my side. "What happened?"

"I'm fine." I'm wound up, but not in a bad way. I didn't stand up to Chance when I first learned the truth, but I did when it counted, and Nik and my family had my back. I feel triumphant; I feel *good*. "I'm fine, he doesn't matter."

"He doesn't matter at all," he says, voice low. "Don't listen to a word he said."

"Yeah," Penny says. "He's nothing, Izzy."

"He's an idiot," Mia says, throwing the boutique a dirty look.

"I'm glad I saw him," I say. Nik raises an eyebrow, but I nod. "Really, I am. He *is* nothing, I knew that, but it's still good to know for sure. And to watch you tell him to fuck off."

"And you," he says, brushing his lips against my temple. He's been doing that a lot recently, probably because of the new scar. My stomach flutters with warmth instead of anxiety. "You were a badass. My little hellion."

"Yeah," Sebastian says. He shares a look with Cooper. "What do you think, Coop? Is it time?"

"Time for what?" I ask.

Cooper ruffles my hair, the way he used to when we were kids. He gives Nik a once-over before turning his gaze to me. His eyes are bright, his expression almost boyish. "Time for the Callahan tattoo."

CHAPTER 47
Nikolai

"A re you sure?" Cooper asks as Isabelle wriggles into position on the table, lifting her shirt so her ribs are exposed. "Really, really sure?"

"Shut up, I'm so excited." She beams at us both. "This is the best present *ever*."

While she agreed—more like shrieked and hugged Cooper and Sebastian tightly—to get the Celtic knot tattoo her brothers have inked on their chests the day we ran into Chance, she waited until Rae, the tattoo artist who did the sword on Cooper's arm, had a free appointment. She's been anticipating this for weeks. Cooper and I met her and Penny at the tattoo parlor right after practice, so I'm exhausted, hair damp from the shower. I roll my shoulder with a wince. Our first game after the holiday break, a winger from Maine flattened me like a pancake, and I've been nursing the ache since.

"It's going to look great," I say. "Although I read that rib tattoos hurt pretty bad."

She shrugs. "It'll be worth it. Shoulder still bothering you?"

I wave her off as I settle into a chair along the wall, close enough that we'll be able to talk while she gets the tattoo. "It's fine. I've played through worse."

"Maybe you should get a massage."

"Maybe you can give it to me yourself later."

"We'll see," she says with a snort. "You might have to distract me so I don't start crying."

"You're going to be fine," Rae says as they wash their hands. "You can pick the music, and we'll chat."

"For the record, we did want to take you to get it with us," Sebastian says through Cooper's phone. He's in Geneva with Mia, but they called to wish Isabelle good luck. James called just before I arrived; he's in on the tattoo plan as well. "But Mom threatened us with the pain of death if we so much as suggested it to you."

I catch the flash of surprise on Isabelle's face. "Really?"

"Yeah." Cooper sits next to Penny with a groan. She looks up from her book, rubbing his knee reassuringly. He's also taken a couple hard hits recently. The end of the season is still a ways off, but around this time, it's impossible to be completely healthy. "I wanted to sneak you out, but James reminded me that you couldn't have gotten it without parental permission anyway."

"Huh. And here I was thinking it was a boys' club."

"No way. It's a Callahan thing."

Even though he's talking to Isabelle, he throws me a look. I guess I really got through to him about Isabelle's insecurities. I'm glad. A family like hers is rare, and she deserves to feel every bit as much a part of it as her siblings.

"I like the sound of that," she says.

"Once a Callahan, always a Callahan," says Sebastian. "Somehow I got that through my thick head."

"Eventually," Cooper says dryly.

"I need to go, but good luck, Iz," Sebastian adds. "I can't wait to see the pictures."

"I'm sending them to the group chat as soon as I can," she says. "Mom is going to *flip*. Tell Mia hi!"

"Ready?" Rae asks, pulling gloves over their tattooed hands.

I wink at Isabelle, who flushes. She nods, adjusting her arm so the tattoo won't look strange on her rib cage when she stands. I wonder how she'll handle the pain. She doesn't mind a little of it in bed, but this isn't the same. She creases her forehead with determination. Even if it hurts like hell, I don't think we'll hear any complaints.

"No tattoos, boyfriend?" Rae asks, glancing at me as they wipe Isabelle's skin with an alcohol swab.

"Nah. Although you make it seem appealing."

The walls are covered in tattoo designs and photographs of finished products on various clients. The small Celtic knot that Isabelle is getting is ridiculously tame compared to the full sleeves some of these people have going on. I rub my shoulder as I inspect an intricate depiction of a dragon curling around someone's arm.

"You should get one," Penny says. "I didn't think I'd be into it, but I love mine." She lifts her sleeve, showing off the small tattoo on her wrist. It's a phrase written in a language I don't recognize. "It's a *Lord of the Rings* thing. Cooper has the same one."

"You definitely should," he says, grinning. "You can show off some ink when you get to your new locker room next season."

I force a laugh. "Maybe."

"Can confirm it would be hot," Isabelle says, turning on a Sabrina Carpenter song.

I'm already thinking about when her tattoo is healed and I'll get to lick it, so that checks out. I cut off that train of thought before it can get too far away from the station. We're going to be here for a few hours; the last thing I need is to spend half of it with a boner.

I pull my phone out of my pocket, intending to check my email, but pause when I see a string of new voice mails. I work my jaw.

I should ignore them. Dad, thank fuck, hasn't made concrete plans to see me yet. He keeps talking about it, but the longer it's just talk, the greater the chance it won't come to fruition. He said the same thing last spring, even went so far as to buy me a plane ticket to Berlin for a hockey expo, but I didn't show, and he didn't force the issue.

I wish I could be excited by the prospect of him coming to see me play. He used to attend as many of my games as he could, in between his own. Sometimes that was a good thing—I can still hear the praise in my mind like a siren song—and sometimes it led to me getting chewed out and punished. But he wouldn't just be here to watch me play hockey, and I can't help the protective feelings that rise up at the thought of him anywhere near Mom and our lives now. Not to mention Isabelle.

I hover my thumb over the delete button on the first voice mail. Before I can make myself press it, though, my phone lights up with a text from Cricket.

"You okay?" Isabelle asks.

I run my hand over her hair quickly, careful not to jostle her. "Yeah. I just need to make a quick call."

She purses her lips, no doubt putting two and two together. "Is it . . ."

"No. Just Cricket."

She relaxes. "Tell her we need to find a time to meet up."

I slip around the corner of the building. It's snowing lightly, just a coating that won't stick, but for whatever reason, the sight of it pricks me with nostalgia. It's stupid; obviously it snows in a lot of the world, including New York, my actual home, but for a brief moment, I'm seven again, walking the few short blocks from school to my apartment building. I used to have this pair of red leather gloves that I liked because they reminded me of what I wore for hockey. I doubt Dad kept them after we left.

"Ooh, a phone call. I feel so special."

Cricket texted me in extremely grammatically incorrect Russian, so I'm not surprised to hear her greet me in the language. I cross my legs, leaning against the building.

"Your accent isn't half bad," I reply in Russian.

"I'm trying!"

"Your grammar needs help, though."

"Eh. Grammar is overrated anyway. Everything okay?"

"He wants to visit."

"Motherfucker."

I bark out a laugh. "When did you start learning the curses?"

"The curses are the fun part," she says, switching to English. "Did he say when?"

"No. He brought it up for the first time a few weeks ago." Before she can bring up New Year's, I add, "I think he's serious, though. He's still trying to make a case for his team."

"Tell him you won't see him."

"Somehow, I don't think that would stop him."

"Tell McKee not to sell him a ticket."

"He'd just come to an away game."

"Maybe Grandfather could get him on the no-fly list or something."

"I think if he could, he already would have."

"Ugh," she groans. Her voice softens. "I'm sorry. Tell me if he starts talking about dates. How's Isabelle?"

"She's getting a tattoo," I say, happy to change the topic of conversation. "Right now, I mean."

"Really? I love her even more."

"You haven't even met her."

"And whose fault is that?"

"It's not my fault that she wasn't at the game you saw in the fall."

"We should get dinner. Come to the city."

"I'll see if we can work something out. She's busy right now with wedding planning stuff."

"Wait. Did you—"

"Jesus, no." My stomach flips, not unpleasantly. "Her brother's wedding. She's working on it with my mom."

"Oh, nice. That's cool."

"She's really talented at it." I clear my throat. It's snowing heavier now, slowing traffic. "Not just at keeping track of everything and making sure all the details are correct, although that, too. But it's more meaningful than table settings and color schemes. She has this ability to make a story out of the event. It's an art form."

While I've always respected the business my mother built after her divorce, I never paid too much attention to the details. Not until now. Even last summer, I didn't understand the point. After Isabelle walked me through her thought process on James and Bex's wedding tone—not a theme—the other day, however, I started to get it. She's creating a story, a celebration, a promise for the future. And she's damn talented at it, even if she's still learning.

"Aw, are you blushing?"

"What? No."

"I'll bet you're blushing. You sound so different when you talk about her, by the way. It's cute."

I scuff the toe of my boot against the ground. "I'm hanging up."

"It's nice, Nikolai. Really. It's nice." She's quiet for a minute, and I stay on the line, even though the back of my neck is burning. Cricket texts me all the time about her various short-lived relationships—she has the busiest dating life of anyone I know, queer or straight—but we don't usually talk about me. "You sound like she's the best thing you've ever experienced."

I peer around the corner. Through the window, I can't see

much of Isabelle, but something loosens in my chest anyway. She stood up to my past—demanded to hear the truth of it—and didn't even flinch. I don't deserve her, and when I've lost her, that's what I'll remember.

Because she is the best thing, and that's terrifying.

CHAPTER 48

Izzy

"He called again, didn't he?"

The soles of my shoes crunch against the ice melt on the sidewalk as Nik and I loop around the quad. After all the runs on the trail, it's still a novelty to do this on campus, in full view of anyone passing by. Same as when I stop by the rink during practice, or kiss him before heading to class. It makes me want to explode with happiness, which I know sounds cheesy, but I didn't realize how *nice* it would be, having Nik in my life without reservations.

I have him. I have a break from volleyball. I have a chance to prove myself with Bex and James's wedding. If Nik's dad would just leave him the fuck alone, life would be perfect.

But he hasn't. He keeps calling, keeps trying to plan a trip to see Nik. I know it because of the way Nik acts after he gets a call, that panic edged in exhaustion that knocks him out for the rest of the day. He slept over at my house last night, and sometime early this morning, he slipped out of the room, phone in hand. I found him in the kitchen later, pale and sipping coffee as he stared at his computer.

He looks over with a sigh. "It's fine."

"You should stop answering."

"He just keeps calling."

I nearly snap that I hate him—because I do—but I know that despite everything, Nik doesn't hate him, so I hold my tongue. I dance around an icy patch, sniffling from the cold.

"He has to know by now that you're not going to play for his team."

The thought of Nik back in Russia, alone with his father . . . I can't entertain it. I know that Nik doesn't want it either, so I have nothing to worry about, but I wish he'd kick him to the curb and never talk to him again. How can he call his son, much less want to look him in the eyes, after what he did to his mother? To *him*? The evidence is on Nik's face.

"I don't know. I keep telling him, but . . ."

"He's trying to wear you down until you say yes."

"That's not going to happen." He stops in place, chest heaving. Despite the cold, sweat trickles down his temple; we've pushed each other on this run, choosing the hillier parts of campus. After halting exercise for a week to let my tattoo heal, it's been nice to get back into the routine. "But he's my father, Isabelle."

"I know that."

"It's just—it's complicated." He tucks a lock of hair underneath my headband. "Did you get the invitation samples?"

Whenever we talk about it, he says it's complicated. I give him a look, but don't press the issue. "Bex and James want to go with the cream and lavender."

"That sounds nice."

"We're still deciding on a font, though. So many script fonts are very formal, and you know they're going with more of a semi-formal vibe, so it's been tough to settle on something."

"Am I going to get an invitation?" he asks, pulling me against the side of a building, ostensibly to clear the path for a tour group walking in our direction, but really, I know, to kiss me in front of other people on campus.

I let him do it, then poke him in the stomach. "Plus-ones don't get their own invitations."

"Plus-one. I like the sound of that."

"You'll come, won't you? James and Bex want you there."

"And you, I hope."

"Of course." My brother and Bex settled on an early May wedding date, hoping to take advantage of the springtime weather in New York and have time for a long honeymoon before prep for next football season kicks into gear. It's a tight timeline to get everything together on the scale they want, but I'm throwing myself into the challenge. Katherine gave me full creative control and is just acting as a sounding board. I want her to feel confident about hiring me again this summer, and maybe even beyond.

"Then I promise I'll be there." He smiles, squinting in the winter sunshine.

I rise onto my tiptoes, pressing my lips against his cold cheek. He winds his arms around my waist. One hand slips low enough to squeeze my ass. I yelp, making him snort into my hair.

"Ugh, look at you two. Disgustingly adorable. Aaron, babe, you owe me twenty bucks."

I turn at the sound of Victoria's voice. "Torie!"

Over the past few weeks, I've been busy with wedding planning and she's been focused on spring league, so we haven't seen each other *nearly* enough. Now that I think of it, I need a margarita-and-movie night, stat. She weaves through the tour group, yanking me into a hug when she's close enough.

Aaron trails behind her, swiping a hand through his long hair before settling a beat-up Tigers cap on his head. A smirk plays on his lips as he gives Nik a back-thumping bro hug. "Can't believe you're doing that with Callahan's sister in public."

"Hey," I say, my voice muffled by Victoria's shoulder. She's wearing a ridiculously puffy black coat, plus a bright green knit cap. "For the record, I think PDA is very healthy. Not that it matters to you *or* Cooper."

"I can totally tell what that one girl is thinking," Victoria says, jerking her chin in the direction of a prospective student literally stopped on the sidewalk, looking at the four of us. I like her sense of style; she'd fit in on campus. "'If I go here, maybe I'll get with a super-hot hockey player too.'"

"Aw, I'm flattered," Aaron says.

"*Obviously* I meant Nik."

"There's no way that Abney is hotter than me."

"Wow," Nik deadpans.

"I like your shoes," I call to the girl, who startles, nearly dropping her map of campus. I shrug at Nik, who pulls me against his chest, hands over my ribs. He nuzzles my ear, murmuring something about me being the super-hot one here, and that distracts me enough that I nearly miss what Victoria is saying.

"—a certain rugged charm."

"Last night, you couldn't get enough of my *ruggedness*, Yoon," Aaron replies.

My eyebrows fly up to my hair. Damn, Aaron. It takes a lot to make Victoria blush, but that does it. She glares at him. He just grins, clearly unrepentant. Hockey players and their egos. He's the one in sandals and tube socks, despite the fact it's February.

And yet, if Nik's reports are anything to go by, he's been having a monster season. As long as he keeps delivering shutouts, I suppose he can wear whatever he wants. And it's not like I have to look at it; I'm lucky to be dating the guy with an actual sense of fashion. I could drool at the way Nik's shoulders look in the tight, long-sleeved gray shirt he's wearing.

"Izzy and I are going to get breakfast," Victoria declares. "I'll take that twenty now."

I PULL MY legs to my chest as I settle into a booth in the corner of the Purple Kettle. I take a sip of my whipped cream–topped cherry mocha, wiggling happily. Pumpkin spice might be the ultimate seasonal drink, but the Valentine's Day possibilities aren't too shabby, either.

I didn't put up much of a protest when Victoria stole me away, although I could tell that Nik was sad that we didn't get to finish our run. We haven't had that much time alone lately. I'll have to make it up to him when we celebrate Valentine's Day next week. Despite how packed the semester has been so far, I have a plan in the works.

"So?" Victoria says, bouncing eagerly on her side of the booth. "Show me the tattoo."

"And flash the entire café?"

"It's not up that high, is it?"

"It's just under my bra line." I pull up my shirt, turning so she can see my rib cage. The black ink stands out starkly against my fair skin, identical to my brothers' tattoos. I look at it fondly before letting the shirt fall. Apparently, Nik told Cooper something about how I can't help but compare myself to him and James and Sebastian. He might've been overstepping, but I couldn't bring myself to be annoyed about it, not when it led to them gifting me this tattoo.

It's silly, since it's just a couple lines of ink, but it means more than they know. I can still feel Sebastian's tight hug on the street in downtown Port Washington, Cooper promising that I'm always going to be part of the family, and James adding in over the phone that it has nothing to do with sports, and everything to do with love.

I wish that Nik had the same support from his family. One cousin isn't enough.

"It looks amazing!" Victoria exclaims. "Was it painful?"

"I cried."

"Oh no."

"It was . . . yeah. Worth it, but ouch." I scrunch my nose.

"What's up with you? I feel like I haven't seen you at all outside of Shah's class."

"I know, right? Organic chemistry has been killing me."

"Ugh, science." I shudder. Organic chemistry sounds terrible. Right up there with the complicated poli-sci classes Nik is taking.

"No, no, it's yay, science." She takes a sip of her matching mocha. "How about you?"

I fiddle with my headband. "I've been doing wedding stuff in all my free time."

"And getting it on with your sexy Russian?"

"Like you and Aaron haven't done worse."

"Fair." She drums her silver-polished nails against her mug. "Are you sure you don't want to come to spring league?"

"I'm too busy."

"Is that really why?"

"Yes." I pull the lid off my yogurt parfait and give it a stir. "It's not— I just really want to do a good job on the wedding. It's a lot to keep track of, especially with school. And the break has been good."

"Everyone misses you. And no one likes the way Alexis handled what happened."

"I know. You've said." I swallow a spoonful of yogurt. "She didn't kick me off the team, Torie."

"Which is why you shouldn't be hiding from us."

"I'm not hiding."

She arches an eyebrow. "Really?"

"Really." I fish my phone out of my pocket and pull up the notes app. "Look at what I need to do for the wedding."

She scrolls through the long, detailed list. "Damn, this is a lot."

"And that's just what I have to get done over the next few days."

"I thought Nik's mom was helping you."

"She is." My heart twinges at the thought of Katherine. I have zero idea if she knows I know what happened during Nik's childhood, but if she does, she hasn't brought it up, and I'm content to follow that lead. It makes me sad to think about, though. She's such a vibrant personality, it's hard to imagine her trapped in that situation. "But it's still my project. It's something I can really put a lot of thought into. I want James and Bex to have the perfect wedding, they deserve that."

"Will you think about it? You could even just come to the practices and not do the games. A couple of the girls are doing that because of class commitments."

The thought is tempting—I haven't so much as touched a volleyball since I got back to campus—but I just shake my head.

"I don't know. Maybe. But we should hang out."

"Want to do something this weekend? Or are you and Nik celebrating Valentine's Day early?"

"I'm touring venues with Bex and James."

She sits back, mocha in hand. "How about tonight? We could just study together, or watch a movie."

"I've been dying for a margarita," I admit.

Her eyes light up. "Margaritas and *Bridesmaids*?"

"Make it *27 Dresses* and you have a deal."

CHAPTER 49

Nikolai

I knock on Isabelle's front door, adjusting the flowers and gift bag in my arms. I'm not sure why my stomach is doing a gymnastics routine—it's just Valentine's Day—but I barely have a chance to take a breath before she flings open the door.

"You didn't have to knock," she says, eyes alighting on the flowers. "It was unlocked."

"Sounds like a great way to get murdered."

She shrugs as she leads the way to the kitchen. "I knew you were coming." As she searches for a vase, she adds, "And I want you to feel comfortable here. It's so much better than your dorm."

When she straightens, I tug her into my arms. The vase is wedged between our chests, but I don't pay it any mind. "Happy Valentine's Day. I thought we were staying in and watching a movie?"

"Happy Valentine's Day." She rises onto her tiptoes for a kiss. "What, I can't show off my new dress?"

I'm not sure I'd call what she's wearing a dress; it reminds me of the fancy nightgowns she wears to bed sometimes. It's a soft, gauzy pink, held together with a bow over her breasts. It barely reaches mid-thigh. My mouth goes dry as I take in the perfect way it clings to her curves. She tilts her head to the side, clearly aware of the way she's affecting me. If the not-dress wasn't bad enough, she's wearing sheer black knee socks, also adorned with bows.

I actually rub my sternum; this is too fucking much. "I was

under the impression we were watching that movie you really like—"

"—*The Wedding Singer*—"

"—possibly with your brother and Penny and the cat—"

"—they're gone for the night. We have the house to ourselves."

That stops me in my tracks. "Wait, really?"

"What, you think I'd be wearing this in front of my brother?" She busies herself with the flowers, trimming the ends before putting them into the vase. "I didn't think burning down the house sounded that romantic, so I got takeout from that Greek place you like. Also, I know you don't really eat dessert, but the red velvet cupcakes in the bakery window looked too good to pass up."

She sets the vase in the middle of the kitchen table. My heart does a funny hiccup at the sight of the candles and place settings. We discussed having a low-key Valentine's Day, and all along, she had a plan.

"This looks so nice. Although you didn't have to go to this trouble."

"I wanted to be domestic with you," she says, pecking my jaw. "What's this?"

Domestic. It's a nice thought. I lean against the kitchen island, watching as she opens the present. Like I expected, she gasps at the delicate gold star and moon earrings, but it's the bag of M&M's in all shades of pink that makes her face light up like a sunbeam.

She does a happy dance as she pops a few candies into her mouth. "You remembered!"

"The great pink M&M rant of last summer? How could I forget?"

She rolls her eyes, but she's smiling. "You like my rants."

"I do," I say, playing with the utterly tempting bow framing her cleavage. She's not wearing a bra underneath, so if I untied it, I'd be greeted with the sight of her perfect tits. "Although I like everything about you." I lean in, whispering in her ear, "You're killing me, sunshine."

Her breath catches, sending a zing of electricity through me. "We should eat dinner."

I nip her earlobe. "Later."

"Nik," she chides, even as her fingers, tipped in a fresh pink manicure, curl in my shirt.

"It's your fault for surprising me like this," I say, tugging her in the direction of the living room. "I was expecting to sit through an Adam Sandler movie, of all things, and keep my hands off you in front of Cooper, and instead, you answer the door wearing the sexiest fucking thing I've ever seen, acting all innocent—"

"I'm not seeing the problem," she interrupts, chin angled playfully. She squeaks when I drag her into a rough kiss. "You're not the only one who can spoil someone."

Her hairbrush rests on the end table. My mind spins in a new direction at the sight of it. I snag it, pulling her into my lap on the couch. The dress rides up as she settles her legs on either side of mine, giving me a glimpse of her panties.

Or rather—the fact she *isn't* wearing any. I practically growl as I haul her closer, one hand tangling in her silky hair, the other digging into her perky ass. The mere sight of her had me aching, but now that her weight is on top of me, I'm starting to strain against my zipper.

"You want domestic?" My voice is low, measured. Part of me wants to flip us over and push right into her, but a greater part wants to tease her back. To lean into the fantasy she laid out the moment she lit those candles and pulled on those knee socks. I finger the ribbon over her breasts, loosening it. She arches her back, instinctively seeking more of my touch. "You want to play house, sunshine? Then I just came home from a game, and you've been waiting for me in that silly excuse of a dress, acting like an angel when we both know you're my slut."

I emphasize the last sentence with a rough rub of her clit. Her breath hitches, eyes wide, showing off that endless blue.

I hold up the hairbrush, letting the silent question hang in the air between us. I've spanked her plenty, but never with an object, just my hand. She nods, swiping her tongue over her bottom lip.

"Use your words." I trace the bristled side of the hairbrush down her back, relishing the way she shivers. It feels like all the blood is rushing to my cock at once. "I think you want it to hurt before I kiss it better, but you gotta tell me."

"Please," she says, voice breaking on that single word. "Please, I need . . ."

"I know." I kiss her so deeply, I can taste the chocolate on her tongue. I smile against her lips. "I know what you need."

And it's a need that fills something in me, too. A shared desire to mix a pinch of pain in with the pleasure. Nothing gets me hotter, but only when it's her. Only ever her.

I give the dress ribbon one last pull, groaning when it unravels. She gasps as I massage her tits, pressing the small, soft hand-fuls together. I kiss a path from her mouth to her throat, her chest, then catch her hardened nipple between my teeth roughly enough, she cries out. Her nails dig into my thigh, making my cock jump in the confines of my pants.

"You want to take a break, or stop, you tell me," I murmur.

"I know," she says shakily. "I trust you."

"Good girl." I pull the dress over her head, tossing it onto the floor. I stare shamelessly at the sight of her. The curve of her breasts, the tattoo gleaming on her rib cage, the contrast between the knee socks and the smooth skin of her thighs . . . she's a pic-ture of goddamn perfection, and better yet, all mine.

I roll my sleeves to the elbow. "Put yourself over my lap."

She does as she's told, tossing me a cheeky look as she wriggles her bottom. There's no fucking way she didn't have a scene like this in mind when she got ready earlier; she's already dripping, inner thighs shining with her arousal. As soon as her ass is nice and pink, I'm going to devour her.

I groan at the thought as I gather her hair over her shoulder. "So goddamn pretty like this, Isabelle, all on display for me."

"Nik," she breathes, pressing her face against my thigh. I rest a hand on her back to steady her. "I wanna feel it."

"I know, sweetheart. You're good like that."

I pick up the hairbrush. It's pink—no surprise there—with an oval shape and a handle I can grip comfortably. I run the edge down her spine, stopping just before her ass. I flip it around, slapping the smooth side against one cheek. She whimpers, her hand slipping down to dig into my calf.

"Tell me how it feels."

"So good." She spreads her legs wider. "Give it to me harder."

I smack the other cheek, then flip the brush and hit her with the bristled side. She gasps sharply, grinding against my leg as best she can in this position. I build up a rhythm, alternating between the two; she sobs as I spread her cheeks and spank over her hole. I shudder at that beautiful sound, my free hand digging into her firm thigh. I'm so fucking hard, my dick jolts with each breath.

But even though I'm feeling the ache bone-deep, I stay focused, controlled. She's at my mercy, and that comes with responsibility. I murmur praise all the while, soothing her skin with my palm in between smacks.

When her ass is a gorgeous deep pink, I slip my hand between her legs to widen them, then smack over her cunt with the back of the hairbrush. It comes away glistening with slick as her body jerks with surprise.

"Look at you," I whisper. "My perfect fucking girl, so messy already."

"More," she says breathily. "I need more, please—"

I don't think; one moment we're on the couch, the next on the floor. I slot my mouth against hers, hands roaming everywhere they can reach. She runs her hands through my hair, jerking on the ends. I wrestle out of my clothes, kissing her all the while.

"Need to taste you," I rasp against her stomach. I lick her belly button. "I can't believe how wet that got you."

"Wait, wait," she says before I can dive lower. "I want to taste you, too."

It takes a little maneuvering, but eventually, we both end up on our sides. My head's buried between her legs, which are clamped tightly around me as she mouths at my dick. The position is new, but it's worth it for the dueling sensations. As she sucks me, I lose myself in the utter heaven of her soaked pussy. Every moan, every gasp, every whimper—I feel it as well as hear it, heightening my pleasure. I know she's feeling the same way, judging by the way her body shakes.

She cups my balls, massaging them as she takes me into her throat. I clench my ass with a moan. My tongue's inside her, and she must feel the reverberations of my voice, because her grip around my head tightens deliciously. I'd be content to stay here forever, caught between her legs, marveling in her seductive, almost sweet taste. I press my face against her inner thigh, digging my blunt nails into her sore bottom, and bite, hard. She comes with a cry, half-muffled by my cock.

"Fuck." I laugh breathlessly against her skin. My balls tighten; her honeyed voice is too much. "You take what I give you so goddamn well."

As if in answer, she urges me deeper into her mouth, sucking hard. I explode, panting against her pussy as I spend down her throat. It's too quick to pull back, but she swallows, her moan answer enough about whether she likes it. My blood roars with near-feral satisfaction at the thought of her drinking my seed. We might be coming down from the peak, but part of me is still inside her.

For a long, sweaty minute, neither of us speaks. Then the cat breaks the silence with a plaintive meow. We burst into laughter, rolling away from each other.

"Way to ruin the mood, Tangerine," she says as she sits up, shaking out her hair.

"You're the one who wanted domestic," I say, kissing her temple. Her face is flushed, lips pleasantly swollen. I haul her into my lap, double-checking that I didn't hit her too hard. She won't bruise, but her skin's still a beautiful shade of pink. Whenever we do something like this, I always need to make certain that I kept myself in check. I can't let it go too far.

"Good?" I check quietly.

"Perfect," she says with a shiver.

Tangerine inches closer, swiping a paw at my arm. I scratch her behind the ears.

"Do we have a cat, then?" she asks. "If we're playing house? I thought you'd want a dog."

"I would like a dog," I admit. "My dad never wanted an animal in the house. Grandfather didn't either."

"What would you name it?"

"Maybe something hockey related."

"That sounds nice."

I half smile. Yeah. It does sound nice. "Dinner?"

When she tugs the dress into place again, I tie the bow for her. She straightens my collar, blushing when my hands slip down to her bottom.

"Go use the bathroom, and when you come back, pour the wine."

"Yes, Daddy," she teases.

"Isabelle," I growl, swatting at her.

She laughs, dancing away from me. When we settle at the table a few minutes later, I sit her on my thigh, holding her in place with my arm around her middle.

She tilts her head back, squirming. "Really?"

"You didn't think I was letting you off that easy, did you?" I skim my nose over her shoulder. I should give her a bite to match the one on her thigh. I settle in the chair comfortably, watching as she adjusts to the position. The adorable splotches of blush on her cheeks make me want to take her all over again. At this rate, I'm going to be hard as stone by the time we get to dessert. And I'll bet she's going to ruin my pants. "You're sitting here all meal so you can feel that hairbrush. If you're going to tease, you better be prepared to handle the consequences, solnishko."

She half turns to kiss me, a wild, bright light in her eyes. "As long as you're the one giving them."

CHAPTER 50
Nikolai

I narrow my eyes as I stare at Tangerine. She stares right back, her eyes unnervingly bright, tail swishing on the notebook I need. When I try to slide it out from underneath her, she stomps her paw down. She must have decided she liked me on Valentine's Day, because now whenever I'm at Isabelle's, she refuses to leave me alone. Cooper had a bunch of the guys over earlier this week to watch the Devils-Rangers game, and she plopped herself in my lap the instant I sat down.

"Really? What are you going to do with that?"

She meows at me.

"Are you going to write my paper? What are your thoughts on China in the global economy?"

She licks her paw, blinking slowly. While she doesn't move, she welcomes a scratch behind the ears. I reach for the notebook again, hoping to snag it while she's distracted.

"She has a rich inner life," Cooper says from the doorway. He takes off his Yankees cap and tosses it onto the kitchen island. "I wouldn't put it past her. Is Izzy still here?"

Tangerine cranes her neck around to look at him. He picks her up—I grab the notebook while I can—and kisses the top of her head before setting her on the floor. She leaps onto the windowsill, lounging on it like it's a throne. He gives her a faint smile as he sits across from me.

"No," I reply. "She left a few hours ago."

"Her car's in the driveway."

"I arranged a car for her." I flip to the right page in my notebook. My notes are a disaster, but I need all the help I can get for this seminar, the last of my major requirements. "She seemed anxious about driving that far."

"Yeah, I was surprised to hear she was going all the way to Philly again. Thanks."

I pull up my half-finished essay. I make a face at it, then push the laptop away. Even if the end of college means committing to an office job, it has to be more interesting than finding a way to make bullshit arguments for the sake of grades. "There's a specific store Bex wanted to shop at for the dress. I think the owner is connected to the Eagles somehow. Is it okay that I'm here? I offered to go, but she said you wouldn't mind."

"Yeah, of course." He eyes the spread of papers around me. "I don't envy whatever this is. Although I'm reading *Crime and Punishment* again. I thought I escaped that when I took a class on Russian literature sophomore year."

"I've never read it."

"No?"

"What, do you think they hand it out in kindergarten? Here, have some pencils, *Prestupléniye i nakazániye*, and the complete works of Chekov?"

"Of course not. It's Marx, isn't it?"

My lips twitch at the smirk on his face. "And what, you've read all of Maya Angelou and Mark Twain?"

He snorts with laughter. "A good chunk of both, actually."

"This is rough," I say, holding up an article I annotated a few days ago, when Dad called yet again and I couldn't fall back asleep afterward. "It's about China's bureaucratic structure."

"Sounds riveting." He tips the chair, balancing on the two back legs with a practiced air. "God, I can't wait until this is over. Next year is going to be so much better."

"Don't wish away the rest of the season."

"No, definitely not." He lets the chair fall back into place. "And thank fuck it's been going well, Remmy's been a beast in the net since the second half started. But don't you wish you were already playing for real?"

My chest tightens. He's looking at me earnestly, clearly thinking about skating onto the ice at MSG or TD Garden. Imagining both of us, probably; we've spoken a lot recently about the Sharks, never mind the fact that it's not in the cards for me. The uncomplicated way he talks about it, eager yet level-headed, makes me so jealous, I have to keep the conversations short.

"Yeah." I clear my throat. "It'll happen soon enough."

"Want to get a beer? The Rangers are playing your future team in a bit."

The paper is due in a few days, but a beer sounds fantastic, actually. Even though I'm sure he's just missing his brother, I'll take it.

I stand, shrugging on my leather jacket. "Fine, but you're buying, Callahan."

COOPER SETS DOWN his beer with a thud, raising his arms in a half cheer. "Come on, come on—shit."

"Didn't set it up," I say, watching as Panarin skates in a loop around the Sharks goal, shaking his head. "That was sloppy."

"He's been scoring a ton of goals recently." Cooper takes a sip of beer. "And they've had opportunities this game. Sharks could use another weapon on defense."

At that, he elbows my side. I just roll my eyes, pushing my empty beer across the counter and gesturing to the bartender for another. It's ironic, considering how much Dad drinks, but I'm sure if he saw me have two beers in a row, he'd tell me it'll give me a gut.

"And that's me?"

"I don't know what they're waiting for."

"You should be happy they're waiting. We're dominating Hockey East right now."

"On the hockey team?" the guy sitting next to Cooper asks. He's middle-aged and gray-haired, wearing a Rangers-era Gretzky jersey. "I've been to a couple of your games this season."

Cooper raises his glass in a salute. "Thanks, man."

"Hey, you're Richard Callahan's kid," the guy says, snapping his fingers.

I watch Cooper to see if the immediate connection to his father bothers him, but he just flashes the guy a smile.

"Guilty." He claps me on the shoulder. "And this is my team-mate, Nikolai Abney. Listen for his name on the Sharks, like, next week."

"He's exaggerating," I say, even though technically speaking, they could call me up. Especially as the season goes on and they keep staying in the mix for the playoffs.

"The Sharks are good, but if they want to make a run, they need more defense."

"My thoughts exactly," Cooper says.

The bartender passes over another beer. I take a long sip. Cooper and the guy are talking about stat lines, and I chime in with a few comments, but for the most part, I keep my eyes on the game.

It's a weird thought, what it would be like to play a game that's televised. It's happened a few times over the years, and I just flat-out ignored the cameras, but something tells me the atmosphere of an NHL arena—and all the media personnel—would make it a much different experience.

I know I'd be able to handle it. No offense to the other teams we play, but there's no competition. I carve up the ice whenever I step onto it; I have every bit of my father's instincts and more raw athletic ability. It would be a weird transition, yeah, but a completely doable one. Let me beat Panarin in man coverage, I could fucking do it. I could surprise him with some Russian trash talk, too.

I finish my second beer. I shouldn't think about it. And I should stop drinking, especially in the middle of the afternoon. The next time the bartender swings around, I ask for a seltzer. The guy shakes our hands and moves along.

I sigh, tilting my head back. The ceiling in Lark's is made of hammered metal. Never noticed it before now, despite coming here regularly with the team.

"You okay?" Cooper asks. "You've been quieter than usual."

"Fine."

"Come on, man." His voice sounds light enough, but I catch the worry. Damn Callahans. "Want to go home?"

I keep my eyes on the television. "It's not happening."

"What do you mean?"

"I'm not going to the NHL."

"Wait. Not the Russian league, right?"

"I'm going to work for my grandfather when I graduate."

He's quiet for so long I squirm on the barstool, wondering if I miscalculated confiding in him. Shit. Maybe the moment we shared outside his family's house on Christmas Eve was a one-off.

"Does Izzy know?" he asks eventually.

"No," I admit, teeth scraping the inside of my cheek. Part of me has regretted that I didn't just bite the bullet and tell her about it on New Year's. I don't know why I didn't do it. I think part of me knew how disappointed she would be and didn't want to have to face that. Of course she's going to hate it. I don't like it either. But I made a promise, and I need to be the kind of man who keeps his promises.

"You have to tell her."

"She'll be happy, I'll bet." I fiddle with the tab on my seltzer can. "I'll be in New York permanently."

"I fucking hope that's sarcastic. You can work for his business when you retire, if you want. You can't put off a shot at the NHL."

"That's the deal I made with him. He got me into McKee, but I agreed not to play hockey professionally."

"Jesus Christ." He sits back, mouth open in disbelief. "What, does he hate hockey or something?"

"Something like that."

"Can't you just tell him to fuck off?"

"I'm fine with it."

"Like hell you are." He leans in, lowering his voice, his expression open and earnest. "I don't know what moment it was for you, but the instant I understood what hockey was—what it felt like to play it—I knew I wasn't doing anything else."

I wish I had something stronger to knock back. "I was three. First real memory."

The curve of my father's smile, his taped fingers lacing up my tiny skates. When he taught me to skate, he pushed me onto the ice and let me figure it out. Then he put a hockey stick in my hand, dumped a bunch of pucks around, and let me figure that out, too.

"Your dad, yeah?"

I shrug. "He wanted his son to play hockey."

"Is he okay with you giving it up?"

"He doesn't matter," I say, my voice clipped enough that Cooper puts his hands up.

"Okay," he says. "I'm just saying, I know you love it as much as me."

I glance around the bar. It's the middle of the afternoon, so it's not too crowded. Other than a few solo drinkers, we're alone.

I assumed that when I told Isabelle everything, that would be the end of it. It took everything I had to force the words out. But with Cooper . . . I don't know. I want him to understand the whole story. Maybe talking to Isabelle loosened whatever lock and key I've kept the past under even more than I realized.

"Look," I say. "Isabelle already knows this. And I'll tell her about the hockey, I will, just . . . give me some time to do it."

"Okay," he says warily. "What is it?"

Fuck it. I signal the bartender again. Even if alcohol sometimes makes me nauseated—a holdover, no doubt, from seeing Dad abuse it—I could use a stiff drink for this. I pick up my shot of vodka, clinking it gently against Cooper's as I toast to us in Russian.

I make a face as the sharp liquid hits my tongue. It should be chilled, not room temperature. I might not drink it very often, but I abide by that rule.

All the same, the liquid warms my chest. In Russia, drinking isn't a problem unless you're doing it alone. That, my father did plenty. I wonder if he still does, or if he actually grew up once we left. It's probably too much to hope for, because he's never said so, but I can't be sure.

"What did you say?" Cooper asks.

"To our friendship."

"Aw, Abney," he says, putting his hand over his heart. "I'm flattered."

"Technically, he should have left the bottle."

"Well, we're being good athletes."

"As long as you know that I could drink you under the table," I say, knocking my boot against his.

"We'll have to test that sometime. I come from Irish stock, you know."

I look away, clearing my throat. Time to jump, if I'm going to do it at all. "My dad is a piece of shit, Coop."

The amusement slips off his face. "Oh."

"This scar isn't because of a skate to the face." I shiver, remembering the moment Dad threw the glass. "It was him."

I brace myself for disgust or discomfort, but it doesn't come. Without missing a beat, he waves to the bartender.

"Fuck being a good athlete. We need the bottle for this."

CHAPTER 51

Nikolai

"Y̶ou washed it, right?" Isabelle says, catching the sweater I toss at her. "Not everyone loves sweat as much as you."

"Who do you take me for?" I lean against her bedroom door with a grin. I should be at the rink already, preparing for the game, but I wanted to see the look on Isabelle's face when I gave her my jersey.

"A possessive bastard," she replies, smirking as she pulls the sweater over her head.

It's a home jersey, the one I've lived in for most of the season, at least until the collar got ripped a few games ago. I figured she'd like the lived-in quality, and by the way she sniffs it, I know I knocked it out of the park.

"What do you think?" she adds, twirling around in front of the full-length mirror on the wall. She fluffs her hair, letting it fall tantalizingly over one shoulder as she winks.

Hockey sweaters aren't known for their high-end nature, but in a matter of seconds, she's pulled off an outfit that has me groaning. The tight leggings, the diamonds glittering in her earlobes and the hollow of her throat, and especially the tall black boots, all come together to create a picture of goddamn perfection. Seeing her dressed like this in the crowd tonight will give me an extra push of motivation.

"On second thought, what about wearing a paper bag to the game?"

She rolls her eyes. "Babe."

I fist my hands in the familiar fabric, kissing her deeply. The sight of it—the jersey I've fought in and sweat in and even bled in—on her body is enough to make my cock twitch.

Scratch the motivation. I'm going to have to limit the number of times I let myself look at her during the game if I want to play at all. Maybe only before periods. Or in between shifts. Fucking hell, purple is a good look on her. I love the sight of her in her own uniform, but something hits different with my name across her back.

Isabelle Abney doesn't sound bad at all. I'm sure as hell not entertaining the thought of Isabelle *Volkov*.

But that's what it would be, no matter what we called it. If we went there one day, I'd be tying her to all of me, past included. I stiffen at the thought. I nearly step back, but I'm against the door with nowhere to go, and she smells like orange and lemon, and frankly, it's all too tempting to force it out of my mind and kiss her once more.

She hums happily, deepening the kiss as her hands loop around my neck.

"I have something for you, too," she says.

"Oh yeah?"

"I know you don't normally wear anything on your wrists during games, but I thought you might like it."

She unwinds herself from me, reaching for a small bag on her desk. I shake the bag, making her smile, before pulling out a black leather bracelet.

"If you hate it, I can return it," she says quickly. "Or if it'll mess up your vibe, you don't have to wear it. But there's no metal, so it should be safe for you to wear while you play. If you want, I mean."

I slip it onto my left wrist. "I love it."

"You sure?"

"Yeah." I turn my wrist around, admiring it. It's understated but elegant, and above all, comfortable. "Thank you. I'll wear it to the game."

She puts her hands over her face, peeking through her fingers. "I hope I didn't just give you bad luck."

"Please," I scoff. "You're good luck, you know that."

I back her against the bedroom door, hands playing with the hem of the jersey. She shivers as I skim my fingertips up her sides.

The next time I'm inside her, she's going to be wearing this. I won't have it any other way. I'd love to devour her now, but the anticipation will give me an edge during the game. It never hurts to play starved.

Doesn't hurt to play with your girlfriend's mark on you, either.

"You should get to the rink," she says breathlessly.

"One more thing." I reach into my back pocket, pulling out the flyer I grabbed from the community bulletin board outside Lark's last weekend. I swear I can still feel the hangover that resulted from Cooper and I accidentally getting shit-faced on the most expensive vodka in the bar. Worth it to watch him curse out my dad in a creative string of expletives. "I thought maybe . . ."

She stares down at the flyer. "Nik."

"You'd be good at it."

"A high school volleyball club volunteer? Really?"

"The girls from the high school love whenever you come into the ice cream store. You'd be awesome at it. I thought this could be a way to keep volleyball going without worrying about spring league."

"I'm not *worrying* about spring league," she says, crumpling the flyer and tossing it onto her desk. "I'm worrying about the wedding, because I'd like your mother to hire me again this summer."

"She will."

"I don't want her to give it to me because we're dating."

"It wouldn't be that. You did really well last summer. She'll want you back no matter what."

"Still." She sighs, frowning at the balled-up flyer. "I want my family to see it, too. Volleyball is just . . . it's different, now."

"Promise me you'll think about it."

"I just did."

"Really think about it." I know she spoke with her parents about volleyball—which I'm glad about—and they reached their own understanding, but I've seen what she's like when she plays. The end of the road isn't here, even if she truly wants to shift her focus to her potential future career.

With each game I play, the closer I come to the end of my hockey career. I feel the weight of it whenever I skate onto the ice, especially now, with the end of the regular season in sight. We'll make the playoffs for sure, but that doesn't take away the pain. I don't want Isabelle to lose volleyball a second earlier than necessary.

"Maybe," she says, reaching around me to open her door. She shoves me into the hallway. "Go steal some pucks for me."

IN THE SEATS, she's all I see.

Like that first game, but so much better, because she's mine. My jersey on her body, and my name that she's cheering, although her brother gets a few shouts as well. I manage to put her out of my mind each shift, because I have a job to do, but when I'm on the bench—and okay, for the two minutes I spend in the box, I didn't get away with that tripping call like I'd been hoping—I can't help but stare. That's what she gets for sitting front row at the blue line. She's with the whole group: Penny, Victoria, Mickey's date, Micah's girlfriend, Evan's boyfriend, the other partners of my teammates. After this win—even if we're down by a goal right now, this is ending in a victory, I can feel it—we're going to meet up at Lark's.

If I can manage to share Isabelle for even a second longer tonight, that is.

I all but collapse onto the bench when my latest shift finally ends, sucking wind and wincing; the extra twenty seconds felt like torture. I pull off my helmet and slick my hair back.

Something catches the corner of my eye. Not Isabelle. A man.

I nearly drop the helmet.

"Good effort, Kolya," someone says, clapping a hand on my shoulder.

I whirl around. "What?"

"I said good effort, Abney," Coach Ryder says. He frowns. "You okay, son?"

I wet my lips, resisting the urge to look over my shoulder. It couldn't have been Dad. He still hasn't told me when he's coming to visit, and if I know anything about him, it's that he can't resist making everything about himself. He won't slink in halfway through a game. He'll charm his way into the locker room. He'll force me into a big production, all in the name of fathers and sons.

Kolya. Jesus. I need to get my head on straight.

"I'm fine. That shift was just a little long."

Ryder nods. "Drink some Gatorade."

When I risk another look at the stands, I breathe a sigh of relief. Not Dad. Just a random guy with an angular face and intense eyes. I crumple the empty paper cup, my gaze finding Isabelle in the crowd once more. The squeeze of my lungs eases at the sight of her laughing with Victoria. I adjust the bracelet she gave me, making sure it's safe underneath my glove.

Then I race onto the ice and do it all over again.

CHAPTER 52

Izzy

To the game winner!" Mickey says, lifting his shot glass to Nikolai. "You're next level, dude, seriously."

"Yeah, you're cold as ice," Evan says. Half the guys groan, and the other half burst into laughter. "What?" he adds, spreading his arms. "We play *ice hockey*. It's stupid, but it works."

I snag a shot from the nearest tray, holding it up, too. Across the table, cluttered with empty glasses, Nik catches my eye and smiles. I make a silly face, and he replies by sticking out his tongue and crossing his eyes. I giggle.

He clears his throat as he stands, looking around at his teammates.

The guys are practically high on the victory, courtesy of a perfectly executed shootout goal by Nik. When regulation ended in a tie, they went to a blisteringly fast overtime period, but that didn't force a goal. The shootout had me screaming, holding on to Penny's arm so tightly she yelped. I wasn't expecting Nik to come out for the game winning attempt, but he steamrolled the Lowell goaltender in the blink of an eye. I don't know all the intricacies of hockey, but even I could tell that a shot like that was a thing of lethal beauty.

He's so collected when he plays, his face can be blank, but after that goal, I caught the emotion in his expression. Elated, but a little sad, somehow. Maybe he didn't think he was going to get the goal.

He played *so* fucking well tonight. He deserves these cheers.

He holds up his own shot glass, the bar lights throwing his scar into sharp relief. He had the bartender put a couple bottles of vodka on ice when we first walked in.

"Gentlemen—"

"Iceman," Cooper says, snapping his fingers. "That should be your nickname."

"*Top Gun* vibes all the way," Evan says, nodding.

"Isn't Iceman the antagonist?" Penny says. She's halfway in Cooper's lap, nursing a glass of wine.

"Not by the end. And definitely not in the new movie." He squeezes her knee as he presses a kiss to her cheek. "Although to be fair, when we watched it, we didn't pay that much attention."

"Iceman," Mickey says contemplatively. "I like it."

"I've never seen it," Nik says.

Cooper's mouth drops open. "Okay, next team movie night, we're watching it. *Miracle* can wait; we watch that one every year anyway."

I snort. Now Cooper knows how I feel about Nik and *Legally Blonde*.

"*Miracle* also has Russians," says Micah, the freshman who sticks to Nik's side like a burr. He's holding hands with a pretty girl I vaguely recognize from the communications department.

"Technically Soviets," Nik drawls. "Weird, though, it's almost like Russians have reasons to be good at hockey."

"Even though Canada invented it," Jean says, his French-Canadian accent more pronounced from the alcohol he's been knocking back. "As the only Canadian on the team, I will not let—"

"Can we get going with the toast?" Aaron interrupts. "I'd like to keep the good times rolling, if it's cool with Iceman and Captain Callahan."

"Captain Callahan?" I repeat, catching Aaron's double meaning. "Oh my God. This is the greatest night of my life."

My brother actually blushes. "It's just my name, technically."

"Okay, *Captain America*."

He groans, slumping against the booth. "Iceman, give us this long, poetic Russian toast before we all lose it."

After a toast that does sound pretty poetic to my untrained ears—not to mention sexy; I want to rub against Nik like a cat every time Russian comes out of his mouth—I knock back the shot. Victoria pulls me in the direction of the dance floor, and I let her, even though I can feel Nik following my movements. I'm buzzed enough to want nothing but his touch, yet not quite bold enough to start making out with him in front of everyone.

Before I can get into the song, however, he snags me around the waist. I squeak as he pulls me into his lap. I try to sit up, but he holds me tighter, arm draped over me possessively.

"I can't take how goddamn stunning you are," he whispers into my ear. "Everyone in this fucking bar knows that you're mine."

I bite back a moan at the feeling of his muscular thigh between my legs. He whispers again, this time in Russian, and I don't have to be fluent to realize he just said something filthy. His hand slips underneath the jersey, playing with the waistband of my leggings. I glance around, but no one is paying us any attention. Cooper and Penny are wrapped up in each other, Evan is dancing with Xander, and a bunch of the single guys are shooting their shots with a group of women the next booth over.

I whimper as his thumb works underneath the waistband, swiping across the soft part of my belly. Not low enough to be indecent, but we're in a bar full of people, and his hand is close enough to my pussy, my core clenches. I twist around, cradling his jaw in my hands. Our teeth gnash together as we kiss. He groans, the sound slicing through me like the shot of vodka.

I break away slowly. Deliberately.

If we were alone, he'd sweep the glasses off the table and lay me over the sticky top. His chest would heave as he yanked down my leggings, then cupped my pussy, fingers digging into my slick folds. He'd pour vodka on my tits, my tattoo, and lick it all clean before nosing between my legs.

I whimper; I'm getting soaked at the fantasy. I rock on his leg, even though it's not nearly enough. His eyes flicker, pupils blown wide. His mouth shines with the gloss from my lips, but I pretend it's from my slick. The alcohol hasn't done much to him, he's only had two shots, but he's still drunk on *something*.

On me.

"Take me home," I breathe.

CHAPTER 53

Izzy

Nik manages—barely—to keep his hands off me during the walk back to the house, but the moment we're inside, he presses me against the door. It shuts with a definitive click as he kisses me. I moan at the delicious sensation of his solid body pinning me in place.

He hefts me into his arms, walking us both up the stairs. My stomach swoops low at the casual display of strength. When we reach my room, he tosses me onto the bed, then throws himself onto it beside me. We laugh as we bounce on the mattress. I kick off my boots and roll on top of him.

"Hopefully Cooper and Penny stay at the bar."

"Something tells me they'll be a while," he replies, hands curving over my bottom. I flush, remembering the way he spanked me with my hairbrush on Valentine's Day. I couldn't get enough of him that night. After dinner, we went upstairs, and he worked a plug in and out of my ass while he fucked me.

He must be thinking about it as well, because he smacks me lightly, over the leggings.

I whine into his mouth. "Nik."

"Close your eyes," he murmurs.

I do as he says, shivering as he pulls down my leggings and panties. Instead of touching my pussy, though, he keeps playing with my ass, massaging it, pinching it. I grind against his crotch, whimpering as my sensitive skin drags against the fabric of his jeans. His cock, already getting stiff, strains in the confines.

"You've been torturing me all night," he says, his voice quiet and seductive as hell. "My own personal ray of sunshine. So now you're going to take my cock up your tight ass, sweetheart."

My eyes fly open. He gives me a satisfied smirk. I reach for the hem of the jersey, but he shakes his head.

"I want the reminder of who you belong to." He tugs on the collar for emphasis. "I want you to see it when I fuck you against the mirror and to feel it in every thrust. It's like I said at the bar. You're mine, solnishko. Every part of you."

My core tightens. His fingers have felt so good there, and so did the toy. I don't feel an ounce of hesitation, even at the thought of having sex in front of the full-length mirror on the wall. He tucks a lock of hair behind my ear, a tender move at odds with his dirty words.

"You're a good girl, aren't you?" He spanks me again, harder. "Good girls let their boyfriends fuck them wherever they want."

"Please," I say breathlessly, heat zipping through me. "I'm good."

If only everyone knew what a dirty bastard Nik is. I had my own filthy fantasy at the bar, but it pales in comparison to this. My clit begs for attention, but I don't dare reach between us to rub it. Not without his permission.

He reaches over, pulling out a bottle of lubricant and a condom—and my little bullet vibrator. I wet my lips at the sight of it.

"Show me." He turns on the toy. I press forward, hoping for friction, but he just tsks. "You teased me with that jersey, you can tease yourself. Walk that perky ass to the mirror and play with yourself until you come. Do that, and you get my cock."

My nipples go taut at his words, two tiny points of heat to match my throbbing clit. I curl my hands in the fabric of his jersey, hips jerking forward. He groans, the sound sending a fresh lick of desire to my core.

"What if I can't do it?" I blurt.

It's hard for me to come from masturbation, even if Nik is with me. The last thing I want is to disappoint him, especially when he's ravenous like this. The high of the shootout goal must be lingering in his blood.

He tilts my chin up. "Then we take a break and I make you come however you want." He trails his fingertips over my collarbone, making me shiver. "Either way, you're going to come for me. I promise."

I take a breath. "Okay."

"Perfect girl." He swats my ass. "Go on, give me a show."

My blush only deepens as I walk to the mirror. I can sense him watching me—casual and confident, like a predator stalking prey—as I press one hand to the mirror, planting my feet on the floor. Other than the hockey sweater, I'm bare. I curl my toes, angling my hips so he gets a good look at my curves.

I glance at him, hair falling over my shoulder. He isn't touching himself yet, but he's devouring every inch of me with his eyes. I turn to the mirror, resisting the temptation to shut my own. I want to be good for him. To give him a show that leaves him desperate to fuck me. The thought makes me moan. I settle on a fast, punchy rhythm for the vibrator, tracing it down the front of the jersey.

"There's my girl," he says. "Make yourself feel good."

I gasp at the first touch of the vibrator against my folds. I swipe it lower, to get it slick, before rubbing it in a circle over my clit. Heat begins to build immediately from the direct contact, making my belly tighten almost to the point of pain. I can't help but shut my eyes, then, losing myself in the sensations.

I hear Nik's footsteps. When he stops behind me, I sense him, but he doesn't touch me. I pull the vibrator away from my clit with a pant.

"Keep going." He waits for me to obey before he adds, "Good girl. Your pleasure is important."

He punctuates that with a spank, his touch lingering.

"What about you?" I ask, whining without meaning to when he withdraws his hand.

"You think this isn't turning me the fuck on?" He traces over the shell of my ear with the tip of his tongue, leaning in close to whisper, "I'm hard as goddamn stone, sweetheart. It's taking all I have not to dive between your legs for a taste."

"Then do it."

He laughs. "Nice try, but this is about you. Open your eyes."

Somehow, I manage it. My blush deepens at the sight of his devilish smirk in the mirror. It's one thing to listen to his velvet-smooth voice guide me, but another to look him in the eyes when I'm laid bare like this. When he's inside me, we're sharing the pleasure. This is just about me, with nothing in it for him.

As I continue to tease my clit with the toy, he uncaps the lubricant. He slicks up his fingers, still looking at me in the mirror.

I whimper as he spreads my cheeks. The first touch is chilled, a sharp contrast to the heated friction of the toy. He rubs my asshole with a finger, pushing in just slightly.

"Put a finger in your cunt," he whispers.

I obey shakily. His index finger slides all the way up my ass. I can't help myself; I add another to my core. Filled in both holes, his body pressing against mine, all while we look at our reflections . . . I feel like I'm on fire, but the flames aren't burning me. They're teasing, dragging me to the edge of oblivion.

"Nik," I sob. "It feels—I need more—"

"So greedy," he croons. "Keep going. Make a mess for me."

He pushes another finger into me. The punishing vibrations from the toy, the dominance in his voice—it all works together to send me right to the peak. I curl my fingers, biting down my scream as the pleasure finally, finally crescendos. The tension leaves my body in a blissful rush.

I don't recall starting to cry, but when I blink, a tear streaks down my cheek. He turns my head, his fingers digging into my jaw, and licks it away. The blatant possessiveness makes me whimper.

"Look at yourself. Stuffed in both holes. Dripping with slick." He sucks a mark into my neck as he clicks off the vibrator. "Wearing my number. You're a wreck, Isabelle. A beautiful wreck. Who do you belong to?"

"You." My voice breaks. "Babe, please."

"Please what?"

"Fuck me."

A light slap. "Where?"

"My ass," I stutter out.

"Good girl," he murmurs into my ear. "Lean against the mirror."

I put both hands on the mirror, shivering as he preps me the rest of the way. He gives his cock a stroke, groaning, before he rolls on the condom and adds more lubricant. He wraps his arm around me, rucking up the sweater.

Our gazes meet through the mirror.

"I'm going to go slowly," he says. "If you need me to slow down even more, or stop, you tell me. Understand?"

I nod, then add, "Yes."

"Good." He lines up, pressing against my asshole. I gasp at the sensation of the blunt tip there, so different than when he's sliding into my cunt. "Stay relaxed for me, sunshine. Let me in."

He pushes in inch by inch, rubbing my clit to spark another round of pleasure. I ache at the stretch, but not in a bad way.

When he finally presses in completely, he lets out a breath, dropping his head to the crook of my shoulder. I clench my core as I adjust; it's as though he's splitting me open. As he kisses my neck, scraping his teeth over my skin, a strange sensation settles in my belly.

I've never felt so owned by him. So completely his. It's raw, it's dirty, and somehow, my heart feels more exposed than the rest of me.

"You're so big," I murmur.

"And you're so goddamn tight."

He cups my pussy, grinding the heel of his hand against my clit. He moves, achingly slow, clearly attuned to any signs of discomfort. I will myself to relax further. The sensations ramp up with each careful thrust.

"You can give me more." I look at him over my shoulder. "Take your pleasure too, Nik. It's important, right?"

He thrusts harder at my teasing words. "Such a little brat."

I spread my legs as wide as I can while keeping my balance, arching my back. The angle deepens, making both of us moan. He thrusts harder, building up an undulating rhythm so consuming, I can't breathe when he's inside me all the way. He steadies himself with a hand on my hip, fingers digging into my skin. His other hand covers my throat lightly.

I gasp, heart sprinting. The weight of it settles me, even as it ignites each and every one of my nerve endings. It's one thing to feel it, but another to see it through the mirror. His hand, so large it nearly wraps around all the way, and my leather bracelet on his wrist.

"Look at us." He gives my throat the barest squeeze, punctuating it with a much harder thrust. "We were made for each other, Isabelle."

"Nik," I whisper, emotion crashing over me in a wave. I can't manage anything else.

He doesn't drop his hand, but he doesn't let the pressure linger. Careful and protective, even when he's pushing me. He snaps his hips, driving his cock into me. The sensations bleed together, bringing me closer and closer to the edge. When I come again, it's with a scream. I hope—hazily—that we're still the only ones in the house.

Nik practically growls, driving into me once, twice, three more times. He grunts against my shoulder as he climaxes, sounding so perfectly strung-out, I smile. Nothing is better than the sound of his satisfaction.

"Was I—"

"Fuck, sunshine, yes." He kisses me deeply. "You were perfect."

CHAPTER 54

Izzy

They want to have the wedding at your parents' after all?"

I glance at Victoria as I take out my notebook. Technically, class should have started already, but our professor is still fussing with the projector. This class on Greek mythology is as much a chance to spend time with her as it is an easy way to earn credits.

"Yeah. It's what they were going to do originally."

"Does that make it easier for you? Or harder?"

"A bit of both." I fish around in my bag for a pen. My fingers brush against a crumpled bit of paper. The flyer. I sigh, pulling it out—along with a highlighter, but not a pen. "Venues that do a lot of weddings usually have set ways that they do things, so it makes certain parts of planning easier. With this, we're creating a venue ourselves. I have a bunch of tent companies to talk to later. Once that ball is rolling, I'll apply for permits, all that boring but necessary stuff."

Nik hasn't pushed me about the volleyball thing, but it's definitely been on my mind the past few days. When I finally could think about anything other than the way he fucked me after his last game, that is. I adjust in my chair, ducking my head until I get my blush under control. What we did was intense. If I close my eyes, I can still feel the weight of his hand on my throat. He made sure, after, that he hadn't gone too far, but I loved every moment. I practically cried when I had to take the jersey off for our aftercare shower. If I could, I'd wear his marks all the time.

"What's this?" Victoria asks.

I look up. She has the flyer in her hands.

"Nothing," I say, reaching for it.

"This looks really cool, Iz."

I snatch it away and stuff it into my bag. "It's just some stupid thing Nik showed me."

"It doesn't look stupid." She leans back in her chair, tapping her pen against the edge of the table. "Are you doing it?"

I shrug as I glance at the professor. He's still fiddling with the projector.

"I'm busy. The tent companies aren't going to call themselves."

"I'll go with you. It's tomorrow? I'll bet Ellie and Shona would come, too."

"Wait, really?"

"Of course. Where is it, just at Moorbridge High? That's like ten minutes away."

"Ugh, I don't know."

"Are you scared of a bunch of high schoolers? Don't tell me you're too busy."

"I am busy," I grumble, but without any bite in my voice. "You'd really come?"

"Ladies," the professor says, like *he* isn't the one starting class fifteen minutes late. "If you'd join us, please."

Victoria and I turn to the front of the room. I open my notebook to a fresh page and write the date across the top. When the professor dims the lights and starts the lecture, she leans over.

"I think it'd be fun. Like that summer camp we taught together, remember?"

"Those kids were in elementary school. It was barely volleyball."

She smirks. "You're totally scared of the high schoolers."

"No way."

"So let's go. It sounds fun, I'm all about helping more girls discover how cool volleyball is." She draws a heart on my paper. I pull hers over and add a star. "And then you can come to spring league practice."

"Torie—"

"Just saying." She nudges my shoe with hers. "We all miss you."

"Fine." A guy turns around to shush us. I drop my voice to a whisper, even though it's not like there's anything fascinating to pay attention to. I'm not sure how this professor manages to make the drama of Greek mythology so boring. "Just one practice."

"Hey," I call as I enter the house. I toss my keys onto the table in the foyer, poking my head around the corner. "Nik? You here?"

He should be; he's spent the better part of the week here. He hasn't spent much time at his dorm at all, lately, which I selfishly love. I get to sleep beside him at night, but surrounded by my stuffed animals, with all of my hair products in the bathroom. We don't have to deal with his dorm neighbors, and if Cooper has heard anything he doesn't want to hear, he has the good sense not to bring it up. It's perfection.

"Kitchen," he calls.

I slip out of my shoes and jacket. At the doorway to the kitchen, I smile. He's chopping bell peppers with careful concentration. Penny's at the kitchen table, typing on her laptop, and Cooper's standing by the stove, making a face at whatever is in the Dutch oven.

"I should have paid more attention when Sebastian made this," he says. "How's it going, Iz?"

I kiss Nik on the cheek, stealing a piece of pepper. "What are you making?"

"A Thai-style curry," Nik says. He sets down the knife, putting his arm around my waist so he can give me a proper kiss. "Allegedly. I'm just playing sous-chef, so don't blame me if it sucks."

"They've been very involved," Penny says, a touch dryly. "I was just on the phone with Mia, Iz, she'll be sad she missed you."

I grab a seltzer from the fridge and crack it open as I sit next to her at the table. "I'll text her later."

"How was the volunteer thing?" Nik asks. "You're home late."

I bring my knees to my chest, hugging them as I sip the seltzer. "It was actually really fun." I snort as I remember Victoria's dramatic speech to our team during the scrimmage; Ellie and Shona handled the other team. We pulled out the win, but it wasn't very serious. "The kids were all into it. There were only a few, but still. The gym teacher loved us. We're going back next week."

"That's great."

"But, um . . . I'm later than I thought because I went to spring league practice after. Don't say I told you so," I warn when his eyes widen.

"Wouldn't dream of it." He passes Cooper the peppers, then starts in on the broccoli. "I'm happy to hear it, that's all."

"Same," Penny says, smiling as she shuts her laptop and sets it aside. "It's fun to teach, isn't it?"

"It's fun to be reminded that you're actually good at something," I admit.

It might be silly, but demonstrating skills, cheering from the sidelines—it was a confidence boost. Whenever I've thought about volleyball lately, it's been wrapped in uncertainty, but this brought me all the way back to the basics. I spent a while teaching this one girl, Joana, how to serve the ball, and when she finally got the hang of it, we celebrated like she just won the lottery.

"I like passing on skills," Penny says. "We all had to learn from someone, in the beginning."

"Yeah," I say, smiling at the memory of Joana hugging me before I left. "I'm glad I went."

Cooper looks over his shoulder, a pair of tongs in hand. His shirt is covered in oil splatters. I wince, but don't say anything about missing Sebastian's cooking. Between the two of us, it's a miracle we haven't set the house on fire.

"And I'll bet your teammates were happy to see you," he says.

I smile. They embraced me the moment I walked through the doors with Victoria. I thought it would feel strange, but I fell back into the routine as easily as slipping into my favorite pair of pajamas.

"Don't give me that look."

"What look?" he says, glancing at Nik. They smile at each other.

"Both of you are doing it. *Ugh.*"

Nik comes around the island, flicking my cheek. I blush at the fondness in his expression.

"It's just nice to see you happy," he says.

"Christ," Cooper says, pushing the Dutch oven, now smoking, to the back of the stove. "Okay, this is a disaster. Let's get takeout."

"You're staying over later, right?" I ask Nik as Cooper and Penny haggle over the takeout menu. "Although fair warning, I have more work to do."

"If you'll have me," he says.

"Stay. I like waking up next to you." I turn in his embrace, kissing his cheek as I remember the voice mails we woke up to this morning. "Did your dad call again? Did you talk to him?"

He shakes his head. "The captain of the team tried earlier, but we didn't talk. He's a big name over there."

"He can't come here, Nik." My insides twist into knots at the thought of his father stepping foot on our campus. If I were him, I'd have changed my phone number long ago. He remains frustratingly unable to move on, even with the evidence of why he should on his face. I hate to push him, but I'm terrified of what will happen if we come face-to-face with Andrei Volkov.

He sighs heavily. "I know, Isabelle."

CHAPTER 55

Izzy

A noise startles me out of my concentration.

I pause my music, looking at the bed. Nik went to sleep hours ago, but I've been awake, working at my desk. I told Katherine that I'd handle the permit applications for the wedding, since I haven't done it by myself before, and I need to submit them soon so they can be processed in time. Aside from the halo of light around my desk, it's dark in the room. Pinkie the stuffed bunny stands guard next to my laptop, and a bunch of others are strewn across my side of the bed.

As my eyes adjust to the dark, I hear it again. That whimper.

"Nik," I whisper, sitting on the edge of the bed. He's breathing shallowly. I put my hand on his shoulder, stomach fluttering.

He flinches away from my touch. "Don't."

"I'm here." I reach out again. "I'm right here."

"Don't," he repeats, voice hoarse. Scared, almost. "Don't—Isabelle—"

I turn on the bedside lamp. He's still asleep, his body shaking. He seemed fine earlier, but this has to be a nightmare. Can you even have a panic attack while you're sleeping?

"Nikolai," I say firmly, shaking his shoulder.

"Please," he says, but still, he doesn't open his eyes. A slice of moonlight cuts over his face. "I'm sorry, I'm *sorry*—"

His voice rises by the end, shattering the quiet. I scramble on top of him and shake his shoulders. "Nikolai. I'm here."

"I'm sorry," he repeats, his breath catching on something close to a sob. "Don't hurt her."

I bite my lip hard enough I wince. Maybe he's dreaming about that night on New Year's Eve. Maybe it's something else, something that never happened but that his mind is trying to twist into reality. I need to find a way to break through to him.

Something comes to mind, but I hesitate. I haven't said it aloud before, so I don't know how he'll react. Odds are, he never used the name.

He twists underneath me, chest heaving. The sight of the pain on his face, even asleep, slices through me like a knife.

"Kolya," I say finally. "Kolya, wake up."

His eyes fly open. I sigh with relief, brushing the hair away from his forehead. Like the other times I've seen him panic, his pupils are blown wide, but this time . . . he's crying. My heart sinks straight to my stomach. I touch his cheek.

"There you are," I whisper. "You scared me."

He sits up, working his mouth a few times. I slip out of his lap. He didn't wear a shirt to bed, so I can see the sheen of sweat on his chest.

"How did you know that name?" he asks, voice cracking.

"I guessed." I sniffle, reaching for his hand and squeezing. I'd clamber back into his lap, but he's looking me over like he's not sure if I'm real or part of the dream, and I don't want to upset him further. "Did . . . did you go by that name? It's a nickname for Nikolai, right?"

"It's what my father calls me." His mouth twists, clearly remembering something. "Did I hurt you?"

"What? No, of course not."

"Fuck." He lets his head fall back against the headboard, the tension leaching away from his body. He squeezes the heels of his hands into his eyes, breath hitching. "I just . . ."

"You're okay. You're safe." I can't help it; I pull him into a hug. He's still shaking, but less violently than before. "What were you dreaming about?"

"I . . . nothing. I'm sorry if I woke you."

I blow a bit of hair out of my face. "Nik. Come on."

"It doesn't matter. I'm just glad I didn't—"

Someone knocks on the door, interrupting whatever he was about to say.

"Izzy?" Penny says. "Is everything okay?"

"We heard shouting," Cooper adds.

Nik curses softly. He reaches for his shirt, slipping it over his head.

"I can tell them to go back to bed," I murmur.

He shakes his head. "Won't be able to sleep anyway. I don't want your brother to worry about you."

After we explain what happened to a bleary-eyed Penny and a wary Cooper, there's a long, silent minute. Tangerine steps between our legs, meowing softly. Penny picks her up. She cuddles her close as she stifles a yawn.

Cooper scrubs his hand down his beard. He blinks a few times, as if waking himself up.

"Okay," he says. "Iz, can you make a pot of coffee? I'll get the gear in the truck."

"What gear?" Nik asks.

"Our hockey shit." Cooper claps him on the shoulder. "You know the key card works twenty-four seven."

Nik raises an eyebrow. "It's two in the morning."

I suppress my smile. Sometimes, when Sebastian would have nightmares—remembering the night his parents died in that horrible car accident—Cooper would take him to the batting cages. Nik mentioned that he told my brother a little about his past, but the simple acceptance of it, not to mention the hand he's holding out to help Nik recalibrate, means more than he can know.

"What, never had ice time in the middle of the night?" he says. "Come on, I'll play goalie."

CHAPTER 56
Nikolai

I smack one puck from the line in front of me into the back of the net, then another, and another. Cooper half lunges at the last one—which he could definitely stop—but lets it hit the net with a satisfying swoosh.

"You're terrible at this," I tell him. "Thank God we don't need you in the net, we'd be fucked."

He barks out a laugh as he taps his stick against the ice. "I'll stand here, but I'm not fucking up my knee for you."

When we arrived at the practice facility, we grabbed a bunch of pucks from the equipment room. He's been letting me work out the lingering edge of panic with smack after smack of my stick. Penny and Isabelle are on the bench, splitting a bag of gummy bears, and despite how literally unimpressive this is, my girlfriend cheers whenever the puck crosses into the net.

I shake my head as a shard of the nightmare pushes back into my mind. I used to have them more when I was younger, and they'd center on memories—a fragment of a disagreement between my mother and father, magnified, or a snatch of a negative moment in hockey training. This one, however, wasn't just a memory. I fucking hope it never becomes one.

It started with my parents, slammed doors and shouting and darkness. But somewhere along the line, it morphed. First, I looked through my father's eyes, and then I *was* my father, but I wasn't looking at my mother. It was Isabelle, her hair curled, wearing the blue gown from Boston. Isabelle, crawling away from me with a torn skirt, blood leaking from her lip, a bruise around her eye. Pleading with me in English, in Russian. Her voice entwined with my mother's. Dream me looked down at my knuckles, saw the smear of red, and went in for more.

I force myself to take a deep breath. I don't feel angry now, but in the dream, I couldn't escape the cocktail of rage and hopelessness. I drank it down like poison, and instead of killing me, it went for Isabelle. When I woke up and saw her safe and whole . . . I don't know if I'd ever been so glad to be dreaming.

"Come on," Cooper says, as if he can tell I'm thinking too hard. "Let's keep going."

Instead of winding up with my core and smacking the last puck into the net, I skate towards him slowly, flicking it from side to side.

He lunges when I act like I'm about to shoot, but at the last moment, I fake him out, hooking the puck around him neatly.

He scrambles to his feet, wiping the ice off his knees, and grins. "Prick."

I rotate my stick in my hands as I roll my shoulders. I snag a puck from the net, skating backwards in the direction of the neutral zone.

"Come and steal it!" I call as Cooper chases me.

"Is this a preview of next season?" Isabelle says, raising her voice so I hear it across the rink.

"Yeah," Penny says. "Show us what it's going to be like."

Cooper raises his eyebrows as he skates around me. I catch the silent question—no, I haven't told Isabelle about my agreement with Grandfather yet—but ignore it. I'll tell her soon; I just haven't found the right time and place.

We loop around the ice, skating as hard and fast as we dare without pads. He manages to snag the puck, only for me to check it away from him. He pushes harder, forcing me to pull out all of my best moves to keep possession.

I can't help but smile when he backs me against the boards, pressuring me into a turnover. I haven't played the sport like this in years. It makes me think of evenings at an outdoor rink my father liked; he'd challenge me to race him, to steal the puck from him, to play a little dirty to prevent him from scoring. Sometimes it would be in the middle of the night, like this. He'd carry me out of bed and put me in the car before I was fully awake. Mom hated when he did it on school nights.

Moments like that, tucked away in my mind, make the nightmares even harder. They make it impossible to block his number, even though I know that Isabelle hates every time I pick up the phone. He hasn't tried outright to lure me to his team again—apparently, he's given that task to other people—but he's reminisced with me. Asked how I'm doing. I know he's just playing nice so he can bring down the hammer later, but I'm falling for it anyway. I even mentioned Isabelle to him the other day.

Part of me can't believe that he'd actually set foot in America again. But who knows?

When Cooper and I are finally out of breath, we skate to the bench. I hang over the edge, smiling when Isabelle kisses me. She grabbed one of my sweaters on the way out the door; the dark blue cable-knit looks adorable on her.

"Want to skate?" Penny asks as she laces her skates. "I brought my extra pair; they should fit okay."

"No, no," Isabelle says with a groan, flopping the sleeves over her hands. "You know I'm terrible at it."

"I didn't know that," I say. "And I highly doubt it."

"I don't know, man," Cooper says. "The athleticism doesn't extend to the rink."

She makes a face at her brother. "Dad is the same way."

"Yes," he says with a snort. "At least he's terrible at something."

Penny reaches into her bag and pulls out a pair of white skates and rolled-up socks. "It'll be fun."

"I won't let you fall," I add.

"You have to promise," she says as she takes them, staring like they're an alien artifact.

"Promise," I say, biting back my smile as I rest my hand on my heart. "Let me lace you up."

I can't believe I didn't know this about her sooner. I could've been helping her this whole time. Maybe if she gets confident enough, we can go to one of the open skates at the rink Penny works at. After I get the skates laced tightly, I help her onto the ice. Cooper and Penny are skating together in the middle of the rink already, but I don't take her there. We skate around the edge— she's shaky, but stable enough that she doesn't fall—with our hands clasped together.

"There, you're getting the hang of it," I say, squeezing her palm. "Your body remembers."

She glances up, bottom lip caught between her teeth. "How are you doing?"

"Fine. Better," I add, at her look.

"You scared me."

"I know. I'm sorry."

"Were you dreaming about that night?"

I hate to lie, but I can't tell her what I was actually dreaming about. That's not an option. "Yeah. It happens sometimes. Not so much lately, but I guess . . . I don't know. Something triggered it."

"Your dad?"

"It doesn't matter." I steady her with a hand on her back. "Take longer strides. Good."

She skates with a bit more confidence, her body leaning into the movement. She's quiet for a full lap before she speaks again. "If there's anything I can do to help . . . you'll tell me, right? These attacks—"

"They only happen sometimes," I interrupt. "I'm handling them fine."

"Maybe if you spoke to someone about it, it would help."

I nearly stop in my tracks, but I promised her I wouldn't let her fall, and an abrupt change in movement would definitely make her lose her balance.

Therapy. Like talking about my feelings would lead anywhere. Speaking about that nightmare, bringing it into existence, even to denounce it? The thought makes me sick.

"I'm good," I say shortly. "It's fine, really."

"I think telling me about it helped," she says. "It brought us closer. If you shared some of this with a therapist, maybe then you'd be able to actually cut your dad out of your life."

"I can't do that."

She reaches for the boards, stopping us both in our tracks. I'm the one who nearly falls.

"Come on, Nik," she says softly.

I can't cut him out of my life, but I can quit hockey. It's not a perfect solution, but it's something. It's all I have, no matter how it hurts. I could tell her about my post-graduation plans right now, but I have the sense that it wouldn't do anything but start a fight.

There was anger in that dream. Anger that burst out in a physical way. If I lost my temper in real life . . .

I shake my head, somehow managing a smile. "Let's try skating in the middle of the rink."

THE NEXT MORNING, the four of us slump around the kitchen table, fighting through our exhaustion. By the time we got back to the house, it was nearly dawn. Isabelle rests her head against my shoulder, eyes half-shut as she sips her coffee. I'm trying to avoid face-planting into mine.

"I'm skipping my seminar," Penny says, her voice cracking on a yawn. "I don't even care."

"I have work to do," Isabelle says. "Ugh."

"At least we don't have an early practice," Cooper says. "Ryder would kill us if we showed up looking like this."

"He would," Penny agrees.

"Thank fuck," I say. I accidentally take a sip of Isabelle's coffee, wrinkling my nose at the sweetness. She laughs as she rescues her mug.

"By the way, I have something for you," Cooper says to me. "Figured we might as well make it official."

"Make what official?"

He reaches into his pocket, pulling out a set of keys and tossing them across the table.

Isabelle lifts her head from my shoulder, eyes wide. She looks at her brother, who gives her a half smile before pouring his girlfriend more coffee.

I look down at the keys.

House keys.

I meet Cooper's gaze. He nods at me.

If he knew what I dreamt about last night, I doubt he'd be doing this. He'd want me away from his sister as fast as humanly possible. But I just return his nod, closing my fist over the keys. The cold metal digs into my palm. "Thank you."

Stupid, stupid. And yet there's nowhere in the world I'd rather be than right here. However selfish, I want to be by Isabelle's side. The more time we spend together, the deeper I fall. She's everything I want, everything I thought I could never have. If

I make a mistake—if the switch flicks at the exact wrong moment, proving my grandfather right—I don't know how I'd live with myself.

If she's sunshine, I'm the guy who hopes it never starts raining.

But deep down, I worry that I'm the typhoon.

CHAPTER 57

Izzy

Yeah, I'm sending over their portfolios now." I hit send on the email open on my laptop, juggling my phone between my ear and shoulder. "I think having the wedding video will be really fun. Imagine when Charlie gets old enough to watch it."

"I know, right?" Bex says. "By the way, the Polaroid camera idea was genius. We definitely want to do it, and the photo booth."

I open the notes app on my phone, jotting down reminders about both. "That's so great. We don't want the event to be overly focused on football. It's for both of you, it should represent who you are, too."

"You're so sweet," she says. "And I think it'll be fun to see what everyone decides to photograph, you know? I'm sure we'll all see the day differently."

"Totally." I get up from the kitchen table to refill my coffee mug. "Let me start pricing out the photo booths."

"Awesome." There's a pause, and then a sigh. "Crap, I have clients coming in a couple minutes. Text me if you have any other questions, okay? You're killing it, Iz. Happy to hear about the volleyball, too."

I check the time as I walk upstairs. Usually, Nik is up and about at this hour on Fridays, getting ready for his individual training session with the assistant coaches, but I haven't seen him since I rolled out of bed. I have a million things to do before class later, but I don't want him to be late if—highly unlikely, but still—he overslept.

I open the door to the bedroom slowly, poking my head in. "Babe? You up?"

He isn't in bed, but the bathroom door is open, light spilling into the darkened bedroom. I'm about to head back downstairs when I hear something clatter. I put my coffee on my desk, hurrying to the bathroom.

Nik's standing at the sink, frowning at it. His toothbrush is in the basin. His cheeks are flushed, eyes glassy. He runs a hand through his hair, making it stick up at odd angles.

"Hey, are you okay?" I frown, reaching over to turn off the faucet.

He shakes his head once, violently, as if to wake himself up. "Yes. Sorry. I'm just . . ."

I feel his forehead with the back of my hand.

"Wait. Nik. You're burning up."

"I'm fine."

"You're absolutely not fine. You're sick." I tug him in the direction of the bedroom, but he digs his heels in. "You need to go back to bed."

"I need to get to the rink. What time is it?"

He tries to pull my phone out of my pocket, presumably to look at the time, but I slap his hand away. "You can't be serious. You look awful. No offense."

He snorts. "I've skated through worse."

"Well, not today."

He manages to snag my phone, groaning when he sees the time. "Shit. I'm going to be late."

"Just call your coach and tell him you're sick. I'll make you some breakfast. Do you want toast? We have rye bread."

I block the doorway so he can't slip past me to get dressed. My heart is fond, but my brain is ticked off. Not at him. I'd bet all the shoes in my closet that his father never let him have a day off. He's practically swaying on his feet; there's no way he doesn't have a fever. He needs to rest, and yet by the way he's glaring at me, he thinks he's somehow capable of conducting a full workout right now.

"I can't—"

"Yes, you can," I interrupt. "You don't have to be on all the time. You're allowed to take a sick day."

"Isabelle. I need—" Whatever he might've added is lost in a bout of coughing.

I arch an eyebrow. "Back. To. Bed."

When he finally nods, I let him pass. He slips into bed, on the side that has become his since he's all but started living here, and grimaces through another deep cough. It's probably just a cold, but it doesn't sound pleasant.

"Guys play through things all the time," he says, scowling as I tuck a blanket around him.

"What about when you're in California?" I touch his forehead again, wincing at the feel of his clammy skin. We probably have some medicine around here. If not, I can run to the drugstore.

"You need to take care of yourself, so you play well," I add, grabbing his water glass from the nightstand. I slip into the bathroom to refill it. "And so they won't get mad when you sneak away after East Coast games to see me, of course."

It'll be hard, once he's in the NHL and I'm still at McKee, but it's nice to think about. He'll be doing what he loves, and I'll figure out ways to support him long-distance. And then when I graduate, hopefully we'll be able to settle down together, whether it's in California or somewhere else. People get married everywhere; it shouldn't be hard to establish myself once I have a portfolio and more clients under my belt. If I can pull off James and Bex's wedding successfully, Katherine might let me take the lead on some meetings with vendors and potential clients this summer.

I smile as I set the glass down, hoping he'll give me one in return, but instead, he grimaces.

The attempt at positivity slides right off my face. "What is it? Are you going to throw up? I can get you a bowl. I know, gross, but babe, I really think if you just—"

"I'm not going to San Jose."

I blink, whatever else I was going to say abruptly fleeing my mind. "What do you mean? Did they trade your rights to another team?"

"Sit." He pats the edge of the bed. "Please."

"Why?"

"Sit, Isabelle."

I do as he asks, even though the careful way he's looking at me sends my stomach plummeting. He coughs again, a wet sound that has me itching to hunt for NyQuil, but I don't move. I compromise by taking his hand in mine. I don't care if he's contagious and we're both going to end up sick. I can tell when bad news is coming. If his father fucked something up for him—

"I—look. When I came to McKee, my grandfather and I, we made a deal."

"A deal."

"He pulled some strings to get me into McKee, and in exchange, I agreed to work for his company when I graduate."

"Right after?"

His dark eyes are so serious. He nods.

"Which means . . ." I trail off as the enormity of what he's saying sinks in.

"I'm not going to play hockey after this season. I've been putting off telling the organization, but—"

I yank my hand away. "You can't be serious."

"It's not like I'm happy about it."

"You say that like you don't have a choice."

"You're right. I don't. If it wasn't for him, I wouldn't have been able to finish my degree at McKee. Or any other school, for that matter. This was the only way for me to finish college."

"Don't you have a trust fund? You could have paid for it."

"And who would have taken on someone who just got expelled, no matter how good he is?"

"You could have played hockey somewhere else. They have minor leagues."

"It's not about that."

"Nik—"

"He helped us, okay?" The words burst out of him, as if they've been pent up a long time. "Years and years of watching my mom endure shit from my dad, and then she finally called him, and he *helped*. I owe him, Isabelle, and anyway, he's family. I can't have my father, but he's . . . he cares, in his own way."

I breathe out hard through my nose. "That can't . . . be what you want." My mind races, trying to wrap around this clusterfuck of a situation. I haven't met his grandfather yet, although we've been talking about taking a trip into the city soon. Right now, I'm glad I'm nowhere near him. I'd *eviscerate* him for forcing Nik into this.

He works his jaw. "It's not about what I want."

"Your life should be about that. Quite literally." I huff out a breath. "Does Katherine know about this?"

He just nods.

"And what? She's fine with her father strong-arming her son into giving up the thing he loves?"

"She understands the reasoning."

Scratch that. I'd eviscerate his whole family, even Katherine, despite the fact she's basically my boss. She always says she's so proud of him, but all along, she's known that he's giving it up. I want to pace, maybe kick something, but instead, I crawl onto the bed next to him.

"So what? You win the Frozen Four with Cooper and the guys, hang up your skates, and learn the world of corporate real estate?"

"At least I'll be in New York. I'll be able to visit you here whenever."

"That's not funny."

"It's reality."

"You can tell him you changed your mind. Why does he want you to work for him right now, anyway? You won't be in the NHL forever. You can do it after. *If* you want."

He rests his hand on my knee, and despite the highly flammable mix of emotions pouring through me right now, I lace our fingers together. He meets my gaze. There's a tiredness in his eyes that isn't from being sick. It's deeper than that. It's been there so long, it's nearly permanent.

"Hockey isn't mine. It's my father's. And if there's one thing I can't be, it's like him." His voice is quiet, but intense. "This is the way I prove that I'm not him."

I don't know what to say to that, so I stay silent. My heart aches for him; I feel the pain in every word. I understand why he wants to be nothing like his father—and he isn't, even if he doesn't let himself believe it—but even if he's the one who introduced him to hockey, that doesn't mean he can't love it on his own merits.

I've been around professional sports my whole life. It doesn't matter how or why you fell in love with your sport. If the love is deep enough, you need it in your life no matter what, and if you're able to make a career from it? It's a privilege you hold on to for as long as you can. My dad did it, and James is doing it, and soon Cooper will be, too. It's what Nikolai deserves, and his father has nothing to do with that. No wonder he's been so adamant about getting me back into volleyball. He doesn't want me to miss it the way he thinks he'll be missing hockey, sooner or later.

"I was glad." He presses fevered lips against my temple. "When he said he got me into McKee, I mean. All I could think about was that I'd have a chance to see you again."

Despite everything, my heart skips a beat. "I'm glad, too." I should go make him some breakfast, see if I can find cough medicine, but I stay put. "Thank you."

He looks at me warily. "For what?"

"For trusting me with this." I smile slightly, stroking my hand through his sweaty hair. Even sick, he's too handsome for his own good. "I know that opening up is hard for you."

"I wanted to tell you sooner." He traces over my fingers, my knuckles. I suppress a shiver. "It wasn't about not trusting you. I do trust you, Isabelle."

"You just knew I'd hate it."

He laughs shortly. "Can you blame me?"

"No. And for the record, I still hope you change your mind." I pat his hand before sliding out of bed. "Let me make you some toast. No sneaking out of the house. You're staying put and resting."

Once I'm out of the room, I stop in place, taking a couple deep breaths. I wipe my eyes with the heels of my hands and clear my throat. In the kitchen, I give Tangerine a treat before putting on the kettle and pulling out the rye bread.

He might think this is what he has to do, but it isn't. Not by a long shot. I'm sure that when he's actually presented with a contract, it'll be different; he'll realize he can't say no. Giving up such a special future would be too hard. No one as talented as him should have to think about doing anything but what he was born to do. And as long as the Sharks think he's still going to accept their contract, the possibility is there.

I just have to find a way to help him see it before it's too late.

CHAPTER 58

Nikolai

I turn the key in the lock, stepping into the house cautiously. It would be just my luck if Tangerine made a break for it while I'm the one opening the door. Isabelle's car is in the driveway, but I don't see Cooper's truck.

I'm still not used to the keys, just like I'm not used to the *A* stitched onto my jersey. Alternate captain. Cooper and the guys presented me with the sweater after practice the other day, and I'm not ashamed to say that I got choked up. I've tried all season to put the loss of the captain position at UMass out of my mind, so being able to slip back into the role again in some form is a gift. Cooper acted like the whole team came up with the idea, but Ryder pulled me aside and told me that Cooper insisted. He wants me wearing it for our next game, at the end of spring break—a game that, if we win, will secure us Hockey East and an automatic trip to the playoffs.

I toe off my sneakers, putting them in the hall closet, and hang up my leather jacket.

"Isabelle?" I call. "Are you home?"

I hear a noise that sounds suspiciously like a sob.

She's sitting at the kitchen island, sniffling as she feeds Tangerine a handful of cat treats. Her computer is open next to her elbow, with papers strewn around. My heart thuds with concern.

"Hey," I say, pressing a kiss to her hair. "What's the matter?"

She just grabs a couple more treats, holding them out to the cat. Tangerine gives me a baleful look before nibbling on one of them. I gently pull her hand away. The bag looks suspiciously empty, and I know Penny opened a fresh one last night.

"Trying to poison the cat?" I say lightly.

Her face crumples. "No. She likes them."

"Yeah, but maybe not quite so— There we go," I say, easing the bag away. Tangerine leaps off the island. "Sweetheart, what's wrong?"

"I hate New York State." She reaches for a napkin, blowing her nose. "And *especially* Nassau County."

Of all the things I expected her to say, that wasn't anywhere near the top of the list. My lips twitch, but I wipe the slight amusement away when she looks over. Her eyes are swollen, her face blotchy and pink.

"What happened?"

"I messed up the permits." Her lip wobbles. "I accidentally attached some stupid assignment for that mythology class I'm taking—" She cuts herself off, lurching for her computer.

"Just fantastic," she says as she peers at it. "That's where the permits went. My professor is probably wondering why the hell I turned in a request for a liquor license."

I inch her computer away. "You can email your professor and explain."

"But I have to redo the permits." Her breath catches. "They take *forever*, and we have a ton of them, and New York is literally so unhelpful—and James and Bex will need to pay all the application fees again."

"Wasn't it only a couple hundred bucks, altogether?"

"It's their money. Money that they gave to me so I could handle it for them."

"It's a drop in the bucket for them. Don't sweat the money."

"It's not even that," she says, sliding off the stool and walking around the island. She leans against the refrigerator, wrapping her arms around herself. "It's everything. We're on a tight timeline, and I can't mess it up, but I'm already messing it up, so we're behind schedule—"

"Isabelle," I say, gently but firmly. I join her by the refrigerator, pulling her into a hug. "Take a breath. You haven't messed anything up."

"I messed up the permits!"

"And that's totally fixable. Mom knows who to contact if you need to expedite them. Why don't you call, and I'll—"

"No. I told her I could handle it."

"She's helping you."

She shakes her head. "I told everyone I could do it."

"You're still doing it." I tuck a lock of hair behind her ear. "We've all seen how hard you're working. You're doing a great job."

"I'm not," she whispers. "I'm failing, Nik. And I can't fail again. Not at this."

I study her. She looks utterly exhausted, hair hanging limp, face devoid of makeup. Not that she needs to wear it, of course, but usually she prefers to at least put on mascara. She's in yesterday's sweater, and when I glance at the island, I take in the empty coffee cups, plural. I knew she was busy—it would be impossible not to notice—but I didn't realize just how strung out she was.

"Fail again?"

She swipes her eyes. "You know what I mean. Volleyball turned into a mess. I can't fail at my own brother's wedding, too. But between that and school and volunteering and everything else, there's just barely any time, and now I'm making mistakes, and it's just . . . I don't even know."

Shit. I'm the one who brought up the idea of volunteering, and of course that was just another thing on top of the pile. It's been good for her—she's full of energy and stories whenever she comes back from the high school—but that doesn't mean it's not a commitment. Add in spring league, and classwork, and the massive to-do list for the wedding that never seems to get smaller, and it's no wonder she's a ball of stress.

"If it's too much with spring league and all of that, maybe you can take a step back."

"I want to be doing it," she says, an edge to her voice. "All of it. But you know what I have to prove with the wedding. To your mom, to my family."

"Mom already loves you."

"My original internship with her wasn't something I got on my own."

"So?"

"I want to work for her, but because I earned it."

"You've already—"

"And my family." She takes in a shuddering breath. "I know they say it doesn't matter what I do, but it matters to me, okay? I need them to see I can do this. I . . . I need to see that *I* can do this. For myself."

"Okay." I pause, trying to figure out what would get through to her. "You're already showing that you can do it. But asking for help isn't a bad thing. Let my mom help you with the permits and whatever else you've been stressing over. You need a break."

"Weren't you just sick with the flu and begging to go to the rink?"

I wince. "I get it, Isabelle. But it was the right move, taking a rest."

Maybe it's the acknowledgment that she was right—slowing down hockey for a couple days wasn't the end of the world—but she softens.

"Why don't you call my mom, get her input on the permits, and I'll draw you a bath."

When she's safely tucked away in a bubble bath with a glass of iced tea and her iPad, so she can catch up on *Love Island*, I take a breath. Mom was happy to work on the permits, of course, but Isabelle needs more support than that. Large-scale event planning is hard, and has so many more moving pieces than anyone ever thinks about. I don't want her to get so wound up that any setback will cause a meltdown like this. It's spring break, so at least classwork can wait, but knowing her, she'll just use it as time to get ahead on her to-do list.

One of the stuffed animals on her bed catches my eye. A little koala.

She needs a real break. An acknowledgement of how hard she's working, and a reset.

And I have the perfect idea.

I SIT ON the edge of the bed next to Isabelle. She's still fast asleep, buried underneath her pink comforter. I can't see much but her dark hair and yellow-and-white striped nails, still holding her phone. Even though she followed the bath with a nap, she worked on stuff for the wedding until late last night. I was also hard at work, but for totally different reasons.

I glance at the suitcases standing guard at the foot of the bed. I based most of what I packed for her on these nails. Her favorite color might be pink, but I love her in yellow. She's gorgeous in every color, of course; blue matches her eyes, and pink is adorable, but yellow feels like the color of her soul.

My heart clenches with fondness. Once I decided on a plan, everything fell into place quickly. It's spontaneous as hell, and Isabelle is going to think I'm being ridiculous—a favorite word of hers, when it comes to me—but I don't care. It's spring break. Our lives can go on hold for a few days. Cooper and Penny are going to see Sebastian and Mia in Europe, after all.

What better way to help her relax than to whisk her away to Australia to meet koalas?

"Isabelle," I say, brushing a kiss to the top of her head.

After a few moments, she stirs, sitting up as she rubs her eyes. I grin; she looks cute with messy hair.

She squints at me. "What? Did I wake up late?"

"Nope."

"I have that meeting with the florist—"

"My mom is handling it."

She crosses her arms. To my satisfaction, she's wearing the Rift T-shirt. If we didn't have a plane scheduled, I'd have peeled it off and woken her up with my tongue. "What do you mean, she's handling it?"

"She's taking over things for a few days so you can have a break." I gesture to the suitcases. "We have somewhere else to be."

She narrows her eyes, but rises to the bait. "Where?"

"To hang out with koalas, obviously."

She blinks. "What, at the zoo?"

"Anyone can go to the zoo. We're going to Australia." I grin at the wide-eyed look on her face. I ought to surprise her more often. "There's a koala conservatory in Brisbane, and they're excited to meet their newest donors."

A beat, and then she throws her arms around me, moving so fast she nearly knocks both of us off the bed. "Are you serious? You donated to a koala conservatory for me?"

"Technically, I think we're supporting one koala in particular. Her name is Lovey."

"Oh my *God*. I love her already."

"Then let's go meet her."

She shakes her head with a little laugh. "This is—"

"Ridiculous?"

"As long as you know it."

"You need a break." I brush my lips against her cheek. "A real one. Run away with me for a few days."

She's quiet for a moment, but then she nods. "Okay. Let's do it." She unwinds herself from me, bouncing on the bed a few times. "Seriously, I can't believe you. How are we getting there?"

"I convinced my grandfather to lend me the jet for a few days." I slide off the bed, stretching. "But we have to go to a dinner party he's hosting right when we get back."

It's always something with him. Quid pro quo. At least Cricket will be there. She can finally meet Isabelle.

She does a double take at the mention of the plane, but I just shrug. "Beats commercial."

"I need to pack," she says, staring at her closet. "And find my passport."

"The black suitcase is yours. And Cooper already gave me your passport from the safe. And before you ask, Ryder is taking Tangy, since we'll all be out of the house."

She stops in her tracks. "You packed for me?"

"I know what I like to see you in."

By the way she flushes, she's having fun imagining what I picked out for her. I saunter over, cupping her jaw. She breathes in quickly, eyes searching mine. I lean down and kiss her, morning breath and all. She smiles against my lips.

Ridiculous, yes, but so worth it. A girl like her deserves more than half measures. Hopefully, this trip can be a reset—for both of us—and by the time we get back, she'll be rejuvenated. Hugging a koala has to release a special kind of dopamine.

"Come on, sunshine. Let's go hold some koalas."

CHAPTER 59

Nikolai

How much did you say she weighs again?" Isabelle asks the sanctuary worker, Lex. "She's so dense!"

I lounge against the trunk of a eucalyptus tree, watching as she wrestles with the slow-moving, yet determined, koala in her arms. When we finally arrived in Brisbane, after flying to Los Angeles first, it was morning the next day; we spent the day napping and exploring the city. Early this morning—with enough anticipation she was practically vibrating—she dragged me out of bed, and we headed to Fig Leaf Koala Sanctuary.

Somehow, Isabelle's joy is even greater than I thought it would be. She hasn't stopped smiling since we arrived. During the tour of the sanctuary earlier, she danced with excitement over each new animal and tidbit of information.

Whenever she looks at me, that adorable beam of pure sunshine on her face, my heart feels close to exploding. I've followed her around dutifully, enjoying the warm weather and the sight of her in tight khaki shorts. March in Brisbane is a far cry from New York.

"Lovey is on the heavier side for a female," Lex says, her lips quirking up as the koala presses her paw into Isabelle's chest. "She's about nine kilograms. The Southern koalas are larger than their Northern counterparts, as well."

"And the prettiest girl ever," Isabelle croons. "Does she like me? Can you tell?"

"She'll definitely like you when you feed her later." Lex gestures to the tree canopy. "They're very picky about which leaves they choose to eat, so you might need to try a few times to find some to her liking. They eat nearly half a kilogram of leaves a day. That's a pound."

"I—Nik, you're seeing this, right? I'm obsessed." She gently pulls the koala's hand away from her hair, adjusting her in her arms. The koala blinks, her eyes inquisitive; the distinctive nose and tufts of gray fur make her downright charming. "Did you say a *pound*? Each of them?"

I look at the trees around us. That's a ton of leaves; no wonder half the property is reserved for plant life. We're alone, save for Lex and the koalas. The moment we arrived at the sanctuary, one of the owners—an older man with an accent thick enough that it took us a moment to figure out what he was saying—handed us off to Lex, insisting on a private tour. Apparently, they don't normally get such large donations.

"They're even cuter than I thought they would be." I reach out carefully, stroking one of Lovey's soft, teddy-bear-like ears. "For a bear, I mean."

"They're actually not bears," Lex says. "That's a common misconception. They're marsupials, like kangaroos. The gestation period in the pouch is six months."

"Does Lovey have any babies?" Isabelle asks.

"She had one about a year ago. I'll show you him later, he's really sweet. His name is Striker."

"You should hold her." Isabelle takes a few steps in my direction, swaying the koala like a baby. The koala tries to grip her hair with her surprisingly well-defined claws, but Isabelle patiently pries the strands free. "She'll hold on to your arm like it's a tree branch."

Before she can try to foist the koala-not-bear on me, the older man from earlier walks over, flanked by a woman his age in a tan uniform like Lex's.

"There they are," the man says, gesturing to the two of us with a proud smile. "They gave the largest private donation on record."

"Oh," Isabelle says, glancing at me, "that wasn't me, it was—"

I wrap my arm around her waist, giving it a light squeeze. "We're glad to be able to support your mission. I keep looking around and thinking that you must go through a hell of a lot of eucalyptus."

"Maintaining our own eucalyptus plantation is a huge part of what we do here," the woman says, holding out her hand for us to shake. "I'm Maren. I'm so glad that you met Ralph, my husband, and our niece Lex, already. And truly, we want to give you a huge thank-you. For the donation, and also for making the trip to see us in person, so you can meet the animals you're helping to support directly."

My face is heating up, but I just keep smiling. I'm glad to be able to do this, although if this wasn't for Isabelle, I'd have kept the donation anonymous.

"They're beautiful," Isabelle says eagerly. "We saw the kangaroos earlier, and the raptors. Oh! And the wallabies were adorable."

"Aren't they?" Maren says, with a fond look at her husband. "How long have you two been together?"

"Since last summer," she says before I can answer. She throws me the tiniest wink she can manage, eyes dancing. "And sometimes he goes off and does wonderful things like this."

Since last summer. Even though it's not technically the truth, it's close enough. My life changed the moment I first saw her, over a year ago now, and the only thing that I wish happened differently is how long it took for us to put a label on what we have. By the expression on her face, she feels the same way.

"Do you want us to take a photo of you?" Maren asks. "Both of you with Lovey?"

"Yes," Isabelle says immediately. "Please. You hold her, Nik. It'll make your whole life."

She carefully deposits Lovey into my arms. Isabelle's right; she's heavier than she looks. Lovey stares at me with a slow blink. I adjust her in my arms, more or less holding her the way I was holding Charlie by the end of winter break. She reaches a paw—larger than I'd expect, but still a lot smaller than my hand—to my face.

"They like to cling to things," Maren says fondly. "A couple of them refuse to be weighed in our veterinary office without a stuffed animal in their arms. We have to weigh the toy separately to get an accurate reading."

Isabelle literally squeals, clapping her hands together. "I'm going to pass out from cuteness." She whips out her phone and snaps a picture of me and Lovey. "Ugh, stop, you both look perfect. I'm making this my phone background."

"I thought I was your phone background already," I tease.

"Yeah, but in this one you're literally holding a koala. *Our* koala." She lifts her sunglasses, squinting at me. "Is your background still that horrible picture of me ice skating?"

"You look cute."

"I look like a baby deer in headlights."

"And fawns are cute."

She snorts. "Maybe you can upgrade with this picture."

She holds out her phone to Lex, who shakes her head; Ralph brings out a proper camera. He takes a few steps back, setting up the shot. Isabelle fusses with my hair as Lovey discovers my leather bracelet.

"No, no," she murmurs, pulling Lovey's claws away. "He needs his lucky charm for next game if he's going to clinch Hockey East."

"Taking all the credit?"

She lifts an eyebrow as she smooths the collar of my white linen shirt. "So you do agree it's a good luck charm."

I steady the koala with a hand behind her head as I lean over to kiss Isabelle's hair. Ralph's camera clicks away. "*You're* my good luck charm. I hope you know that by now."

Her smile could outshine the sun. "You can be such a flirt."

"Only for you."

Only and ever.

I freeze, my mind echoing on the *ever*. Maren says something about smiling, and we face forward, snuggling this goddamn koala like it's our kid. Maybe it's Isabelle's laughter, or the way the light catches in her clear eyes, or the fact I'm across the world with her just because I wanted to give her a brief respite from everything going on in her life, but the whole moment slows and expands and crystallizes like a work of art.

I love her.

The realization hits me so hard, I lose my breath.

I've never loved someone like this, but I recognize the truth of it instinctively. I don't just care for Isabelle. I don't just want the best for her. *I love her.*

"What do you think?" she asks.

I shake my head, trying to get my bearings. The words nearly spill out of me, but I stop myself. When I tell her this for the first time, I want us to be alone. I don't want to share it with anyone, not even the toddler-size koala currently giving the love of my life so much to smile about.

But I feel it. I feel it in my fingers, my toes. My chest, beating a wild song. I thought life couldn't get better than skating full speed with cold wind on my face, but I was wrong. Isabelle cut a doorway to my soul, and now that she's there, I know she's never leaving. No matter what happens in the future, she'll be there. A drop of sunshine, just for me.

There are so many things I'm uncertain about, but she's not one of them.

"I think that I want to keep doing things like this with you."

She flicks my cheek playfully. "I meant about lunch, babe."

"Well, I mean forever." I pass the koala to Lex so I can pull my girl into a proper embrace, underneath the shade of the eucalyptus tree. "I want to travel the world with you."

Her lips part slightly. Even though her cheeks are already flushed from the warmth of the afternoon, I swear they get pinker.

"Kolya," she whispers.

Something must show on my face, in my voice, at the sound of that name from her lips. It doesn't hurt. It just makes me feel lighter. For a long time, I thought I never wanted to hear that name again, but it means the world when it's coming from her.

I kiss her. A soft, fevered touch that sends my heart into a sprint. Pressed close, I feel her intake of breath, the upturn of her mouth. I smell her citrus perfume, as bright and inviting as always.

After a moment, I ease away, one palm still on her cheek. She's so beautiful, I can't stand it. I'm about three seconds from sinking to my knees to swear fealty to her. Whatever she wants. Whatever I can do for her.

She shakes her head slightly, as if she doesn't believe what she's seeing, but she's smiling.

"Come on another adventure with me," she says, tangling our fingers together. "Starting with lunch on the Brisbane River."

CHAPTER 60

Izzy

I just realized something."

Nik, lounging across the bed—part of an extremely fancy suite overlooking downtown Brisbane—props his head up. "What's that?"

"I need a new life's dream." I join him on the bed, enjoying the taste of chocolate on my tongue from our shared slice of cake at dinner. I take off my earrings. "I've held a koala. I don't know what's left for me. I didn't expect to experience my greatest wish this early."

He holds out his hand for the earrings and places them on the nightstand. "Hard to top, I know."

The smile on his face is so smug, I have no choice but to pinch his thigh. The spontaneous trip, the amazing day spent at the sanctuary, the donation—I never imagined that anyone outside of my immediate family would care so much about my happiness. He's right, I needed the break. I've been running at full speed since the semester began, and it was starting to wear on me.

I pulled Maren aside earlier to ask about the donation details, and the number made my mouth drop open. That, and the fact it's yearly. It's outrageous, and yet it's not a complete surprise. He's so hard on himself, when in reality, he's one of the best people I've ever known.

I lean in for a kiss, wanting to taste the sugar on his lips. I'm proud that he's starting to let himself enjoy sweets when he wants them. He deserves chocolate cake every now and again. He unclasps my necklace, careful not to snag it on my hair.

"Thank you. For all of it. This has been amazing."

He holds my gaze, his gold-brown eyes bright in the lamplight. His finger traces from my wrist to my elbow with deliberate slowness. I bite the inside of my cheek, pressing my legs together.

"Do you want to go out? To a bar maybe, or a nightclub?"

"Is that why you packed that yellow dress?"

"It's the dress I first saw you in. Last fall, I mean. At the party with Victoria."

"It makes me look like a highlighter."

"A fucking sexy highlighter."

I burst into laughter. "You're so full of shit."

He laughs too, snagging me around the waist and pulling me into his lap. The skirt of the dress I'm wearing—fortunately not highlighter yellow, but rather a beautiful blush pink with a short skirt and sweetheart neckline—rucks up as my thighs settle on either side of his. He's half-hard in his charcoal slacks; earlier, I couldn't stop staring at the way they molded perfectly to his ass. The top two buttons of his white shirt are undone, giving me a tantalizing peek at his sculpted chest.

He finds the zipper on the back of my dress and tugs it down. I'm not wearing a bra, so his hands span the width of my bare back, the blunt tips of his nails digging in. I'm torn on whether I want to wriggle into the yellow dress and dance with him or keep the party going in private, until I see the look in his eyes. It's not yearning, not even hunger—it's practically starvation, as if even this position, with both of us fully clothed, has him close to the edge.

I lean in, letting my breath wash over his lips. He swallows, his Adam's apple moving.

"Is that what you want?" I tug on the lock of hair hanging over his forehead. "To dance with me at a nightclub?"

"This trip is about you, sweetheart."

I let the dress fall off my shoulders. His gaze drops to my tits, unabashedly admiring them.

"Let me thank you properly, then."

Before I can kiss him, he grips my wrist, shaking his head slightly. "You never have to do that. Sex doesn't have to be . . ."

"I know that." And I do; I know he'd never expect anything. "But this is what I want. I always want you, Nik."

I nearly call him Kolya, but I'm not sure if I'd be pushing my luck. I couldn't help myself earlier; it slipped out before I could change course. I could have sworn something changed in his expression when he heard it. Not a bad something, but noticeable all the same.

I push the hair away from his face, suddenly so full of fondness I couldn't stop smiling if I tried. I kiss his scar, then lick it, and he makes a noise in his throat that sounds close enough to a growl, I don't know whether to giggle or moan. He rolls us over, so I'm on my back and he's caging me in with that lithe body I fucking love, and bites my lip before kissing me properly.

"Give it to me like this." I wrestle out of the dress, tossing it aside. "Like this, baby, please."

He pops a few buttons in his haste to take off his shirt. I drink in the sight of him hungrily as he fumbles out of his belt and pants, too. He has a wild look in his eyes, and I bet I'd see the same thing in my own expression. He hooks a thumb in my pink mesh panties and tugs them down an inch, enough to expose some of my trimmed hair. My breath quickens as he slowly, slowly takes them off, freeing one leg, then the other. I expect him to dive right in, but instead he just spreads my legs and *looks*.

"Nik, what—"

"You're so beautiful." He shakes his head slightly, as if in disbelief. "I can't fucking believe how lucky I am, that's all."

Blush creeps up my cheeks. I've been bare for him so many
times now, and in so many positions, but this feels different.
Charged, somehow. He stays still for another moment, just looking, before finally splaying his hand over my tattoo and coaxing
my legs further apart. He seals his mouth right over my clit, making me gasp. I arch my back, hoping for more friction.

He doesn't waste time on finesse or teasing; he licks and sucks
everywhere he can reach. When his tongue slides into me, I bring
my legs up reflexively, but he holds them down. He slips in a finger, too, and I whimper, reaching for his hair. I wind my fingers
through the soft strands and pull. He moans against my skin like
he can't fucking get enough, even though I'm the one at his mercy.

He meets my gaze. "You have the sweetest pussy."

My belly tightens. I'm slick, I know I am, but the sight of his
wet mouth has me panting. He wipes his hand across his mouth
before going back in for more, his thumb stroking my clit in time
to the rough thrusts of his tongue.

He pulls out long enough to add, "Your taste, Isabelle, it makes
me want to bury myself inside you, make you cry on my cock."

I jerk my hips up. He rumbles against my skin. He pushes two
fingers into me, curling them so they brush against my G-spot.

"Please," I whine, bearing down on his fingers. "I need it, I
need it—"

"That's my girl. Let me hear all those beautiful noises."

As he talks, he plays with my clit, his fingers plunging in and
out of me. I wobble right on the edge, my breath coming short
and fast, until finally, I gush with his name on my tongue, clapping a hand over my mouth out of habit. He laughs against my
skin, his fingers still rubbing my inner walls. I twist, oversensitive,
but he holds me in place.

"You're soaked," he says, voice rough with lust. He pulls his wet fingers out of me and wraps them around his cock, jerking with a satisfied groan. "I could slide right into you, just like this, and you would take me so perfectly, wouldn't you? My dirty girl."

I prop myself on my elbows, watching as he fists his cock. I whimper at the thought of how snugly he fits inside me. His thick length gets so deep, pressing against places I hardly know belong to me. He looks sinful like this, dragging his teeth over his lip, forearm flexing with each stroke of his hand. I sit up all the way, kissing his messy mouth—messy with evidence of *me*—and help him jerk himself, coaxing him to that last bit of hardness. He pants into my mouth, our tongues clashing as I taste my own slick.

"So do it," I whisper against his lips. "Fill me up, Kolya. Just like this."

He shudders, his grip on himself faltering. "Let me get a condom."

I stop him, shaking my head. "No."

"No?"

"I want to feel you. Really feel you. Every inch."

My heart pounds as the words leave my lips. I've never done this with anyone before, not even Chance. But we're as exclusive as it gets, and I want to experience this with him. I want to crawl inside his skin and make a home there. To know that he's still inside me long after we finish this particular dance.

His brows knit together. "Are you sure?"

"Remember when I said I was looking into birth control?"

"You said the pill gave you bad side effects, back when you took it in high school," he says, frowning.

"Yeah. But this time, I was able to get an IUD. It doesn't have hormones."

"And it's fine?"

"Totally fine. I promise." I smile at the look of concern on his face. "I want to do this with you."

It must finally sink in for him, because he groans, jerking his hand through his hair. "Fuck. Okay, sweetheart."

He turns off the bedside lamp, letting the deep blue nighttime wash over us. His eyes shine in the light spilling through the window. There's tenderness in his expression, the way he pushes me against the bed. The hunger is still there, that passion that I know by now never leaves him, but I understand, without him saying it, that this moment means as much to him as it does to me.

He strokes my face, cupping my cheek and rubbing his thumb over my lips before leaning in for a featherlight kiss. His other hand slides over my ribs and lower, pressing my legs apart again.

I'm still dripping, but he checks anyway, quirking his lips in a slight smile as he rubs over my hole. My breath hitches as I look into his eyes. He's a work of art, so gorgeous my heart skips a beat whenever I look at him. I'm so familiar with him now, but that just makes me fonder. I've never felt this way for anyone, and I never want to feel it for anyone else. Just him. *Only* him.

Because he's safety. Comfort. Joy.

Because I love him.

Maybe it should feel like a life-changing realization, but it doesn't. It's just the truth, something that part of me already knew. *I love him.*

Love him, love him, love him.

He works into me slowly. Taking his time, grounding us both in this moment. I loop my arms around his neck, kissing him as he presses in inch by perfect inch. The words are on the tip of my tongue, but before I can say them, he pushes in the rest of the way, and I can't focus on anything else. He moans into my mouth. I clench around him, reveling in the slight ache. He rubs my clit with two slippery fingers, sparking an even deeper level of pleasure.

"Good?" he murmurs.

I nod breathlessly, digging my heels into his back, needing him even closer. He strokes his hand through my hair, fingers catching on the ends of the strands. Slowly, he rolls his hips. He snaps them back, then forward, coaxing a moan from my throat as he settles inside me all the way once more.

"You take me so perfectly, solnishko."

"Nik." My voice catches on the word.

Another kiss, soft and lingering. "My sunshine girl."

My sunshine girl. He said that for the first time last summer, forever ago. If I'm sunshine to him, then he's the earth beneath my feet, the grass between my toes, grounding me like nothing else. That feeling has been building for months, upon hundreds of tiny moments. I belong to him, and he belongs to me.

I meet his thrusts with my own, snapping my hips up. A growl, a deeper thrust. I dig my nails into his neck, crying out as he finds a particularly good angle. He lifts my hips with ease, pounding into that spot over and over. I'm shaking, so close to the edge again that I can't stop the moans spilling from my mouth.

He says something—in Russian—into the crook of my neck. Even though I don't speak it, I sense the gravity in his tone. Three words. Three words, repeated like a prayer.

My eyes widen. "Kolya."

His thrusts falter; he's buried deep inside me as he climaxes. He pinches my clit so I'll come over the edge with him, and after a moment, my pleasure blooms, overtaking my senses. There's only him, inside and out. His body pinning me against the mattress. His scent. His groans. His words, echoing in my mind like music.

We're quiet for a moment, catching our breath in the cool dark of the bedroom. I curl my toes, shifting underneath him. I can't help but smile. His seed is inside me. A claim to match the one he said aloud.

"I love you, too," I whisper.

"I realized earlier," he says hoarsely. He lifts his head. "I think some part of me has known for a long time."

I push the hair away from his forehead as I give him a kiss. "Say it again."

"Я люблю тебя." He shifts, but doesn't pull out of me. I'd happily stay like this all night. "I love you."

I try to repeat it, but stumble over the unfamiliar pronunciation. He smiles. He catches my hand and laces our fingers together as he says it once more, slower this time. "Ya lyublyu tebya."

I listen, then try again.

"Good." He eases out of me gently, rolling us onto our sides. "You're getting the hang of it, solnishko."

I tilt my head against his shoulder, shivering as his hand splays over my belly. "It's pretty."

"It's home." He kisses the soft spot behind my ear. "Part of it, at least."

"Maybe one day, we'll go there together."

"Maybe. The country has serious problems—I don't know if I would take you there now. But one day, if we can, I'd like to show you where I grew up." His tone is measured, thoughtful. "You'd like Moscow in springtime."

CHAPTER 61
Nikolai

I help Isabelle out of the car, careful not to mess with the long skirt of her dress. She's wearing green tonight, a warm, inviting shade that runs counter to the still-cold March weather. I miss the warmth of Brisbane already. We landed in New York earlier today and, after sleeping for a few hours, pulled ourselves together for Grandfather's dinner party.

She fiddles with one of her earrings as she looks up at his building. I just look at her. She's always gorgeous, of course, but something about this outfit is making it particularly difficult for me to think. The careful arrangement of her hair, the diamond jewelry, the elbow-length white gloves and fur stole . . . she looks like a princess. I know we make a good pair; I put as much care into my armor for tonight as she did, but I don't feel like her prince. I don't fit in this world. If anyone does, between the two of us, it's her.

"Ready?" I ask, offering her my arm. "You look stunning."

She fixes my tie, a light green that echoes the shade of her dress, before letting me lead her to the door. "You wouldn't know I was just on a plane for a hellish amount of time?"

"Not at all."

"The bags underneath my eyes look atrocious."

"Bags? What bags?"

She rolls her eyes as we thank the doorman. Just before the elevator, someone calls, "Nikolai!"

Not just someone. Cricket. She's wearing slacks and a neat

white button-down, her short hair slicked back. Large red glasses give her face an owlish look.

I smile at her fondly as she pulls me into a hug. "It's been way too long."

"I've been dying to meet you!" Isabelle says as Cricket hugs her, too.

"You must be Isabelle," she says. She adjusts her glasses, beaming at us both. "I'm Cricket, Nik's favorite cousin."

"My only cousin," I say dryly.

"What about that second cousin in Smolensk? No? Thank God you're here. Now it'll actually be a party."

"It'll be something."

"Well, after you ditched us on Christmas, you pretty much had to come to this one."

Isabelle makes a face. "Whoops."

"Oh, please. I'm glad he was with you." She slides her arm through Isabelle's, walking to the elevators. "I want to hear all about the wedding you're doing for your brother. If I tried to plan one it would be a hot mess, so props to you for being able to do it. I've seen pretty much every episode of *Say Yes to the Dress*, though."

"Oh my gosh, then you have to hear this story about Bex's dress."

By the time we reach the penthouse, Isabelle and Cricket are talking like old friends. I always knew they'd get along, but finally seeing it in action makes me smile, despite the knots in my stomach. I trail behind them as we enter the party. A server appears with a tray of champagne.

My grandfather's dinner parties happen a couple times a year, and they're so exclusive, people have begged to get on the guest list. He pulls out the stops for friends, business partners, and anyone else who seems like an interesting contribution to the conversation.

Over the years, I've met politicians, scientists, authors. I don't recognize anyone famous in this crowd, but I do spot Mom chatting with Grandfather and a few people from Abney Industries. I steer us into the next room before they can wave us over.

I wonder how many of these I'll be expected to attend starting this summer. All of them, probably. Grandfather is always quick to point out that most of the time, business happens outside the boardroom. Cricket plays the networking game better than me; as we walk through the party, she recognizes and says hello to nearly everyone. Isabelle's a natural, too, drawing stare after stare.

I resist the urge to chug my champagne. I almost snatch a fresh flute from a nearby server, but manage to contain myself. That's what my father would do. Actually, he'd be several drinks in before the party even started. As much as I'd like to take the edge off, I hate the thought of acting like him even more.

"Ah, there you are. It's been too long, son."

I turn at the sound of Grandfather's voice. I haven't seen him in person since Christmas—when I ditched him for Isabelle and her family—but he looks the same as ever. Black suit, silver hair combed neatly over his temples, a carefully selected watch. He claps me on the shoulder, then steps back so Mom can hug me. She messes with my hair, tutting, but she's already looking past me to Isabelle.

"Katherine!" Isabelle says, hugging her tightly.

"You look lovely," Mom says. "I noticed you wearing the stole when you walked in."

Isabelle gives me a small smile. "Thank you for letting me borrow it."

"It looks better on you than it ever did on me." She squeezes her arm. "We'll talk all about the wedding soon, okay? I'll fill you in on every detail from the week. You're doing great."

Grandfather holds out his hand for Isabelle to shake. "It's nice to finally meet you. I've met your parents a few times. They do wonderful work with their foundation."

"Thank you, sir," she says. "They speak highly of you."

"Isabelle has a wonderful eye for wedding design," Mom chimes in. "You should see the work she's putting in for her brother's wedding—I'm so glad it's getting an exclusive in *People*."

"*People?*" Grandfather says, his brows lifting. "Why a gossip rag like that?"

"Grandfather," I start.

But Isabelle doesn't even flinch as she says, "My brother has become one of the most recognizable faces in the NFL. If you care about sports, you know that players like him are celebrities with fan bases that want to hear about their lives beyond their play on the field."

If Grandfather notices the slight dig at him, he doesn't show it. He does, however, look at her with something akin to approval. "You seem like a suitable match for Nicholas."

She blinks. "Nicholas?"

"Why don't you tell Mom about Australia?" I say quickly.

"Oh, yes please," Mom says. "How was it?"

Isabelle throws me a look, but she just says, "So much fun. I have pictures, let me show you."

As she scrolls through her phone, Mom and Cricket exclaiming over the pictures, Grandfather pins me with his gaze. "No trouble with the jet, I presume?"

I shake my head. "Thank you again for letting us borrow it."

"It'll become commonplace for you soon enough," he says, gesturing across the room to another group of guests. "I have a development project happening in Dubai right now that I think would be the perfect introduction, once you begin with the company."

"Dubai?"

"You'd only be out there a few months at most."

I shift my weight from one foot to the other. Out of the corner of my eye, I see Isabelle frown. I don't blame her. California would have been one thing; Dubai is another entirely.

"I assumed I would be based here in New York with you."

"This project is fascinating. Come, let me introduce you to a few people."

He marches me across the room for a round of introductions and conversation I can barely follow, not that I'm interested in the first place. I resist more champagne, but ask a server to bring me a seltzer, and sip on it while I watch Isabelle command her side of the room with Mom and Cricket.

When we finally, finally sit down for dinner, she ends up next to me. I sigh with relief as she purses her lips, studying me.

"You okay?" she murmurs. "You looked miserable."

"Just bored." I lean in to catch the scent of her perfume. My hand settles on her leg, squeezing lightly. "I'm not going to Dubai."

"He called you Nicholas."

"I know."

"What the actual—" She stops herself with a smile as a server pours the wine. "*And* he called *People* a gossip rag."

"If I could have your attention for a moment," Grandfather says from the head of the table, standing with his glass in hand. "I'm thrilled that my grandson is with us tonight, and so pleased to say that he's following in my footsteps when he graduates later this year."

He raises his glass to me, and everyone else follows suit. Before I can reply to the toast—saying what, I have no idea—my phone buzzes in my pocket. I can't help but sneak a glance at it.

My pulse quickens as I take in the San Jose area code.

CHAPTER 62

Izzy

I stare at Nikolai's retreating back for half a second before my body kicks into motion. I've only ever seen him take calls like that from his father, and that's the last thing he needs right now. He strides down the hallway, into a part of the penthouse I haven't seen yet.

Before I can follow, Joseph Abney steps into the hallway, saying my name.

I halt, looking over my shoulder. "What?"

"I couldn't help but notice you seemed less than enthusiastic about my announcement." He takes a couple steps forward. A Rolex gleams on his wrist. He has a neutral enough expression on his lean, lined face, but I sense his displeasure. "You come from a good family, Miss Callahan. You understand some of this world."

I cross my arms over my chest as I straighten my spine. I barely held my tongue earlier, especially when it came to Katherine, but clearly Joseph isn't interested in fake pleasantries. Fine. I can work with that.

I inspect my nails. "Meaning what?"

"Meaning you understand the future I'm offering Nikolai."

"So you do know his name."

His lips twitch. Almost a smile, but not quite. "I assume by now that he's told you some things about his father."

I dip my chin in assent.

"Can you imagine what it was like for me to learn what had been happening? To realize how badly I failed her and Nikolai, for years? I can't help what happened, but I can give him a real future."

"By denying him his heritage?"

"That sport isn't his heritage."

"His name is." My voice shakes with emotion. I bite the inside of my cheek, hard. "You know he feels like he can't say no to you, and you're using him. You're guilting him into giving up the future he's supposed to have because you can't let go of the past."

"You seem like a girl who enjoys extravagance," he says, assessing my expensive dress, the diamond jewelry. "If you stay with my grandson, which sort of life would you prefer? Parties and fancy dresses and charity events on his arm, knowing he has real power, or watching him labor over an unforgiving sport he feels he's beholden to by his bastard of a father? He'll try to take care of you either way, to be sure, but we know what would be best for him. For you both."

The words hit me like a slap. "What's best for him is what makes him happy."

"Happiness is an illusion, Isabelle."

"If you truly believe that, then I feel sorry for you." I sweep my hair over my shoulder, smiling even though I want to scowl. "And for the record, even though it's not about the money, NHL players are paid well. Not that I'm planning to rely on him financially, but thanks for your concern."

I nearly turn and leave, but then he adds, "I care about my grandson very much. And I tolerated his hobby for a long time. But it's time for him to grow up. You're a smart girl. I'd appreciate your help in getting him to see that."

I laugh in disbelief. "You know the family I come from, right? Would you have told my father to grow up? My brothers?"

"The situations are not at all the—"

"He doesn't just play hockey." I take a couple steps forward, my heels echoing on the marble floor. I'm glad we're away from the crowd, so I don't have to watch my words. "He's amazing at it, one of the best at his position, but I suppose you wouldn't know that, since you never come to his games. I'll bet you never did, right? You looked at him and saw his father and let that fester for years without doing a thing to help him."

Joseph opens his mouth, but I keep talking, the words pouring out of me in a rush. "I've never seen anyone work harder, and the fact you'd diminish it to a *hobby* tells me everything I need to know about you. Nikolai is going to be a top defenseman in the NHL, and whatever stupid deal you forced him into isn't going to change that. In fact, I'll make sure of it."

"Isabelle—"

"Excuse me," I interrupt, needlessly adjusting my necklace. My *lavish* necklace, which apparently made him think I'm a shallow idiot. "I need to go find my boyfriend and make sure he's okay."

"We're not finished talking."

"Oh, we definitely are." I turn, striding to the doorway at the end of the hallway. Just before I cross it, I look over my shoulder at him. The hard set of his mouth does nothing but embolden me. "And one more thing. Never call him Nicholas again."

It takes me a few minutes of poking around, but eventually, I find Nikolai in what looks like a library. He didn't turn on any of the lamps, but the last light of evening illuminates him as he stands in front of the window overlooking Central Park.

My heels click against the floor. He turns at the sound, shoulders relaxing when he sees that it's me. I take a tentative step forward, but freeze at the look on his face.

"Was it him?"

"No. It was the Sharks."

CHAPTER 63

Nikolai

A win today, and we clinch Hockey East.

When I came to McKee, I imagined this moment. A guaranteed slot in the Frozen Four, a final send-off to hockey. I should be excited, at the very least, about the prospect of winning the division, but with the call from last night still echoing in my mind, I haven't so much as smiled.

I adjust my leather bracelet as I stare into my locker. A new helmet, since my old one got too scuffed up. A fresh home sweater, the purple and white gleaming. I run my hand over the sleeve, swallowing hard.

I asked the Sharks' general manager for the weekend to get everything in order. I didn't outright say no to the offer; when I tried, the words wouldn't leave my mouth. It's Saturday. Monday, I have to tell them that I'm not going.

I've never wanted to do anything less.

Cooper glances at me as he straps his shin guards. "For the record—"

"Don't," I interrupt. "Please."

"Fine." He pulls on his skates with a scowl. "But Izzy is right."

"What, don't you want me around for the rest of the season?" I keep my voice low; I don't want to attract anyone else's attention. Thanks to a tense night with Isabelle, I'm barely rested for the game, much less for more unwanted opinions about my future. I'd break poor Micah's heart if I told him I was turning down a shot at the NHL. "You need me for the playoffs."

"Gentlemen," Coach Ryder says, clapping his hands as he strides into the room. "If I could have your attention for a moment, we have a guest."

I glance at the doorway, and the rest of the room promptly fades away.

My father smiles at me. "Hello, Kolya."

My palms go slick as he says my name. Ryder keeps talking, but I can't hear him over the ringing in my ears. I let out a breath as I back against the bench.

He's here. Really here, in my locker room. He looks a little leaner, a little grayer, but his eyes are the same. My eyes. My hair. My jawline. The older I get, the stronger the resemblance. He shakes Coach Ryder's hand, says something in accented English, and walks across the room to me. Cooper doesn't bother hiding his scowl, but I slip into autopilot, trying for a smile. Anything to keep up appearances, to shove down the white-hot rush of panic racing through me.

I need to breathe.

Of course he came at the end of the season, after all. And of course he chose this game, this shot for my team to win the division. I fucking knew he'd take the opportunity to trade his status as a professional hockey player for a public appearance with me. I know how he operates, I've seen it in action, and yet I let him orchestrate this moment perfectly. I can play the good son, or I can look like an ungrateful asshole in front of my team. He's giving me a choice, but it's not really a choice.

And despite all of that, under the layers of anxiety, my heart stutters at the sight of him.

I steel myself with the memory of bruises on my mother's face. That night on New Year's Eve.

"I know I should have called," he says, still in English, for the benefit of my teammates and coaches, "but I thought you'd appreciate the surprise. I've missed you, son."

He holds out his arms. I hug him mechanically. Even if I told him to leave in Russian, it would cause a scene. I just have to grit my teeth and get through this. Then the game. After that . . . I don't know.

"Thanks, Dad. I've . . . missed you, too."

"I'd wish you luck, but I know you don't need it. I trained you well." He breaks off the hug, looking through my locker. He halts momentarily as he stares at the name on the back of my sweater, but just adds, "The entire team has been impressive all season."

"We're a close group," Cooper says flatly.

Dad glances at him before turning his attention back to my sweater. I can't tell if he's genuinely hurt, or just pissed. Either way, it makes my stomach lurch. He doesn't say anything about the *A* on it, naturally.

"And we have excellent coaching," I add, just to say something.

I nearly tack on that he hasn't been my coach since I was thirteen, but hold my tongue. Everyone is staring. Micah looks like he's about to burst out of his skin with excitement. Mickey's beaming the way he does whenever his mom and stepdad come to our games. Evan's smiling at me with some relief in his expression; he's noticed that no one comes to watch me play.

"Nikolai is very talented," Ryder says. "He's been a welcome addition to the team this season."

"Of course," Dad says, narrowing his eyes. Sizing me up, no doubt comparing me to the eighteen-year-old he remembers from the last time we saw each other in person. College hockey has been good to me, and I know it shows. "I expect a good game from him."

I try to think of a safe reply. One that promises nothing, but doesn't shift his mood. He's in good spirits now; he loves being the center of attention. I remember all too well how easily that can change.

"It's been years," I finally say, in Russian. I smirk. "I think I'm better than you by now."

He laughs at that. I relax minutely, panic ebbing away like low tide. Not gone, but contained, at least for now. As he claps my shoulder, I resist the impulse to flinch.

"Prove it and I'll buy you a drink."

CHAPTER 64

Nikolai

I put on a goddamn show.

Every shift, every cut across the ice, every pass and block and check, comes together like choreography. Hockey demands every brutal second of focus, and I don't blink. My shifts pass in blurs, as natural as breathing, and when I'm on the bench, I just chug water and stare at my skates. Isabelle's here, but I don't look at her. I especially don't look at my father. I'm aware of him—he's sitting in the front row, middle ice, his eyes narrowed as he tracks each play—but I don't give him the satisfaction of even a shared glance.

It's the third period. The guys realized early on that I'm not feeling chatty and leave me at the end of the bench whenever I'm on it. We're up by a goal, but Vermont keeps pressing. Unless we stay sharp on defense, we're not going to get out of this with a win.

There's an opening for me and Evan to get off the ice. We haul ass for the bench. Cooper's gloved hand squeezes my shoulder as we trade places. I switch out my stick for a fresh one, fiddling with the tape. My shoulder, newly sore thanks to a check early in the game, throbs, but I welcome it.

I think I secretly hoped for a moment like this, all along. I had enough pride not to ask for it outright, but I wanted my father to see the player I've become. At eighteen, the last time he saw me in person before tonight, my skills weren't as sharp. There's no doubt now that I'm ready to play professionally. This game is a team effort, of course it is, but I've set the tone tonight. I've carved up

Vermont's offense with the precision of a surgeon, and got the assist on the lone goal earlier. It's been a clean, efficient game. Dad will have something to critique, because he always does, but deep down, I know I'm at the top of my abilities right now.

My next shift comes. We've been stalwart tonight, protecting our side of the ice like an army around a fortress. Cooper falls back while I press forward, tracking as Mickey and the others circle Vermont's net. Cooper takes the shot, but it goes wide; he slams into one of the defenders as they chase it behind the net. A Vermont winger comes up with it, picking up speed as he skates to the other end of the ice.

I check him into the boards, fighting for the puck. I don't mean to, but with my face pressed against the glass, I catch sight of Dad.

He's cheering. Shouting, in fact, pounding his hand against the glass. Most of what he's saying gets lost in the noise of the crowd, but my name—Kolya—rises above everything else.

I nearly lose concentration, unable to process what I'm seeing, but the Vermont player's elbow catches me in the stomach. I grunt through the burst of pain, managing to take possession of the puck. I smack it to Cooper, who gets it out of our zone.

The moment the horn sounds a few minutes later, ending the game, the entire arena erupts into frenzied cheers. Cooper shakes my shoulders, shouting with excitement; he pulls me into the middle of the celebration forming on center ice. I try to focus on my teammates—my Hockey East champion teammates, I realize as my heart leaps—but I can't help risking another look at the seats.

He's already gone. From cheering and shouting to *gone*. Evan pulls me into a hug, and Jean starts a *McFucking McKee* chant as he pounds on my back, yet I'm utterly frozen, unable to stop staring at that empty seat.

"We fucking did it!" Cooper says, hugging me tightly. "Holy shit, Nik, we did it!"

I twist away from him, skating for the bench. We did it. I should be fucking elated. I was elated three seconds ago, watching Dad cheer me on, but now the tight, panicked feeling I had in the locker room comes rushing back. I spin in a circle, looking for Isabelle, but I can't find her in the crowd of cheering fans. I rub my chest. I need to get out of this gear.

An empty seat. I know who he is, I know I shouldn't care, but part of me thought that maybe . . .

"Son?" Ryder asks me as I pass. "You okay?"

"I'm great," I manage to force out. I even smile. "We did it."

He claps me on the shoulder, eyes bright with excitement. "What are you doing? Get back out there, celebrate with the guys."

I take off my helmet, tucking it underneath my arm. Sweat drips down the side of my face. I wipe it away with a trembling hand. "I have to find my dad."

"Of course." His eyes soften. "He'll be so proud of you."

I don't know what to say to that, so I just nod.

"And I'm proud of you, too. You played a hell of a game, just like you have all season." He clears his throat, glancing at the ever-growing celebration on the ice. "I know the Sharks got in touch. If this was your last game with us—I want you to know it was an honor to coach you. You're a special talent, son."

I blink once, hard. "Thank you."

He gives me another pat on the shoulder before letting me pass. I tear through the tunnel.

There he is. Waiting.

Part of me wants to turn around and head back onto the ice. But I'm too curious for that, and anyway, if he doesn't talk to me now, he'll just find a way to make it happen later.

He hasn't cheered for me like that since I was thirteen.

He hasn't hurt me since then, either.

I have to keep my head. Maybe he's changed, but I doubt it. It's not fair that he gave me this talent, this love, without being a good father. I can wish all I want that things were different. That doesn't make it so.

"Kolya!" he says, pulling me into a one-armed hug. He presses a kiss to my sweaty hair. "I definitely owe you that drink."

He half drags me down the hallway, around a corner and away from the crowd. I let him, dazed by the tone of his voice, the display of affection I haven't gotten from him in so long, I'd nearly forgotten what it felt like. As the sounds of the crowd fade into the background, I finally wrestle myself away from him, backing up a few steps.

There's a hint of alcohol on his breath. Of course. It was too much to hope that that part of him had changed.

"No critiques?" I swipe my hand through my hair. My palms were already sweaty, but now my fingertips are going numb. "I expected more feedback."

"You played an excellent game, start to finish."

"I doubt you actually think that."

"You were sharp and focused. You've gotten so clever, Nikolasha. You're exceptional at reading the offense." He laughs in disbelief, shaking his head. "I was so proud to see that—"

"Stop."

"Stop what?"

"Stop—doing that. Praising me."

"You earned it."

"I know I did," I say shortly. I flatten myself against the wall, letting the hallway act as a chasm between us. I shove down the tiny sliver of my soul that wants to embrace him again, and stay there as long as he'll let me. The Russian rolls off my tongue the way it did the other night, with Isabelle. "I know I'm talented. I don't need you to tell me that."

"A father can't tell his son how proud he is of him?"

"Not when I remember how much you liked to point out my mistakes."

"To make you better." He takes a step closer, his gaze soft and beseeching. "To get you to this point. You know that."

"Is that what it was? Encouragement?"

"Of course."

"And what about the rest of it?"

"The rest of what?"

I never should have left the ice. "You know what I mean."

He doesn't take the bait. "I pushed you from the very beginning because I knew you could be great. And I was right. I've been patient for so long, Kolya—but now it's time to come home."

Scratch that. I never should have let it get to this point at all. "Home? I was born here, I've lived here—"

"Your childhood memories are in Russia. It's where you belong. Not here."

"You can't actually believe I think that." My voice hardens. "What about everything else? Or do you think I've forgotten by now?"

"Think about how good it would feel to come home. You've been away for too long."

"This has nothing to do with being Russian," I finally burst out, my voice rising. It echoes in the hallway. "It has everything to do with you. *You're* what I don't want anything to do with, Dad. Not my heritage."

Something ugly crosses his face for the barest moment. Then he wipes it blank, forcing another smile. "Of course I have regrets. If we could just talk about this—"

"Regrets? That's a funny word for abuse." I push away from the wall, getting in his face. After years and years, the anger is finally pouring out. I can hardly think over the rush of blood in my ears. "Here I was thinking maybe you changed, but I see you're still the same piece of shit you were when we left. How many drinks tonight, Dad? How long until you snap?"

A muscle in his jaw twitches. The calculated hint of warmth leaves his eyes.

We're the same height now, I realize with a jolt. He was my age when he met my mother, when he tried his hand at the NHL and failed miserably. Let him take a swing at me. I couldn't fight back properly at thirteen, but I can do it now. It doesn't fucking matter if someone walks in on us brawling, because I'm not going to California.

"Son—"

"Don't call me that. I'm not your son."

He hustles me against the wall, hands fisted in my jersey. A wild lick of panic punches through the anger. The scar on my face twinges with phantom pain. I swipe my tongue over my lip, chest heaving.

Instead of taking a swing, he cups my jaw. Traces my scar. I try to twist away, but he leans his weight into me, pinning me to the wall.

"You might wear a different name on your uniform, but you're still my son. Nikolai Andreyevich Volkov." He says my full name slowly, lovingly. "The name I gave you. The name your mother called beautiful. You can't change blood, Kolya."

I shove my elbow into his chest. "Fuck you."

He grunts with pain, but he just smiles, self-satisfied. "You're my son. You will always be my son."

"Then guess what, Dad? You just saw your *son* play one of his last games. Congratulations."

His grip loosens. "What?"

Before I can twist the knife, even if it's a wound for me as well as him, someone says my name.

Out of the corner of my eye, I see her. My sweater on her body. Glitter on her cheeks. Blue eyes, wide with shock.

Isabelle.

CHAPTER 65

Izzy

For a moment, I just stare at Nikolai and his father. I blink, trying to unscramble the image, but it remains the same. Nik, pinned to the wall by Andrei. Like that night so long ago.

I might be sick. I inch closer, pressing my hand to my mouth. Maybe I should scream. There's security here; they could throw Andrei out. Joseph Abney and his stupid ultimatum is one thing, but this is another entirely.

Andrei hurt his son. The man I love. He can't just walk in here and act like that never happened. I should have pushed Nik harder to cut him out of his life. I should have figured he'd come to a game like this, an important one, and I ran as soon as I saw Nik leave the ice. He doesn't look hurt, but I wouldn't put it past Andrei to try. He had no qualms about hitting his wife and teenage son, after all.

"Sweetheart," Nik says, sounding remarkably calm, "I love you, but you don't need to be here. Go wait for me by the locker room."

"Like hell I don't," I snap. "Get away from him. Right now."

"Ah," Andrei says. "You must be Isabelle."

I press my lips together. He looks so much like Nik, it's unnerving. A vision of my boyfriend, twenty or so years from now.

"He didn't want to say much about you," he continues. "He definitely didn't mention how pretty you are."

His tone is warm, as if he's a normal father who is happy to meet his son's girlfriend. Nik did say he has no trouble being charming when he wants. I swallow, fisting my hands in the sleeves of my borrowed jersey.

Nik shoves his dad, hard, breaking them apart.

"Don't look at her," he says, his voice low.

I take a couple more steps in their direction. They were talking in Russian before, and I didn't understand a word, but I caught when Andrei said Nik's full name. "I know all about what you did to him. I can't believe you'd show your face here."

He ignores Nik, lip curling as he straightens his jacket. "I can imagine why he doesn't want to come home, if you're here. But giving up hockey—"

"This has nothing to do with her," Nik interrupts. His eyes blaze as he steps in front of his father, cutting off his view of me. "I'm not playing for you, and I'm not playing in the NHL, either. Your shitty legacy in the sport will have to die with you."

My heart drops to my stomach. Somehow, when he got the call from the Sharks, I still had hope that he'd change his mind. I tried to talk to him about it last night, but I didn't get anywhere. By the hard tone of his voice, though, he made his decision.

"You can't be serious," Andrei says.

I'm loath to agree with him about anything, but I feel the same way.

"I don't want to be anything like you," Nik says, glancing at me before turning his focus back to his father. "Even if it means giving up hockey. You're right; I can't change blood. But I can change what I do with my life."

This is wrong, all wrong, but I don't interject. Not here, when Andrei could easily twist my words. His eyes flash, but he doesn't make a move for Nik. Maybe my presence is keeping him at bay.

"When you regret that decision, I'll be waiting," he says finally. "You can't escape your destiny forever."

"Have fun waiting the rest of your miserable life, then. Because I'm done."

"Come on, Nik," I say, reaching for the sleeve of his jersey and tugging. "Let's go."

He doesn't move. I tug the sweater again, harder this time.

He spits on the floor in front of his dad's feet. "Get out, or I call security."

I stifle a gasp.

Andrei blinks. Glances at the floor, then Nik's face, and says something in Russian. He looks defeated, as if Nik finally landed a killing blow.

"No," Nik says in English. His voice trembles, but there's strength in it. "But don't come here again. Don't call me, either."

I press my face against Nik's shoulder, listening as Andrei's footsteps echo into the distance. The moment we're alone, I twist around. Nik's eyes are wet. He wipes roughly at his face.

"What did he say?" I whisper.

He gasps softly, screwing his eyes shut. "He asked if I hate him."

I wrap him in the tightest hug I can manage, given the bulk of his gear. He sobs into my shoulder—once—before shaking his head, pulling himself together. He's still flushed with exertion from the game.

He ought to be celebrating right now. Making plans to go to Lark's with the rest of the guys. I doubt he'll be in the mood for that now, but there's no way I'm leaving him alone. If he wants to sit in silence all night, we will. If he wants to cry, he can. He might not hate his father, even after everything, but I recognize that moment for what it was.

A goodbye.

"Go to the locker room." I step back, sniffling, too. "At least get out of your gear. I'll go to your room, okay? I'll be there waiting."

He looks as if he wants to protest, but after a moment, he nods.

"I love you." I stroke his hair lightly, hating how he flinches. "And I'm proud of you."

I watch as he walks to the locker room. People keep congratulating him, and while he stops each time, I breathe out with relief when he finally disappears behind the door.

He's nothing like his father. Nothing. He inherited Andrei's talent, sure, and learned to love the sport because of him, but that's ancient history. One conversation with Andrei was more than enough to know that for certain.

If he actually quits hockey, he'll be ruining his life.

I might not be getting through to him, but there's someone else who can.

I pull out my phone. She should have been here tonight. I asked her at the dinner party if she was going to attend, and she shook her head and said Nik wouldn't want her there. Bullshit.

"Katherine? It's me, Izzy." I look in the direction of the locker room. My heart quickens. "We need to talk about Nikolai."

CHAPTER 66

Nikolai

Isabelle is waiting, just like she said she would, when I arrive at the dorm.

I'm exhausted, completely and utterly. The guys jumped on me as soon as I entered the locker room, and protested when I said I didn't feel up to drinks, but a look from Cooper silenced them. He cornered me before I left, made sure I was going to be with Isabelle.

I don't deserve his friendship, and I definitely don't deserve Isabelle's love. Tonight finally made that impossible to ignore. I might've told Dad to get out of my life—for real this time—but he still won, in a way.

Blood is blood. The moment I looked into my father's eyes and realized how deeply I wanted to take a swing, it all clicked into place. I'm no different from him. I might give up hockey, I might try to keep a tight lid on my emotions, but that doesn't change a damn thing about who I am at my core.

Isabelle rises from the bed. Without a word, she wraps me into a hug. I don't lift my arms; they feel like bricks. She sniffles as she steps back, blinking her red-rimmed eyes.

"Are you okay?"

"Fine."

"That was a lot."

I rip off my jacket and toss it on the desk chair. Push up the sleeves of my sweater. Isabelle fusses with my hair. I gently pull her hands away, stepping around her to sit on the bed. I groan, pressing the heels of my hands into my eyes.

In the locker room, and in the car, I kept the panic at bay. I breathed through my nose. I counted to ten. All that bullshit. Now, though, alone with Isabelle, the too-tight, panicky sensations rush to the surface. It's as if someone welded iron around my torso. I rub my sternum as she curls next to me.

Normally, her presence helps calm me. Right now, I feel like one wrong move—from either of us—could set me ablaze.

"Breathe," she murmurs as her hand squeezes my knee.

I'm sure she means it to be reassuring, but I flinch away from her. I have no idea where my father slunk off to, but his words won't stop echoing in my mind.

You can't change blood, Kolya.

I stand, pacing the small room. Isabelle says my name. My fingers tingle. I curl and uncurl them, but they're on the verge of going numb.

You will always be my son.

My stomach lurches.

Panic and rage, entwined in a violent embrace. I pushed, and he showed his true colors. Whatever hope I had that he was different now, that he had really changed, faded the moment I smelled the vodka on his breath. Saying goodbye was the hardest thing I've ever done. Even harder than protecting my mother, finally, after years of being silent. And why couldn't I have said it? Why couldn't I have told him that I hate him, to complete the break between us that started the moment he lifted his hand in a fist?

"It's going to be okay," Isabelle says. She doesn't leave the bed, but she watches as I pace like a caged animal. "But Nik—you have to know that you don't have to quit hockey. No one believes you're anything like him."

"You don't understand."

"I think I do." She catches me as I pass the bed. She must have washed her face, because there's no glitter on her petal-soft cheeks. "Look, if you're not going to listen to me, at least listen to your mom."

I laugh shortly. "What?"

"I called her. Told her about the offer to join the Sharks. And . . . and your panic attacks."

I wrench myself away. "You did what?"

"You never really talked to her about your dad. I think if you did, it would help you. Really help you."

"You went behind my back to talk to my mother."

"Don't say it like that." She twists her hands in her sweater. My hockey jersey, the gift I gave her. I'm suddenly aware of the leather bracelet on my wrist. It feels tighter than usual. Constrictive. "I'm just—I'm trying to help you not ruin your life."

"I'm not ruining my life."

"You *are*." Her eyes look as fierce as they did on New Year's, when I couldn't keep the panic at bay and she saw my breakdown from start to finish. "And I don't care if you're mad at me for saying that, because it's the truth. You don't have to prove to anyone that you're not like your dad. We already know. All of us, your mom included."

"You have no idea what my mother thinks. There's a reason we haven't— I can't believe you would . . ." I trail off, shaking my head. I rub my chest again; it's getting harder and harder to breathe. If I'm not careful, I'm going to puke.

Isabelle reaches for my arm, but I shake her off. I can't. I can't do this.

"Nik," she pleads. "I'm trying to help. You encourage me, you remind me my passions are important—why won't you do that for yourself?"

I struggle to keep down the rush of emotion, but it's building. It's building, and I can't fucking stop it. I'm spinning out, and like hell am I going to let Isabelle be collateral. Goodbye to my father, goodbye to hockey—she doesn't understand that I have to do this, I *have to*—

"You need to go." I get as far away as I can in the small room, clenching my trembling fists and pressing them against my stomach. My shoulder aches, my chest aches, my goddamn soul aches. Isabelle blinks, her expression shuttering.

I never should have dragged her into this.

She pulls herself together. "What are you talking about?"

"Go." My voice breaks on the word. It's a struggle to force anything out, much less speak in English. "I don't—I can't—"

She takes a couple steps in my direction. "I don't want to leave you alone right now."

"And I don't want to hurt you!"

She freezes. "What? You'd never do that."

My heart lurches as I imagine it. I feel like a monster, hell-bent on destruction. This close to cracking open. I shake my head shortly, turning away from her.

She rests her hand against my back, in between my shoulder blades. "Nik—"

"I mean it." My voice comes out as a snarl as I twist around. I can't control anything right now. Not my voice, not my breathing, not my body. I'm burning from the inside out, and if Isabelle gets caught in the inferno . . . "Just go. Now."

"You'd never hurt me," she says stubbornly.

"I don't trust—"

"I trust you," she interrupts, her voice gaining steam. "What about in bed? You make it hurt, but you're not hurting me."

"It's not the same as this." Never the same, because I'm not panicking when we're in bed. This is the furthest thing from that. It's skirting right on the edge of the rage I can't shake. The inheritance from my father that I'll never be able to distance myself from, no matter what I tell myself.

"Why not? You trust yourself then, trust yourself now. You're not a violent person. You're not your father. I promise."

"Isabelle."

"I know the man I fell in love with," she whispers. A tear slips down her cheek.

"Please, solnishko. If I did something I couldn't take back, I'd never forgive myself. Never."

She flinches at my harsh tone. I nearly heave. I turn to the wall again.

Such a coward. A selfish fucking coward.

But if she goes, I'm protecting her.

"Fine," she says, her breath catching on the word. "But talk to your goddamn mother."

Finally, finally, I hear her leave.

I grab the nearest object—a paperweight with a hockey puck in the middle—and hurl it across the room.

CHAPTER 67

Nikolai

I'm not sure how much time passes.

After keeping such a tight lid on myself for so long, it's not hard to find other things to break. Glass sparkles on the floor in the moonlight, crunching underneath my boots as I pace. My mouth tastes sour; I heaved into my wastebasket when I saw the shattered paperweight. I sweat through my clothes long ago, and chewed the inside of my cheek long enough to make it bleed.

Still, I pace. I pace and try to breathe.

At least I'm alone. At least the nightmares running through my mind aren't reality.

I'll be alone forever if it means not hurting her.

Someone knocks on the door. I tense, imagining Isabelle, but it's my mother's voice that I hear.

"Nika?" she says softly. "Are you in there?"

Another old, well-loved nickname. I stare at the door, ignoring the throbbing in my shoulder.

This is what Isabelle asked of me. The last thing before I pushed her away. I might've fucked everything up, but I can do this for her.

I pull the door open.

Mom's gaze sweeps over me. I open my mouth, unsure what excuse to muster up, but before I can speak, she yanks me into a hug.

"You're okay." She pushes my hair away from my forehead, inspecting me. "Thank God you're okay."

I'm frozen. She hasn't hugged me like this in what feels like forever. I'm not sure what's more surprising: the embrace, or the fact she's here at all.

She peers around me, taking in the glass, the trashed room. "Where's Izzy?"

I clear my throat; my voice is rusty. "Not here."

"Are you still panicking?" She leads me to the bed and sets me on the edge, fretting needlessly with the collar of my shirt. "Was this the first time, or has it happened before?"

I just stare as she sits next to me. She's usually so put together, but right now, she isn't wearing makeup, and she's in leggings and a pullover sweatshirt.

She turns on my bedside lamp, giving the room a yellowy glow. "Should we do a breathing exercise together?"

"I'm fine," I say automatically. "You didn't have to drive all the way here."

"I left the moment Izzy called."

My throat constricts as I remember the look on her face when I told her to leave. The way she jumped when my voice got loud. My mind refuses to shut off that particular memory.

At least I didn't hurt her. I could feel myself shaking apart, utterly out of control. I'd never been so terrified—not for myself, but for her. If she refused to leave, I don't know what would have happened.

"Why?"

Something crosses her face, too fast for me to parse. "Is this new, Nika? How long has it been going on?"

"You haven't called me that in ages."

"It's one of many things I haven't done in way too long."

"A long time," I finally say. I'm too exhausted to filter myself. "Sometimes pretty bad. This was—he was here, Mom."

"I know." She reaches for my hand, squeezing tightly. "I know, honey, Izzy told me everything. I hate to see you like this. He triggers them?"

I manage a short nod. The tightness in my chest hasn't fully gone away, even if I can breathe normally again. Now that I have some distance, I feel like a fool. A fool for thinking—hoping— that Dad might've changed. A fool for letting myself get swept up in him, even to shove him away. A fucking fool and a bad son and *his* son, on the edge of shaking to pieces.

She shuts her eyes for a long moment. When she opens them, they're glassy. "The same thing used to happen to me."

SHE SENDS ME to shower and change into clean clothes before she says another word. When I return, she's sweeping up the glass with a broom. I step around the pile carefully, taking in the sight of my room. She changed the wastebasket, made my bed, and put the hockey puck from the paperweight back on my desk.

"Where did you get the broom?"

"I found it in the hall closet." She sets it aside, blowing the hair out of her face. "Did the shower help? They always helped me."

I sit on the bed. "You never told me you had panic attacks."

"Have some water, that'll help, too." She holds out my water bottle as she sits in my desk chair.

At my look, she keeps talking. "I didn't want to worry you. But I struggled with them for a long time." She swallows, looking at her lap. "I remember I had one once . . . God, it must have been a couple weeks after we came back to New York. It was at one of your first hockey games here. I don't remember what triggered it. Maybe the rink, or—"

"Me."

Her head jerks up. "What?"

My heart sinks to my stomach. I always assumed she left that game just because the sight of me playing hockey reminded her of Dad. If I actually caused a panic attack, that's even worse. "I know you don't like me playing hockey."

She's quiet as she fiddles with the gold bangle on her slim wrist. "Is that what you really think?"

"It's Dad's thing."

"I did watch you play for a long time, you know." She shakes her head, smiling wryly. "You probably don't remember half of it."

"I remember you arguing with Dad about training."

"I wanted you to have a normal childhood. And I stand by that. Andryusha was so insistent, though. He didn't just want you to play hockey. He wanted you to be the best."

I startle at the sound of my dad's nickname.

"Was I always into it? When I was little, I mean?"

"Of course."

"But you don't like it. It . . . it reminds you of Dad. Like when you look at me."

The back of my neck burns at the admission. I've never said it to her before, but it's not hard to tell that when she looks at me, she sees my father. Especially now that I'm the same age as he was when they met. I'm his son, through and through. No one would know that better than her.

"What?"

"You always . . ." Fuck it. If I'd opened up sooner, maybe I wouldn't be in this mess with Isabelle. She told Mom about my panic attacks; there's not much else to hide. "When you look at me, you . . . you flinch. Like you're looking at Dad and then remember it's me. Am I really that much like him? Do I bring up those memories? Make you panic?"

"No." A tear runs down her cheek. She wipes it away impatiently. "I remember things, yes. But not because you remind me of him. Nika, I look at you and remember how I failed you."

I shake my head. "I should have protected you. He terrified you. If I had just said something, then maybe—"

"No, sweetheart. That wasn't your responsibility." Her tone is soft, but firm. "I was your parent just as much as him."

"But—"

"I don't regret meeting your father," she interrupts. "I don't regret it, because he gave me you. But I do regret not leaving sooner. I regret letting him control us for as long as he did. I tried to keep it behind closed doors, especially since he left you alone physically, but I should have known that eventually, he would . . . I'm so sorry." She breathes wetly, blinking back more tears. "And I'm sorry I didn't know you've been struggling, either. I know how much it hurts."

Bone-deep exhaustion settles over me. When we left, she retreated into herself, and Grandfather took me under his wing. This whole time, I thought she couldn't stand to look at me because I was lingering proof of what she lived through, when really, she was panicking, too. Drowning in her own memories.

But when she panics, I'll bet she doesn't worry about hurting anyone.

"I can tell you're thinking of something." She clears her throat. "Just tell me. Whatever it is."

"Something's wrong with me." I twist my fingers together, wincing at the pain in my knuckles. The night has been such a blur, I can't remember how I bruised them. If it was the game or my meltdown.

"Nothing is wrong with you." She squeezes my shoulder. I tamp down my wince. "Nothing, Nika."

"No, Mom. I mean it. I have these nightmares." I ease away. "In them, I'm him, and I'm . . . I'm hurting people. You. Isabelle." My chest twinges sharply, as if someone hooked it with a fishing line. "I felt out of control, with her. I thought I might do something bad."

The admission hangs in the air, like the night on the beach when I told Isabelle about my past. It's as if saying it aloud purges something from my body, my soul.

Mom lurches forward, pulling me into a tight hug. I breathe into her shoulder, blinking as the intensity of her embrace sinks in. When she lets go, tears streak down her face. She brushes them aside impatiently, then fusses with the collar of my shirt.

"I tried to give you space to process things on your own," she whispers thickly. "We all thought that would be best. I should have known you needed more support."

"I don't want to be like him."

"You're nothing like him."

"I am." I squeeze my eyes shut, trying to calm down. "I'm just as angry, and there's hockey—"

"Don't let yourself spiral," she says firmly. "Let's take this one step at a time."

"Even after everything—I miss him, Mom. He asked me if I hate him, and I couldn't say it. I couldn't, even though I should have. I should have quit hockey years ago, too. It's his, it's always been his."

"Deep breaths." She looks into my eyes, her gaze steady. Calm. "I don't hate him either."

"You don't?"

"I don't hate him. I don't feel much of anything when it comes to him. But honestly, Nika—I'm glad you don't either. No son should feel that way about his father. You're allowed to be angry. You're allowed to have complicated feelings. You're even allowed to miss him." She laughs, self-deprecating. "Lord knows my feelings were complicated enough. Feeling these things, feeling out of control—that doesn't mean you're like him. It doesn't mean you're going to go through with whatever you're thinking, even if it feels impossible to break the pattern."

"I don't trust myself not to be like him."

"Is this really why you don't want to take the contract?"

I give a short nod.

"Hockey doesn't belong to him."

"It's his dream."

"So all the work you put into hockey in high school, in college—it was for his dream?" When I don't reply right away, she presses further. "You're not your father. You never have been, and you never will be."

I let the words wash over me.

"You're you and no one else," she adds. She reaches out, then hesitates with her fingertips an inch from my face. I nod once, tightly. She cradles my cheek, brushing against my scar. "And I love you. More than anything in the world."

I clear my throat as tears prick my eyes. "So it's not . . . you're not going to be disappointed . . ."

"The only way I'll be disappointed is if you don't sign that contract."

Somehow, after all of this, I still didn't expect her to actually want me to go through with it.

"I spent so much time rebuilding my life, my whole sense of self, after the divorce, that I didn't question as much as I should have. I didn't make sure you were okay. That's my failure. My own guilt just made things worse."

"Mom, I don't blame you. You deserved to be happy."

"And so do you. What do you want, Nikolai? You, not Andrei or anyone else. What do you want to do with your life?"

"I want to play hockey." There's no question, no debate. At my core, it's what I want. It's what I've always wanted.

She nods. "Good. Then you're going to play hockey."

"Grandfather will hate it."

"I never should have let him talk you into quitting." I'm taken aback by the fire in her voice. "If I'd known why you agreed . . . I love him, but he can be such an asshole sometimes."

Despite myself, I laugh. "I don't think I've ever heard you curse."

"There's a lot we need to catch up on," she says, laughing, too. Her eyes soften as she nods, almost to herself. "Let me handle your grandfather. On Monday, you're getting on that plane to California."

Finally, I nod. "Okay."

"And Nika—I want you to go to therapy."

"Isabelle has been saying that."

"She's a smart woman." She sits next to me, tucking me against her side. I lean my head on her shoulder, torn between exhaustion and the tendril of anxiety that ignited at the mention of therapy. "It's scary at first. And it's hard work. But it helps."

Talking to Isabelle about my past. Cooper. Now my mother. It's taken something from me each time, but I can't deny that I've felt lighter after.

"I don't know."

"Keeping it locked inside just makes it worse." She rubs my back. "You need to face what you're feeling."

"Does it really get better?"

I feel stupid for asking it, but she just hums thoughtfully. "It does. It's not always linear, but over time . . . it does."

Something shifts in my heart. The last piece of resistance, falling away. I'm terrified to start, but I'm more terrified of staying this way forever, constantly on edge, constantly worried I'll fuck everything up irreparably. Unable to love hockey the way I want, unable to love *Isabelle* the way I want.

I can't live like this anymore, but I can try to change. For her. For myself.

For us, and the future I imagined in Brisbane.

CHAPTER 68

Izzy

H eads up, Iz!" Shona shouts.

I look up from my phone in time to smack away the volleyball rocketing in my direction. Shona jogs over, a sheepish expression on her face. "Sorry, sorry. You okay?"

I just nod. Technically, I'm fine. I spent the day in class, and now I'm at Moorbridge High's volleyball club, and later this evening, I have to finalize the catering arrangements for the wedding. A totally normal Monday, if not for the fact that I haven't spoken to my boyfriend since Saturday night. Since his father crashed into our lives. Since I left him alone, if only to keep things from falling apart beyond repair.

I felt sick the moment I shut his door. I knew he wouldn't hurt me; the thought didn't even cross my mind. But I kept envisioning his panicked eyes and the strung-out tension in his voice, and it took all my willpower not to cry until I left the building.

It's only been a day, but it feels like a year. When I called Katherine, I played the last card I had. She went to see him; she called to tell me so yesterday, but Nik hasn't reached out.

I hope he's packing for San Jose. If he isn't, after all this, I don't know what I'll do.

Shona tosses her braids over her shoulder, dribbling the volleyball. "Come on, leave it for a few minutes."

"He might text."

"Turn up the volume."

"Ugh, fine." I adjust my ponytail as I jog onto the court after her. "What are you doing?"

"I vote contact drill," Victoria says, jumping in place on the other side of the net.

"You always want to do that."

"Because it's fun." She turns to the high schoolers milling around; we've been getting a bigger crowd every session. "Want to play against us? See who can keep the rally going the longest?"

Joana waves, giving me a braces-filled smile. I wave back, trying to return her expression. I glance at the bench, where my phone rests on top of my bag. I don't care if I'm trying to give Nik space. I don't care if he's mad that I called his mom. If he doesn't get in touch by the end of the day, I'm marching to his room and banging on the door until he opens it.

Ellie turns on a playlist while Victoria sets up the game. Me, her, and Shona on one side, Joana and two of her friends on the other. I serve—a perfect floater that gives Joana plenty of time to react—and the rally gets underway. First, we get to ten touches. Then fifteen. At twenty, we're all in stitches at the way Ellie and the rest of the club members are cheering us on. The girls rotate, and we start afresh. It takes most of my concentration, and finally I sink into the game.

Then my phone starts ringing.

The volleyball nearly hits me in the head again as I dash across the court.

I almost sink to my knees with relief when I see Nik's name. Victoria catches my eye, giving me a reassuring nod, as I slip out of the gym. She told me about what we missed at Lark's on Saturday night—including all of them nearly getting kicked out when Jean started dancing on a table—and I couldn't help spilling the story to her. Nik should have been there, celebrating with his teammates, after all.

"Isabelle?"

I shut my eyes as I lean against a trophy case. It's only been a day, but I missed the sound of his voice.

"Hey. How are you doing?"

"Better." He sounds exhausted. "We need to talk."

My heart speeds up. "Can I come over? Or I can meet you at the house."

"I'm actually . . . on my way to the airport."

I don't say anything for a minute. I don't even think anything would come out of my mouth if I tried. I let out a shaky breath, finally, tears pricking my eyes as I speak. "That better be because you're getting on a plane to San Jose."

"You were right, sunshine. About all of it."

"I'm sorry I called Katherine, but I was so worried, and—"

"I don't blame you." He clears his throat. "Things can't go on like this forever."

"Yes," I say with relief. I didn't regret calling Katherine to tell her how he's been struggling, but it was a risk. Thank God it led somewhere good. Just like when he talked to my brothers. I press my hand to my tattoo, hidden underneath my tank top. "We can work on it. I can't come to San Jose today, but maybe this weekend? Do you know where you're staying yet? What's the game schedule?"

"I don't think that would be a good idea."

"What do you mean?"

"I need to sort out my shit."

"I know. We can figure out next steps this weekend. What did Katherine say?"

He's quiet for a moment. "No, sweetheart. I mean that *I* need to. I don't trust myself right now. I can't be with you if I'm constantly worried I'm going to do something I'd regret."

"Nik. No." I blink, freeing a few tears. I wish he were here, if only so I could shake some sense into him. I'll bet that's why he called me from the car instead of saying goodbye in person.

Goodbye.

"If you try to break up with me because you're scared, I'll end you."

For some reason, that makes him laugh. "There's my girl."

"I'm serious."

"We're not breaking up," he says, a bit of a growl in his voice. "Definitely not. But I can't pretend I don't need help. I can't live like this anymore, shoving everything down and waiting for it to explode."

"So let me help you."

"I can't put that responsibility on you. I need to sort myself out, and I can't expect you to do that for me. I don't want to."

"Why? I'm not enough?"

My voice cracks at the admission, the vocalization of the thought that's been echoing in my mind since the moment I left his room. Not enough. Never enough. I gave him everything, and he's slipping through my fingers anyway.

"That's not what I mean."

"Then what do you mean?" I sniffle, pressing the heel of my hand against my nose. I shouldn't make it about me, I know that, but I can't help the jumbled feelings rising to the surface. California is one thing. Leaving me—even if he says it's not forever—is another. "You know I trust you, right? I meant what I said. You'd never hurt me like that."

"I need help, Isabelle. The professional kind." He takes a breath, as if readying himself. "If I'm going to be a good partner for you—a man you can spend your life with—I need to learn how to manage my . . . my panic disorder. My past. And if I don't have the distance, the space to reflect, I don't know if I'll really change."

"So you'd rather be alone than with me."

"Not forever."

I laugh derisively. "Sure."

"I'm doing it because I love you," he says, voice thick with emotion. Quiet, intense. Just like him. "I'm doing it for us."

I know him. I know when he's made a decision, and I know how steadfast he can be when he sets his mind to something. I should be happy right now. This is what I've wanted for him. But he feels so far away, and he hasn't even left New York yet.

"If you do this, you have to promise you're coming back." My voice breaks. "You have to promise."

"I'm coming back. This isn't goodbye."

I hear it, but I hate it. I hate it so much I want to scream.

"When you do, it has to be for real." I wipe roughly at my tears. Distantly, I notice the sounds of the gym. The world going on around us, as if this moment isn't delicate and breakable and right on the edge of shattering. "You have to be coming home to me, Kolya. Not for now, not for a little while. It needs to be forever."

Even over the phone, his voice is velvet soft. Russian first, then English. "I promise, solnishko."

Our love has felt like springtime. Warmth chasing away shadows, light spilling into the open. I imagined sun-drenched days ahead, but the frost hasn't left the ground. The flowers haven't bloomed. I've never wished for his embrace more than right now. I'd hold on so tightly, he couldn't pry me away.

But instead, I have to trust for both of us until he trusts himself.

CHAPTER 69
Nikolai

Another new team. Another facility tour. Only instead of a college rink, this one is SAP Center. And instead of a college team, it's the San Jose Sharks.

The NHL. The National Hockey League.

Despite everything—despite leaving half of my heart three thousand miles away—I can't deny the enormity of this moment. When I was little, I'd pretend I was Zdeno Chára, Ryan McDonagh, Pavel Datsyuk. I'd close my eyes on the bench and daydream about playing in the last period of a playoff game. Now I'm walking around as a rookie, about to be thrown into a late-season push for the postseason.

I trail after Hal, my new head coach. He's been talking a mile a minute to get me up to speed before tonight's game. His assistant offered to give me the tour instead, but he insisted. He hasn't outright said it, but it sounds like he had been angling to get me on the team for a while.

"Let me show you the stage," he says, clapping me on the back on the way out of the locker room. "I love when every seat is full, but there's something about when it's quiet."

"It's the fresh ice."

He snaps his fingers. "I think we're going to get along, kid."

We walk down the tunnel. He's right, the moment I actually see the ice from this perspective, I feel weak in the knees. Putting on the Sharks jersey at the press conference yesterday was nice, but this is better. Way better.

I just wish that Isabelle was by my side.

After Mom helped me pack—and told Grandfather in no un-certain terms that I was signing the contract—I nearly went to Isabelle's place. It took all of my self-control to head straight to the airport instead. I feel the distance like a physical ache behind my ribs. I know she's upset, but if we have a shot in hell at mak-ing it, I need to get my head on straight. I love her too much to be selfish about this.

When I've started to untangle the knots in my head and my heart, then I'll come home to her.

Forever, like I promised.

"Kid?" Hal says, giving my back another thump. "You listen-ing?"

I blink. "Sorry, what?"

"Think you can handle this? It'll be fast. The contact will be harder."

I just nod. It's not my job that I'm worried about. I've been ready for this for months. It might take some getting used to, but if there's one thing I know how to do, it's play hockey.

I wonder if Dad will find a way to watch it. If he's back in St. Petersburg by now.

I'd be lying if I said I wasn't curious, if I didn't care—but tonight, I won't be playing for him. I'm playing for my old team-mates and coaches at UMass. My McKee teammates. Coach Ry-der. Cooper.

Isabelle most of all.

"YOU DON'T HAVE to stay, you know," I tell Cricket as she follows me down the sidewalk. I pull open the door to the building, ig-noring the lurch of my stomach. "I thought you wanted to check out the Winchester Mystery House."

"One, we're going there together." She holds the door open

for an older person with a walker before catching up to me. Her glasses are a cheery pink today, which keeps reminding me of the whirlwind of pink that follows Isabelle around. "Two, therapy is exhausting, so it never hurts to have someone else to drive you home. And three, when I'm in Dubai for six months, it'll be a little hard to hang out."

I stop on the threshold of the therapist's office. "Dubai?"

"Whenever I want to strangle the old man, I'll just curse him out in Russian." She beams as the receptionist whips up her head. "Maybe I can bully him into an early retirement."

I sign in with the receptionist. "Ignore her. She doesn't know how to behave in public."

"Ooh, Nik, they have *Coastal Living*. You know I love the Nancy Meyers aesthetic."

I drop into the seat next to her. I have to admit that it's nice to have her here with me. When I made the appointment, I nearly called the office back right away to cancel. However necessary, nothing sounds more uncomfortable than telling a stranger about my past.

"Maybe getting a dog would be enough. That might heal me."

"No. Shush." Cricket pulls my hands away from my face. "Nik, this is a good thing. A really good thing."

"Nikolai?" The receptionist walks around the desk. "I can bring you to Dr. Reyes now."

My cousin gives me an uncharacteristically serious look as I stand. "I'll be here waiting. You got this."

When I asked the team's performance coach for therapist recommendations, it took all of my grit to clarify that I was looking for someone who specialized in childhood trauma. Domestic abuse. It was the first time I said it aloud that way—that ugly phrase—but she just nodded once and gave me Dr. Reyes's name.

I wipe my palms on my jeans as the receptionist shows me to the right door.

It's just one session. One session to try it, to hopefully set me down a path that will make it possible to move on with my life. Playing in actual NHL games the past week and a half has been hard, but this is ten times harder.

This is for me and for Isabelle and I can do it.

I knock on the door.

A woman my mother's age opens it. "Hi, Nikolai. Come in and make yourself comfortable, okay?"

My heart has started to sprint, but something about her welcoming smile helps me walk the last few steps into the room. She gestures for me to sit on a love seat. I settle on it stiffly, taking in the room. It's done up in shades of blue and gray. There's a framed photograph on her desk of her at a Sharks game, wearing a home sweater and cheering.

I fiddle with my leather bracelet. Will myself to relax.

"It's nice to meet you." She sits across from me, clasping her hands together. "Let's talk a little about therapy."

CHAPTER 70
Izzy

I park my car in the driveway, silencing Taylor Swift midsong.

For the past two weeks, I've done nothing but throw myself into work and school. Finalizing plans for the wedding, going to volleyball, writing papers—anything to keep from thinking about Nikolai too hard. He asked for space, and I'm trusting him with that space, but that doesn't stop reminders of him from peppering my life like ghosts. A doodle he slipped into my planner. Rift headlining my "on repeat" playlist. The clothes he left behind in my room, the koala stuffies on my bed. The other day in class, I pulled out a pen he lent me and felt heartache so acute, I couldn't listen to a thing my professor said.

The distance is one thing. I could take the distance happily, if only we were talking. But it's been two weeks since we spoke. Two weeks since we so much as texted. If Katherine wasn't updating me, I don't know what I'd do.

I sit in my car for a long time before finally dragging myself into the house. I have homework to catch up on. A couple small wedding-related fires to put out. I owe Mia a phone call.

All of that flees my mind the moment I see what's on the television.

I know that Nik is playing every game—and doing well, according to Cooper—but I haven't been able to bring myself to watch any of them.

Tears well in my eyes as I stare at the broadcast. I drop my bag, shuffling to the couch. Cooper's here, of course, and Penny, but so are Evan, Xander, and Mickey. I bite my lip, so the tears don't spill over.

The camera pans to the Sharks bench. I press my fist to my mouth.

He looks good in teal. Really good.

"Shit," Cooper says. "I'm sorry, Iz. I thought you had a game."

"Just a practice." I wipe quickly at my eyes. "How . . . how's it going?"

"He scored his first goal," Penny says, untangling herself from Cooper and hurrying around the couch to me. "From the blue line."

"It was fucking awesome," Mickey says eagerly. He sees the expression on my face and clears his throat. "Uh, sorry."

I lean my head on Penny's shoulder as she strokes my hair. I haven't spoken much about this break that Nik and I are on, but it's not a secret. He left, and I haven't visited, even for a weekend.

"I got the chocolate chip cookies you like from Trader Joe's today."

"Thanks." I straighten my shoulders. "I'm fine. I just hadn't seen him in his new uniform."

"It's a good look on him." She gives me a half smile. "Want to watch some of it with us? They're winning."

I draw my legs to my chest as I settle into the armchair, popping a cookie into my mouth. Maybe I'll feel closer to him if I watch him play. Maybe some of the hurt that I wish I wasn't feeling will fade away.

"Do you think they're making it in?" Evan asks Cooper.

Cooper's answer, whatever it is, fades into the background as the camera pans away from the game, showing the bench again. A bunch of guys I don't recognize, and then Nik at the end, hair flopping over his eyes. He works his mouth guard with his jaw as one of the coaches shows him something on a tablet.

He takes off his glove to point at something on the screen, and my heart stops.

He's wearing the bracelet I gave him.

I can't breathe. I get up, somehow, and manage to run upstairs without succumbing to the emotions beating a painful rhythm in my chest. I put my hand over my mouth, trying to catch my breath without sobbing.

My bracelet, underneath his glove, just like it had been the night everything came crashing down. Somehow, I didn't expect to see it on him. Not like that, so casual, a mark of me from three thousand miles away.

It takes me a moment to notice Cooper standing a couple feet away.

I wrap my arms around myself, clearing my throat. "What?"

"You should be really proud of yourself." He steps closer. His eyes are soft, too soft, with kindness. I don't want to see it right now. "You gave him the push to live his dream, Izzy. That's huge."

I stare at my feet. "I am proud of him."

"You should be."

"He deserves this so much." I risk a look at my brother, hating how I can't stop my runaway thoughts. "But what if . . ."

"What?"

I press my lips together, shaking my head. He might not trust himself yet, not with his emotions or with me, but I trust him. Worrying myself to distraction about impossibilities won't help.

"You can tell me."

"What if he doesn't . . . come back? What if he realizes he likes his new life better without me in it?"

The words leave me before I can tamp them down. After he called me on the way to the airport, I felt so certain that I'd see him again, but even the sight of that bracelet on his wrist isn't enough to quell the thunderstorm in my heart. He might slip out of my life the way he did the first time, only now, it would be so much worse.

I used to tell myself that I could handle him becoming a stranger. I know better now. The memories run so deep, I wouldn't recover.

"Oh, Izzy," Penny says as she reaches the top of the stairs.

"That's not going to happen," Cooper says firmly.

"You can't know that."

"Actually, I can." He tugs me into a hug. "He's doing this for you. He told me so."

"You spoke to him?"

"Called him after his first game."

I pull away, searching my brother's eyes. "How did he seem?"

"Like he got his ass kicked." There's amusement in his voice, and a hint of envy. "But good, too. He had an appointment with a therapist."

"Katherine told me he found a good one."

"Which means he's working on himself," Penny says.

"I know." I wipe my eyes again. I've locked these thoughts away for a fortnight, throwing myself into distractions. Now I can't keep the emotions at bay. I adore him, and I understand why he did what he did, but if he doesn't come back, if he realizes I don't fit into his new future . . .

It'll still be worth it. If I lose him because of this, but he has his hockey career, then I'll suck it up and be grateful. I'll put on a smile whenever I see him play, because I'll know he's doing what he loves, and healing in the process.

"He's one of my best friends now, you know." Cooper makes a face. "Still not sure how that happened."

"Blame my dad," Penny says wryly.

"You trust Nik, right?" He waits for me to nod before continuing. "I trust him, too. And I'm glad he's with you."

"He cares about you so much," Penny adds. "I could tell that the moment he came to visit you in the hospital."

I open the door to my bedroom, newly exhausted. I notice the fresh vase of flowers on my desk—Penny gives me a quick hug and tells me to enjoy them, before she and Cooper give me privacy—but my attention lingers on Nik's leather jacket, thrown over the back of my desk chair. He left it behind, and I haven't had the heart to put it in my closet.

I shut the door and slip on the jacket. I press my nose to the collar and breathe. It still smells like him, clean and masculine and slightly spiced.

I shove my hands into the pockets as I sink onto the end of my bed. My fingers brush a piece of paper.

It's a photograph—tiny, folded up twice. I smooth it out.

My eyes sting as I stare at it. It's of me at the High Line, a purple coneflower tucked behind my ear. I'm beaming, arms flung out, while the sunset fills the sky behind me. The High Line. Nik and I went there what feels like ages ago. I remember him taking the picture. He said he'd delete it, but I guess he liked it enough to print it.

I flip the photograph over. The messy scrawl looping over the back is in Russian. The Cyrillic letters are still foreign to me, even though I've started to look into Russian lessons, but after a few painstaking minutes with Google Translate, I manage to work out a translation.

мой любимый

My favorite.

CHAPTER 71

Nikolai

"What do you think about the pink?" I ask Tempest, who wags her tail with barely contained energy. I took her for a run earlier, but she's already itching to go out again. I set aside my paintbrush, checking my watch. "No time for another run, little lady. I'm sorry."

Tempest cocks her head to the side, one dark, sleek ear flopping inside out. I could swear that she lets out a disappointed, if understanding, whine. When I adopted her, the woman at the shelter told me that she'd be clingy. I think between the two of us, I'm the clingy one. Whenever I'm home—or at least in the downtown apartment I bought my first week in San Jose that I'm trying to convince myself feels like home—I can't shut up. Maybe it's the therapy, but all I do is talk to Tempest, even if she can't reply. She's getting the hang of commands in Russian and English, and has figured out quickly that when the harness comes out, I'm about to take her to the trail that runs parallel to the Guadalupe River. She's a German shorthaired pointer; she loves running even more than me.

And she listens.

Either I talk to her, or I battle the urge to call Isabelle.

"I know," I say sympathetically. "And I have a road trip tomorrow. I'm sorry."

She nudges my hand with her nose, accidentally smearing pink paint all over it. I sigh, wiping it away.

I didn't set out to paint the bathroom blush pink, or decorate the kitchen with yellow accents, or keep a vase of fresh-cut flowers on the coffee table, but once I put a photograph of Isabelle on my nightstand, it's like the floodgates opened, and now I can't stop. I have shoes for her, still in their boxes, and dresses line the half of the walk-in closet I'm not using, and I know she'd approve of the pink candy dish on the marble-topped island. I even have a koala stuffed animal on my dresser.

It's not a substitute for her. Nothing is. No matter how many citrus candles I light, or cozy blankets I put in the living room, or pieces of jewelry I collect, it's not the same as having her around. It's not a home.

All the same, the reminders help. One day, she's going to share that closet. She'll appreciate the walls in the bathroom. We'll take Tempest on walks and dance in the kitchen and join a gym with a pool we can swim in together. She'll put stuffed animals on the bed, and leave her beauty products on the bathroom counter even though that means I keep knocking them over, and ask me to zip up her dresses before we go out. We'll make love on every surface in this apartment, and fight in it, too, and it will be okay because I'll have learned to manage myself.

The thought of that future steadies me. Grounds me. I'm going to therapy twice a week, and adjusting to my anxiety medication, and playing my ass off every shift I have on the ice. I'm finishing my classes virtually, and even though I'm keeping my distance from Isabelle, I'm thinking about her all the time. Everything I'm doing is for the future we deserve to have together.

I just wish it didn't hurt so much in the meantime.

I wrap up the painting for now, slipping my leather bracelet back onto my wrist, and get ready to head to the practice facility. With the regular season ending after these last couple of games and the postseason looming, I need all the practice I can get.

My phone starts to ring as soon as I shut the door to my car. I glance at the number on the touchscreen, expecting it to be Mom. Things are still stiff between us, but they're slowly loosening up. She came to my game the other day, with Grandfather, of all people—he still doesn't approve of my choice, but he understands why I made it—and has kept me in the loop regarding Isabelle and the wedding.

Instead, it's a number I don't recognize. My stomach clenches, panic overtaking me in an instant. After my first game on the Sharks, Dad tried calling from a different number, since I finally blocked his, and I'm still jumpy.

It takes a few tries, but I manage a deep breath. If it's my father, I will calmly hang up the phone and block the number. Dr. Reyes reminds me every session that I can and should continue to reinforce that boundary. It probably isn't him, but just in case, I have a plan.

I loosen my grip on the steering wheel and remind myself that the car is in park. I let myself notice the lingering new-car smell, and the way the sun is hitting the windshield, and the feel of the leather seat. The spike of nausea fades. My head feels clearer. It's not a perfect system yet, and I'm still panicking more than I'd like, but at least I'm really learning how to handle it now.

I answer the call.

"Nikolai? It's James. Izzy's brother."

I blink with surprise, even though he can't see me. I'm not sure who I expected, but Isabelle's eldest brother wasn't at the top of the list.

"I remember," I say dryly. "You threw me into a snowbank."

"It all worked out in the end, yeah?" he says, amusement in his tone.

"If by worked out, you mean a friendship with your brother

that involves way too many movie references I don't understand, then yes." The panic might be at bay, but that doesn't mean I'm not still on edge. "Is everything okay?"

"Yeah. Sorry to call out of the blue. Is this a good time?"

"I'm just heading to a training session, but yeah, I can talk."

"Cool. How are things going with the new team?"

I pull out of the parking space, considering my answer. I don't know him too well, but I have the sense that he wouldn't ask if he didn't want the truth. "It's great, but exhausting."

"Yeah, my rookie season was—sorry." I smile as I hear a baby's shriek. "Charlie has been so fussy lately. Daddy's here, I've got you."

"She must be so much bigger now."

"Oh, wait until you see her. She can roll now, which has turned her into a little menace." Charlie shrieks over the line again. "Sorry, chickpea, it's just the truth. Anyway, my rookie season was rough, and I didn't come into it a month before the playoffs."

"Maybe we'll get knocked out in the first round and I'll wish I'd been at McKee for the Frozen Four win."

"Pretty spectacular, huh?"

McKee's victory came thanks to a last-second goal from Mickey, with an assist from Cooper, and yeah, it was fucking incredible. I watched it on television and FaceTimed everyone after, but it wasn't the same.

"I'm proud of the guys," I say, slowing the car at a red light. "But I'm assuming that's not what you called to talk about."

"No." He pauses for a moment. "The wedding is soon."

"Right."

"Are we going to see you there?"

The thought of returning to New York kicks my heart into high gear. Of course I want to be there, but Isabelle told me to come back only once, the right way. I intend to honor that.

"I admire what you're doing," he adds. "I don't know all the details, and I'm not asking for them, but I know the gist of it. My sister has always deserved someone like you. Someone with integrity."

I clear my throat. "That means a lot."

I didn't need the distance to decide whether Isabelle is it for me, but I feel it even more deeply now. She's the first thing I think about in the morning and the last thing I think about at night. I dream about her twice as often as I have nightmares. I'm sure she's been busy with her own life, the wedding and school and volleyball—with limits and my mother's continued support—but I hope that I cross her mind just as often.

"And I just want you to know that Bex and I want all our family, present and future, at our wedding."

Months ago, I promised Isabelle I'd be her plus-one. I've made other promises since, weightier ones, but I haven't forgotten it. I've kept an eye on the potential playoff schedule.

I wonder which bridesmaid dress she settled on.

I wonder what she'd look like in white.

"You're future family, right?" James says.

Before Isabelle, I'd have said I had no plans to get married. Watching my parents' marriage crash and burn was more than enough. I didn't need to experience it myself, especially when I didn't trust myself not to fall into the same traps.

One day, though, I'd like Isabelle to wear my ring. One day, I want to be the one standing at the end of the aisle, watching her walk to me. Dr. Reyes has encouraged me to think that far ahead, even if they're just daydreams. The more often I think about it, the more possible it feels.

"Yeah." I busy myself with switching lanes. "I mean, if she'll have me."

"She misses you. She says she's fine, but I know it's eating her up."

I wince, even though he can't see me. "Me too."

He hums thoughtfully. Charlie whines, getting fussy again. He whispers something to her, too quiet for me to catch.

Maybe one day, Isabelle and I will even discuss children.

"Whatever you need to do, keep doing it. But Nik—we'll save a spot in the wedding party for you."

CHAPTER 72

Izzy

"Want to get drinks with us later?" Brooklyn asks me as we corral the volleyballs strewn around the court into a mesh bag. "Celebrate the end of the semester?"

I kick a volleyball to her as I scoop two into my arms. For our last spring league meeting, we just listened to music and played a few casual sets, laughing and chatting the whole time. Brooklyn and the other seniors didn't give big speeches about how much they'll miss us, but I wonder how they feel. If they're happy with how their college volleyball careers went.

Despite everything going on, nothing sounds better than unwinding for an evening. Nik would be proud to hear I'm taking a break.

"Yeah, that sounds great."

"The wedding is next week, right? You must be so excited."

"I'd be more excited if the landscapers would finish transplanting the dogwoods."

"Izzy?" Coach Alexis calls from the entryway to the gym. "Can we talk?"

Brooklyn raises an eyebrow. "I'll finish up here. Wear purple tonight."

I wipe my palms on my shorts as I follow Alexis out of the gym. Aside from a few short conversations, I've kept my distance from her. She said all she needed to say at the end of last semester, and it's not like spring league wins you bonus points.

"Your blocking is improving," she says, holding open the door to her office. "I've noticed that."

"Oh, thanks." I perch on the end of the chair in front of her desk.

She sits back, crossing one leg over the other. "I've noticed you've been volunteering at Moorbridge High School, too. I don't think they expected actual volleyball players from the university to show up."

"It's been fun." I'm not sure of her angle, so I just add, "Rewarding, too. At first, only a couple of kids showed up, but now we have enough players to do actual matches."

"That's what they're hoping to do in the fall," she says. "They're planning to hold tryouts and everything, put together a team."

I smile. Joana will be so excited. "That's great."

"And they're hoping that we'll continue to be involved, of course." She lifts an eyebrow. "You could have a future in coaching."

That's a nerve-racking—if not entirely unappealing—thought. "I definitely want to keep volunteering."

"That's good to hear." She drums her nails on her desktop. "I have to admit that I underestimated you, Izzy. Spring league, the volunteering—it would have been easier to stay away. Especially since I was so hard on you last season. Harder than I should have been."

I blink with surprise. I volunteered at the high school for myself, and went to spring league for my teammates, but I didn't expect her to notice any of it.

"I still love volleyball." I throw back my shoulders, meeting her gaze. "And wherever you want to play me next year, I'll be excited to tackle it."

"I know you will." She gives me a long look. "What about setter?"

As SOON AS the door shuts behind me, I press my hand to my mouth, jumping in place. I meant what I said, but there's no way in hell I'd turn down a starting position at setter. I have to call my parents. Nik is going to be so excited.

Nik.

I deflate. Normally, I'd leave ten texts in a row without a thought, but we still haven't spoken. I pause in the hallway, pulling up our text thread for what feels like the billionth time. That last game—the last time I watched him play hockey in person instead of on the television—I texted to let him know I was almost at the rink. I even included a dumb little heart emoji.

I stare at it. It's so normal, so boring and presumptuous.

If I texted him, would he answer? If I called, would he pick up the phone?

The first time he left without saying goodbye, I thought it was final. So much has changed since then. I didn't love him then. I hadn't yet given him my heart for safekeeping. But by then, he'd taken that photograph of me. He'd already called me his favorite.

I type out a text, but I can't make myself press send. He has a game later. He's probably deep in pregame mode.

Then I see three little dots.

I freeze in the middle of the hallway, watching those dots disappear and reappear. When the text finally comes through, I stifle a gasp.

Nik

Remind me what the groomsmen are wearing to the wedding?

CHAPTER 73

Izzy

The night before the wedding, I'm a ball of nerves.

I've been running around all day, ironing out last-minute details. There will be more tomorrow, but for now, at least, I can catch my breath. I pour myself a glass of wine, nudging the refrigerator shut with my hip.

"Nervous?" Katherine asks.

I smile as she walks into the kitchen. She takes off a pair of reading glasses, tucking them into the front pocket of her shirt.

"A little." I sip my wine. "Okay, a lot."

She returns my smile. "The first wedding I planned was for a friend. That would have made it nerve-racking enough, but of course I wanted it to be extra perfect for her. It's no wonder you're feeling this way."

"Yeah," I say, joining her at the table in the breakfast nook. "I just hope James and Bex are happy with it."

I'm glad she's going to be by my side for the event. Managing a guest list of a couple hundred—with a rain forecast in the morning—won't be a walk in the park.

"They'll love it." She clasps her hand over my wrist. "I know it was hard, but you did a wonderful job."

"You always say to wait until the last guest leaves before making declarations."

"I'm confident." Her eyes shine. "And I'm proud of you. For so many reasons, Izzy. I haven't had the chance to properly thank you for telling me about what was going on with Nika."

Nika is such a cute nickname. I smile whenever I hear her say it, even though I prefer Kolya. I know things aren't perfect between Nik and his mom, but based on what she has shared, they're trending in the right direction.

"I . . . thank you." I shake my head slightly. "I'm sorry you went through so much."

"I'm sorry I let myself believe he was fine for so long." She presses her lips together as she leans back in her chair. "At least he's getting better."

I look at the tabletop. "Do you think he's really going to come?"

"He loves you, he—"

"There's my favorite sister-in-law," Bex says. She dashes across the room, giving me a squeeze. James follows behind her at a stroll, shaking his head fondly. "We wanted to say thank you before all the chaos."

"Everything looks amazing, Iz," he says, leaning in for a hug, too. "Thank you for being the best wedding planner we could ask for."

"The absolute best, right?" Bex asks Katherine.

"I was just telling her that tomorrow is going to be perfect."

"Fingers crossed," I say.

"It will be." Bex gives me another hug, as if she's so full of energy, she can't contain myself. "I'll be walking down the aisle to my husband and daughter, what more could I want?"

"Ah," Mom says, peering around the corner. She walks into the kitchen with Dad. "We thought we heard voices."

"You should be so proud of Izzy," Katherine tells them. "She's tremendously talented."

I'm blushing, but no one contradicts her. Mom just kisses the top of my head, and Dad smiles at me. The validation warms my chest. I did it. In the end, everything came together, exactly as I had hoped.

"We've loved watching her passion for this grow," he says.

"Thank you," Mom says. "Truly, thank you."

"She earned it all on her own," Katherine says. "I've never met a harder worker."

"Stop," I say, wiping my eyes. "You're going to make me cry."

Everyone laughs with me. I don't think it'll sink in until James, Bex, and Charlie actually leave for Bermuda, but I really did put it all together. Meltdowns and missteps and koala hugs aside, I did it. My entire family will see months of careful planning come together tomorrow, all in celebration of James and Bex and the life they're building together . . . and hopefully Nik will, too.

CHAPTER 74

Nikolai

The last time I was at the Callahan family home, it was snowing. Now springtime blooms all around me. I adjust my tie, the exact shade of light purple that Isabelle requested, and start down the hydrangea-lined path. The wedding isn't until the afternoon, but the house bustles with activity. Caterers in white shirts. Men in coveralls hauling ladders and electrical wiring. An extremely stressed-looking woman carrying an enormous box of flowers.

"Do you need a hand?" I ask, helping her steady the box. "I can carry them."

"Oh, that would be fantastic. Watch the mud there. It rained last night."

I wince. Hopefully Isabelle isn't too panicked.

The woman opens the back gate for me, then directs me to put the flowers on a table at the entrance to the huge white tent on the lawn. A quick glance around makes it clear that there are already enough flowers to rival a greenhouse—even the pool has floating bouquets—but it does look beautiful. Two white dogwood trees stand like sentries behind what I assume will be the altar, and a chandelier hangs over the dance floor in the tent.

Even incomplete, I can tell that this wedding will kick the ass of the wedding we crashed in Boston. And no offense to my mom, but it blows the Heyman wedding in the Hamptons last summer out of the water, too.

My heart swells with pride. Isabelle did a wonderful job. I don't want to get in her way, but I'm dying to see her. I loop around the tent, hoping for a glimpse of her.

Things aren't perfect yet, and they never will be, but I can't deny that I feel steadier now. Stronger. I don't know if it's the medication, or the therapy, or just the change in scenery—probably all three—but the past is staying put, and I'm looking to the future.

I want the future to start now, with her by my side.

"Nikolai." I turn at the sound of Richard's voice. "I wasn't sure if we should expect you today, son."

I turn to him, shaking his hand. He's also dressed in a gray suit. A silk pocket square matches the light purple of both our ties. He smiles, clapping me on the shoulder, and I find myself smiling back.

"I did promise Isabelle that I'd be her plus-one, sir."

"You look good," he says, giving me a once-over. "No game today?"

"I'll have to fly back tomorrow. We're between games in the second round."

He nods, guiding me out of the path of a couple people carrying chairs into the tent. Mom rushes by, muddy boots contrasting with the neat skirt of her dress, but she stops dead in her tracks when she spots me.

"Oh, Nika." She wraps me in a hug. "I'm so glad you're here." As she steps back, she squeezes my arm, her eyes shining. "When you're ready, she's inside."

"Are you?" Richard asks. His voice doesn't hold any judgment, but I know there's weight behind the question.

"Yes." I glance at the house, resisting the impulse to run inside. If my mother is dashing around, then so is she. I don't want to get in the way. "I've been imagining this since I left."

"I felt that way about Isabelle's mother from the moment I left for games until I got home. I still feel it, whenever we're not together." He shakes his head, as if marveling over that. "Son, I want you to know that I trust you with my daughter. You make her happy, and that's what she deserves most of all. Both of you."

I swallow around the lump in my throat. "Thank you."

Those intense eyes settle on mine. "And if you ever need advice, or have something you wish you could ask your father about— you know where to find me."

"Sir, I— Thank you." I pause, unsure what to say to even begin to cover the emotions rushing through me, but before I can un-scramble my thoughts, the patio door opens.

It's her. I know it before I even see her.

Unlike my mother, she's wearing delicate heels, but that doesn't stop her from sprinting across the lawn to me.

"Your shoes, darling," Richard calls.

"Fuck my shoes!" She darts around yet another display of flow-ers, her skirt catching in the breeze. Her hair is loose, but curled; it streams behind her like a mane. I hold out my arms, heart beating so fast it might make a break for it. But a couple feet from me, she skids to a stop. She brushes the hair out of her face and stares.

"Isabelle," I start. I had a whole speech, I practiced it on the plane, but now I can't remember a single word. Not when she's staring at me, more gorgeous than ever, the tears in her eyes glit-tering like the diamonds around her neck.

"Your beard is atrocious." She claps a hand over her mouth, laughing helplessly. "Please tell me this is a playoffs-only thing."

"Come here."

She drops her hand, shuffling the tiniest bit closer. "You're here. Really here." Her eyes search my face; she wipes the tears away without a thought to her makeup. "I swear to God, Kolya, if this isn't—"

"It is." I take a step in her direction. There isn't much distance between us now. "I wanted to come home."

"Forever?"

I nod. I don't know whether I can speak.

She finally lurches into my embrace, throwing her arms around my neck. I hug her tightly, the tension rushing out of me as soon as I catch a hint of her perfume. I'm home.

"I missed you," she whispers thickly. "I was afraid maybe—maybe you'd change your mind."

"Never." My voice is rough with emotion, an unending well of it that I can't stop falling into. I don't care. I don't want to stop falling, not when it comes to her. I ease far enough away that I can look into those calm, beautiful eyes. "You're everything to me, Isabelle. You're stubborn warmth and wild summertime. You're sunshine." I put her hand against my heart so she can feel its staccato beating. "I feel your light here, always."

"I love you." She cups my jaw, stroking over my beard, and repeats the phrase in Russian, her voice strong and steady. "You're my favorite, Kolya."

I kiss her with abandon, with heat, with everything in my soul. "You found it?"

"Did you know even then?"

"Yes," I whisper against her lips. "Even then."

It's a beautiful wedding.

I stand next to Cooper, Sebastian, and James's friend Bo—plus their dog, Kiwi—on the groom's side during the ceremony. Isabelle, holding Charlie in her arms so she's part of the action, stands in a pair of backup heels next to Penny, Mia, and Bex's friend Laura. Richard walks Bex down the aisle, to my surprise, and she's so excited that she kisses James before the officiant gives them permission.

Even though I want nothing more than to sweep Isabelle

into my arms the moment the reception begins, I let her work. The elegant decor, the live band, the subtle nods to football and photography—it's all her doing, and it all comes together like a richly woven tapestry.

When the first dances wrap up and the floor opens to everyone else, however, I can't help myself. I catch her elbow, tugging her to my chest.

"Let's dance."

She squints at me. "I need to make sure things are set for dinner."

"My mom can do it." I rub my thumb across the inside of her wrist. "I have so much to tell you."

"Like what?"

I kiss her softly. "Dance with me and you'll find out."

"Wait. Not here." She leads me to the tent entrance. "Look how pretty this is."

Now that it's later in the day, tendrils of sunset reach out across the sky. She makes a beeline for the dogwoods, lit with fairy lights. The music fades into the background. Even though the sunlight is slipping away, the air is pleasantly warm. Springtime bordering summer.

"Maybe we should have a sunset wedding."

Her mouth drops open. "Shh! You can't talk about your own wedding at someone else's."

"So you agree, then?" I press her against one of the dogwood trunks, kissing her soundly. "We're having a wedding?"

"I don't recall a proposal."

"When the time's right, solnishko."

She bites her lip as she smiles. "What did you want to tell me?"

"You go first."

"I didn't say I had anything to share."

"I'm sure there's something I missed."

She pretends to think as she plays with my tie. "I'm playing setter in the fall."

Cooper had hinted that she had volleyball news, but I figured that'd be too much to hope for. "No way."

"And I'm talking with my parents about putting together a volleyball scholarship for McKee through the foundation."

"Holy shit." My heart pounds with pride. I squeeze her, lifting her off the ground in my excitement. "That's incredible."

"Also, your mother is very interested in expanding her business to the West Coast." She tugs me into a kiss by the tie. "I told her I'd be happy to explore the idea after I graduate."

"Come back with me tomorrow." I brush a lock of hair behind her ear. This early evening light makes her look unfairly tempting. "At least for the game. Meet Tempest. See the apartment."

"Who's Tempest?"

"Our dog."

"Our dog," she repeats. "She doesn't even know who I am."

"Sweetheart, all I've done is talk to her about you. She knows your name better than she knows her own."

The band starts a new song, perfect for slow dancing. She shakes her head again, eyes sparkling.

"Is that enough of a forever for you?"

"Dance with me," she whispers.

I can't change my past, but I can shape my own future. She's the only one I want by my side. My partner. My future wife. My home. I sweep her into my arms, my heart settling at the way she smiles. "Always, Isabelle."

Izzy

Five Years Later

I pull the hockey sweater out of my jeans and re-tuck it, chewing on my lip all the while. On the ice, Nikolai and Cooper and the rest of their teammates are warming up, but they look tiny from this angle. The team practically tripped over itself to offer us a box for opening night; they wanted the whole family together for Nik and Cooper's first NHL game as brothers-in-law.

The box is still filling up, but as I look around, I spot Katherine and her fiancé chatting with Mom and Dad. Cricket and her wife walking arm-in-arm. Bex, laughing at something Penny just said while she wipes Charlie's face with a napkin. Penny holding her son, Lukas, on her lap. He's wearing those adorable baby headphones, which highlight his mop of gingery hair.

I give Joseph a nod as he enters. I've never forgiven him for what he tried to do to Nik, but we've reached an understanding. We both love him. We both want him to succeed. And considering the fact that Nik has led all defensemen in the league in points the past two seasons, I'd say he made the right career choice.

James walks over, holding his younger daughter, Harper, on his hip. When she sees me—her favorite aunt, of course—she reaches her arms out. The little Rangers jersey she's wearing looks unfairly cute on her.

"Oof," I say as James sets her on my lap. "You're getting so big!"

"How is Uncle Nik going to play, Harps?" James asks. "Good, right?"

"Bad!" she declares, brushing her strawberry-blond hair, so like Bex's, out of her face.

I burst into laughter. James looks at her helplessly.

"Sorry," he says. "She's in this phase where everything is bad. It's her favorite word."

I blow her a kiss anyway. "You're lucky you're so cute."

James takes a seat next to us. "You okay?"

"Just nervous." When we found out that the Sharks were planning to trade Nik, it came as much of a surprise to us as everyone else that the Rangers won out. He wants this to be a long-term thing, considering Cooper's recent contract extension. Even if it isn't, I can't deny how exciting it'll be to see them on the same side of the ice again. "You remember how banged up he was by the end of last season."

"He's healthy now," he says reassuringly. "He'll get back in the groove of things."

"Auntie Mia!" Harper says, pointing at the door. I crane my neck around, watching as Mia hugs Penny.

"Are we late?" she asks, kissing her nephew on the head. "This is when I regret being all the way in Boston."

"The traffic was rough," Sebastian adds as he embraces Bex.

"No, you're perfect," Bex says.

"How are things going with the restaurant?" Penny says, untangling Mia's hair from Lukas's grabbing fist.

"Uncle Sebby!" Charlie exclaims, holding up her arms.

"Charlie girl!" Sebastian scoops her up, spinning her around. "It's great. We finalized the drinks menu."

"I'm still impressed that you worked so many space puns into the names," Mia says dryly.

Harper wriggles out of my lap, a determined look on her adorable face. I don't blame her for wanting to join the group. I'll never get enough of moments like these.

"I can't believe you're doing it all again," I say to James as we follow Harper across the box. Mia picks her up, letting her play with her necklace. "Do you know yet?"

"Another girl," he says.

I stop short. "Seriously?"

He just nods, a quiet, pleased smile on his face. "I guess that officially makes me a girl dad?"

I throw my arms around him.

"Izzy, do you want a glass of champagne?" Penny says.

"Do it for me," says Bex, pressing her hand against her bump. James winds his arms around her, kissing the side of her head.

I hold up my drink in answer. It's just seltzer, but they don't need to know that yet. It's barely sunk in; life has been so busy lately. Between my own wedding this past summer—in the Hamptons, of course—the trade, Nik acclimating to the new team, and wrapping up my last West Coast clients' weddings while moving across the country with a dog, I've barely had time to breathe, let alone really think about the positive pregnancy test I stared at in private the other day. We only just started to try, so I had no idea to expect it so soon.

One thing I do know? Our baby will have plenty of cousins.

The thought makes me smile. Sebastian and Mia won't be having kids, but I wouldn't be surprised if Cooper and Penny gave Lukas a sibling at some point. I fiddle with my wedding ring—an heirloom from Katherine that she gave to Nik the moment he mentioned proposing—as I take in the scene.

My family. The family I was born into, and the family Nik chose. Literally chose, since he took my family's name when we got married. It was sad to say goodbye to San Jose, but I can't deny that this homecoming feels good. Sebastian and Mia in Boston, Bex, James, and the girls in Philadelphia, and the rest of us in New York—it's close. It's perfect.

"Let's go down for a quick hello before the game," Penny says to me. "Luke likes seeing Cooper on the ice."

When we reach the boards, I tap on the glass, waving at my husband.

Nikolai Callahan, my husband. I'll never get tired of thinking that.

He skates over, pulling off his helmet with a grin. His hair flops over his forehead, eyes dancing with warmth.

I practically swoon. Six years together, going on seven, and he still gives me butterflies. If there wasn't glass separating us, I'd have jumped into his arms the moment he got close enough. He looked great in teal, but dark blue isn't half bad, either.

"Hey," I say, pressing as close as I can, anyway. "You ready?"

"I'm always ready. Everything good in the box?"

"Yeah. Luke wanted to see his dad."

We look over. Cooper's in the middle of playing peekaboo with Lukas, who giggles wildly, trying to grab him through the glass.

"Is Daddy marching into battle?" Penny says, bouncing him on her hip. "Is he going to defeat the evil Bruins?"

"I'm looking forward to that," Nik says.

"Oh," I say softly. I nearly press a hand to my stomach, but manage to contain myself. I shouldn't tell him here. He'll be distracted for the game, and that's the last thing he needs on opening night.

"Whenever you're ready," he adds, his smile taking on a teasing edge.

I hesitate, twisting my wedding ring around my finger.

"Everything okay?"

"It's just—I guess we need to be ready," I say in Russian. I'm not fully fluent, but I've worked at it long and hard enough that we can hold whole conversations in the language.

I'm sure he'll want to teach our child how to speak it, too. The thought of that fills me with joy. We haven't been to Russia yet, but maybe one day. There's always hope for a more peaceful future.

It takes a split second for it to sink in. "You're serious?"

"I took five different tests to make sure."

"You're pregnant." His voice drops, taking on a rough edge. He clears his throat. "Isabelle, you're really pregnant?"

At my nod, he smiles, so widely it takes my breath away.

"Yes," I whisper, crowding even closer. I press my palm to the glass, and he does the same with his gloved hand.

"Are you okay? Do you feel good?"

I nod tearfully. I knew he'd be happy; we've spoken enough about it that we're certain it's something we both want, but all the same, this is unexpected. "Do you feel good?"

"I'm scared," he admits. "Scared, but excited."

"You're going to be a wonderful father." My heart soars at the truth in those words. If there's anything I'm certain about, it's that. He has spent so much time working on himself, for us, and hasn't wavered from my side since that morning at James and Bex's wedding. "You deserve this, Kolya."

"You're the only one I'd ever want to do it with," he murmurs. "I can't wait."

"I love you," I whisper back. "Ya lyublyu tebya."

That phrase he taught me so long ago, back when we were just starting to imagine our shared future.

Even though the game is starting soon, he leaves the ice, wrapping me in his embrace. Gently. Carefully. His kiss lingers; his hand cradles my belly. When we finally break it off, tears glint in his calm, reassuring eyes.

There's so much love and joy in his expression, it shines through like gold. I blink away my own tears as my vision blurs.

After all, I don't want to miss a single moment of our forever.

Acknowledgments

First of all, Reader, thank you for taking a chance on Izzy and Nik's story. Whether this is your first introduction to the Callahan family or the long-awaited conclusion, I appreciate you! I hope this gave you all the feels the way it did for me when I wrote it.

Writing a book is always hard, and this one was particularly challenging. I wanted to get it just right—Isabelle, Nikolai, and the whole Callahan family deserved that—and I was fortunate to have the support of so many people as I strove to make it happen. My publishing team, my readers, my friends and family—thank you to the moon and back for helping me live out my dreams. Maybe it's cheesy, but even on the tough days, I wake up grateful that this is my career.

Let's start from the beginning, then.

Thank you, Dad, for giving me a love of sports. One of my favorite things in the world is connecting with you about our teams. Thank you, Mom, for being my first cheerleader, and for keeping the family updated with all I do. Thank you, Moira, for being the best sister I could ask for, and for sharing my love of reading and romance. To all of my family—thank you for being my biggest fans.

Stephanie, Lily, and Olivia, thank you so much for supporting me as I wrote this book. The voice notes, the memes, the unhinged GIFs, the brainstorming sessions—I'm so grateful that Discord connected us. You make me a better writer with each conversation and frantic voice note. I am so lucky to know you!

Brittany, Maren, Veronica, Peyton, Ally, and Sarah—forming friendships with you has been one of the best parts of this journey so far. Thank you for all your support.

Anna, I am forever grateful that a random Tumblr message turned into a friendship as deep as ours. Thank you for always being willing to imagine with me.

Catherine, thank you for being such a steadfast friend. From that initial Twitter group to now, look at us! We're living our dreams! And to everyone in the LlamaSquad, thank you for supporting me as I took the leap into romance.

Elizabeth, thank you for keeping me steady, one conversation at a time.

This book would not be nearly as fabulous without the help of my beta readers, whose awesome feedback and cheerleading brought it to the next level. Thank you Jos, Ronnie, Catherine, Lauren Brooke, Kristen, Caroline, Shelby, Joanna, Lauren, and Candin for giving me the push I needed to get Izzy and Nik's story right.

Transitioning from indie publishing to traditional publishing has been an adventure, and I have been so blessed to have the full support of my publishing teams at Avon and Headline Eternal every step of the way. Thank you, Sylvan Creekmore and Priyal Agrawal, for digging into the heart of *Wicked Serve* and giving me the tools to make it shine, and Priyanka Krishnan and Sophie Keefe for bringing it to the finish line with such enthusiasm. DJ DeSmyter, Samantha Larrabee, and Kalie Barnes-Young, thank you for championing this book—and the entire Beyond the Play series—so hard through marketing and publicity.

It's extra-special to have a friend create such gorgeous cover art. Thank you, Gabriela Romero Lacruz, for capturing the essence of Nik and Izzy in that stunning illustration, and Elsie Lyons for shaping it into the perfect cover. Diahann Sturge-Campbell, thank you for creating beautiful interior formatting, and Brittani DiMare, thank you for managing everything through copyediting and proofreading. Madelyn Blaney, thank you for coordinating as the book went through final tweaks.

Valentine Grinstead and the entire team at Valentine PR, thank you for working so hard to get the news out about the Callahan family!

To everyone at The Bent Agency and Azantian Literary Agency, especially Emma Lagarde, Victoria Cappello, and Brent Taylor, thank you for working so hard to get this series to readers around the world.

To all of my readers—thank you to the moon and back for your love of this series. Since the very beginning, so many of you have championed these books through your reviews and posts and recommendations, and I appreciate each and every one of you. You helped bring this series to the finish line. That epilogue—finally one set in the future!—was for you.

And as always, thank you to Claire Draper, agent extraordinaire, who, in the spring of 2022, asked me: what if you wrote a sports romance?

What if I did, indeed.

About the Author

GRACE REILLY writes swoony, spicy contemporary romances with heart—and usually a healthy dose of sports. When she's not dreaming up stories, she can be found in the kitchen trying out a new recipe, cuddling her pack of dogs, or watching sports. Originally from New York, she now lives in Florida, which is troubling given her fear of alligators. She is the author of *First Down*, *Breakaway*, and *Stealing Home*, the first three books in her college-set sports Beyond the Play series about the Callahan siblings.

 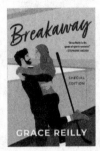